KARISMA

KAYOS

- - -

OUT OF TIME

An
Unfortunate
Lineage

- - -

Finale

VOLUME
VII

A Novel

Books by Delaine Christine
through
Kimerah Publishing

AN UNFORTUNATE LINEAGE
Terrible Karisma – I
Kayos Effect – II
Karisma Trouble – III
Total Kayos – IV
Deadly Karisma – V
Kayos Knows – VI
Karisma Kayos: Out of Time
Vol VII (Finale)

A HAYDEN CLARKE MYSTERY
*Title To Be Announced

*Forthcoming

KARISMA

KAYOS

- - -

OUT OF TIME

An
Unfortunate
Lineage

- - -

FINALE

VOLUME
VII

A Novel

Delaine Christine

Karisma Kayos: Out of Time
An Unfortunate Lineage VII

Copyright © 2020 Delaine Christine

ISBN-13: 978-19505563319

Book and Book Cover by D Johnson
Model Pic by Maksim Toome, used with permission
Scenic Cover Image by Igor Zhuravlov via 123rf.com

Kimerah Publishing, Elkhart, IN

Printed in the United States of America.

Dedication

In loving memory
of
Janet Hersom

A woman of unparalleled character.

She lived her life with grace,
with dignity,
with an abundance of love,
and she had the forethought
to instill those very same traits
within her children as well.

Thank you God for taking her home.

PREFACE

From the dawn of time mankind has been haunted by the past; a history of our origins, arguably the most debated among mortal man.

But what if we're all wrong? What if the written accounts aren't as simple as we think? What if our origin story is the culmination of fabricated tales by mortal men who are desperate to find and possess a gifted few?

This is the story of one such family of extraordinary individuals with a lineage spanning over three millennia. Their blood runs red, their hearts beat strong, their minds are keen, their gifts are real and yet, for their own protection, they hide their true selves from the rest of the world.

If you were them and you knew the truth...

You would too.

Chapter 1

Indiana, Pennsylvania

Ten years. Out of time.

The five words had an ominous ring to them. Their repetitive unrelenting chant overwhelmed Karisma Kayos to near hysterics. Panic, fear, and dread knotted her insides and tore at her heart. Instinct told her something was about to happen, and whatever it was had to do with the repetitious phrases.

Karisma paced the room and waited. The need to keep moving welled within her the moment she applied the box of hair color and set the timer. With every passing second, she could see the numbers receding on it.

This was taking too long.

Losing patience, she knocked the alarm to the floor, flung the curtain back, and climbed into the tub. Cranking the knob all the way, she dove under the shower head.

The lukewarm water washed over her and along her back, helping to sooth the tension in her shoulders. Rivulets of inky black streamed down her body, puddling near the drain in the tub. She held her breath, watching the liquid swirl around her feet.

Another rush of trepidation struck her. She sank to the floor of the bathtub, desperate to ignore the confusing flash of pictures in her head. Tears came unbidden to her eyes as she wrapped her arms around her waist in despair. The water chased away the remaining hair dye as she hugged her knees to her chest. Eventually the spray turned frigid, forcing her to get out.

What was now black hair clung to Karisma's neck as water dripped down her body to the mat. Her swollen eyes from crying, and the remaining steam from the shower, made it hard to see. She fumbled for her towel only to realize it was on the other side of the room. Sopping wet, she stepped toward the bathroom counter and reached for the hazy mirror. She hesitated.

Bucking up the courage, she cleared the fog from the glass with a shaking hand. What she saw was frightening. Her ebony mane now contrasted with her pale complexion, and the pinpoint lights once reflected in her eyes were gone. Her dulled irises appeared dead and listless.

The view shifted suddenly, becoming warped as the left half of her face disappeared. In its place, she could see the half image of another woman with tan skin and a crystal-clear blue eye. Gasping in surprise, she leaned back and blinked several times.

Jiggling her head to clear her bleary vision, she moved forward and took a closer look. Her own face peered back at her now, looking as confused and scared as she felt.

With an overwhelming surge of panic, she grabbed up her husband's shears. Fear had her pulling her waist-length hair taut. Dread had her slicing through her hair. She shuddered to a stop when the first section of long black strands tumbled to the tile floor. She stared briefly, before hacking away at the rest. The wavy locks swirled and came to rest on the floor.

Her hands quivered. She dropped the shears in horror over having chopped off a foot and a half of her length. They fell to the floor with a muted clang, the sound diminished by the cushion of hair. With an urgent need to sort out what she saw, she gaped at herself. Was it her in the mirror? She wasn't so sure anymore.

Haunted by the reflection, Karisma snatched the metal shears back up from the floor and threw them at her likeness. She was angry, determined to regain control of her mind, and had expected the mirror to smash. Instead, it cracked from top to bottom down the center, splitting her image in half.

Chapter 2

"You have to tell him." Dr. Sum Ting Wong's insistent nature was born of the need to stay on good terms with his father-in-law.

"Why? Why should I tell my father anything about them? They're my dreams." Megorah Wong unbraided her long ebony mane while she sat in bed. As far as she was concerned it was too early to be fighting, but her husband wasn't easily dissuaded.

"Because you never dream, Meg. We both know there's a reason when you do." Frustrated and worried, the doctor known as ST due to his unfortunate name, paced their bedroom at the Blackthorne Estate. His pajama bottoms rode low on his waist, and he hadn't bothered with a t-shirt yet.

Meg huffed, her features splintering into a dubious frown. Disinclined to explain herself, she stayed silent, grateful he hadn't lost his temper to the point of using her given name.

He stopped pacing and locked eyes with her. "Go downstairs and tell him now. I won't pack to head home, leave for the clinic, or step foot from this house, until you do."

"Fine! I'll go, all right?" Crawling from under the covers, she flounced out of bed and padded toward the door. Sensing him behind her, she peered back at him. "Where do you think you're going?"

"To make sure you tell him."

Meg stomped out of their room and down the hall, halting outside her father's office door.

"What are you doing?" ST asked.

"If you must know, I think he's already in his study."

"You are correct, *he* is," Rafe Blackthorne said, from behind his desk. He could hear them squabble from down the hallway. Gesturing for his daughter and son-in-law to enter, he took note they were still in their nightclothes. His eyebrows rose in question. "To what do I owe the pleasure of this meeting so early?"

Meg slowly headed into the office, hating she couldn't have this conversation over coffee. She longed for something she could sip and hold, to help ground her emotions.

"Dr. Sum Ting Wong has a bug up his butt this morning," she said.

ST's eyes shot daggers at his wife. "You go too far, Megorah."

Aware of how much his daughter hated being called by her given name Rafe sat forward in his seat. "As do you, ST. That said, I'd wager, calling your husband by his full name would be as great a source of aggravation as your own is to you, Meg. Now, what is it you're not telling me?"

Meg slid uneasily into one of the matching leather seats in front of his desk. "How did you know I've been keeping something from you?"

"Because, I've been hearing you two argue from your room for the past ten minutes." Exasperated, Rafe noted his daughter's usually vibrant pallor faded. "What are you so worked up about?"

"I've been having dreams for a couple of weeks now."

"Why am I only now hearing of this?" Rafe asked with concern.

"She didn't even tell me about them," ST said. "I only found out on Monday, because I overslept and happened to be in bed when she woke from one."

Alarmed at the news, Rafe's attention moved to his daughter. "What's so bad you can't tell me?"

"Do you paint?" Meg's abrupt inquiry sounded more like an accusation than a question.

Rafe froze in his chair. He didn't respond.

Turning in her seat, she glanced behind her at the portrait on the wall. Her mother looked back at her in her ankle-length ivory velvet wedding dress. The sight of her, as always, made her nostalgic and sad for she'd passed away many years before.

"I never thought about where the paintings in this house come from. It didn't occur to me to ask until this past week."

Leaning over toward his wife, ST asked with a deep growl, "Why are you badgering him about paintings?"

"Because, I think it's important to my dreams."

Rafe became noticeably agitated. "I doubt there is relevance between who rendered the portrait and your visions. Now, what are they about exactly?" His hands steepled together over his desk as he patiently awaited their reply.

The couple frowned. Their eyes shifted toward each other than back at Rafe. He was evading her question.

"I'm not telling you until you answer me. Do you paint?" She turned in her seat, suspecting from the panicked sensation she was experiencing from her father, that he was keeping something from them. She pointed at her mother's portrait. "And did you paint the picture of mom?"

Rafe didn't like being caught off guard, especially when the subject matter was over his secret evening pastime. But if his daughter was having dreams then they were likely prophetic in nature, and she was asking about his hobby.

Without warning, a memory from long ago popped in his head. He was painting his first portrait ever of a woman in her mid to late twenties wearing an ivory velvet wedding dress. His heart constricted painfully in his chest. It couldn't be. He was sure there were at least two more years. Or had something unforeseen happened?

Rafe splayed his hands against the desk, trying to stay calm. "Are you dreaming about a woman? One with midnight blue eyes and long strawberry blonde hair down to about here?" He indicated his waistline, then waited expectantly for her answer.

His daughter pursed her lips and fidgeted in her seat. "No."

"Meg," Rafe said dangerously.

"I said no, because I'm dreaming about a woman with shoulder-length black hair." Slumping in her seat, her arms and legs crossed as she scowled.

Rafe heaved a relieved sigh and relaxed in his chair. The feeling was short-lived.

"Funny thing though, she had dark blue eyes, and I keep glimpsing the image of her in a portrait wearing mother's wedding dress while sporting reddish-blonde hair instead. Your name is signed on the bottom of the painting dated two years before you married mom. Hence, my question."

Erupting from his chair Rafe emitted such a guttural sound from his throat, it frightened Meg at its intensity. "Are you sure the woman you're dreaming about has black hair now?"

"Yes, and much shorter. Why?"

"I'm a closet painter," Rafe said in a rush, "been painting for years. Before you were a thought in my head; before any of you; even your mother. Everything hanging in this house - I painted it. Including the one in the front room. On the back of it, as with all the rest, it'll say the name, David Pearson. That's the name I paint under." There was only one painting he'd ever put his real name on before. If his daughter was dreaming about the woman in that portrait, and her hair was black now than it was a very bad sign. Making a drastic decision, Rafe ordered them to follow him then rushed toward his study door in a panic. He ran to the end of the hallway, veered around the corner, pulled the attic steps down, and began to climb.

"What in the world?" ST raced after his wife and father-in-law, still in shock over learning the man had forged the Van Gogh in the living room. As confused as Meg, he pulled himself up into the attic as a light flicked on. The sound of something scraping across the wooden floor and a thump led to another breach of bright light which flooded the room.

"There's a hidden door to another room in our attic? Dad!"

Meg and ST ducked through the once concealed doorway and gasped. Inside were multiple easels, a whole row of shelving, and cabinets littered with paints and paintbrushes. The floor was lined with drop cloths and there was a pedestal chair in the center of the room. It was situated before an easel with a landscape which was drying from recent touch-ups.

Against a far wall spanning the entire length of the room, almost twenty feet or more, were hundreds of canvases in varying sizes. They were all finished works. Meg's mouth dropped in dismay. Her father steered her to the end of the room and opened a set of blue velvet drapes. Behind them was a life-size portrait of the woman she dreamed about.

The woman smiled serenely out at her from the canvas as she wore her mother's bridal gown. Her deep blue eyes danced happily and her long strawberry-blonde hair blew in an imaginary wind. Meg's eyes were drawn to the base of the artwork. Her father's signature rested above the date. The image was produced prior to her mother's? How could that be? She thought her father had only been married once, and the woman was wearing the one of a kind wedding dress he'd always claimed he had made for her mother.

"Is this her? Is this the woman you're seeing?" Rafe's face lit up with a mix of excitement and worry.

Eyes burning with a jealous heat, Meg couldn't help herself. Her answer was simple. "No."

Chapter 3

Burrell Township Library
Black Lick, Pennsylvania

"You're welcome to make the effort if you think you can do better," Karisma said under her breath. Out of the corner of her eye she noticed the retreating customer pause and glance back. Did she overhear?

Eyes widening, she cringed inside. Being more careful, she grumbled softer. "Could've at least put the book back in its place. There's an order after all."

Karisma couldn't help being irritated. She had heard the advice about the book covers before. Having designed them herself, she knew they needed work. Frustrated, she checked the clock on the wall. Three hours at the author event and she hadn't sold one book. This was getting her nowhere.

A half-hour later a new wave of people entered the room. Many walked by her table looking for the novelist two tables down who'd been selling and signing a lot of books. A few people took a quick look at her table on their way to his. She tried calling out to several.

Attempting to engage them in conversation wound up being an awkward experience for all involved. Socializing had never been an easy thing for her. She had an abrasive unwelcoming personality which tended to put people off, but she tried. Managing to gain someone's interest they asked about her novels. She tried to give a description without oversharing.

"So this is faith based romantic fantasy with some supernatural aspects, and this one is paranormal fantasy?" The clean-shaven man who asked wore glasses, tan pants, and a V-neck pull-over shirt. The educated white-collar worker had an air of entitlement about him.

"That's right."

"The series titles are almost the same, and you have two author names? Why is that?"

Karisma became defensive. "There is a similarity, but they're not the same. An Unfortunate Lineage has religious undertones and Lineage is a secular set. Plus, the individual book titles themselves are each different."

"The way they're laid out I couldn't see the first part of the series title on this set." The man began reading the book description of one, then switched to another. "I get it now. Same stories, but with the sex and violence cut out for those who don't like it. I suppose trying to cater to both viewpoints helps reach more people."

Tired of craning her neck she opted to stand as she corrected him. "They aren't the same. They're different."

The man was confused. "What's the An Unfortunate Lineage about?" He grabbed one of the paperbacks back up again.

"It's about two families and their father's. Each one has six gifted adult children. Both patriarch's struggle to keep everyone safe from those who would use their children for dark purposes."

"And Lineage?"

"That one is about a different family with powers which stem from an extensive lineage."

"Hence the title."

Karisma's face flamed. She continued with an edge to her voice. "What I mean is, Bastion was taken away at a young age and raised by the RavenCroft's. He and his fully-grown kids have powers, not discerning gifts like the Blackthorne's of An Unfortunate Lineage."

The man's eye's roamed heavenward. It looked like he was having trouble with the explanation.

"See, the RavenCroft's are an extension of the Blackthorne's in the An Unfortunate Lineage and their tales are told by way of a narrator. The Lineage collection doesn't have a narrator." Noticing she was getting a few people standing around listening, she became self-conscious. The man went on to ask more about them. She tried to describe them as best she could. When he asked about the new novel, he became annoyed.

"You have a final book in the works combining both series, but the stories aren't the same? Do you plan to write anything without the Blackthorne's and RavenCroft's in them?"

"I'm a Ghostwriter for a living, so yes; I keep pretty busy. To clarify, I didn't come up with the An Unfortunate Lineage. Someone hired me to edit, proofread and polish the manuscripts of another writer. But I have their permission to sell them, of course." She said the latter hastily, noting his questioning look.

By this point, Karisma had taken a seat again, not keen on standing in front of the eavesdropping bystanders. Some of them smirked. One woman shook her head and walked away. Distressed, she could feel the heat of embarrassment flooding up and down her body in waves. What possessed her to come here?

The man shook his head. "Not trying to give you a hard time or anything, but it all sounds like the same story to me. Hits too close to being plagiarism, if you ask me."

Fuming, she snapped at the man. "People get ideas from other people all the time. How about I take the book back from you since clearly you're not interested, right?" Her tone was blasé and sugary sweet. Reaching across the table she snatched the book back from the man and set it down hard on the table.

Startled, the guy attempted to take a few steps back, only to realize he'd drawn an audience. "Sorry, no. Not interested." The man walked quickly away.

A tall woman with a baseball cap smirked as she watched the man meander away. "I imagine that guy isn't used to women being so bold with him. You certainly put a lot of work into the stories. A dozen novels with another to come. You must have been writing them for a long time."

Head held high, Karisma glanced at the woman as she walked off too, taking the throng of voyeurs with her. "I wrote them in a couple months, but thanks so much to you all for the humiliation," she said in an undertone.

"You wrote all twelve of these novels in two months' time?"

Karisma's head jerked around. Nearby, a woman in her mid-fifties with chin-length brown hair and an unpleasant stern face stood waiting. The middle-aged woman had way too much make-up on and appeared out of place. She missed seeing her standing among the crowd before.

She heaved a huge sigh, exasperated at having to repeat herself. "I did half of them. Someone else came up with the others.

The woman eyed her curiously with an intense stare. It made her uneasy.

"That gentleman doesn't understand what you're doing, but I do."

She gave the stocky woman a grateful smile. Finally, someone with intelligence. "You do?"

"It sounds to me as though you have something in your head you're desperate to get out into the real world." The woman set a Louis Vuitton purse on the table, covering a couple books in the process. "When you were little, were you happy? Just think about it. Did you obsess about certain things?"

Karisma winced, afraid now of where the woman would go with this. "I don't understand what you mean."

"Did you sing all the time and get berated for it, draw the same pictures, read the same type of book all the time or maybe you couldn't stop watching the same type of movies and TV shows all the time as a child?"

If the woman didn't pose the question, it never would have occurred to her. She used to do it all. She peered at the novels and the announcement board which displayed the first book for her next series to come.

The woman tapped Karisma's hand. The noxious scent of floral perfume nearly knocked her out with its potency when the lady leaned closer.

"It's a bit obsessive dear," she said in a sympathetic hushed tone. "Some people create their own little world and live there. I think it's what you did with these stories. Take a look at your provider list. I'm sure someone can help figure out a way to get you to stop writing the same tale." Smiling sweetly, the lady patted her hand again with ice-cold fingers, eliciting a chilly shiver down Karisma's spine. Then she walked away and disappeared in the sea of people as if never there in the first place.

Shocked into silence, Karisma sat for a moment, completely stupefied.

The woman had called her crazy without using the word. That took talent.

Or pure nerve.

Either way, it had been embarrassing as there were two different authors on either side of her table. Their wide-eyed expressions made it obvious they heard everything. Angry and dejected, she pulled more than one box from underneath the table and repacked the paperbacks. Opening her convertible folding dolly, she placed the boxes on top of each other. Then she pushed the overburdened cart out of the room, leaving the skirt and tablecloth behind.

With the humiliating conversations and now packing, she was receiving too much unwanted attention. She had to get away. Pushing her way through the entrance she almost made her escape when the leader of her writers' group stopped her.

"Why are you leaving? Did something happen?"

Karisma kept moving, forcing the woman to follow after her at a rapid pace. She laughed bitterly, all the while her heart felt hollow in her chest.

Karisma whirled about to face her. "Why did you bother to invite me in the first place? I have no business being here."

"Of course you do. You wrote six novels and published secular versions of each one."

"I told you someone hired me to write half of those. The other ones I wrote myself, and they are so not the same." Karisma's eyes rolled, and she shook her head angrily. Turning back around she headed toward her car. Not even the head of her writers' group understood.

"What's the difference?" the woman asked. "You're making yourself visible and giving people a chance to buy them to read."

Karisma stopped near her vehicle. She clicked the locks and opened the back end. "I haven't sold a thing today, and I'm no longer interested in trying to anymore. Huh, obsessive!" She fumed. A single tear spilled down her cheek. "It was a stupid dream. I have no idea what possessed me to write my own story; it always turns into chaos when I try to put it all down." As she said it something within her, around her, above her felt off. And her wording.

She turned about the parking lot as though spooked but didn't see anything out of the ordinary. Had that been a shadow above the tree line? No, impossible. The sky was sunny and clear, and her ideas never came to her when awake. She only received the images while sleeping. The man, however. She saw him night and day. "To think anyone would want to read my stories."

"What's the matter with you Karisma? I don't recognize you anymore."

Ignoring her, she loaded her stuff, shut the back door, crawled into the driver's seat and took off. She left the woman standing in the lot, looking stunned and more than a little peeved.

She didn't care. Karisma wouldn't be going back to the writers' group, because it all didn't matter. Nothing mattered.

There was no such thing as individuals with powers, let alone discerning abilities or otherwise. Characters with those traits worked in comics, but not in real-world type stories unless they were vampires, Lycans, or witches. Her tales were unrealistic even for fiction. What possessed her to write about people like that in the first place?

Oh, right, Vortigern Black.

She hadn't thought to write about the elusive black-haired blue-eyed man in such a long time. The moment she read the job request to fix the manuscripts she had been lost because they reminded her of her own. The mere thought of him sometimes made her feel so guilty. She was married - had been for almost four years - and yet this other man, whether real or not, always seemed to be in her head which was unfair to Matthew.

She pounded on her steering wheel in as she drove. Why couldn't she get the revolving images to go away? She tried so hard to ignore them. Especially when in the middle of one story, she would get an idea for another. She had a dozen more novels in varying stages because of it, and they were always about the same people.

When she attempted to write her own stories they always came out in a jumbled mess. Was it because of the accident years before that messed up her head for a while? Matthew thought so.

If she didn't know better, she'd say what she was seeing was real, but that would be absurd. It'd be like saying she were aware of the lives and daily happenings of a family of gifted men and women who lived in Montana and Colorado. While, at the same time, she spent her life in Indiana. Somehow she knew of them without having met. Is it possible?

Distracted by a honking motorist who sped past her, she jumped in her seat.

Thinking she saw something out of the corner of her eye, she cast a glance in her rearview mirror toward her back seat. Seeing what appeared to be someone else looking back, her body jerked, causing her to swerve near the dividing line of the road.

In the next instant, no one was there. Alarmed and wigging out, she shifted her gaze away. Karisma knew who she thought she was seeing, but it was not possible. Her characters weren't real. Besides, no one was there. The moment the thought coursed through her mind, she dispelled it as ridiculous.

Bah!

Knowing anything real or imagined was making her crazy.

Overwhelming despair had her suddenly pulling off to the side of the road. Leaving the air conditioning running, she sat within her vehicle trying to calm down. Somehow she knew something bad had happened. The image of it had hit her full force and shaken her to her core. What the vision was she couldn't say for sure anymore. No sooner had it come to her then it was stripped away. It reminded her of waking from a dream, but not recalling what it was an hour later.

Whatever she saw instilled within her the uncontrollable need to cry which was uncharacteristic of her. She couldn't stop, so she was no longer able to safely drive. The engine idled for the next thirty minutes before Karisma attempted to move the vehicle again. Her haggard state didn't improve, and a thought kept racing as though on spin cycle in her mind.

Ten years. Out of time.

The mantra was back again, and she had no idea what it meant.

Chapter 4

Megorah!

She came awake. The jolt sending her to the floor.

Disoriented and panting for air, Meg's chest heaved. Sweat glistened across her forehead and down her face. Her hair plastered to her cheeks and neck, and her face flushed with heat. She was too weak to push up from the floor to a seated position. Eyes wide, she blinked rapidly, taking in her surroundings.

It all came back to her. She was in her father's home, and she fell asleep while reading. The disturbing vision in her dream startled her awake. The soft carpet beneath her knees took most of the impact when she fell off the couch. Her head shifted to the hearth. The low crackling flames soothed her roiling emotions.

The vision repeated in her mind, preventing her from being able to forget the woman in the portrait.

Horrified her indifference over the painting might have adversely affected another, her stomach churned nauseously. She needed to tell her father. If they were real, then the woman and her family were in grave danger, as well as the entire Blackthorne family.

But she couldn't move. When the nightmares were this bad, they often paralyzed her for a time. She hated to be, and feel, helpless, but she didn't have a choice, she needed to get help.

"Daddy! ST, help me!" Her hoarse voice and dry throat made swallowing and moistening her own tongue difficult. Desperate to get the images out of her head, she called out again, screaming at the top of her lungs as best she could.

"Meg? Is everything okay?" Having heard his daughter's cries, Rafe had ran from his study to investigate. He looked down from the second floor into the front room. The sight of her crying in a heap on the floor had him leaping from the balcony down into the foyer. He ran to the living room.

"Your agility at your tender age of fifty never ceases to amaze me," ST said, racing to his wife's aid from the hallway.

Reaching her first, Rafe picked his daughter up from the floor. Laying her on the couch, he cupped her face with his hands. He could tell she had another nightmare.

"Tell me what you see." Concern etched lines into his brow.

"I lied to you. I'm so sorry. I'm seeing the woman in the painting, but her hair is short and black now. Something's wrong. I'm jumping in and out of time as I sleep." Meg's wild eyes darted about the room.

Rafe's heart plummeted to his feet.

"One second I'm here, the next I'm not. I'm there, with her; the woman in the portrait."

"You can't do that, Meg. It's dangerous," Rafe said.

"I'm not trying to. I think she's pulling me there to her."

"No, that's not possible. What you speak of is a rare form of Borrowing, akin to an out-of-body experience. It isn't her gift," Rafe said.

Startled by his words, Meg and ST both gaped at him.

"Are you saying this woman has special abilities like your family does?" ST asked, regaining his voice.

Head bowed both in thought, Rafe closed his eyes and tried to regain control. He needed to be careful how much more he shared. There was only so much they could know, even now.

Sensing the answer in his emotions, Meg stared up at her father in surprise. "Who is this woman? How can she be gifted like us? I thought we were the only ones."

"To believe we're the only humans blessed with such talents would be presumptuous," Rafe said. "You need to tell me everything. What have you been seeing?"

"Something to drink first, please. I'm so parched."

ST moved her to the kitchen and tended to her most immediate need with a glass of water, Rafe determined chamomile tea with lavender would be beneficial. It would allow her to relax and eventually sleep soundly.

Meg began explaining while her father filled a teapot with water and set it on the nearest burner. She slumped over the counter, her eyes drooping. Her hands circled her water cup. Every once in a while she lifted the glass to her lips for a tentative sip.

"The first time, I saw her in my mirror, not while asleep."

23

Rafe stopped near the fridge, his hands still resting on the door handle. He turned, giving his daughter a questioning look.

Quickly defending what she said, she told them about the incident two weeks ago when she was getting ready for work. When she first glanced up after adding her colored contact to her left eye, she had to look twice at her reflection. For a brief moment, her waist-length hair looked chopped off on the left side of her face to below her shoulders. Blinking, she could see half an image of another woman, but then it disappeared. At the time, she thought it a trick of the light.

The same day after heading to bed she dreamed she was in a random bathroom. She'd just pulled the tan shower curtain open and stepped down on a blue folded towel on the floor. Confused, she walked the few steps past the toilet and wiped her hand over the fogging mirror. A different face then her own looked back at her. It was the woman from earlier in the day only with black hair nearly as long as hers. Meg had watched helplessly as the woman hacked at her hair. The face before her crumpled the more she cut, tears springing from her eyes as she cried.

"What is her name, Dad?"

"I called her Inara, but I believe she now goes by another name."

"Inara. That's pretty." ST Grabbed several mugs from the cupboard, put them on the counter, and dropped tea bags in each one.

Meg hesitated. "I woke devoid of all emotion. The next night I dreamed of her again as she's cutting her hair. The image of a portrait popped in her mind and, by extension, my mind. I'm seeing her, but I'm also able to view what she sees in her head. The portrait image became more detailed each night, allowing me to figure out the dress she wears is Mom's wedding gown. I have been able to make out your signature for the past week."

The teapot began whistling loudly. Rafe turned off the stove and poured the hot water over the bags in the coffee cups. Setting the pot back on the stove he set the timer for each one and passed them around to their respective owners.

"I suspect I know why you didn't say anything sooner." He cautiously peered in her direction.

"Were you married to her before Mom?"

"No." Rafe chuckled at the implausible notion. He could tell Meg wasn't thinking clearly, considering how old Inara would have been at the time he'd painted her.

Meg was disappointed at the lack of further explanation. She could tell he was upset by what he heard so far and didn't understand the significance of the hair being black and cut. An uneasy silence filled the kitchen.

"Does she do anything else?"

"She trims her nails. Pretty low too, practically to the quick."

Rafe winced. He took a sip of his tea in an effort to calm his nerves. "What about today? Something changed?"

Getting worked up again, her face scrunched up, a renewal of tears pooling in her eyes. Her hand shook as she covered her lips and nodded. "I'm so sorry. I should have said something sooner."

ST tried to soothe her. "Whatever it is, it'll be okay."

She sobbed and shook her head. "No, I realize now she was in trouble. I think she sensed something bad was about to happen. She didn't know how, why, or from what, but she knew."

Rafe took a long shaky drink and set it down, trying to stay calm. His hand trembled when he released his mug. "What's happened?"

Hearing the timer ding, Meg pulled her tea bag out and took a much-needed sip for courage. She didn't want to talk about the last dream, but she had to. "This time was different." She explained how she found herself in the driver's seat of a vehicle while driving along an unfamiliar road. Then she relayed how she, as Inara, looked through the rearview mirror and saw her real self in the back seat.

"The image of me in the back seat disappears. Then I'm looking out through the windshield again, but I'm not seeing what's in front of me. Instead, I'm seeing quick snippets of time. One minute I'm seeing an adept hand painting a landscape with a tree and pond. The next I'm watching someone stare at her portrait as they're holding the blue curtains back. Then I'm in our kitchen looking at you, Dad, as you open the fridge. In the reflection of the fridge door, I see her image as if I'm there, seeing everything through her eyes. That's when I realized she knew."

"Knew what?" Rafe asked.

"I think she believes we're a figment of her imagination for some reason. Like she made us up. But not anymore. She knows we're real now and not in her head."

"What do you mean? She didn't know you, but you are aware of her?" ST asked of Rafe. The left side of his father-in-law's lip twitched. He didn't respond.

Continuing on, she described another snippet of time. There was a flurry of one book cover after another being place on a table for display. Meg read off the series titles then caught the Blackthorne name in the description on the backs of a couple books.

"But that's not the worst part."

"What could be worse?" Rafe said, his tone harsh. His daughter flinched.

"Suddenly, I'm peeking in on two kids as they sleep. The next, I'm in an entryway waving goodbye to the same children, and then I'm standing beside the car I'm sitting in, looking in the window. Her reflection, as well as that of a black truck, is behind me." She wept unable to look her father and husband in the eye. "The last thing I see is a mangled black Chevy truck."

Rafe's daughter sobbed as if her heart had been broken. It occurred to him, that she'd relived what Inara went through.

"Are you still sitting in the car when you're experiencing this?" ST asked. He suspected Rafe had pieced everything together in a neat order. "She isn't driving at this point, is she? Was there an accident?"

"Yes, but not her. I think her family was though?" she said, not sounding entirely sure. "Or, maybe she's seeing what's about to happen. I'm not sure. I've had both present and future dreams before. But, in that instant, I think she became aware."

"Of?" ST probed.

"Knowing," Rafe said. His son-in-law looked at him questioningly.

"Knowing what?" ST asked.

"That what she saw was real and had happened in real life. Both in our time and hers." Rafe gripped the chair in front of him, desperately hoping the dreams weren't real. This was not supposed to occur yet, and certainly not like this. A variable changed the intended course of events. Nothing was predestined after all. He only hoped the transition would be much smoother than what it sounded like it might be.

He needed to find out for sure if the accident happened yet. His daughter was right. Sometimes the dreams were precursors to events not yet transpired. He might still be able to prevent the this from occurring. Rafe needed to locate Inara first. She lived in the same country, but at one point, her adopted parents moved. He had more than one problem though. The book covers his daughter mentioned concerned him. Their content led him to believe his own families safety might be at risk.

"Do you think you can remember those book covers? Both the series and book titles. Author name too?"

She hesitated. "Must I?"

Rafe could relate to part of what she experienced and understood her aversion to relive it. Though he had never been pulled as his daughter had been. He didn't like having to ask her to do this.

"This is important or I wouldn't ask."

Meg took a deep breath. "I think so."

Pulling a pad of paper and a pencil from a drawer near the China cabinet he prepared to write.

"As I mentioned there are two series titles." She relayed them to him and Rafe wrote them down.

"What does is the author's name on them?"

"That's what is so confusing."

"Why?"

"An Unfortunate Lineage lists a Delaine Christine, but for the Lineage series it says Vortigern Black."

"The first might be her real name, the second a what? Pseudonym? Sort of like you utilizing David Pearson for your paintings."

"It's a fair guess," Rafe said. "What else?"

"There's a board with a book cover pic. Looked like an advertisement for the finale to both of the book series. Every time I try to focus on the author it keeps going back and forth between three names," Meg said.

"Three?" ST's eyes grew wide.

"You've mentioned, Vortigern Black and Delaine Christine, what's this third one?" Rafe asked.

"Karisma Kayos, spelled with K's and Y's."

Rafe paced, running his hand along the back of his neck as he pondered on this news. "What's the title?"

"Out of Time."

ST whistled softly.

"We don't have much time. I need to find her." Rafe pointed toward Meg. "You need to rest. Go take a nap if you can. Before you do, call your brothers. I all hoped to avoid coming home this summer, but we're going to need them here. Some of you may even have to go with me to get her."

"I'll call everyone, but I'm not terribly keen on the whole napping aspect. I don't want to dream again."

ST took her hand in his, gently rubbing the back of it with his fingers. "If you do, I'll be here. Okay?"

Still fatigued, Meg tried to stand. She steadied after a few steps then left the room to grab her cell phone to make the calls.

Watching her go Rafe halted ST from following after her. "I may need your help, if you're willing."

His response came quick. "Whatever you need."

"You might change your mind once I ask of you."

There was a momentary silence. Then, "Understood."

- - -

Disturbed. There was no better word for how Rafe felt when he learned what Inara was writing.

Locating all of her books, they discovered she self-published them. Anxious to learn what was in the books, Rafe bought them all in both paperback and digital, so they could start reading right away.

They sifted through the eBooks for several hours before Rafe fully grasped where she was going with the stories. From what he could tell, the tales revolved around a prophecy his late wife, Lilyandhi made.

Three of the novels were about his family, which bothered him a lot. She used all of their real names in the stories. Inara wrote about all their abilities and everything that happened to them in the past four years. She also wrote about a similar family, she called RavenCroft. Three volumes were dedicated to them within the same series as well.

The characters in the Lineage collection appeared to be a confusing mess about his children as well, but with different names. After speed reading those short descriptions, he promptly disregarded them and moved on to the Blackthorne books in the An Unfortunate Lineage series. He realized each volume covered the story of one of his eldest three sons so far. Her descriptions of them were uncanny.

"I don't get it," ST said finally, looking perplexed. "Inara is clearly writing about all of you, but at the same time everyone's story is completely off. Dante, Dart, and Drin. None of them have met the women she described."

Concurring with his son-in-law, Rafe mumbled as he continued to read the author biographies, trying to filter through Inara's words for some clue to her actual whereabouts and current identity. One of her names originated from Pocahontas, Iowa. Another lived somewhere in Indiana, Pennsylvania, but the last one was located near Elkhart, Indiana. After that discovery, Rafe suspected he knew her real name and where he could find her.

He doubted her name would be Vortigern Black, so he disregarded that one. The chances of Karisma Kayos being a real name seemed unlikely, although he knew he couldn't discount it. Parents sometimes had a warped sense of humor when it came to naming their children. Case in point, his own son-in-law, Dr. Sum Ting Wong.

ST had been a little black boy with brown hair and eyes, stranded among a small Japanese town after he washed ashore from a tourist boating accident. Since the couple who found him didn't live near an American Embassy there was no way for them to return him to the United States. They couldn't have children of their own, so they assumed their prayers to Kami, their local water spirit, had been answered. The Wong's took him in and raised him as their own until he turned seventeen when they took ill.

"Her parents might have a sick sense of humor like mine," ST said dryly as he read.

"I doubt your adopted parents understood anything about the English language," Rafe said while chuckling. He knew the name to be a source of aggravation over the years. He'd been impressed ST opted to keep the name all this time, out of respect for the Asian parents who raised him. He could have resumed his given name at birth when he returned to the United States to go to college and earn his medical degree. Things would have been easier for him.

"I'm not mentioned in the stories about the Blackthorne's at all."

31

"I think Inara put you in the RavenCroft volumes for some reason. Oddly, she gave you a different last name."

"Oh? What is it?"

ST sounded so hopeful, Rafe almost hated to burst his bubble. "F.u.n.n.i.e."

The man gaped. "Inara called me Sum Ting Funnie? That's just wrong on so many levels."

"To be precise, she calls you Dr. Some Thing Funnie. But it is wrong, isn't it Wong? But funny?"

ST groaned. "Even you? Really?"

An unmistakable slight smile crept at the corners of Rafe's lips and his eyes sparkled. "You have to give me this one. I was very understanding about it when we first met, after all."

"Right, because forcing me to give you my driver's license and social security number so you could run an in-depth background check was you being understanding?"

"You, a black man claiming to be from South Dakota, presented yourself as a suitor to my daughter, with the name Sum Ting Wong, as you stood next to a red Maserati while wearing orange and lime green Hawaiian print shorts, a black shirt with kissing lip prints, and sporting hair as well as hands stained with red ink dye. I realize it may sound racist as well as narrow-minded for me to have questioned it, but it came on the heels of finding a bong and tin of marijuana in Meg's bedroom. Seriously, what did you expect?"

"You know full well she took it off of her former College roommate whom she was trying to reform. And is it my fault it turns out my American grandparents are rich and very grateful I'm alive?" ST splayed his arms and hands in the air as he shook them.

"So thankful, that when they asked what they could do to make amends for not having scoured Japan for you, you asked them for said, Maserati," Rafe said.

"I was joking. I didn't know the old man would take me seriously. As for the clothes, I was no more thrilled about that then you were, but I presumed you'd be more annoyed with me showing up naked when I discovered my not-so-funny co-workers had placed red dye packs in my locker among my things."

Rafe laughed, pleased nonetheless in his daughters choice. Growing up the way he did made ST humble, and he'd developed a good sense of humor. Plus, he was kind and respectful to Rafe's daughter. It also helped that he was capable of making authentic Japanese Yakisoba and Hayashi Rice, two of his many food-related weaknesses.

Realizing they'd gotten off track, Rafe tapped on his laptop. "But there is a doctor married to Meg here. A, uh, what was it? Oh, right, Dr. Chase Ryans."

"Hmmm."

"What?"

"I'm trying to decide if I'm offended by that or jealous. Why do you suppose she switched me out with that guy?"

Rafe sighed heavily. "I have a bad feeling Inara is terribly confused. It's not the only discrepancy I'm finding between this and the Lineage volumes. There are name misspellings as well. In addition, she has both Meg and Breydon married already and I have no daughter named Crisalya. According to her books they have children too."

"I see Breydon's are adopted though." ST peered up from his tablet. "I think we both can agree he's nowhere near ready for that sort of commitment with Hailey yet.

Besides, she only has one son, not two. I do find it interesting the author has him married to Hailey here. Do you suppose there might be something to it?"

"Anything is possible." Deep in thought, Rafe leaned forward, wanting to get a closer look at the monitor as he read. Was he reading book six correctly? Wondering if he missed something in the other two about his family as he read, Rafe decided it was high time to continue a more in-depth search for the woman he knew as Inara.

Karisma Kayos supposedly lived in Elkhart, Indiana but Delaine Christine was listed in Indiana, Pennsylvania. He had the impression she was attempting to keep her real-life persona hidden. In his mind, it fairly screamed the real author name was likely in the latter state rather than the former. Entering search parameters for Karisma Kayos, he started sifting through the biography picking out anything he could about her life in Elkhart. Then he homed in on Indiana, Pennsylvania, putting the information in there, looking for anything he could find listing that name, rather than Delaine Christine. He even searched the town of Indiana's past and present news articles.

In no time at all he found her, though he wished he hadn't the moment he did. Rafe hung his head in despair, distraught over the local news posting about a Matthew Kayos and his two children having been killed by a drunk driver in an auto accident yesterday morning. Karisma Kayos, the mother, was listed in stable condition, having been rushed to the hospital requiring sedation after learning of her husband and children's deaths. She had been returning from a book signing at the Burrell Township Library in Black Lick, Pennsylvania when the accident occurred.

He was too late.

Erupting from his leather chair so abruptly that it bounced on its casters then began spinning rapidly, Rafe banged through his balcony doors. Desperate for fresh air, he leaned against the deck railing, his shoulders shaking with barely repressed sorrow.

"What is it?" ST called after him. Taking tentative steps toward his father-in-law's computer screen, he saw the article that upset Rafe. He cringed, instantly knowing his wife would not take this news well. He knew she would blame herself for not having told her father about the dreams sooner.

- - -

A few minutes later, Rafe peeked his head out from the stairwell near the kitchen. "Where's Meg?" he called. Three of his son's arrived and were making quick work of foraging their way through his fridge and cupboards for sandwich fixings and snacks. The fourth worked undercover with the CIA and couldn't be reached at present.

Dartanian's head popped up from his hunched position over his plate at the table. "She's sleeping in the living room."

Rafe noted the deputy sheriff's uniform he wore. "Are you on duty right now, Dart?" he asked, utilizing his son's nickname.

"Yes, but I haven't eaten lunch yet. Meg called, said you needed us?" Dart gave his father a questioning look as he took a bite of his roast beef sandwich.

Rafe stepped the rest of the way into the kitchen, ST following close behind with four tablets in hand. With regret, Rafe watched the second born of his triplets, take a plate loaded with three roast beef sandwiches along with a beer and bag of chips to the table. Drin - short for Drinian - sat his brutish bulk in a chair next to his brother. It groaned under his weight. Everyone froze momentarily, waiting to see if it would finally break. Nothing happened.

Not for the first time, Rafe marveled at his son's enormous size. All of his boys were big men, ranging from six-foot-three up to the tallest, Drin, at six-foot-eight, being the largest. The man was big, burly, and brutish, but he was also the best looking of all his sons. The stories accurately portrayed their descriptions, from their jet-black hair and crystal-clear blue eyes, right down to their personalities and tastes, to their extraordinary abilities. If Drin wasn't so tortured by the shadows, he might have found a woman and settled down by now. Rafe couldn't, see how any woman would be able to look past those pesky creatures to the teddy-bear of a man within.

"We've got a problem," Rafe said, bemoaning the loss of the roast beef he planned to eat for dinner.

"What's up?" Breydon asked while pouring a heavy dose of barbecue sauce over the food on his dish.

Rafe became further annoyed with his youngest son who managed to ruin the left-over General Tso's chicken he picked up from Charlie Wong's the night before.

"You all moved away and are living in your own houses, yet I'm still unable to keep food in my own house?" Every last one of his sons gave him a sheepish look.

"Can't help it. Everything always tastes better from home." Dart wiped his mouth with a napkin then took a drink of his cream soda. "Now, what's this about our having a problem again? I don't have a lot of time before having to get back out on patrol. When Meg called, she said something about a woman in a painting and you lying about being an accomplished artist? What's that all about?"

"She would leave the important stuff out." Rafe said. He took a seat at the head of the table while ST passed around the tablets to view.

Rafe gave his sons a quick rundown on Meg's dreams then expressed his concerns over the novels Inara wrote. Realizing his mistake when he mentioned her name right away, he corrected himself for both his and their benefit.

"It would seem her name changed when her parents adopted her. Inara's real name is Karisma Kayos," Rafe said.

"That is a horrible name," Dart said between mouthfuls.

"Why?" Drin asked.

"Because it sounds like a porn stars name," Breydon said.

Thumping his hand on the table Rafe regained their attention. "Focus please," he said as he continued, omitting for the moment the news about her family. Out of the corner of his eye, he noticed ST looked like he was about to speak. Suspecting he meant to relay the information, he gave him a quick head shake not to just yet.

"It's more than a bit concerning," Dart agreed. "I'm not too keen on my name being in a book, fictional or otherwise, especially when it's describing our gifts. Who knows what would happen if it got out we were capable of seeing aura's, knowing people's thoughts, or seeing shadows, and sensing a person's emotions. People would-be all-over Breydon for his ability to know when people spoke the truth." Dart had been doing a cursory run-through of one of Karisma's novels as his father had talked. "Wait a minute. According to her story, I'm married to a woman named Lylia? Whoa, and we have a daughter?

Drin's head shot up over his sandwich. He appeared to want to say something, but his mouth was too full of food. He was also running through one of the novels on a laptop ST brought down for them.

"None of us can have children," Breydon reminded him, trying to keep his brother from getting too excited. "I'm confused. What's our biggest concern here? The fact Meg's consciousness is somehow being pulled to this woman - by this woman - as she sleeps? Which, in my mind, is the most pressing concern, or are we worried about this woman and what she's writing in her books? So Karisma's hair is black and short now. What's the significance in that?"

"Slow down," Drin said, having finally swallowed. "You're not giving the man a chance to respond. Besides, I personally want to take a look at this portrait first. I noticed something in the novel I'm reading through that has me curious about something in regard to it."

Breydon and Dart both looked at Drin, having not thought to ask to see it until he mentioned it.

Rafe scowled as all three of his sons hastily erupted from their chairs and made a dash for the stairs. "I'm not done yet." He yelled after them as they disappeared up the stairwell to the second floor.

"For obvious reasons, they're bound to be curious. You might as well let them see it," ST said.

Grudgingly agreeing, Rafe moved to follow after his sons. He paused when he noted his son-in-law still in his chair. "Are you coming?"

"No. I want to stay close to her in case she needs me." ST nodded toward the door leading to the living room where Meg slept.

Understanding and appreciating the man's need to be protective of his wife, Rafe headed on up. Finding Dart, Breydon, and Drin in the attic blindly searching for a secret door, he blustered at them.

"All of you, turn around and face the entrance. There's no need for you to see how I open it from here. A man needs some privacy, after all."

"Clearly," Dart said.

"He kept this from me for years," Breydon pouted. "Me, of all people!"

"Been sleeping on the job from the looks of things," Drin said.

Breydon gave his brother an annoyed look as they all turned about and waited to be let inside.

Finally allowed entry, they were directed through the long room. Marveling as they passed by their father's artwork, easels, paints and canvases, they were all equally awed at the extent of his hobby. It went completely beyond anything they imagined.

"There must be over a hundred paintings in here," Dart said. "Dad! You did all of these?"

Drin harrumphed. "I'm guessing more."

"Easily," Breydon said. "How in the world did you keep this from Dante, our family mind-reader?" He wondered as they were brought before the painting in question. The curtain had been left open after its last viewing.

Rafe didn't respond.

"She's beautiful," Dart said in wonder. "I think she'd look better as a blonde though." The deputy was transfixed by not only the image but the meticulous care his dad took with the brush strokes. The paint job on the portrait was even better than the one done of their mother which hung in their father's study.

"Who is she to you, Dad?" Breydon asked, sounding suspicious.

Distracted by Drin's not too careful foray among his easels, Rafe didn't answer right away. He was concerned his son's clumsy wanderings near and around his easels as he investigated the paintings, would take out one of his landscapes. He watched his son's head swivel around the room in wonder.

Drin finally found his way to his brother's side. The painting took him by surprise when he saw it. He suspected this was the case after what he read, but it still startled him when he saw the painting. The person in the portrait looked like the woman he met several days ago.

"Why are you painting a portrait of my new tenant, Lylia Minnosa?" Drin asked.

Rafe looked momentarily confused. "No, this is the Karisma I've been speaking of."

Drin's eyebrow rose. "It looks an awful lot like the woman I just rented an apartment to." He turned his head toward his brother Dart. "It's funny too, because I read in Karisma's book that I did the very same thing; rented the same apartment to a woman with this author's description. Only Lylia has golden blonde hair. You know? Like the Lylia in volumes two, four, and six? The same Lylia you're supposedly married to in her stories, Dart." His brother became animated.

"Are you messing with me?"

"I'm as serious as a heart attack. I wouldn't kid about such a thing," Drin said.

The youngest of the Blackthorne men was unconvinced. "Yes, you would. In a heartbeat. It's always been in your nature," Breydon said.

"Maybe," Drin said sheepishly. "But this seems a little too important to be messing around with right now."

"Are you telling me you know this woman?" Rafe pointed to the painting.

"Know her?" He shook his head. "I wouldn't say that so much as I met a woman who looked like her yesterday. Pretty lady but with lovely long golden locks about to here." He indicated the middle of his back. "I showed her the open apartment at the old hospital because Meg couldn't. She decided to rent it as soon as she saw the claw bathtub - most people do. She's probably moving in as we speak."

"This Lylia is here in Montana right now?" Rafe was confused. Why would Karisma look like this Lylia? "I need to see her," he demanded.

Thinking his father didn't believe him, Drin conceded to the request, looking forward to proving him wrong. "I'll call her and set something up for tomorrow."

"No, today. Now."

Drin looked stupefied. "How am I supposed to explain why my Dad wants to meet my new tenant?"

"Tell her I need to see the apartment for some reason. I'm doing an insurance estimate or investigating water damage. Anything. Give her some excuse, so I can get in to see her."

"That's dishonest." Drin gave his father a sly grin, thinking he must be pretty desperate to suggest something so underhanded. "You've always said such behavior was not becoming of a Blackthorne."

41

"Just do it. No wait, I know. Tell her the tenant next to her sprouted a leak. We had this same problem last month when you were in Billings picking up supplies. You asked me to make sure it wouldn't affect the unit next to it. This will get me in to see her, and it must happen today, too."

"Why such urgency?" Dart imagined there was a lot their father had failed to tell them yet.

Rafe cast a glance down at the tablet in Breydon's hand. His face became ashen. He suddenly looked every bit his age. He stumbled as though about to fall. Alarmed, Dart reached out to assist in keeping his father erect. Never had he seen the fear in his father's eyes as he did now and it worried him.

"What is the significance of Karisma cutting her hair and dying it black?" Breydon asked again, becoming concerned by the way his father behaved. He had always been a formidable sight to behold from childhood to adulthood, but now his mortality was readily apparent even though he was only fifty years old.

Rafe winced as though in pain. "We can't let 'knowing' kill her too." He held tightly to the counter behind him.

Drin's eyes narrowed, suspecting he knew what was eating at his father; the shadows. "Snap out of it. Don't let them get to you." Usually, he could see them clearly, but recently he discovered they learned to masque themselves from him when bent on being underhanded. It was an unsettling development.

Shaking his head as if to clear it, Rafe regained his composure. "If this Lylia, is the same one Karisma speaks of in her books, then it means there's less time than I thought."

"Time for what? You're not making any sense," Dart said.

Taking a deep breath, Rafe finally got around to the hard part; the fact that they were already too late to save Karisma's family. His sons blank but horrified and sympathetic expressions left him even more frustrated.

"I thought you always said the shadows couldn't kill a person," Breydon said in alarm.

"They can't directly kill anyone," Drin answered for his father. "But indirectly, sure. The shadows can mess with a person's head. To the point where people will make choices that can affect the lives of others. You know that firsthand. Need I remind you of the mushroom incident?"

Breydon adamantly shook his head, recalling the day he'd accidentally eaten poison mushrooms with distaste. "No reminders are necessary."

"Don't you see?" Rafe cut in. "There is a prophecy. To be accurate there's more than one. You and your sister, Drin, tried to tell the rest of us when your mother died. You were both right. Have been all this time. The one about the three of you is right here in book two which means I'll be pulling all of your mother's journals from the library shortly. Lilyandhi foresaw this. It's in her journals somewhere, according to this. None of this was supposed to happen yet and not like this. A choice by someone, somewhere affected everything, and Karisma is the key to it all. Something got to her though, and it's making her feel like a captive woman, so she's cut and dyed her hair." Rafe could see the reference went straight over their heads. He wondered if they retained anything he taught them. Fortunately, Breydon renewed his faith in them.

"You mean like in Deuteronomy? Where it speaks of if a man takes a captive woman for a bride?"

Dart snapped his fingers in recognition. "She must cast away her captive clothes, cut her hair..."

"I thought it was shaved their head?" Breydon said.

"Depends on what version you read," Drin said, recalling the verses in question. "You know. New International, and English standard, versus King James, etcetera."

"But I thought that was in reference to war. Where men would go off to war and, by God's grace, defeat their enemies, take them as captives, and if they found an appealing woman among them they could take them for their wives with those stipulations in place. Our country's not at war with anyone, are we?" Breydon asked, at the same time pretty sure he would have picked up on something in the news recently if they were.

"Not that I'm aware of," Drin said. His dad didn't say how many children Karisma lost, but he guessed at least a couple from the excited chittering sounds the shadows were making. He could see them now, hovering above his father. "Nowadays, women and children are being kidnapped and held captive all the time, because they're being sold as sex slaves. Or for other more disturbing purposes."

Rafe rolled his eyes heavenward. His boys could get distracted so easily. "It's symbolic for heaven's sake. At least, I think it is in this case. The point I'm trying to make here is, she's dying inside."

Processing everything he learned so far, Dart frowned, still confused about one aspect in particular. "And the black? There's no mention of coloring hair, as I recall."

"Dart, you of all people should know this." Rafe countered. "What does black signify?"

"Regeneration, riddance, transition, and pro ... oh." He turned to each of his brothers in turn.

"Protection." Rafe finished his son's thought. "I fear all of that applies here, but I think initially she dyed it black in order to protect herself. I doubt she realized what she was doing. But now she's aware." He took the tablet from Breydon and shook it as if to make a point. "Which puts her in danger."

"Danger of?" Breydon wanted to know, taking the tablet back.

Drin inhaled sharply. Finally, understanding the real threat to her, and to their family. "Knowing what she does invited the shadows into her life." Drin managed to wrap his head around why his father was so upset. "You said before, that Karisma's name was Inara before being adopted. Her parents changed it to Karisma afterwards. But Inara means ray of light, doesn't it? I remember you telling me once a long time ago that one day a ray of light would come and save me. That it'd be heaven-sent. I was so desperate for a reprieve at the time, so what you said always stuck with me. "

"Yes," Rafe said.

"But if the shadows take control of the light. Destroy it. Destroy her somehow," Breydon said.

"Then your torment, Drin, will never end," Rafe said.

"Because Karisma is the key to unlocking the prophecy," Drin finished.

"If we can go get her. If we bring her here, is that how it all begins?" Breydon appeared as hopeful as his brother Drin.

"I believe so, yes."

"Believe? Or know?" Dart wanted to know.

"I know it." Rafe said fiercely. "Just as I know Meg will not take the news of how it must begin well at all. It's why these dreams are affecting her so adversely."

Dart and Breydon looked at each other, still a little confused, but Drin figured it out. He pointed at the woman in the portrait. "She's wearing mom's wedding dress."

They all looked at each other than back at their father in astonishment. A captive woman taken for a bride. The knowledge of what must happen for the prophecy to begin truly hit them for the first time.

"I have to go get her and you're all coming with me. Her family won't let me bring her here without proof, so we must make them believe."

Chapter 5

Indiana, Pennsylvania

Much to Rafe's irritation, getting everyone's affairs in order before leaving took over forty-eight hours. The delay did allow for Karisma's paperback books to arrive before they left. He packed them in a duffel bag along with his late wife's journals, to bring with him. Then they took off before sun-up, the best hour of the day to return to time.

Disoriented, coming off the white noise of the flight, Meg held one hand to her stomach, and the other to her head. "I didn't realize traveling by plane so soon after returning to time would be so unsettling."

ST groaned and pinched the bridge of his nose. "At least you didn't get a migraine the size of the Statue of Liberty." Laying on the bench seat behind them, he attempted to read one of the novels. By Pennsylvania time, it was now past the lunch hour, because Drin insisted they needed to stop to eat a late brunch.

"I warned you to take something for headaches before you left. Now quiet, I can't hear the GPS instructions from google maps. Drin has enough trouble following me when I'm not lost." Having the foresight to have two rental vehicles waiting once they arrived at the Indiana County Jimmy Stewart Airport, Rafe was now headed toward the home of Karisma's parents. The police took her to the local hospital for sedation, but she had been released into their care the next morning.

Lush trees, well-kept yards, and homes gave them a pleasant view as they drove along Fulton Road. Soon it curved through a densely wooded area. Sharper bends had him lowering his speed bit by bit.

"Do you realize we're meant to have at least three children, Meg?" ST sounded tickled by the revelation. "Two girls and a boy."

Meg huffed in response. "According to that I'm married to Dr. Chase Ryans rather than you. I doubt it's accurate."

"Maybe, but what if this foretells of what's to come? Once Dart and your Dad met Lylia, the other day, Rafe struggled to get your brother to leave to come on this trip. The two are already infatuated with each other."

Shifting in the front seat, Meg sighed. She rested her head against the window of the car as they drove, her appearance wistful.

Rafe patted his daughter's knee. The curse affected not only his sons, but his daughter too. When she met and married ST, it became a source of great disappointment for them. Not wanting to give her undue hope he stayed silent. They had no way of knowing whether Karisma would help them for she had lost a lot. His most pressing desire was to help her through the trauma. To do that, he had to convince her parents to let them in the front door.

"Head northwest on Pennsylvania 954 North," the GPS droned.

Anxious to arrive, Rafe dreaded it as well. He had to handle Karisma's parents properly or things would go south for them fast. "Not much further everyone."

- - -

Karisma lay in a dark room, her eyes barely slits as she stared at a wall where shadows played. They bounced around a portrait recently returned to its place of honor after being removed when she moved after graduating from high school. The picture was one of two additions to the room, the other being her family portrait. She didn't wanted anything else from her house, not even her clothes. The only thing she wanted was gone, forever, and they would never come back.

She stared at their picture.

Somewhat catatonic, she'd been unable to cry since her fears had been confirmed. The police were at her house when she arrived home from the library.

Her children and husband were dead. Gone. Taken from her, from the world.

Once sedated, Karisma shut down and stopped speaking, only communicating through small scraps of paper. The doctor released her since her health insurance didn't cover more than one day.

From her old bedroom, she heard the doorbell ring. She lay motionless, staring at the charcoal drawing on her wall, unaware of who the visitors were at her parent's front door.

Curled on the pillow next to her, the fur ball purred. His head popped up at attention, captivated briefly by the noise. He stared at the door. Deciding the sound unworthy of investigation, he snuggled closer to her, recognizing its masters need for comfort.

- - -

Pulling into the drive of a one and a half story home with white siding and a porch, Rafe parked the vehicle near the two-car brick garage. Through the windowpanes on the old-style garage door he saw two cars parked within. With relief, he saw another vehicle parked near the garage which meant the Millers' were home.

Behind him, Drin pulled his car into the drive. Swerving to the right, he parked next to him after revving the motor. They argued as they got out of the vehicle.

"Enough," Rafe said, gaining their attention. "No more arguing. This is going to be challenging enough without the three of you bickering. And remember, let me do the talking." Triplets, they never changed.

"Right, because we wouldn't want to be honest about everything." Drin slammed his door shut. Nothing about his tone was veiled sarcasm. His father eyed him, giving him cause to temper his outburst.

"I wish Dante was here." Dart trudged up the walkway to the front door.

"The presence of your identical twin may or may not be helpful. There's no way to know for sure. Four of you are here, plus ST. That should be enough." Not wanting his children to see his own nerves, Rafe pushed the doorbell.

Moments later the door opened. A short woman in her sixties greeted them. She didn't appear to be in the best of moods for guests.

"This isn't the best of times if you're salespeople. We've had several deaths occur," she said with difficulty. Her lip quivered and she struggled to hold back tears.

"I am terribly sorry for your loss. More so than you might imagine. I'm here, because I'm hoping we might be able to help each other. Are Janet Miller? Karisma Kayos' mother?"

"Yes, I am," the woman said, taken aback.

"Your husband Dan is home as well?"

"Janet, who is it?" Near the kitchen, Dan overheard his name being mentioned.

"As is my son from Philadelphia," Janet said, a bit anxious at his inquiries. She waved her husband over.

"My name is Rafe Blackthorne. We have traveled here to visit you and Karisma from Montana. These four here behind me with the dark hair are my children; Dart, Drin, Breydon and Meg. My other son Dante, is unable to join us today. The gentleman next to my daughter is Dr. ST Wong, Meg's husband. Though you may be familiar with him as Dr. ST Funnie."

Dan Miller stood with his hand against the small of Janet's back for both comfort and support. She swayed a bit upon hearing who they were meeting.

The woman did a double take at the familiar names, having read about them among her daughter's books. She took in their black hair and striking crystal-clear blue eyes, as well as the pleasant-looking black man who stood in the back.

"This isn't funny," Janet said, her expression harsh.

"I assure you, Mrs. Miller, there is nothing amusing about this situation."

Her mouth pursed angrily.

Noticing his wife becoming upset Dan whispered next to her ear. "What is it, Janet?"

She whispered a biting response back. "Blackthorne, Dan. He's saying he's Rafe Blackthorne, the main character in Karisma's fictional book series." Her glare turned back to Rafe. "How did you come by these names anyway? Did you buy one of those books of hers?"

"An Unfortunate Lineage, that's right. The Blackthorne family. I thought their name was Black?" Wary, but curious, Dan was nowhere near as threatened by their presence as the mother.

"The Blacks are in her Lineage series, the one she claims she didn't remake from the other one."

Rafe cleared his throat, regaining their attention. "We don't mean to impose at such a difficult and painful time, but I wonder if we might come in. I can explain why we're here, and who we are."

"You mean who you really are?" Janet asked crossly.

Pulling his wallet from his pants pocket, Rafe extended the billfold toward Dan. "I assure you; I am Rafe Blackthorne. Please, check for yourself." He hoped the gesture of relinquishing his wallet would help put them at ease.

Uneasy about leafing through another man's belongings, Dan tentatively opened the wallet. He noted the Real ID compliant driver's license for Montana. The address on the ID listed Rafe Blackthorne, as being a resident of Kalispell.

At Rafe's prompting, Dan continued to search, seeing half a dozen credit cards with the name Rafe Blackthorne, a social security card, and an FBI badge. The sight of which garnered a raised eyebrow from both he and his wife. It shook in Dan's hand.

He handed the billfold back. The closed wallet had been thick, the stack of bills within noticeable. Dan's palms began to sweat. Unsure what was going on, he became anxious.

"Let's invite them in, Janet. They seem harmless enough."

Janet balked. "Karisma is in no condition for this visitor."

"So they visit with us for now, not her. They've come a long way, Honey."

Giving in, she beckoned for the tall, broad gentleman in front of her to enter. She had the look of a woman cross at being challenged. The Blackthorne men raised their eyes at each other as if to say, "tough crowd."

Rafe stepped into the Miller home, needing to stoop a bit as he entered. The door height seemed shorter than the standard measurement. Drin nearly whacked his head on the door frame as the rest followed suit. They filled the tiny entryway, their bodies smashing together uncomfortably.

"Please watch for her..."

"Karisma's cat, Haven? I suspect he is comforting her in her room. There's no need for concern at present," Rafe said, surprising the mother.

Drin, Dart, and Breydon exchanged looks, understanding why their father took a last-minute trip to a pet store before their flight. All three wondered how their Dad knew she had a cat. Did he have a vision and not tell them?

They were led around the couch through the open living room to the dining area. The sound of a car pulling into the drive had everyone turning their heads to peer out the window. Dart reached for his waistband, but Rafe shook his head. He mouthed everything was okay.

"That's our daughter and son-in-law with their kids," Janet said. The exchange had gone unnoticed.

"Karisma?" Dart asked in confusion. Everyone but Rafe craned their necks.

"No, Crystal, her older sister. Karisma is in the bedroom," Rafe said.

Dan gave Rafe an odd look. "How do you know?"

"I can sense her presence." Rafe shrugged as if the statement explained everything. Internally, he fought the desire to make his way down the hallway to her room. Instead, he concentrated on the cream-colored walls of the living room and dining area. The older furniture had been well cared for.

A woman with short blonde hair entered the house from the side entrance near the dining room. She carried a petite young girl about eight years old with the same blonde hair as her mother. The child's face was streaked with tears, as though she couldn't stop crying. A man came in behind the woman with a little boy. The innocent, wonder-filled expression in the child's face made it obvious, he didn't understand what was going on.

Startled by the large men in her parents' home, Crystal halted upon entering, causing her husband and son to collide with her. "I didn't realize you had company."

"Wow, you're huge!" The boy said to Drin.

Drin bent down and said, "You know what? I get that a lot."

"I'm gonna take Annette back to the spare bedroom." Crystal moved to head down the hall only to find her way barred by Drin, who stepped in her way. He smiled but didn't budge.

"Karisma's in there," Janet said.

"They can nap together."

"Not wise, I think." Drin glanced around the room with concern. "There are too many shadows in dark rooms. You should put her in a room with more light so she won't be frightened."

Crystal frowned. "You might be right. Downstairs, Mom? She fell asleep crying in the car on the way."

"Put her in our bedroom for now," Janet said in a strained voice.

Drin stepped out of the way and Crystal disappeared down the hall.

Seeing his wife struggling for control of her emotions, ST guided her to the front door. She appeared ready to faint. "If you'll pardon us, I think Meg and I will step outside for a bit of fresh air. We'll wait there, Rafe, okay?"

"Why don't you head back to the plane for now?" Seeing his son-in-law nod with understanding, Rafe turned to the Millers as Crystal returned to the living room. "My daughter is a bit sensitive to emotionally charged environments. May I sit at your table?" He recognized the need to take the lead.

The Miller's and Rafe took a seat at the table.

Determining something serious was going on Crystal's husband took his son to the basement to play with computer games. He returned moments later with his brother-in-law, Eric, who appeared to be in his early thirties.

In need of aspirin Rafe pulled a small aspirin bottle from his pocket and popped a couple of pills in his mouth. He took some before leaving Montana, but with the strain of the trip, he needed more.

"Apologies, I'm afraid I have a headache." Rafe gestured for the duffel bag Breydon carried. "I've come here to speak with you about your daughter, Karisma." He pulled out book after book, filling the table with her novels. Then he laid out a tablet with her website open on it, listing the announcement of the finale soon to be published. "I am aware of what's happened in your family. You have my sincerest condolences. If I may be so bold, please tell me first her present condition. How is she holding up?"

- - -

In the bedroom, the motor continued to purr. Haven shifted, curling around Karisma's head, wrapping his paws about her neck and brow. The cat kissed her forehead, resting its own head against hers while continuing to purr.

There was a sound; a familiar voice. Karisma's insides did a flip-flop, as she stared at the portrait. She might wish he were real, but he wasn't. The only thing real was pain.

- - -

Darkness filled the bedroom.

It was the first thing Rafe noticed when he opened the door several hours later to peer inside. The drawn curtains left the room shrouded in nighttime, but it was only mid-day. It bothered him to see his light hidden in the dark.

Karisma's mother didn't want him to venture in to see her. Permission or not, he intended to. Citing the need for a restroom, he found his way to the bedroom and took a tentative step within.

"Karisma?"

She didn't respond.

"Karisma, do you know who I am?"

Still, no response. He sat down on the bed and whispered in her ear.

"Inara?"

She flinched.

Scanning her drawn tired profile, he noted she blinked as well. He stayed close and spoke again. "Inara, Honey. It's Rafe. Rafe Blackthorne."

She whispered, her head shaking in denial.

"He's not real. Can't be. I made him up. I'm hearing things. Always things in my head; can't be, couldn't be." Afraid of what she might see, her unusual pale gray eyes turned toward him. Hands covering her face, her body shook. She began to cry. "No, no, no, no. He's not real, can't be. If he's real, it means they're really gone. Am I imagining him?"

Rafe took her by the wrists and pulled them away from her face. An uncomfortable zinging sensation tingled through the palm of his hands and up to his shoulder. He could tell she felt it too.

She looked at him in surprise, shocked and a little confused. Her mouth dropped, forming a perfect circle as she reached up toward him. Taking her soft hand in his, Rafe raised it to his cheek, so she could touch him.

Karisma shivered as the man hovered above her. Could it be him? Her gaze flickered to the charcoal gray portrait on the wall and back again to the man above her, comparing the two. His jet-black hair was peppered with white above the ears and his beautiful pale blue eyes stared back at her with sympathy. His gentle gaze about undid her. Big and broad-shouldered the attractive man leaned over her, his weight almost pinning her slender frame to the bed.

It looked like him, but how? Rafe Blackthorne and his family were fictional characters. They didn't exist. This had to be a joke, one done in poor taste.

Rafe searched her face. She was not what he expected. He could see the grief, doubt, and fear in her eyes and wanted to reassure her - to help her.

"I know what you're thinking. It's not a joke or a trick, nor am I fake. If I were imaginary, could I do this?" Bending down, he kissed her on the forehead, as the cat watched.

Shuddering beneath him, she whispered. "Please say it again."

Confused at first, it dawned on Rafe what she needed. She didn't respond to him until he called her by the name.

"Inara," he said gently.

A relieved sigh escaped her lips. "Is this real? Are you here to take me to Montana?" She dared to hope, thinking her reality and fantasy world had somehow collided.

"Yes ... Inara Kingsley, I am here to take you home."

Her face crumbled. Tears streaked from her eyes into her hair. She sobbed, afraid what he said was only a ruse to get her to come out of her room and eat. She had refused to eat for days and knew her mother worried about her.

Not knowing what else to do, he pulled her up from the bed and into his arms. He held her as she cried, shifting her thin frame to his lap to make her more comfortable. Crumpling into him, Karisma clung to him, as if she never wanted to let go. Pain and grief rolled off her in waves as she wept. He sensed her heart had been steel for so long, she wouldn't allow herself to feel until now.

After a while her crying subsided and her body went limp in his arms. When he tried prodding her to speak, her response was listless.

"Don't shut down again, please. You have to let yourself feel. You can't just shut down." Nothing he did seemed to work.

"Let me take it for you," he said, unwilling to lose her. "Give the pain over to me."

This time he clung to her, wrapping his arms around her as he cupped her head in his hand. Her eyes drooped, the light within appearing to flicker on and off within. Face going lax, her eyelids closed. Tears sprang forth from Rafe's eyes for the first time in over ten years. A mournful sound escaped from deep within his throat; a desperate cry of one in anguish. Tears poured down his cheeks in waves. Something wrenched at his chest, trying to claw its way inside.

A shadow.

The room was too dark.

Despair had him wrapping her in the blanket along with her family picture and lifting her into his arms. He carried her from the bedroom and down the hall, shocking everyone at the sight of him holding her as he cried. Rafe was more than willing to bear the embarrassment if it helped.

Dart met his father at the end of the hall near the dining room. Alarmed, his eyes grew three times their normal size. Were those streaks of silver sprouting from the side of his father's temple's? They weren't there before. Then he saw Karisma's hair.

"Dad?" Concerned, Dart's gaze shifted between the two.

"Outside. I have to get her into the light, now. Or we'll all lose her." The urgency in his tone was unmistakable.

Hearing his father's request Drin got up and opened the door near the dining room, allowing his father space to exit. He exchanged confused and worried looks with his siblings as his Father disappeared with the woman. They had no idea she'd be this far gone.

"Where is he taking my sister?" Eric didn't like what was happening at all.

The Blackthorne men made their way into the kitchen and peered into the back yard. They suspected he would go there as the sunset would be viewed best from that location.

"He's taking her outside into the light. She's been cooped up in a dark room for too long." Breydon said, alarmed by his father's eyes. They had the same look as the day their mother Lilyandhi passed away from cancer. He glanced over at Dart, noticing his brother stood ramrod straight.

"Mrs. Miller, when did she put the silver highlights in her hair?" Dart touched his forehead, then turned to the older woman and stared, willing her to answer.

"She didn't."

"Mom, did you help her do that, because it looks unnatural," Crystal said.

"You don't understand." Janet shook her head. "Her hair has been black since she dyed it two weeks ago. When I went in to check on her this morning and brought her lunch, it was all black. I don't know how that happened."

Reaching across the table Dan comforted his wife by taking her hand. Worry creased his brow as he sipped on a small amount of Scotch.

"Guys, what's going on?" Breydon asked.

"Something is wrong. She's not what we expected and either way, I'm afraid we might be too late." Drin glanced back and forth between Dart and his Father out in the yard.

The Blackthorne men stared out the window at their father who stood holding Karisma in his arms. His face rose to the sky and his eyes were closed as if in prayer.

The uneasy silence in the kitchen and dining room was interrupted by Breydon's cell phone going off. The Brady bunch ringtone signified the caller was his twin sister.

"Yeah, Meg, what's up?"

"He's coming, Breydon. I don't know how he knew, maybe through Dart, but he's coming, and he's anxious - no, scared. Which is unlike him."

"What are you talking about?" Breydon put the phone on speaker. "Who's coming here?"

"He was here when we arrived at the jet, and he is not alone. Oh, never mind. The point is, he's here in Indiana, Pennsylvania, and he'll be on the Miller's doorstep any minute."

A car screeched to a halt in the driveway.

"I would have warned you sooner, but ST left his phone in the other car, and I couldn't find mine until now."

A car door banged closed and someone's hasty steps pounded up the sidewalk to the front door.

Dart grabbed for his holster at his waist. "Meg, who in the world are you talking about?"

"Dante."

The front door flew open causing Dan and Eric to erupt from their chairs in alarm. "How dare you charge into my home?"

"Your daughter is in danger; we must get her out of here now." Dante raced around the living room, drawing the blinds and curtains so no one could see through them.

Crystal's wide-eyed gaze shifted between the man who'd entered her parents' home and Dart, who stood with a gun ready in their kitchen. They looked identical.

"Where is he?" Dante popped his contacts out in front of the Miller's, wanting to show them his unusual crystal blue eyes indicative of a Blackthorne. "Blasted things were driving me crazy." He pocketed the colored lenses, not wanting to leave them behind to be found.

"How did you know where we were?"

"None of that matters, Breydon. We have to take Dad and the author out of here now."

"You mean my daughter, Karisma. Why must she leave with you now?" Dan became upset. With the arrival of the twin, he could no longer deny what Karisma wrote to be true, but he just lost two grandchildren and a son-in-law. Must he also lose their daughter too?

"Mr. Miller, the only safe place for her is within our valley. The men who are after her will find her anywhere else. Now, do you love your daughter?"

"What kind of question is that?"

"A simple one, requiring a simple and quick answer, we don't have much time." Dante waved at his brother as if shooing him out the door. Getting the message, Dart

62

took off outside. He softened his tone. "Mr. Miller, do you love your daughter?"

"Of course I do. I may not have given her life, but she is my daughter."

"Then you must allow her to come with us."

"No." Dan thumped his hand against the table. "The way Rafe talks we'd never see her again."

"Then she'll die."

"Dan, no, I can't lose her too, I can't," Janet said in distress.

"Make a choice. Let her go, she lives. Make her stay, she dies. Your call. Either way, we must go now. We're running out of time."

"Why? What's happened?" Dan wanted answers to the man's sudden appearance and insistent behavior.

Snatching up one of the books on the table, Dante leafed to a page several chapters in, and thrust the book in Dan's face. "Jericho Hensley is on his way here."

Crystal gasped. She blanched as her hand flew to her mouth. "The man from her book is coming here?"

"You are familiar with her story. Good. Yes, this man; a monster. He hunts down the gifted few he can find then subjugates, enslaves, and breeds them like pedigree dogs. If they're women he will often rape them himself, all in the hopes of spawning more like him. If they disobey or displease him he tortures and beats them. He's discovered who your daughter is and knows what she's capable of. Henley won't hesitate for a second to kill anyone in his way; man, woman, or child." The look he tossed toward Crystal's husband sent the man racing toward the basement for their son.

Dan crumbled before them. "You must take her with you, keep her safe."

"You have my word, and my fathers too. Karisma will always be protected."

"Rafe said at some point she is meant to..." Dan stuttered to a halt, struggling for the best way to ask what he needed to. "In the portrait, she wears a wedding dress?"

Face twitching, unaware until that moment of this news, Dante hedged before answering, not catching his brother's uneasiness before answering. "Rest assured, he will give her time to grieve and the choice to do what she wishes in the end. He would never force any decision upon her."

Dante turned to leave but Crystal stopped him as her husband came tearing up the stairs with their son in tow. Tears welled in her eyes.

"That was horribly wrong of you, telling my father those things to get what you want."

"No, horribly is how she would have died," Dante said. Circling his hand in the air, he indicated the need to leave right away. "Now go. Disappear from this house for the next several hours. Separate and go different directions. Once we're out of time, you will be safe."

- - -

On the way back to the airport, they watched out windows in all directions for anyone who might be following.

"You never did explain to us how you came to know Karisma," Breydon said from the front passenger seat.

"It's complicated." In the back seat Rafe held Karisma partially in his arms out of necessity. There wasn't a lot of room, because Drin was next to him. Still not coherent, he figured it was for the best considering the way Dart drove.

"When did you meet her the first time?" Dart asked. Drin scratched his head in confusion. "Is Karisma this Inara Kingsley of yours then or not?"

Sighing, Rafe realized he would have to answer some of their questions. Feeling a bit off, he opted to choose the most benign of the queries to respond to.

"I met Inara Kingsley the first time at the age of fifteen. She was three years old at the time and the sweetest little precocious imp I'd ever seen."

Dart frowned from the driver's seat. "When did you paint the portrait in your art room?"

"Good question. Isn't she supposed to be a strawberry blonde? Breydon asked, recalling her image in the painting.

"I suspect she dyes her hair, as I imagine your new girlfriend does, Dart. They do it because their natural coloring is unusual." The comment elicited a raised eyebrow from Dart through the rearview mirror.

"How is it unusual?"

"As a child Karisma's hair was black, but streaked with silver and gold," he said, surprising all three of his sons. He was glad they were distracted. Maybe he wouldn't have to answer the question of when he painted her portrait. "Her hair received a lot of attention, some not so pleasant." Rafe went on to describe how when the light would hit it just right, it would shimmer in the sun's rays. A year later the fire started streaking her hair. Physically shaking himself to stop his trip down memory lane, he rolled down the window to get some air.

Dart punched the child lock on the door, raising the window up again. "I'll turn up the AC, but the fresh air will have to wait until we reach the airport."

"Yes, of course." Rafe had to get his head straight, but he was struggling with her so close to him. Every bump they hit made it harder. "How soon?"

"Right about now." Dart pulled into the drive for the Indiana County Jimmy Stewart Airport. Moments later he drove around to the appropriate hangar.

Shifting Karisma from his lap, Rafe slid her over to his son.

"What are you doing?" Drin raised both his arms, splaying his hands in the air as though he were being held at gunpoint.

"She's unconscious. I need you to carry her to the plane."

Drin made a face. "You want me to carry her in that state?"

Giving his son a dangerous look Rafe yelled. "I need my hands free in case Henley shows up here."

"You don't know he's out there."

"And you don't know he isn't."

Drin stared down at the woman now in his arms as his father pulled out a Glock and checked its chamber. Some days it was so weird being in his family.

"Why can't Breydon carry her? He's strong too."

"He is, but he's more adept with a gun then you. Your talents lay elsewhere."

Drin grinned from ear to ear at what he viewed as a compliment, then quoted his favorite movie, but with a slight variation. "Drin smashes." He flexed his enormous biceps for show.

Rafe heaved an exasperated sigh. His son never seemed to want to act his age. "I need you to do this for me."

The vehicle came to a stop in front of the small jetliner. Breydon and Dart got out of the car and surveyed their surroundings for signs of trouble.

Dart's gut suddenly clenched. Something was wrong. He could sense his twin's anxiety. The abrupt vision of a car's interior dashboard with a speedometer exceeding seventy miles an hour in a residential area nearly knocked him over. His brother's quick glance in a side view mirror showed a dark blue sedan coming up on him hard and fast.

" Get her to the plane now. Dante is trying to tell me we need to take off. We have company coming, fast."

Without further argument, Drin kicked open the door. He didn't want to have to carry her, but he also refused to let anything happen to his potential salvation. He still didn't understand how it all worked, but he didn't need to. All that mattered was, it did.

Sliding out of the vehicle Drin pulled her carefully up into his arms. His Dad would clobber him if he hurt her with his brute strength. He moved fast, her medium height and slight weight, not an issue for him. He almost had her through the doors of the plane, when he heard cars racing into the airport. The first was Dante's. His brother veered to the right, hoping to draw the pursuer away from them. The hoax worked, but only for a moment.

Getting Karisma inside the plane, Drin came to an abrupt stop at the sight of a pretty blonde woman. She sat by the television with three small children at her feet. They were watching a superman movie and eating his popcorn. They all turned toward him and stared in wide-eyed fascination. It was the usual response he received because of his size.

"I'm Drin." He laid Karisma on the couch. "More introductions later." Making his way toward the cockpit he rapped on the door to gain the pilot's attention.

"We gotta go. Punch it," Drin called.

"That order from Rafe?" Mitchell asked.

Scratching the back of his neck, he thought quickly how to respond. "Uh, yup,"

There was a pause. "Understood."

Drin heard the engines whine into motion as Breydon and Dart raced up the stairs and into the plane. Rafe wasn't far behind. "Let's go, Mitch," Rafe said, punching the intercom. Swearing filtered through the cockpit doors.

"I still got steps down," said the voice over the intercom.

"Just do it. I have another visitor hopping on," Rafe said.

"Like Montreal all over again." Mitchell said through the speaker. They heard Meg in the background hollering for Dante and wanting to know when her father had been in Montreal.

"Where is Dante?" The blonde woman with the children asked. She appeared alarmed at the sight of all the men on the plane.

Confused by the presence of the unknown woman and three children, Rafe didn't have time to question it. Poking his head out the door at the sounds of gunfire, he saw the missing son in question pull a one eighty-shift with his car. He then sped towards their moving plane. The driver in the pursuing car was shooting at him.

Rafe pulled back inside to keep from getting hit by a stray bullet. Dante's car shot past the plane as it picked up an excessive amount of speed. Racing a stretch down the runway, his tires squealed as he skidded to a sudden stop. The car door flew open and Dante exited the vehicle at a dead run.

Shaking his head in exasperation, Rafe ducked out the open plane door. Taking several shots at the windshield of the oncoming car, he could see Jericho Henley peering out at him from within as his son ran at an angle toward the plane. Rafe blew several holes in the windshield, forcing Henley to swerve. Dante reached the stairs, leaped on, and grabbed hold of the stairwell handle with both hands. Stumbling, his feet came out from under him, but he managed to right himself on the steps.

Several more shots rang out and Rafe fired back. Barreling up the stairs Dante knocked his father up against the wall just inside, and they both tumbled to the floor. Reaching up Rafe punched the button for the door. The steps folded up and the door closed.

"Do I want to know how you've come to learn such driving techniques?"

Dante sat up, relieved to feel the plane beginning to rise. "Eh, seeing as we have present company, it might require later explanation." He winced, realizing he had been grazed. Ten to one it was one of his Dad's bullets simply for spite over his unexpected and dramatic arrival. He holstered his gun, as did his Dad, when the little girl got up from her seat near her mother.

"Hey there, little one, no need to fret. All is well with the world." Dante gave her a winning smile. "Your bleeding Daddy Dante." The girl pointed at his arm.

"Yes, Daddy Dante," Astraia said waspishly. "You're bleeding from your arm."

"Oh, well. Just a scratch. A stray piece of metal on the stairs jumped up and bit me." He barked at the little girl, startling her as he played at having taken her nose. She laughed as her brothers giggled in unison.

"We're dispensing with formalities today, ladies and gentlemen. Until we are at a safe flying level, seat belts please." Mitchell said through the intercom, garnering everyone into motion toward their seats. "And Rafe, should I presume I'm to tunnel a rabbit hole today?"

Grateful for his pilot's discretion in present company Rafe said with a hearty, "Yes." It was important to him the pilot lose any and all potential tracking Henley might have on them. He was confident Mitchell would be able to create repetitive deviations to their normal flight pattern before heading for home. He'd done it numerous times before.

"Mommy! Does that mean we get to see rabbits today?" one of the little boys asked.

"No, I don't think so, Honey. I believe it was an expression." Astraia glanced in frustration toward Dante.

Rafe assisted in belting in one of the children, then sat next to Karisma, holding her in place on the couch.

"Is she like me?" Astraia asked Rafe.

"Sorry?"

Dante jumped in. "Different scenario there, Honey, but, uh, yeah. You could sort of say so." The response had everyone's attention.

"Who's the pretty lady?" Drin took a seat furthest from the children, so he wouldn't intimidate them.

"Everyone, I'd like you to meet, Astraia. Uh, Smith, my fiancée. These three lovelies are her children; Aimee, Jake, and Adam." Dante noted the startled expression on his "fiancée's" face. He intended to warn her of his plans concerning her witness protection relocation. There just hadn't been time.

"Fiancée?" Astraia's eyebrows lifted. She looked less than pleased by the announcement and more than a little surprised to be meeting his family. Probably because she had no clue they were engaged.

Breydon whistled softly. "Holy crap."

"Dad, she's in book one." Dart wished he had more time to read through that particular story. He recalled the woman and children were supposed to be escaping a drug lord for some reason.

"What book? What's going on?" Dante looked around at everyone on the plane. "I knew something was up, I sensed it. But I haven't been able to piece it all together yet."

The questions were met with silence.

Astraia was less than thrilled with his family's lack of response. "Did you say I'm in a book?" She directed her first inquiry to Dart. "What happened to your eyes Agent Frank Kastle, and would you mind telling me where we're going?"

"Frank Kastle, The Punisher?" Breydon laughed. He thought Karisma's use of the alias name for Dante had been a joke. He looked over at his Dad. "You gave Dante the name from a comic book when he left?"

Covering his face with his hands, Rafe fought the urge to break something. He was aware of what Karisma wrote in book one and wondered how much of it happened so far. Things were going from bad to worse. He extended a hand to Astraia.

"Welcome to the family Ms. O'Kahner," he said, startling both Dante and the woman, for he used her correct last name. "Rest assured you and your children will always be in safe hands in my home. No doubt my son will make an effort as well."

Dante smiled until his brothers started smirking and he realized he'd been insulted.

"Hey!"

Chapter 6

In Flight

The men huddled in rapt discussion over the first book of the An Unfortunate Lineage Series Dante now held. Worrying over what he learned had him holding his forehead in the other hand. They continued to discuss the books in hushed tones while Meg attempted to distract, Astraia, and her three children with a game. Unable to dissuade her curiosity, Astraia began asking questions about the woman still sleeping on the couch.

"What's wrong with her,"

Meg sighed. There was no getting around telling her. The way Dante talked when he made introductions, Astraia would be coming to live with him.

"Her name is Karisma. Her husband and her two children died."

Stricken by the news Astraia hesitated in rolling the dice. She related to losing a husband. She became a widow herself barely a week ago. Astraia couldn't imagine the grieving for children too.

"How sad. What happened?"

Meg explained how they were killed by a drunk driver in an auto accident. She opted to leave out why Karisma was now with them.

Sensing Meg failed to tell her the whole story, Astraia became frustrated.

"How much did Dante tell you about us?" Meg asked, fully aware of the woman's anxious emotions. She couldn't wait to arrive home and find a quiet place. Her own emotional state as a result of the day's events was already stretched thin.

"His name is Dante? I knew him as Frank for the past week."

"In other words, he told you nothing."

"I don't even know where we're going," Astraia said.

"Home."

"And where is home?"

Meg smirked. "It's more like when."

"Sorry?"

"My father owns a horse ranch in Kalispell, Montana," Meg said, figuring she better leave the rest for Dante to tell. "I understand you're upset but try not to be too hard on him. Our lives are complicated at best. I assure you; you'll understand better when he gets a chance to explain everything."

"Meg, is it?"

She nodded.

"How can I be upset when I don't even know who he is? Is Dante his real name?"

"Yes. Dante Blackthorne."

"Enough for now, Meg," Rafe called across the plane. All five of the Blackthorne men along with ST stared in their direction. "We're unclear yet how long Astraia will be with us."

Astraia could tell Dante appeared more than a little upset. His eyes raged at his father in indignation.

"From what I understand, I'm to be attached at his hip until death parts us." She smiled sweetly, "Isn't that right, Frank, sweetie? Oh, my mistake, Dante!" Her face flamed. "If you'll excuse me, is there a restroom?" She disappeared in the direction Meg pointed, leaving behind an agitated fiancé and a worried soon to be father-in-law.

- - -

Blackthorne Horse Ranch
Kalispell, Montana

Whispering.

Astraia noticed it was all the men did once they boarded the jet in Indiana, Pennsylvania. Occasionally, they stopped to read only to begin their discussions all over again.

Once they arrived at the airport in Kalispell, Montana they shuttled everyone to the Blackthorne horse ranch located on the edge of Kalispell. It was hidden in a valley nestled within the Flathead Valley. The mountains and surrounding trees gave the place a picturesque quality upon first being viewed. She expected her children would love the place and wondered if it was the permanent solution Dante promised her.

Astraia was still angry over his deception, confused about why he enlisted under an assumed name, and perplexed by how he managed such a feat in the first place. As Meg requested of her, she tried to be patient with the man who protected them from Kobi Radford and his men.

The drug lord's name alone sent a shiver up her spine.

From what Dante and Jericho said, her late husband interfered with a drug deal in an attempt at becoming a witness needing protection so he could give them a new life. His idiocy got himself killed and placed her and their kids in danger of being killed by the notorious drug lord in retaliation. If not for Dante, they might be dead.

Astraia new she owed him a lot, but after a week of being on the run with no answers to why he forced them to disappear from witness protection, she got fed up. Dante had yet to explain anything to her. She still didn't have a clue why they had to go to Pennsylvania, other than to meet up with his family, and the circumstances behind Karisma's presence among them troubled her.

The woman slept fitfully the entire flight. She was still asleep when they arrived, so Rafe carried her upstairs to the library next to his room where he kept watch over her through the night. Astraia overheard Karisma talk in her sleep several times during the flight. One of those times she swore she heard Karisma say Astraia would be the start of it all.

Beyond what she heard her say, all she managed to get from the men's conversation between last night and the morning were snippets here and there. They'd been in a heated debate over books written by Karisma that they were studying. Having caught her own name a couple times, she became determined to get her hands on one, particularly when Dante tried to play them off as being nothing. Which of course meant there was something going on with them.

Deciding she had been more than patient, she meandered into the front room of the expansive ranch home, while her children played in a room Rafe called the 'rumpus room.' They arrived late the night before, so Dante showed her and the kids their new rooms. Then he disappeared to the living room to sleep for the night. When morning came she found out he placed her in his old bedroom. She learned the information when she walked in on their conversation.

All the men were going over the mysterious novels again when she discovered them, but they disbanded for a while. She hoped they left the novels behind and had not been disappointed. Spotting one called 'Kayos Effect,' tucked under a magazine on the table, she picked the paperback up. Catching sight of her name on the back cover, as well as Franc Kastle and Dante Blackthorne, she began to read.

Her confusion was soon replaced by an unsettling sense of panic in her gut. The book read like her life. She lived through and experienced most of what the author wrote. Parts changed, but some conversations she had with Dante, were now out there for all the world to read. How was that possible? The story read like a romance novel with paranormal phenomena. The Blackthorne's were supposedly gifted and she was meant to marry Dante.

Astraia gulped. And they are to have children?

Rafe entered the room from the kitchen. Halting his speech at the sight of Astraia, he regarded her with a cautious look, when he saw what she had in her hand. "What are you doing here?"

"Thought you heard. I'm living here indefinitely now. According to this, I'm also to marry Dante. Which is funny, because he hasn't asked yet. I guess I'm a foregone conclusion." Astraia bit self-consciously at her lip. She didn't intend to blurt out what she said, but what she read upset her.

"How did you come by the book?" Rafe asked.

Outraged, she shook the book in her hand. "Someone is careless. They left it under a magazine. How does the author know all of this? Is this for real? If so, how is this even possible or fair? I don't have a say in my fate, is that it? The way the story reads, my life sounds predestined." She stopped talking, testing her theory as she thought the following, 'Oh, and you can read my minds, can't you Rafe?' The alarm in his expression gave her the answer she needed. She took a tentative step back. How did he do that? What was written in the book was now happening in real life. Somehow Karisma foresaw it all.

The man appeared distressed. His response made it clear he had no intentions of denying anything within the book.

He raised his hands as though attempting to calm a child. "No, you misunderstand. There is always a choice. This is one possible course of events, and obviously they didn't go the way the story is written."

"Of course it did. My husband shot Lionel. They shot and killed him in return which is why I'm here now. I mean, this is real. The woman up in the library knew. How? And this was published a month ago," she said upon leafing to the front and reading the copyright information. Her expression turning to bewilderment. "Why do I have the feeling the timing on this is off somehow? If this is for real, did those events occur sooner than anticipated for some reason?"

"Parts of the story may be real, yes, but she's not seeing an accurate picture at times. Or, to be more accurate, she sees one possible version of what might happen. Other people's choices are what's affecting the outcomes." Rafe opened the book to the end of the fourth chapter and turned it toward her to see. He flipped the pages as she attempted to speed read the section he referenced. Her face colored. "I don't mean to be indelicate, but did this happen?" he asked, softening his tone.

"No. No of course not. We didn't. I mean, we haven't." Flustered, Astraia took a deep breath. "Dante has been a gentleman from the moment he brought us to safety. He was strong in a moment when I was frightened and weak, but nothing happened. At least, not the way she wrote."

"Did he take you to the safe house as it says here?" He flipped a few pages and jabbed his finger at the passage in question.

She frowned. "He separated us from Agents Pegueros and Henley. We never went to a safe house."

"Why not? Do you know?"

"He told me he sensed something was wrong."

"With both of them, or Jericho Henley?" Rafe asked.

"No, you don't understand. Henley drove, not Agent Pegueros. He said the wrong person was in the driver seat. Then they made an unexpected stop at a gas station where they both got out. While they were gone, Dante crawled up into the driver's seat, hot-wired the vehicle and took off. I asked him if something happened, but all he would say was, he needed me to trust him. 'Something isn't right with everything,' he'd said. 'Too much déjà vu, but in some way out of order.' Then he said something about a book cover. He didn't make a lot of sense. Why are you asking me this? I'm sure he's told you all of this too."

"Two stories are always better than one. The why's and wherefores are often in the details of differing perspectives."

"I still don't understand how you think I have a choice when the book says otherwise."

"Bah! Ignore what the book says. It is, but one possibility of many. You always choose your own fate."

"Yes, but according to this, choosing to stay would help your son, Drin. Am I right?"

"Indeed, but your presence here isn't the only thing required in order to benefit that situation."

Astraia's face flamed redder. "What other choice do I have?"

"There is more than one option here. Only you can decide which one is the best course for you and your children. Would your marriage to my son, benefit another of my sons? From the way this book sounds, yes, but don't base your decision upon that alone, even if doing so would be advantageous to securing safety for your children."

Astraia was confused. So much had happened in a short amount of time. Her head felt like it suffered whiplash from being smacked in the face with so much new and disturbing information. She was still trying to wrap her head around being a widow and on the run from a drug lord. To learn the Blackthorne family had special abilities, and she a part of some prophecy laid out by Dante's mother before she died was more than she could take.

Rafe chuckled, a half-smile playing on his lips. "Let me guess, you want to know what to base your decision on?"

She gave him a half-hearted nod.

"Do you love him, Astraia?" he asked gently, startling her. He paused, "The book in your hand, Kayos Effect? I read the whole thing. I've the impression you felt, you didn't have a choice. In the story you're living now, you do. I can't help but wonder if that is why all of this happened. To allow my children the chance at a better love story maybe? Who knows. What I can tell you, is you have the right to choose with your heart what you desire. Don't let your decision be about what everyone else might want. One way or another, I will make sure you and your children stay safe. Even if what you decide doesn't benefit my family."

"You would do that?"

The man hedged. She sensed Rafe didn't like the idea, but was honor-bound to do so, if she chose to be elsewhere.

Sitting on the edge of one of his plush chairs in the living room, Rafe bowed his head in contemplation. "If you desire to leave and be placed elsewhere, other than with Dante, I will make sure that happens. I'm capable of doing that, but it would be with stipulations."

Astraia gave a short barking laugh, "Of course there are conditions."

"What do you expect? You're now privy to information about my family that would be deadly in the wrong hands. I would need some kind of assurance from you, our secret would never escape those lips of yours. Ever."

She blinked, recognition and understanding finally dawning on her. "Is that what happened in Indiana, Pennsylvania?" She stared at the book in her hand, then dropped it on the coffee table anxiously. "You weren't aware she wrote these. Somehow you found out and went to get her. You're trying to protect her, but you're also trying to do the same for your family, because this got out there on the internet. Am I right?"

"Is there anything, Astraia, you wouldn't do to protect your own children?" Rafe gave her a hard, knowing look.

Distressed, her hands shook. "Who is Jericho Henley after?" She presumed when she heard the gunshots outside, that they were coming for her and her children. She thought the men were after them, because of what her late husband did to Kobi Radford's brother.

Rafe sighed. "I think he would have been happy to get his hands on any number of the people present yesterday."

"But he wanted Karisma, didn't he? Because of what she's capable of with these books of hers." She stared at the book, not sure she wanted to know any more of her potential future. Would knowing in advance be a good thing, or would it frighten her away?

The dilemma coursing through Astraia's expressive eyes was almost painful to watch.

"Now do you understand why Dante's been so tight-lipped with you? I believe he feels he has a connection with you, and naturally, he wants to help his brother."

"I don't understand. How is our marrying and having children together helpful to his brother?"

"Oh, you didn't read that far yet?"

"What?"

Giving her a calculating look, Rafe got up, grabbed the book from the coffee table and placed it back into her hand. "Volumes two and three are clear, the prophecy isn't all about you, but from the sounds of things, you may be the start of it all. Keep reading, don't make a hasty decision, think about what you want, and give yourself a chance to get to know my son a bit. For all his faults, he's become an exceptional man in my eyes. One, I daresay, you can trust regardless of his most recent deception."

Moving away from her, he headed back the way he came. The discussion made him antsy to check on Karisma. He needed to speak with Drin as well.

"I forced the alias upon him, by the way. I did not want him out in the world with the family name."

"Which begs the question, of all the names to choose from, why Franc Kastle - the Punisher?"

Inhaling, he became momentarily retrospective. His mind reverting back forty-seven years. "Mostly, I was being spiteful over his choice to leave, but to be Franc..."

"So not funny."

He chuckled, sobering suddenly. The memory of when he was three, playing with his brothers along the stream out back behind his house, replayed in his head once again. The nostalgia made him sad. "It is my way of keeping a promise to one who died long ago."

Finding what he said odd, she opted to let it go. "There's a prophecy and a timeframe, isn't there?"

"Hmm. Is there? Or did the author herself feel she ran out of time?" His meaning couldn't have been clearer.

Astraia exhaled with a horrifying understanding of what occurred in Pennsylvania. Karisma foresaw what would happen to her family before the accident. She couldn't imagine the terror of foreseeing an event that would hit so close to home. Worse, not being able to stop it.

- - -

"Wake up sleepy head."

Hearing the voice among her dreams, she wavered between sleep and waking. Why wake up when the life in her head was better than the one she lived? Especially now.

In her visions, she could still see them. They laughed, smiled, and circled around her while holding hands and bringing joy to her heart. Then they waved at her to say goodbye. Her heart skipped between her breasts nearly shuddering to a halt as they both disappeared, taking with them a little piece of her lifeless broken heart.

She reached for them, crying out their names in distress.

She sobbed. "Please don't go!" Her vision blurred as her eyes filled with tears. No, not her children. Why had they been taken from her? What did she do to anger the heavens into stealing them from her?

"Maybe it's because you did something right," a voice said.

Karisma, who was coming to terms with the fact she was the Inara from her book series, didn't realize she spoke her questions out loud. Through swollen eyes, she struggled to see who comforted her. When she realized who held her, she sank into him.

Rafe Blackthorne.

She knew he would keep her safe. The long arms encasing her were solid and strong, containing within them a measure of both control and restraint. It felt good having them around her waist. His large hands splayed across her back, rubbing her between her shoulder blades in an attempt to soothe and comfort her roiling emotions.

She found she couldn't answer him.

"With me, you don't have to say anything." Rafe turned her so she faced him. His heart broke to see her so distressed, so unhappy. Placing his index finger against his forehead he then pointed at hers. "I can hear you fine this way too." He gave her a gentle smile and she burrowed into his chest. "I know all you want to do right now is sleep, and I do understand, but you still need food and water or you'll disappear." Her head shook against him.

I'm not hungry.

Her mind had reached out to him. Resting his chin against the soft black hair on her head he grinned when her stomach growled loudly.

"I think your belly disagrees with you. Besides, I promised your father I would take care of you. I wouldn't be keeping to my word if I let you starve, now would I?"

She groaned.

His own stomach growled. Karisma gave him a questioning frown.

"I don't eat unless you do."

Her face scrunched into an adorable scowl, and her cheeks were red from crying. She pushed at his stomach trying to put distance between them.

"I mean it, Karisma. If you don't, neither do I."

She poked at his belly as if to say he were getting soft.

This time he frowned. "Now, now. You're not being nice."

She sighed heavily, resting her head against his chest. She reveled in the feel of him next to her like this. He was real. She'd been right.

"Are you going to dinner with me?"

She hedged and reluctantly nodded her head.

Hungry.

Lifting her off his lap he took her by the hand and steered her toward the library door. She shook her head.

No, not in the kitchen, here, please.

"Karisma, Honey, you'll have to see everyone eventually." He sensed her anxiety and worry. "They don't bite. Besides, every kind of food you'd want is downstairs. ST is making quesadilla's for us," he offered, hoping to both entice and test her at the same time. According to her books Inara loved Mexican food, quesadilla's and taco's in particular.

She started to move with him then stopped. A horrified look crossed her features. She peered down at herself, for the first time realizing she wore a man's baggy shirt and oversized sweatpants rolled up around her ankles. Her head turned. She gazed up at him, her eyes wide as her mouth dropped open in surprise.

"What?" He knew full well what she was trying to say and intended to let her mind wander. "Is it my fault you sleep naked? I wrapped you in a blanket when I pulled you from your parent's house. I'm sure they are horrified I didn't bother taking the time to bring any of your clothes either. No doubt, no more so then Drin when he carried you into the jet."

Why didn't you?

"Why didn't I what?"

"Carry me," Karisma exclaimed.

"Ah, she does speak."

She shoved him in the shoulder. "Being the perverted voyeur you are, I'm guessing you're the one who dressed me in this?" She indicated the blue and white plaid flannel shirt and baggy sweatpants.

Rafe leaned down to her eye level. His own eyes crinkled in amusement as he spoke.

"Would you rather I entrusted the job to Dart? Or Drinian perhaps?"

Her eyes grew wider. She walloped him in the arm for good measure.

He stood erect and tousled her hair playfully. Whistling, he took her hand in his in order to help encourage her down the hall. Sneaking a peek at her, he caught the goofy expression on her face. She bit her lip and her cheeks flushed pink from embarrassment.

"I'm sorry you couldn't be awake to dress for yourself. But, I couldn't allow you to wake up alone in the library with only a blanket for cover. It wouldn't be appropriate. There are children in the house now." He helped her down the steps into the kitchen.

Karisma took in the expansive kitchen. Clean and well kept, it had been organized to promote efficiency during meal prep. There was a double stove along the one wall with countertops on either side. At each end of the counter stood an enormous double door fridge. A large island held the double sinks with two dishwashers on either side allowing for several people to work at once on the lengthy space. Six bar stools were set around the island so people could eat at the counter if they wished. A long maple wood table with a dozen sturdy-looking matching chairs sat parallel with the island. Windows stretched on either side of the French doors which led to the enormous patio deck. In front of them in the corner stood another, smaller table which seated about eight people.

She imagined it would be exactly like this. Karisma could even feel the cool tile beneath her socked feet as she walked.

Wait, socks?

Ignoring the curious stares of those present she pulled her sweatpants leg up. A pair of men's socks stretched all the way up to her knees. She gazed up at Rafe who couldn't stop laughing.

"Geez, Rafe. How big are your feet? I'm swimming in these."

"Fifteen and a half to sixteen depending on the brand."

"That's nothing," Dante cut in. He snarfed another bite of his quesadilla and filched a French fry, shoving it in his mouth. He spoke between chewing. "Drin's a seventeen and a half. Hi, Karisma. Good to see you're up and about. We've been a bit worried about you." He waved, and she gave a half-hearted wave back along with a nervous laugh.

"I hear foods ready." Drin blustered through the French door, bumping his shoulder on the way in. "You need to let me widen these doors, Dad." He halted at the sight of Karisma standing next to his father in his shirt and sweatpants. She was holding up one of the pant legs showing a foot, ankle, and most of her knee encased in one of his socks.

Drin desperately searched the kitchen. Seeing ST and Meg near the counter prepping more quesadilla's he noticed a platter filled with a half a dozen of them already made. Making a beeline for the food, he snatched it up along with the pitcher of lemonade.

"Hey!" ST and Meg yelled in unison as he took off running for the door.

He stood staring at the door, suddenly realizing his dilemma as he had no more hands to open the door. His pleading eyes found his brother, Dart, sitting near the French doors.

Smiling openly all the while shaking his head, Dart got up and opened one of the doors. No sooner did he have it partially opened when Drin smashed the platter of quesadilla's against his chest and wedged his way through the door. He started running when he hit the porch. Lemonade sloshed from the pitcher as he ran.

"How soon you figure it will take him before he realizes he forgot to grab his beloved salsa and sour cream?" Breydon marveled between bites of his own food. His eyes rolled heavenward.

"I'd say right about now." Dart pointed toward the yard, and Dante began to laugh. They could all see Drin through the windows as he stopped cold in his tracks. He looked at the quesadilla's, looked back at the house, shook his head as if to say, oh, heck no, and continued on toward the horse barn.

"What in the world was that all about?" Karisma asked.

"You recall I told you he carried you to the jet?" Rafe said.

She peered up at him as though awaiting further explanation, grateful in that moment for her five-foot nine-inch height. Any shorter and she would get a kink in her neck.

"He said you were nice and soft all over," Breydon said.

"Yeah, smooth skin and all that," Dante said. "Like a baby's bottom."

Dart leaned back in his chair, unable to help himself from egging it along. The woman looked so cute all flustered and wearing his father's clothes. "He said something else about ample..."

"Oh, my gosh! Rafe?" Karisma's horrified groan filled the air. "You need to talk with your son. You do realize he must go get her right? You want that bundle of mess on Veta's doorstep trying to convince her to come home with him?"

Everyone froze, including Rafe. Cocking his head at her thoughtfully, it occurred to him what she meant. "These stories of yours, they have not played out as you wrote them. Are you saying instead of Veta coming here, that he will need to go get her?"

Karisma spoke before she realized what she was saying. "I'm here almost ten years earlier then what I'm supposed to be. Something changed. It affected and caused whatever is happening now. And before you ask, I've no idea who and what caused the change. It might not have been among this family or me, but elsewhere. Drin's big beefy manly exterior hides a teddy-bear at heart. A man-child who needs to be able to treat Veta as a wife and not a mother. He needs to go find her and bring her home. It'll help his cause more than if she were to come to him. Ten more years of maturing would have been more helpful in his case. That boy's a mess."

"Ten? Try more like twenty," Breydon said under his breath.

"He's hardly a boy at thirty years of age," Rafe said.

"His exterior is all manly for sure. Shoot, he's pin-up worthy. But his maturity level is that of a gnat."

Trying hard not to take the woman's comments about his son's emotional state personally Rafe's mouth thinned. "You believe these stories of yours tell us who we're meant to marry?"

Karisma shook her head, knowing what she was about to say was the truth, and yet not sure where the knowledge came from. She seemed to be falling into the role as a guide to them. "It is only one possibility of many. And having access to this knowledge now." She indicated the paperbacks laying on the table. "If you're not careful, knowing too much might affect your outcome adversely if you do not handle yourselves properly. More so in Hailey's case." She garnered Breydon's full attention. "Though I suspect Astraia might be the most challenging to overcome initially."

"What makes you say that?" Dante dropped his food on his plate as though no longer interested in eating.

"Are you an idiot or just plain clueless about women?" In response, Dante leaned back in his chair and gave her a hard glare. "What? Did I stutter? Think man! I'm not seeing either her or her children here while you're sitting on your butt eating lunch. I suspect you failed to mention to her the food is ready." She gestured around the room. "Does she know you're eating?" she whispered as if he needed further clarification.

Dante sat for a moment. He had the look of a man having an epiphany. "Oh, crap."

"If you want her to take you serious, you should consider becoming your old self again," Karisma said.

"What? You mean you want I look like my brother? The whole sharp useless appearance Dart's got going for himself isn't my thing."

"Hey!"

"What? I said it was sharp."

Karisma turned toward Rafe in wonder. "It's like I'm dealing with twelve-year old's."

Rafe could only chuckle and smile for he struggled to hold his tongue. "She means you need to be yourself, not Agent Franc Kastle," Rafe said for her.

Karisma twiddled with her hair, becoming distracted by its uncharacteristic black color and shortness. She noted the silver streaking through the strands became more pronounced overnight. She wrote that would happen to a character in her Lineage series, though she didn't anticipate she would be the one referred to in the story.

The sounds of children jabbering happily with Astraia caught Karisma's ears, as they came down the hall. Her face fell and fresh tears welled in her eyes. Her head adamantly whipped back and forth in denial. Not wanting to see other children right now, she turned toward the stairs.

"Karisma?" Rafe called in concern.

"I'm sorry, I can't." Panic-stricken, she raced toward the stairwell, adeptly leaping up the first three, disappearing up the stairs.

Rafe sensed her emotions were raw but was still troubled by her reaction. If she couldn't handle the sound of children in the house then how would she heal?

"She needs to eat, Rafe." ST pulled out from the microwave a platter of quesadillas and proceeded to serve four more plates for Astraia and her kids as they entered the kitchen.

First marveling at his son-in-law's capacity for foresight and to adapt, Rafe chuckled over the quesadilla's the man hid away.

ST caught the look Rafe threw at him. "What? You saw what Drin did. There was no thought to anyone else when he took it either. I have learned not to put all the food out when Drin hasn't shown up yet. The man inhales food like a garbage truck. Had I done that; these kids wouldn't be eating."

"Or us, for that matter," Meg said, managing to grab her own plate. She leaned up and gave her husband a peck on the cheek. "As usual, you are right."

ST smiled. "Too true, my love. Too true. What about you, Rafe?" He suspected the answer but asked anyway.

The man eyed the disappearing food. "No, I'll wait to have dinner with her," he said finally. Grabbing a couple of fruit-flavored water bottles from the fridge he headed upstairs after Karisma. He was determined she would at least stay hydrated. Then he knew he had to hunt down his son. He needed to have a talk with him about the trip he would be taking tomorrow.

Chapter 7

Baltimore, Maryland

Nervous, and unable to control his rapidly beating heart Drin knocked on the door. How did he let his father convince him to do this? Wiping his sweaty palms on his jeans, he tried for nonchalance as he waited for someone to answer. He could hear small feet skidding to a halt near the door. A woman's voice, chastising the racing children, deterred them from answering his knock. The door opened and his heart dropped through his stomach to his feet. The little switch in his head that kept him from saying stupid things stopped working.

"God's teeth you're gorgeous," he said the instant he saw Veta Rohann.

Drin knew beyond a shadow of a doubt it was her. Karisma's description didn't do the woman justice for she was breathtaking. He never saw such a beautiful creature in his life. Tall for a woman at about five foot ten, she had long shapely legs, curvaceous hips, a tiny waist.

He couldn't be sure, but he swore drool dripped from his lip at the sight of her.

God help him, if she came to the door in shorts or a bikini, he would have been done for. The notion made him sweat. Thankfully, she wore a straightforward pair of denim jeans and a three-quarter length sleeved green t-shirt with partially undone waffle snaps.

Drin fisted a hand at his side, crushing the paper with her address by accident. The slope of her neck looked so kissable. Her black eyelashes, brows and straight black hair down to her shoulders made her emerald eyes stand out against her pristine olive complexion.

It was wrong for a woman to be so beautiful. Drin's his eyes shot past her nervously into the house.

Startled initially at the sight of the full-on behemoth before her, Veta's eyes and lips shifted into an easy smile. His black hair and haunting crystal blue eyes got her attention right away as did his vast size. At six foot six, the man barely fit through her door.

"Is your h-husband home?" Drin's tongue felt tied in knots.

The woman frowned. "You want Mitch? I kicked him out seven months ago."

"Good, cause he sure as heck doesn't deserve you."

Veta laughed in spite of herself. "Language, please, small children are in the house."

Drin grimaced. "Right, sorry. So, I realize you don't know me, but my name is Drin Blackthorne."

"I know who you are."

"You do?" He was more than a little surprised.

"Yes. I figured you would be here sooner. Though, I thought you were the lawyer when you knocked. He's supposed to be here soon, so I can sign the finalized divorce papers."

Drin couldn't help but notice numerous boxes stacked in her entryway. "You're moving."

"Of course. That is why you're here. Aren't you?" Her face fell, and she sounded disappointed; oddly a bit anxious as well.

He hung his head. She thought he was the mover. This would be much harder than he thought, and he imagined it would be impossible. "Where are you going?"

"Montana, of course. Silly! Aren't you taking us home with you?"

Her response confused him.

Out of the corner of his eye, Drin noticed a life-sized hand-drawn color portrait hanging on the wall in her entryway. His mouth dropped. The picture was of him from the chest up, wearing his favorite flannel shirt.

Turning in the direction of his gaze, she smiled. "Yes, I've had you on the wall since we moved here after I gave birth to the twins." She laughed, the sound rich and inviting to Drin's ears. "Mitch always used to hate it. Now, I understand why. I suppose no man likes hearing their wife is dreaming of another man. Particularly, when he looks like you."

Stunned, Drin found himself tongue-tied once again.

With a nervous giggle, Veta reached out and took his hand. She tugged him further inside her home. "Come on in, Handsome, and meet the kids. The boys are dying to see you in person."

"So all this..." Drin indicated the packed boxes, confused by what was happening. She dreamed about him? Could she be gifted too? What were the odds of that?

"I promise. I won't be bringing a ton of stuff because I know you own your own place. This house is sold. We have about sixteen days left to vacate. I figured if you didn't arrive by then, I would rent a moving vehicle and head your way. Somehow I knew the dreams were not wrong. He clearly wants me at your side for a long time."

"Wait, who does," Drin asked, thinking he would gladly be at her side for an hour, let alone forever.

She hesitated. "God does, Silly. Who else?"

His face alight with hope, he gave her a big toothy smile.

Veta responded as instructed in her earpiece, though the words spewed from her mouth with great reluctance. She hated having to lie to him the way she did. The expression on his face afterwards of pure innocence and excitement nearly undid her. She couldn't understand how he could be a horrible man. Sure, she got an unsettling sensation being in his presence. The agent told her she would. But her response to Drin was not as bad as the one she had of the man who showed up on her door yesterday from Homeland Security.

"Boy, I'm sure glad you were aware I'd be coming for you, Veta," he said, as she guided him into the kitchen.

She found herself being silly, thinking how much she liked the way he said her name.

"You've made this so much easier on me. I must admit I'm not very good with women," he stuttered.

"Oh, why is that?" she asked. His admission seemed odd to her. Looking the way he did, she couldn't imagine him having any troubles with the opposite sex at all. He was an exceptionally attractive man, which made her nervous. Bending over to pick up one of her children's many toys from the floor, she heard him gasp behind her and turned around. "What's wrong?"

The man's face turned crimson. Between his high cheekbones and tan skin, she wondered if he had a bit of Native American in him.

"Nothing." Drin struggled to remove the image of her backside from his head. "So, uh, where are those kids of yours? Can't wait to meet little Casey, Aaron, and Sarah."

"Sarah?" She dumped the toys from her hands into a bin against the wall near the kitchen.

"Did you name her something else?"

"Who? How many children do you think I have?"

"Three?" A bit confused, Drin became antsy.

Veta peered at him curiously. "I only have two boys; Casey and Aaron."

Drin fidgeted. He swore he remembered reading about three children. "How old are they?"

"They're a little over two years old."

"It all makes sense now. You wouldn't have had her yet. I bet you would have a beautiful little girl. Seeing as your gorgeous." Realizing too late what he said, he scrunched his eyes closed, bowed his head, and tapped his forehead against the paneling. He played with the loose corner trim on her wall, pulling it away and back repetitively. Suddenly, it snapped. A foot and a half long piece broke off in his hand. Gaping, he then banged it on his forehead. "I'm so sorry. I can fix this. I'm very good with my hands."

Veta giggled. She bet he would be. If the agent who appeared yesterday didn't scare her so much, she might be having a very different conversation with him. She planned on trying to ask her lawyer about him when he arrived with the divorce papers. Rushing over, she took the trim from him. Placing a hand on his shoulder, she reassured him. "If you're able to fix it, that would be helpful."

"Right, because you sold the place."

"Sorry?" She appeared confused.

He noted her blank expression. "The house, you said someone bought it."

"Oh, yes," she laughed anxiously. "Right, I did."

Drin paused, getting the sense something was not right. Her nervous mannerisms and a little twitch above her right eye tipped him off. She wiped at her jeans with one hand and lay the trim on her counter. When she did, her hand trembled. He sensed it wasn't from nerves, but from fear. Turning back, she gave him a weak smile that didn't quite meet her eyes. She had the look of a frightened mama deer with her doe in the crosshairs of a snipers rifle.

Shifting his gaze around the room, it occurred to him, he had not seen the shadows in a while. They were curiously absent in the presence of a woman. Not just any female either, but one who might be able to help him find peace. The alarm in his head went off. Dear Lord, please don't let this be like Stacey Lynn. He had such a crush on her years back, but she died in an awful accident the shadows had contrived.

Drin strode over to her. She took a slight agitated step back. The moment he got close to her she whirled about the counter, placing distance between them as she spoke. "Would you like something to drink?" she asked, giving him another winning smile.

"No thank you. I would love to meet your kids though." He pulled his phone from his pocket. "If you'll give me a minute, I need to respond to a message I received."

"I didn't hear the ring."

"The phone is on vibrate." Eyes shifting about the room uneasily, he shook the cell in his hand. This had been going way too easy. Nothing for him ever went well. His shoulders slumped. Sending off the message he tucked the cell back in his pocket for the moment. "Can I meet them? I promise I won't hurt them. Children are so innocent. They should never be messed with."

Veta hesitated, sensing the man's exuberance at meeting her had waned a bit for some reason. "Uh, of course. That's why I invited you in. This way." She led him to the living room where the large playpen was set up for her boys to crawl around in while she worked. Casey began to fuss, so she moved to pick him up, but not before glancing out her front window and then at the clock. The little boy batted at her ear as he fussed, causing something to drop from it. Grabbing for the item, she tried to play it off as having nearly lost an earring.

Reaching for his phone from his pocket again, Drin tapped off another message.

Yup, I'm being played here for some reason. What do I do?

He ran a hand across his face in agitation and cracked his neck. The sound agitated her. She made a startled noise, which caused her other son to start fussing. Reaching down, he picked the boy up for her, trying to help. Becoming choked up Drin smiled down at the handsome young man. "Which one is this?" He asked with a gentle smile all the while forcing back tears. His heart ached, knowing he would never have one. This had likely been his only chance.

"That is Aaron and this one with me is Casey." Her response was shaky.

Wrapping the boy close to him with one arm, he couldn't help but place a kiss on the boys' forehead. Gazing with tenderness down at Aaron, he held the cell in the other as he checked for a text.

'See if you can find out anything from her.'

He responded back. 'Not sure should bother. Casey knocked something from her ear.'

Drin waited. 'Get out NOW!'

Grimacing, he tried desperately to keep from humiliating himself in front of her by shedding tears. Lifting the boy back to the floor, he spun around.

"So, I should go. But, I'll be back when you're all packed." He headed for the door, but he could sense someone race toward him from behind.

"Please, don't go so soon."

Spinning around unexpectedly, he grabbed her by the arms, backing her up against the wall of the stairwell. A startled cry escaped her lips and her eyes flooded with frightened tears. The pain within had him wanting something fierce to squeeze her tight, but he tried hard to be gentle,

"Sorry, I didn't mean to startle you. Did I hurt you, Veta?" His eyes darkened. After seeing the terror he instilled in her, they softened. He didn't want to frighten her, yet he couldn't help but look upon her with such wanting; like an abandoned little boy with no one to love him. Absorbed in his own thoughts it took him a minute to realize she had mouthed words at him, but he couldn't understand what she tried to say.

"No, of course, I was only startled. I know, you would never hurt me." He released his grasp on her, finally starting to comprehend she was afraid of someone else. The expression on her face made it clear. But, if not him though, then who?

Popping the earpiece from her ear, Veta showed it to him. She gave him a look, hoping he understood, then pointed toward her sons.

Someone was listening in on them? And she feared for her children. Peering around the room, he worried about what she indicated. The shadows were finally making their presence known. The blasted Houdini's managed to trick him again. He needed to figure out how they were doing that. His ability to see them helped him protect himself as well as others from them.

Noticing a small whiteboard in the boys play-pen, he grabbed it up and motioned for Veta to sit on the stairwell where they couldn't be seen through her bay window.

'Is something wrong? Are you in danger?' Drin wrote.

She nodded her head yes.

"I suppose I could stay a little longer," he said aloud. "I can help pack."

Erasing the board, he scrawled out, 'Because of me?'

Raising her shoulders, she indicated an 'I don't know' sort of response. "Oh, I can do that myself," she said, catching on to his intended ruse.

'Who's listening? Who are you afraid of?' Drin wrote next, in an attempt to determine what he was dealing with. Then he said aloud, "Those are a couple of handsome boys you got there."

"Thank you. I think they're cute too, but I'm biased, being the mother and all." She giggled trying to sound normal, but her body trembled as she took the marker and responded.

'Agent Jericho Henley. He says he's from Homeland Security, but?'

Drin inhaled sharply. The agent's name came from the books. He took his phone from his pocket and texted his dad, then asked another question via the whiteboard. 'Is he here now? In the house?'

Aloud he said, "No, those little guys of yours are cute cause they get it naturally. But don't worry, it comes from you, not their father." More concerned with trying to keep track of the two conversations, he missed seeing her confusion as she wrote her response.

'No, he bugged the house, made me wear an earpiece.'

"Oh, Mitch isn't their Dad," she said, sounding a bit embarrassed.

"It's okay, Veta. I'm aware of what happened in College with the football players, and I know about him. No need to feel bad." He proceeded to text his father the information. Getting a text, he showed her the phone.

'Ask her if she has a garage, if so, is it attached to the house and is anyone waiting in it? Where is her car?'

Not getting a response right away, he gazed over at her. She seemed cross and acted as if her head was spinning. He touched her shoulder and she flinched. Drawing back he waved at her, garnering her attention.

'Are you okay?' He mouthed to her.

She shook her head, appeared more agitated than before. Taking the phone from him, she texted his dad back. 'Garage attached, Car inside with car seats. Don't think anyone is inside.'

Picking up the whiteboard, she wrote Drin a question. 'Why do you think Mitch is their dad?'

Retrieving the marker from her, he scrawled a reply. 'Cause he was the fourth guy.'

She gave him a very confused looked. She erased everything so far and drew a giant question mark.

Taking the phone back from her, he decided to answer her first. 'That's why you divorced Mitch, right? You found out he was one of the men who assaulted you and he went to jail.'

Getting a new response from his father he read the message as Veta stared at the whiteboard, shaking her head. Suddenly she gasped. Clasping her hands over her mouth, she got up from the floor and with a horrified cry, snatched up the family photo on the mantle. Glancing at the picture, she threw it, smashing it to pieces. Agony raged across her face, somehow knowing what Drin said was true. She dropped to her knees, struggling to keep from tipping off Agent Henley. Her husband had been a liar, a cheat, and a scoundrel. He lost his Professorship because he got involved with a student. It was why she was divorcing him. But now to learn this?

Seeing her reaction, Drin's gut clenched. He thought she knew, but she had no idea. Thinking quickly, he tried to come up with an excuse to explain the crashing noises and her startled cry. "Oh, Veta, Honey, I'm so sorry. I'm so big and bumbling. I didn't mean to break your picture." He lifted her from the floor and pulled her to him, cradling her against his chest, so she could sob quietly into his arm. "Don't you worry, I'll take care of this mess, and I'll fix the frame too," he said loudly. Taking her face in his hands, he wiped the tears from her shimmering green eyes. He hated being the cause of the pain in them now. "The photo will be so much nicer by the time I'm done. You have my word, and a Blackthorne's word is everything."

She nodded her head, having the capacity to realize she needed to pull it together until they figured out what they were going to do.

"So tell me, where do you keep your dustpan and broom?" he asked, showing her his phone.

She read what it said aloud at his prompting. "The garage," she said, clearing the catch in her throat.

"Why don't you continue packing your stuff," he pointed around the room trying to tell her to get anything she needed to take with her because they were leaving. "I'll pick up this mess and fix the trim I broke. I'm going to take care of these big pieces of glass first and then I'll go get that dustpan and broom." Within a couple of minutes and with Drin's help, Veta managed to grab up what she needed to get by for a while along with some baby food from her pantry. He took the bags, lifted Aaron out of the playpen again, and between the two of them, carried the children to the garage. "I'll be right back." He yelled into the empty house, slamming the door behind him. Turning around, a two-door red Chevy Cobalt sat in front of him.

His mouth dropped.

Seeing his expression she mouthed, "What's wrong?" as she began latching the kids into their car seats. He tossed the bags in the back seat. Indicating his height and breadth he pointed at her tiny car in dismay. "Don't you have a bigger car?" he whimpered, hoping he couldn't be heard.

She snickered at him and shook her head.

Drin slumped against the car in defeat.

Opening the front door, he reached down and shoved the seat back as far as it would go. He discovered it wouldn't go back all the way, because Aaron's car seat hindered it. Groaning, he struggled to get his legs and body inside the car.

Covering her face, Veta fought to contain her laughter. Her emotions were on a roller coaster today.

Somehow, in her anger and terror, the man was making her laugh over his predicament. His knees were forced up past the bottom of the steering wheel and his shoulders were wider than the seat. He accidentally elbowed her in the side as he attempted to pull the seat belt around him. Much to his dismay, it stopped within an inch of him being able to secure it. He groaned and grunted, trying to get it to clasp, then gave up in its futility. His head kept hitting the ceiling every which way he turned, and he had to scrunch down to see through the windshield.

"Keys?" he silently asked, pointing to the ignition. He held out his hand.

She shook her head and whispered. "Mr. Henley took them."

He stared. She looked so vulnerable, and he knew she was taking a chance on him. The fact she entrusted herself and her boys in his care said volumes, for how frightened the agent made her. Anger surged within him. She had no means of escape other than him. What would Henley have done to her if he didn't show up today? Not wanting his mind to go there, he hunched forward, awkwardly reaching under the steering wheel. It was an older model so this would be easy. He refused to let her down.

"No problem." Ripping wires out from under the dash, he hot-wired the car, handed his phone off to her, and punched the remote for the garage door. "Now, tell me what Dad says next," he whispered.

Startled to learn his father directed him, she peered down at the screen. "He's saying, don't wait for the door to go up. Punch it and go left. The element of surprise is best. Is he serious? He knows we have precious cargo, right?"

Slamming his foot on the gas pedal, Drin squealed tires as he raced from the garage out on the street, busting the bottom portion of the door as he went.

"No worries Veta," he shouted over the radio he turned up. "If my Dad taught us Blackthorne children anything, it was how to run if things ever got dicey. I promise I'll get you all out of here safely." In the back of Drin's mind, he was kissing his father for putting them all through those ridiculous, as he called them, 'life lessons.' At the time they seemed absurd and unnecessary.

Careening around the subdivision corner, he observed from the rear view mirror a van trying to follow. Thinking now, the lessons had been a Godsend, he knew exactly what he needed to do to lose this guy.

- - -

Hiding out in a public parking lot became necessary once Drin managed to escape Veta's house. The van attempted to keep up, but fortunately, he managed to get ahead of him. With a series of dizzying turns, not even Veta could figure out where they were. Staying in contact with his father the whole time, Rafe had been able to pull up a satellite image of their location from his home office in Montana. He directed them to a high school parking lot about twenty-five minutes away from her home. He turned in and parked in the center of the lot. The two boys, lethargic from the ride in the car, rested peacefully for they fell asleep in their car seats.

A heated argument ensued when Rafe told him to choose a small car and switch vehicles. He got out of the car and stepped away a bit to keep from waking Casey and Aaron.

"I won't steal a car," he said while hunching low among the parked cars, "and if I did, it sure isn't going to be a small one." He yelled into his phone.

"I understand you don't want to be the cause of someone else's bad day," Rafe argued, "but do you intend to let that poor woman and her children get caught by Henley? You promised her you'd get her to safety."

Drin's gut clenched. He scowled and cast a glance over his shoulder. "There has to be another way. Can't you wire money to an auto dealership for a used car?"

"That will take too long, plus, it would leave a trail. And what are you gonna do with the vehicle once you arrive at the airport? Henley has resources you don't. And the airfield is still over an hour away. You need an inconspicuous small car."

"All right fine! But why's it gotta be a small one? This dang Cobalt put a kink in my neck and my nether regions aren't doing so great either." He whispered the last part nowhere near as quiet as he thought. Much to his horror, Veta began chuckling from the car. He chose to squat down as he talked a short distance from the car, afraid if Henley passed by, he might see him from the street. Attempting to hobble further away while still in a squatting position, he found himself squished tightly between the two cars in front of where he parked. He didn't want to go too far in case they needed to leave in a hurry. He felt boxed in where he was. "And how am I supposed to make a decent impression on her when you have me stealing stuff? She's going to think I'm a common thief."

"Trust me, son, there is nothing common about you. You're like a pearl from a clam or a black rose among a flower bed of carnations."

"Black roses. Clam pearls. What the heck are you talking about, Dad?"

Rafe groaned. "Small is better because with your size and stature he won't be expecting it. And if Henley catches the two of you before you arrive at the plane, he will make her his mistress."

"One stolen car, coming up." He hung up on his father. Still hunched down near the ground he spun around and glanced back at Veta. She hung out the window looking at him.

"Drin, trust me, I won't think bad of you." Her face had gone chalky white.

"I take it you heard all that?"

"Um, it was a little hard not to," she said.

"Why?"

"You talked with your speaker on."

"I did?" He looked down at his phone. "Oh! Well, crap." He got up and walked over to her, feeling more than a little self-conscious. "I'm not stupid Veta. I scored higher than all four of my siblings combined, on the intelligence tests they give you in high school and college. The commonsense stuff is what I have trouble with sometimes."

"You went to college too?" She stared up at him, marveling over the breadth of his shoulders and a tapered waist. He nodded in response. "I'm an accountant. I passed my CPA test first time around which is hard to do. What did you study?"

"I wanted to go for art and structural engineering, but Dad suggested I add some business courses. Hated every last one of them, but in the end, it was a smart idea. I was able to start my own company after college. I'm my own boss and I don't need to work along a lot of other people, if I don't want to. You know, cause most people can't handle being around me for long." At Veta's questioning look he decided to change the subject. "I should pick one of these cars, and fast too before someone notices us." He scanned the assortment of vehicles closest to him. He wanted to choose the Ford truck with the extended cab, but according to his dad, that wouldn't be wise. Raising his arms above him, he clasped his hands behind his head. Exhaling, he released them, opting for the muddy colored Volkswagen Beatle in front of him. It made more sense than the blue Nissan Sentra a couple of cars down from them. Older models were easiest to hot wire.

Between the two of them, they switched the diaper bags and car seats with the sleeping kids, to the new one without too much trouble. After he squeezed himself inside, he realized upon closer inspection the muddy color was because the person had sanded it down in preparation of painting it. The owner was in the middle of attempting to refurbish the entire vehicle. Feeling more than a little guilty about the misfortune he was doling out, he checked the visor first, on the off chance there would be a key, so he wouldn't have to damage the car.

"Jackpot." He started the car and took off.

Fifty-three painful minutes later, Drin pulled into the Hagerstown Regional Airport having made better time than anticipated. Making his way around to the hangar, he observed the pilot outside the jet talking with a distinguishing older gentleman. He couldn't see the individual well from his angle, but the man appeared familiar to him somehow. The man held a long knobby wooden cane, and he had an air of refinement and superiority about him. Mitch shook his head angrily as if he were arguing with the man. Drin slowed his vehicle to a crawl, trying to determine what was going on.

Without warning, Veta gave a startled yelp and leaned back in her seat reflexively.

"Stop."

He brought the car to a standstill.

"Please tell me that isn't the plane you told me about." She gestured toward his father's private jet and the two men standing outside it next to a black Lincoln Town car.

She sounded uneasy and was making a funny face.

"Yeah, the jet belongs to Dad and the man with the rag in his hand is the pilot. I'm not sure who the other guy is, but I feel I should know him. Why?"

"Drin, why is my ex-husband piloting your dad's private jet? He's not a pilot. What's going on here?"

Alarmed, he parked behind a fuel tanker for cover then turned toward her. "Are you telling me the man with the baseball cap and blue polo shirt is your ex?"

"Yes."

His mind raced, trying to figure out what was going on. "Do you have more than one?"

"No! I've only been married once. I'm saying, he is Mitch."

"Yeah, the pilot's name is Mitchell."

"Didn't you catch the resemblance in the family picture on my mantle?"

Thinking back, Drin recalled passing by it, without so much as a glance. When he picked up the photo after she broke the glass and frame, however, he saw it then. He'd been so worried about getting her and the kids out of the house, it didn't register to him the man seemed familiar.

"Dad's been using this pilot for years. His name's Mitchell Gaylord. Not Rohann."

"Drin, Rohann is my maiden name. I had no intention of keeping that man's name, and I'm sure as heck not getting on any plane with him. How did I not see this?" She moaned, leaning forward in her seat while covering her face. Pulling her hands away, her cheeks flamed with humiliation and anger. "How do you know all this?"

"Uh, from Karisma's books," he said, unsure how to respond.

Veta didn't understand what he said. Waving her hands in the air, as if it didn't matter, she continued to vent. "The police always said there was a fourth guy, but they never could figure out whom. But what you said makes total sense, because his office had been in the same building as the library, and pictures don't lie." Everyone always said her boys looked so much like Mitch. Some who knew her, and what happened would say it too. He'd been a Professor at the college she attended. His classroom had been next to her Economics class. Between classes, he often flirted with and teased her about going on a date. She always politely turned him down because, at the time she was a student. It wouldn't have been appropriate.

Stunned to his core, Drin couldn't believe his bad luck. There was no way his father's long-time pilot being Veta's ex-husband was a coincidence. What concerned him more was that he didn't know who the other man was. He squinted through the windshield between the cab and the tanker he parked behind. He could see Mitch being handed an envelope. Was he pulling money out of it? Rage surged within him. The pilot appeared much happier now too, as though pleased with himself.

Drin's first instinct was to hightail it over to Mitch and give him a sound beating. Once he managed to get his temper under control, he took a more sensible approach and drove out of the airport, grateful they weren't seen when they pulled in.

"What are you doing?" Veta asked, confused about where they were going.

"I'm going to jump on interstate eighty-one south, and you're going to call Dad back for me."

Veta dialed and Rafe picked up on the first ring. "Are you in the air or not?"

"Uh, Dad?"

"And by the way, I hate it when you kids hang up on me."

Drin cringed, realizing he needed to leave it on speaker as he drove. "About that."

"No, no. Don't you dare tell me you haven't switched vehicles yet." Rafe sounded close to irate.

"We did."

"Then what? What is holding you up?" The man was fit to be tied.

"We tried going to the airport, but our pilot, Mitchell Gaylord, also happens to be Veta's ex-husband," he said quickly, hoping it'd be like ripping off a Band-Aid.

There was silence on the other end.

Veta leaned her weary head against the window. A half sob escaped her lips, because part of what he said was untrue. "Legally, he's not an ex yet. Remember what I told you when you arrived? I thought you were my lawyer with the final divorce papers," her voice wavered. She struggled to keep from crying. "He never showed, and I still need to sign them."

More silence as the news sank in. He heard breathing though, so his dad hadn't hung up.

"Take me off the speaker."

Veta started to cry, unable to hold it back anymore. Tears fell down her cheeks and dripped on her lap. She handed the phone back to him.

Punching the button on his cell, he held it to his ear while driving with one hand.

"Why is Veta crying? What's happened?" Rafe asked.

"She didn't know yet." Drin tried to speak softly, not wanting to upset Veta further.

Rafe was confused. "Didn't know what?"

Pausing, Drin attempted to find the most tactful way of voicing it without hurting her more. He took a deep breath. "About Mitch being the fourth guy."

"I see." There was a long pause. Then, "Where are you now?"

"I'm on the interstate heading south. What do I do? Kind of wishing I were Dante right about now." He was getting nervous about whether he could get her home safely.

"You're more than capable of doing this. Head toward Chicago. I'll purchase your flights. But you're going to need to switch cars again since you're driving now, and soon."

"Can I choose a bigger vehicle this time?" The cramped quarters of the Volkswagen were getting to him.

"Yes, Drin." Rafe's voice had an edge to it, and he sounded testy. "Just no trucks, understood?"

"Right. I should tell you before we hang up, there was an older gentleman present arguing with Mitch. He gave him an envelope filled with money. Was that a guy of yours paying him?"

More silence.

"Dad?"

"No."

Drin exhaled, only then realizing how close a call he and Veta may have had. "Oh, and Dad?"

"What now?" Rafe said.

He could hear his father sigh. He sounded tired and stressed like he was at his wit's end. "There are two kids, not three."

"She didn't have twins?"

"No, she has twins."

Rafe sighed again through the phone, knowing full well what that meant. "Understood. Come on home and take your time. No speeding. You got your cash on you right?"

"Yup, three different places."

"Text me with updates and call me when you're close to Chicago."

"Yes, Sir." Disconnecting, he set the phone down and glanced at the woman next to him. "I'm so sorry, Veta. You never should've found out that way."

Not responding right away, she stared out the window and cried. She never shed a tear in front of people but felt comfortable doing so with him for some reason. Or maybe she didn't care what people thought anymore.

Wiping at her eyes, she pushed her hair out of her face. "You're not the one who should be sorry." In the back of her mind, she couldn't help but wonder how her soon to be ex-husband had come to be the pilot to Drin's father. And when? She didn't realize he could even fly.

Chapter 8

Blackthorne Horse Ranch
Kalispell, Montana

Rafe turned off the speaker on his phone. It was so quiet; a person could hear a pin drop in the kitchen.

"Did I hear you right?" Karisma asked from the bar stool across from him. "Rafe?"

He didn't move or speak for the longest time. His whole family stared at him, waiting to find out what he would do.

When Drin called, everyone was eating breakfast. Without thinking Rafe put him on speaker, a bad habit of late. This meant everyone overheard the call.

Picking up the nearby pitcher, Rafe's hand shook as he poured himself a glass of orange juice. Carrying the juice with him, he moved around the counter away from the fridge.

Karisma reached out and touched his right shoulder ever so lightly. "Rafe, hand me the pitcher." He didn't move, so she tried again. "How about we put the pitcher down and you can go take that prized horse of yours for a ride."

"Yes, a ride on Mocktail. That would be good."

His voice, low and quiet made Karisma shiver. "Yes, go take a long horse ride." Not sure what possessed her, she leaned toward him, startling them both as she gave him a kiss on the lips.

It was their first kiss, and she wished it had been under different circumstances. Maybe then he wouldn't be so stunned right now.

Karisma blushed at her brazenness in front of his family. She hoped the show of affection would make things better, by giving him something else to occupy his mind. His head no doubt reeled with the disturbing news of being betrayed by one so close to him.

He took her hand, squeezed gently then let it fall away. "Yes, I think I'll do for a run."

He started toward the patio, spun back around, and headed to the hallway instead. Moments later they all heard the pool room door bang open. A loud splash resounded down the hallway before the door closed behind him.

"There is only one way he'll calm down," Dante said. "To find this out after knowing the man for almost ten years is a huge betrayal. But I'm sure he appreciated you trying."

With pink cheeks, Karisma thanked him in a small voice, left her plate on the counter, and headed upstairs. No longer hungry, she figured he would find her later if he wanted to talk. Somehow he managed to allow a predator around his family. Rafe, of all people; a man whose paranoia was so great he dug into the past of anyone he came in contact with. Yet, Mitch, a predator slipped under his guard. No doubt, the knowledge was killing him for Rafe's only daughter, Meg, flew in the cockpit with Mitch when they returned from Pennsylvania. Karisma doubted he worried about the loss of the plane which might never be returned, because he secretly owned another private jet.

Four hours later, feeling restless and lonely, Karisma wandered out to the hallway and stood near one of the interior windows. The view from there allowed her to gaze down into the pool room. She saw Rafe had returned to swim more laps after attempting a three-and-a-half-hour ride on Mocktail. She leaned against the glass pane of the window with a heavy heart and watched as he, once again, swam laps in his clothes. He didn't even bother to kick off his shoes before diving in. Thinking on what they learned, she counted off two fingers on her hand, then a third. Closing the third finger, she wanted to internally kick herself for not considering the time frame sooner. Veta and Mitch were not married long enough for her to have Sarah.

Karisma never came up with a last name for the pilot when she wrote about him in her Lineage series. She used the name more than once in her stories, and it never occurred to her.

Mitch is Mitchell Gaylord.

The pilot is Veta's husband. Karisma wondered briefly if the supposed author who hired her to edit the An Unfortunate Lineage series - that Vortigern Black character - might have known. It felt like their two series might be linked somehow.

Against her will, the movie reel in her head began to play again. Her stories always came to her during dreams, but since she arrived within the valley, disjointed bits of imagery started to leak out during the day while awake. She shook her head violently. No, she wasn't ready yet. Whether she wanted to view them or not they formed anyway. With a heavy heart, she closed her eyes, deciding not to fight the visions. Money exchanged hands and yet, he waited. Her eyes flew open. Rafe didn't know yet. She must warn him.

- - -

Rafe Blackthorne kicked off the wall of the pool. His long arms pulled him through the cool water, as he clumsily tried swimming the breaststroke with his tennis shoes and clothes still on. At one point he became fed up at being hindered by the weighty footwear. Kicking them off, they now lay at the bottom of the pool.

Fueled by his anger he managed a dozen laps in a short time before slowing to a steady pace. His head came up and out of the water periodically for air, out of sheer necessity. The strong scent of muggy chlorine filled his nostrils each time he re surged for the much-needed oxygen. Otherwise, he kept his head burrowed within the cold liquid for it acted as a balm to the heat raging within. On autopilot, his mind raced over what he learned.

Could Mitch be working with Jericho Henley? He quickly disregarded the notion. If Mitch worked for him all this time, Henley would have come after his family by now. If Rafe read the situation properly, Henley became aware of his children due to the fiasco in Indiana, Pennsylvania. The discovery of Rafe assisting in Karisma's escape meant Henley now knew his true loyalties lay somewhere other than with Phenom or the FBI. The unavoidable result cost him, for the traitorous old "friend" now tested theory's outside of Phenom's control which was dangerous. The man's reckless actions when he went after Veta and Drin made him nervous. More so then when the agent went after Karisma. He wouldn't be surprised if he found both women the same way.

Wincing, Rafe fisted his hands in the water, wishing he thought of this sooner. He bet he knew how Henley learned of Karisma and Veta. Most writers and authors did a lot of reading. He would ask when next he saw Karisma, but he guessed she stumbled upon and purchased several copies of a certain book series. The same with Veta.

Over twenty years ago Phenom commissioned a novice agent and author within their ranks to write a collection of paranormal novels. Through the tracking of those book sales, they located a majority of their so-called "new recruits." Gifted people often found themselves unconsciously seeking out stories they could relate to. Phenom hired the author to write them for that reason. The agent who wrote them used his alias within the agency, David Pearson, as her pseudonym upon Henley's request. Though aware Henley meant the pen name as a joke, Rafe had not been amused.

A horrifying thought started forming within his already too burden-filled mind, the idea of which left his insides filling with ice. He needed to speak with Drin and Veta before they arrived at the airport. No one in the Phenom organization fit the description his son gave of the man talking with his pilot. It could mean a new faction. A whole new group of people, seeking out gifted individuals whose motives are unclear.

Turning at the end of a lap, he pushed off from the wall again, allowing the cold water to soothe his temper. Fear fought to take hold of him. When he got this way nothing calmed him down. Taking a ride on his prized steed, Mocktail might have worked before Karisma tried to help. Her surprising and gentle kiss sent him over the edge, confusing the heck out of him.

That kiss. Her lips were so soft.

He swam a lap and a half, not allowing himself to come up for air. His lungs burned by the time he burst up from the water. Taking a deep breath, he promptly dove right back in, allowing the slap of the water on his face to bring him back to his senses. Rafe couldn't afford to be distracted with those thoughts. Besides, he needed to determine what her true role within his home would be. Her name didn't fit with the story. The last book in the, An Unfortunate Lineage series listed the name of the Inara woman as being Ciara Biardon, and she lived in Edwardsburg, Michigan. Finding Karisma Kayos in Indiana, Pennsylvania meant something definitely went wrong. He conceded part of the story might be incorrectly written for her other series of books were a mess.

Whirling about as he swam, he switched to the backstroke. A sudden gigantic eruption of water sent a wave spewing him forcefully forward against the wall at the end of the pool. Knocking his side against the steps leading out, he resurfaced in time to see Karisma splashing around in a panic. Shoe less, but still wearing clothes like him, she floundered at the opposite end of the pool. A hallway window above the pool room hung open. Had that daft woman risked jumping into the pool from there?

"Rafe. I need. To tell you." Karisma's head went under, and she came up spewing water, thrashing about as if she couldn't swim. She appeared to be in trouble as she tried to speak again. He swiftly swam toward her.

"He's coming. They. I mean. Need to. Akpfhew. Help!" She cried out in distress before sinking back under.

He swam the rest of the length of the pool. Diving where last he saw her, he grabbed her by the waist. Forcing her head up and out of the water, she spewed some from her mouth. Adjusting her in his arms, he carried her up the steps and out of the pool. Water dripped from their sopping wet clothes. By the time he managed to get her out of the pool, they had an audience.

Dante and Dart raced through the pool doors with ST not far behind. They arrived in time to watch their father carry her across the tiled floor and set her down.

"Are you okay?"

The worry etched in Rafe's features made her feel bad. She didn't mean to add to his burdens. Coughing, she spasmed in his arms. The thin shirt she wore plastered to her bra less chest, leaving little to the imagination.

Rafe grabbed a towel from the pool rack in order to cover her. "Why in the world did you go and do that?" His panic over seeing her sinking in the water started to abate, but she still looked fragile, extremely thin, and very tired.

"Needed to. Had to." She tried to speak between coughing fits, to no avail.

Cupping her face in his hands, Rafe then ran them the length of her to make sure she didn't injure herself.

"Try taking a few deep breaths," ST suggested, bending down next to her. "And don't lay her down, Rafe, sit her up so her diaphragm will stay open and make it easier to breathe. I could see her from our bedroom, but I didn't have time to stop her."

Dart shook his head, having trouble believing what he witnessed. "I was coming up from the kitchen when I caught the tail end of her leaping out."

"I heard her going in from the study. Almost sounded like an explosion went off here in the pool. I figured I better check things out," Dante said.

"What were you thinking? It's a miracle you didn't end up on the side of the pool. Leaping from up there like that could have killed you."

"I w-wasn't th-thinking. I n-needed to t-tell you," she said between chattering teeth. The moist air gave her the chills. She shivered violently.

"Tell me what? That you can't swim? Because, that became obvious real fast."

Her eyes begged him to understand. "N-no, I d-didn't know I c-couldn't," she said, surprising all three of them. "I t-took the kids to the pool just this summer and sw-swam laps while th-there with them."

"How could she swim then, but not now? What's changed?"

Leaning against Rafe for support, Karisma managed to regain control of her speech a bit. "Who knows? I need to warn you," she gasped between breaths, slowly beginning to breathe better.

"Warn me about what?"

"Your b-brothers are coming," she managed to spit out. She scowled at him. "I figured you would appreciate the heads up or am I wrong?"

Closing his eyes, Rafe felt a new surge of anger. He inhaled deeply, trying to calm down. "You saw this?"

Her head bobbed vigorously up and down in answer.

"Is that what possessed you to leap from the second floor into the pool?" Rafe asked.

"It sure seemed like a good idea, at the time. I figured you would want as much warning as possible."

"Any idea when his highness is going to grace us with his presence?"

Karisma could tell Rafe didn't catch the full meaning in what she said. "You don't understand."

"I'd say right about now," a man said imperiously from the open pool doors.

Turning to look, Rafe groaned aloud at the sight of his brother. The man looked identical to him in every way, but for his hair. Thick and black, it was peppered with white above the ears like his, but where Rafe shaved his facial hair daily, Rourke maintained a distinguishing beard. He also wore glasses, dark blue trousers, and a light blue dress shirt, rolled up to his elbows.

"Clearly we don't stand on ceremony in this house." Rourke peered around the pool as he kept hold of a knobby wooden cane for support. His gaze eventually found its way back to Rafe and Karisma huddled on the floor. His eyebrows rose in disdain. "Not only do you not answer doors when people knock, but when greeting people you do so in sopping wet clothes."

"We really need to work on your timing Karisma." Rafe absently rested his head against her forehead. It had been so many years. What was his addled, delusional brother doing here anyway?

Rourke walked with a slight limp into the pool area. "What? Did I interrupt you while trying to have a moment?"

His brother looked old. Older than him, Rafe mused with a small amount of satisfaction. Though, he guessed he couldn't blame him. Last he heard, Rourke lived with their father, Rathbourne and their grandfather, Alestair at the Blackthorne Estate house in Scotland. Living with those men would likely age anyone.

"No, you're impeding him from being able to calm down," another voice said from the opposite side of the pool. "I gather he's had a recent shock to his system."

Rafe glanced between Rourke and the other man standing just inside the other door, thoroughly baffled by what he saw. The other man looked identical to them as well, only this guy wore a short goatee instead. He wore black work boots, jeans, and a trim-fitting black t-shirt that bunched at his shoulders.

"Though, staying calm while seeing a ghost in your home is likely to be a challenge," the man continued. "I like what you've done to the place, Rafe. Looks a lot different from what our Dad originally built, though I see you maintained the carved lilies on the mantles throughout. A sentimental homage to Sapphire? There are definitely quite a few more rooms now to hide and play in."

Rafe squinted at the man in disbelief. "Randulf?"

"I tried to warn you," Karisma said loudly next to him. She coughed again several times, prompting Rafe to pat her back absentmindedly. "You know, hence the not so graceful swan dive into the pool. I realized too late you didn't read his stories yet," she said tiredly.

"Actually, it's Bastion now. Has been since Sapphire moved me to Colorado to be adopted and raised by the RavenCroft's."

Rourke grunted, tapping his cane on the ground to gain their attention. "You couldn't wait one more day to show up here?" He scowled at Bastion, somehow looking like a thwarted man.

Rafe thundered. "All this time he's been alive, and you knew?"

"How could you have, Rourke?" Bastion wondered aloud. "Sapphire said not even our father, Rathbourne was aware." He strolled lazily into the pool area, taking up a seat on one of the lounge chairs near Rafe and Karisma. Acknowledging the other three men present who stood with their mouths agape, he rattled off their names as though he weren't meeting them all for the first time. "Dante. Dart. Nice to see you again. ST, congrats on the wedding. Meg's an impressive young woman; an excellent catch on your part." His attention drawn by the woman shivering on the floor next to his brother, he said, "We should really cover her with more than the one towel." Grabbing another towel from the rack he haphazardly tossed it over her. "There you go." He smiled warmly at her, the twinkle in his eye giving him the appearance of a man attempting to flirt.

Rafe gave Bastion an annoyed look as Rourke responded in his usual patronizing manner. "I see all and know everything," he said, giving Bastion cause to snort loudly over his claim. "But to be fair, I did not become aware of your, resurrection, until about three months ago when grandpa Alestair finally died."

"Grandpa Alestair passed away? Why didn't you call me?" Rafe asked, irritated to find this out after the fact. "How's Dad holding up?"

One eyebrow rose in question. "Admirably considering he had a mild heart attack upon finding out Randulf is still alive. As to Alestair, I'd wager Dah would be dancing on the man's grave if he could. But I digress. It took me a while to verify certain details or I might have visited sooner for such news shouldn't be given by way of a phone. Our mother, kept you hid well."

"She insisted on the name change," Bastion agreed, still staring at Karisma. "Though I do wish, at times, ma and pa came up with a different one. The name Bastion is much too similar to the word bastard for my tastes. The name has been a source of great aggravation and trouble for me over the years. I'm betting you know full well what I speak of, eh, my little angel?" The intensity of his gaze started to make Karisma anxious. She shifted uneasily, tightening her grasp on the increasingly damp white towels. She attempted to crawl up from the floor. She barely made it to her feet when she became lightheaded and slumped back down.

All three men leapt toward her as she slid back to the floor, with the intent to catch her. Being the closest, Rafe got there first, catching her about the waist and shoulders.

"Oh, whoa. No, you don't." Bending down, Rafe swooped her up into his arms with very little difficulty.

Rourke grumbled. "Show off."

Bastion grinned, watching the heads of Rafe's sons move back and forth among the three of them. "Now, Rourke. Is it our fault you sat behind desks for the past umpteen years as we've been out tending to horses and the land?"

"You have horses?" Intrigued, Rafe studied his long-lost brother with interest as he held Karisma.

"Yes. In fact, many years back, you bought stock from my adopted father's ranch."

"Did I?" Thinking back, Rafe recalled he went to Colorado for some new breeding stock right around the time he and Rourke parted ways.

Yawning loudly, Karisma's eyes flickered drowsily. She struggled to stay awake for her visions made her sleepy. She shivered, then leaned her head against Rafe's shoulder. Both Rourke and Bastion scowled over the familiar behavior, but they each regarded Karisma curiously.

"She needs dry clothes and a bed," Bastion said.

"Indeed," Rourke said.

"I'll take her up to the library now. She can rest there until I can find her something dry to wear that will work better than my clothes. Maybe Astraia has something?" Rafe gave Dante a meaningful look.

"I'll check," Dante said, speaking for the first time since his uncle's sudden arrival.

"Your clothes?" Bastion erupted from the seat he retook on the lounge chair. "Why in the world is she wearing your clothes?"

Rafe faltered, confused by the suspicious look Rourke cast in his direction. He began walking toward the doors. "It'll take a little explaining. Suffice it to say, she came to this house, having cut and dyed her hair black and without any of her own possessions. Both of you, the Scotch is in the liquor cabinet. You know where to find it, Rourke. The same place the poor excuse for a father of ours kept his. Feel free to pour yourselves a glass, and one for me. I'll be back soon."

"Rafe!" Rourke called, forcing him to halt in the doorway and glance back. "I trust this charismatic widow will be tended to by your daughter? Hmmm? Do not tarry, unwisely, there is much to be discussed between the three of us over her situation here."

Rafe blustered. "Did you say, not to tarry? Bah! I'm not one of those pompous aristocrats over in Scotland you so enjoy entertaining like royalty. I dawdle or procrastinate."

"Linger. Or maybe loiter?" Bastion offered with a smirk.

"Definitely delay," Rafe agreed, "but I never tarry. Nice to know some things never change, Rourke. You're still the same egotistical, condescending, self-important ass I remember." He continued out the door, shouting the latter as he went.

Rourke and Bastion locked eyes the moment Rafe disappeared.

"Charismatic, eh?" Bastion said.

Rourke snorted knowingly, "Indeed,"

"Hmmm. Looks more like an angel if you ask me, regardless of the hair," Bastion said.

"The hair has been colored to fit the individual, and I didn't ask you," Rourke said in answer.

"He has no idea, does he?" Bastion asked. His eyes brimmed with the same expressive wise and cunning look he shared with his brother.

Rourke glanced back in the direction Rafe disappeared. Concern filled his eyes. "That is, as yet, unclear to me, though I dare say, he may now have a suspicion. Come Bastion, let us drink to your resurrection," he said imperiously.

"Did he say Scotch?" Bastion asked.

"Mmm. Yes, unfortunately. I personally would rather have Brandy."

Bastion glowered at the man, looking astounded at his misfortune for having an aristocrat for a brother. "Brandy? What sort of drink is that?"

"A dignified one."

"Eh. Though I do like my Scotch, I'll take a beer any day over Brandy. That said, on a day like today."

"Hot toddies." They both said in unison, disappearing through the pool doors.

Dart, Dante, and ST stared after them.

"Honestly, it's like living through a frelling soap opera around here. I really hope they convene in the kitchen. Or maybe even the living room," ST said.

"Why?" Dart asked.

"Cause then we can eavesdrop, of course."

"Something tells me we're gonna wish Drin was here," Dante said as they walked down the hall toward the kitchen. The other two men looked uneasily at him. Noting their expressions, he grimaced. "I hoped it was my imagination."

"No, it wasn't," ST said.

"We won't know for sure until Dad gets down here, but I'm pretty sure they are fighting over her," Dart said.

Dante sighed uneasily. "We better find Breydon and update him quick."

- - -

Randulf lived. Struggling to wrap his mind around this newest revelation, Rafe took a shaky breath as he carried Karisma up the steps to the library. How could it be possible? He fumed.

His brother Rourke became aware of this information three weeks ago and never said anything to him. Nor did he call when Alestair died. He could understand why he didn't bother informing him of the latter, as in truth he never met the man, but keeping the news about his brother? He knew they didn't ever speak, but to find out their brother was alive, well, and living in Colorado after forty-seven years should have warranted a phone call.

Another thought made him pause outside his study. Their father had a heart attack upon learning the news, but still lived. He was fully aware how much the man loved their mother and could only imagine how painful it must be to learn of Sapphire's betrayal. Though, it still stung that he blamed him for the loss of the Blackthorne book of lineage, he wondered briefly if he should try to make amends with Rathbourne.

Rafe's thoughts darkened his mood. He didn't want to share his prized Scotch with his brothers anymore. A selfish notion for sure, but they showed up unannounced; one of which he didn't even know existed. He would question whether Bastion was his brother if they were not identical, a fact that could not be disputed.

The man clearly had been aware of him and Rourke, in addition to his children, for what sounded like quite some time. That along with the sudden appearance of both of them within a few days of Karisma's arrival, bothered him. It couldn't be a mere coincidence. Both arrived with agenda's, of that he was certain. The thought weighed heavily on him, for he didn't like the way they looked at her - like some prize to be won.

And what exactly did Rourke mean when he said he wished Bastion waited another day to show up? Why would twenty-four hours matter?

"I should have jumped sooner." Karisma said softly against his damp shirt, prompting him to resume his pace. She shivered, despite the two towels now covering her. He couldn't really blame her. He too had become chilled. "If only I remembered what I forgot to tell you sooner."

Before realizing what he was doing, he gave her an affectionate peck on the forehead then turned slightly to be able to fit through the library door. He suspected she became tired after having visions for her eyes kept opening and closing as though she were half-asleep. It was mid-morning, and she hadn't had much activity yet, regardless of her excursion in the pool. There were often side effects to the abilities. Nothing too problematic usually, but being aware allowed them to be prepared for the aftereffects.

"No worries." Rafe laid her on the floor next to the pull-out couch which had been made into a bed for her when she first arrived. He adjusted the towels over her, in the hopes of aiding to keep her warm. "I'll be right back."

Thinking twice about utilizing his secret entrance to his room from the library, with present company in the house, he quickly exited the library. He headed the short distance down the hall to his room. Hastily changing out of his own wet clothes, he threw on a pair of lounge pants and socks. Grabbing two t-shirts, a pair of sweatpants, another pair of socks, and a towel, he left his room and headed back to the library.

"I'll get you dried up and changed before you know it, Karisma," he said as he re-entered the library. He stopped, taking in the scene before him. Rourke stood next to the makeshift bed holding Karisma in his arms. The towels were now in a heap on the floor. His brother's face flooded with barely restrained pleasure as he stared down upon her, taking in every detail of her appearance. Rafe's blood ran cold. "What do you think you're doing?"

Rourke didn't flinch. Adjusting her in his arms, he looked up. His face as florid as his brothers. "You left her on the floor? You were always so inconsiderate. The bed would be more comfortable, don't you think? Not that I would call this a proper bed. And as for you changing her, I don't think so."

"No don't." Rafe tried to stop him, but before he could finish Rourke laid her on the mattress. Her head shifted on the pillow, her wet hair leaving a sizable damp mark. She fell asleep in the short time he was gone. Considering how she was being manhandled, he had to presume she would sleep deeply for the next few hours. "You idiot. I put her on the floor, because she wet. I went to get her clothes and another towel. Thanks to you, her bedding and pillow are now saturated with chlorine water."

"No matter. Now she can be put in a proper guestroom with a real bed rather than a library." Rourke's disdain over her accommodations was obvious. "Who puts a guest in a library anyway?"

"Since Karisma is an author, she had no qualms about staying in this room. Besides, I offered her another room. She said she felt safer in this one."

Rourke's eyebrow quirked as though in disbelief.

"They were her words, not mine. You can ask her yourself when she wakes."

"I intend to."

"What are you doing in here anyways, Rourke? And where is this Bastion who claims to be our brother? You didn't leave him wandering alone in my house, did you?"

"His sudden resurgence may be a little troubling and hard to accept at first, but he is our brother," Rourke insisted.

"And no wandering is necessary," Bastion said. Popping his head into the room, he proceeded to meander in, his eyes falling on the woman sleeping on the sofa bed. "I knew exactly where to find Dante's young lady, Astraia, and I located Meg too in the process." Unable to take his eyes off Karisma as she slept, his mouth curled as though he were struggling to suppress a smile. Then he frowned. "Rafe, why in the world did you put her on the bed in wet clothes? Now everything is wet."

"I didn't." Rafe insisted. "That idiot did."

"Boy, he really doesn't think much of you, does he, Rourke?" Bastion asked, stepping out of the way of Meg and Astraia as they came into the room.

"She's already out cold?" Meg huffed. "How are we supposed to do this with her asleep?"

"I'm sure we'll manage," Astraia said nervously, wandering in after Meg. She carried a pile of clothes in her hands and another towel. "I'll run for more bedding."

"Why bother? She will be put in one of the other guest rooms," Rourke demanded, prompting Rafe to wonder why he insisted so adamantly.

"We tried yesterday," Meg said, as she stared between the two uncles she never met before. Her eyes were wide with wonder, still marveling over learning the news of their presence in the house. But for their choice in facial hair or lack thereof as in her father's case, they were the same in every way. She always knew they were identical triplets, but viewing the three of them together for the first time was overwhelming.

Rafe turned to her in surprise. "You did?"

"Yes," she said sheepishly. "I'm sorry, Dad. Her being right next door to you bothered me. Anyway, changing rooms didn't go over well. I managed to move her in across from us on the opposite side of the house, but too many things in there were reminding her of her kids. After seeing the look on her face I decided not to push it."

"What are you doing in here anyway? There are too many people here. We're bound to wake her up. She needs rest." Rafe's protective instincts were in full swing. He tried shooing everyone out.

"Bastion said we were needed to help her change," Meg said since Astraia had already left for the linen closet.

"Why did you bother going and getting them?" he asked of Bastion.

"She's recently widowed. Surely you didn't intend to strip and redress the woman while she was in such a vulnerable state," Rourke said before Bastion could, giving his brother an accusing glare. "After all, you are not married to her."

"Neither are you," Rafe said.

Suddenly appearing cross, Rourke got up from his chair and assisted Bastion in hastening their brother out the door.

"This will be debated at another time. Now, I believe you promised us a hearty Scotch." Rourke patted him on the opposite shoulder, forcing him to continue to walk down the hall toward the stairwell.

"She's all yours, Meggy." Bastion winked at her, closing the door behind them.

"Let's make hot toddies instead," Rafe said, having no intentions of sharing his Scotch any longer.

"Now that I can live with." Bastion exchanged knowing looks with Rourke.

"Come, come. To the kitchen. We'll get our drinks made up and retire to the living room. We have much to discuss."

"Do we?" Worried about Karisma, Rafe was in no mood for Rourke's manipulation games. "Last I saw you; your backside was having no difficulty walking away. You left with Rathbourne, our father of all people, to go back to Scotland, without a backward glance, thumbed finger, or even a heartfelt..."

"Rafe, language. You do have young ones in the house now after all. Besides, that was long ago. You still, to this day, don't have all the story. Besides, the need for the three of us to discuss matters of current mutual concern has become pressing."

"Why has it become so all fired necessary now?" Rafe asked suspiciously, wondering how his brother could be aware of Drin's current whereabouts. "And why Bastion, after all this time, have you made your presence known? It was nearly thirty years ago when I took that trip to Colorado for horse stock. You have been aware of us for some time now or you wouldn't know the names of my children and who they are. What are you doing here now?"

"I'm here, because the next generation will continue to suffer if we don't start communicating." Bastion stopped at the bottom of the stairs, forcing the other two to halt where they were at three steps up. "It recently came to my attention that the lack of contact with you two was a mistake. Something one of us has done messed things up royally. From what I understand, the woman up there was never meant to lose her children, nor was her husband meant to die, or at least not this soon. Correct decisions need to be made from here on out, regardless of how hard they might be. They may not be the most convenient, or the most desired choices by the heart, but they need to be the right ones for everyone involved."

"Hm. Agreed."

Rafe stared at Bastion and Rourke.

"What in the world are you talking about?" Thoroughly annoyed, Rafe hated when people answered in riddles. It was like having his father in the house all over again.

"Let's get him the hot toddy," Rourke said.

"Yes, I think this is going to require more than one." Bastion rapt him on the back good-naturedly and moved into the kitchen. Rubbing his hands together, he passed by Rafe's boys who were hunkered together over the table next to the island. They appeared to be in a deep discussion until Breydon's head popped up at the sight of Bastion.

"Holy crap!" Breydon's eyes flew open in shock.

"Now," Bastion continued, ignoring his nephew. He began searching the kitchen cabinets. "We're going to need some honey, lemon, cinnamon sticks, Rum and water."

"Nice to see you're making yourself at home in my house there, Bastion."

Intentionally misconstruing what his brother said, Bastion replied in answer. "Why thank you, Rafe, it's good to be welcome after all this time. Particularly after you stood silently by as Rourke tried to kill me when I was three."

"Are you daft man? There will not be Rum in the hot toddies, but Bourbon," Rourke said. He limped the rest of the way into the kitchen, his cane tapping loudly on the tiled floor. "And let's get our stories straight. I didn't try to kill you. Dah did. Now," he paused, his head peering about the kitchen, knowing full well he gained everyone's attention with the statement. "Where's the Bourbon?" Spying a row of cabinets on the opposite side of the main table between the kitchen and the hallway, he headed straight for it. "Good man, Rafe. You hide your alcohol stash in the same place Dah did." He headed straight for the cabinets as ST palmed his head in his hands.

"Dad? You have an alcohol stash?" Dante's mouth dropped in shock. How did he manage to keep that hidden from them all this time?"

Rourke foraged through the cabinet, getting more and more agitated as he searched. "Spiced Rum, Scotch, Wine. There's no Bourbon man. Blimey, where's the Bourbon?"

Grabbing up one of the bottles his brother had set on the counter, Rafe shoved it into Rourke's face. "You don't make toddies with Bourbon you lying, cheating, woman beating cur. Here in America, you make them with Rum. Personally, I prefer Spiced." Sticking a finger in Rourke's face, he shook the bottle in his hand. "Now sit. I'll make the hot toddies while you talk, because you have explaining to do."

Rafe shoved none too delicately on Rourke's chest as he turned, causing his brother to drop into the nearest chair. Rourke blustered, dumping his cane on the floor with a loud thwack. "That's just like you. Ruining a solid drink with that blasted Rum. And no need to be so rough on a partially disabled man of fifty years. For shame on you, I had surgery not long ago."

Bastion took a seat across from Rourke. His brows knit together, thinking through what had been said. "That doesn't jive. You're saying my birth father, Rathbourne, made the attempt on my life, not one of you? According to the letter Sapphire left with me, along with the other stuff, she claimed the culprit was one of you two who tried to drown me. She said she suspected Rourke."

Rafe listened as he pulled out the rest of the ingredients required for the drinks.

"Of course she had to blame me, the one who sees the shadows. Our mother was a wonderful, gracious, and loving woman, but as with anyone she had her faults." Rourke leaned back in his chair. Making a face, he readjusted in his seat, and leaned forward. "One of which was misconstruing her visions at times when she didn't have the whole picture. She often came to hasty judgement of a situation."

Rafe snorted loudly. "That, at least, we can agree on."

Smiling openly, Bastion's head bowed briefly. "I do wish I had the chance to meet her."

"I am sorry," Rafe offered with true regret. "Mom's been gone for some time."

"Thirty years. I know. I received the box left for me within days of you leaving the ranch, Rafe. Once I learned the truth and found out who you were I followed. By the time I arrived, she had already died. I did some investigating at the local tavern and learned what had happened between the two of you."

"Hm. I'm betting the story is inaccurate." Rourke tapped the overly large ring on his right hand against the table. Those closest could tell the giant bauble had the Blackthorne family crest on it. Out of the corner of his eye, Rourke could see his nephews staring in rapt attention at the ring. He grunted. "Things didn't go down as that thick brained buffoon over there thinks. We might as well get this all out in the open before moving on to what really matters. Let's straighten this ignorance out."

Trying to ignore his brother, Rafe pulled three tall brown mugs from the cupboard. He added a splash of cherry syrup, a bit of honey, a cinnamon stick, a touch of clove, nutmeg and a couple of ounces each of Spiced Rum. Adding the ginger tea would have to wait until it came to boil.

"I loved Sarah, regardless of what you might think, Rafe. I never hurt her; it was Dah. Her poor excuse of a father dumped her off at the ranch the day she found out. He told Sapphire that Sarah was my problem. By the time her Dah left her on the porch, she was terrified, in tears, and thought she was hallucinating evil beings. She and Mah started talking and good ol' Dah overheard. He became enraged, more so when he discovered she was aware of our gifts, then over the fact she was pregnant. I was down at the barn when the beating started. He hauled off and struck her, calling her a whore then chased her out into the yard and assaulted her there. He accused her of trying to marry into a wealthy family and attempting to destroy us. Dah was the one who beat her, not me. I tried to stop him. It's why I had the black eye and bruises when you arrived home."

"Very convenient there Rourke. Dah is in Scotland. He isn't here to defend himself and neither is Sarah to confirm your story. Though, you say she was frightened of what she was seeing?"

"Yes, she started seeing the very shadows I do, because she was pregnant with my children. Not equipped to deal with it, she became hysterical. And you're right, they aren't here and able to confirm any of this. But I'm sure if you talk with your old friend Misham Howard, you'll hear the correct version of the story. He married Sarah and kept her hidden from us. From me. A fact I might never forgive him for. I searched for her a long time, even after returning to Scotland."

At this news, Rafe spun around. "What in the world are you talking about? Misham married someone else."

"You never met his first wife, did you? Didn't receive an invitation to the wedding, eh? The judge came to his house. They were married there. Come on Rafe, think. Why else would the man stop coming around? For years, he was your best friend, then all of a sudden, poof. You lost contact. You never once bothered to find out why? Well, now you know. Misham found her. He found her at the divide between our properties. She was scared to death, being tortured by the shadows she was seeing, and still pregnant. Sarah was also in serious trouble too, because she left the hospital mighty quick, trying to escape from us Blackthorne's. He brought her back to his home and helped her give birth. She had triplets, a boy and two girls. Then the selfish arse married her shortly after."

Rourke spoke with such regret and contempt, the emotion gave Rafe a moments pause. Was it possible what his brother was saying was true?

"The boy, he was the only one who survived the bastard's beating. One girl was stillborn, the other died shortly after she was born." Rourke said, his ring tapping becoming a loud thump of his hand. He had become agitated which was never good. Shifting in his seat he cleared his throat, making attempts at the pretense of not getting worked up. "My son doesn't have eyes as the rest of us do though. They're emerald green like Sapphire's for some reason, only with a bit of silver in them."

"You met him?" Rafe asked, startled to learn he had a nephew.

"Oh, yes. Two months ago I received an urgent call from Misham while I was in a meeting. It was only a couple weeks after learning Randulf was alive. Or Bastion as is now. Sorry ol' chap. Anyway, he told me everything and had the nerve to ask me for help to save our son who was diagnosed with AML."

ST made a noise. "Acute Myeloid Leukemia."

Rourke turned toward ST. His brow rose. "Ah yes, the doctor, of course." For some reason, he smirked. Giving the man a quick assessing glance, he turned back and continued. "A blasted scoundrel, Misham is. I was skeptical initially until I arrived at the hospital and met him. They called him Edwin; a Welsh name of all things meaning rich or blessed friend. An intolerable name for a Blackthorne, if you ask me. That alone nearly had me denying him as mine, but in truth, there could be no doubt. He's a brute of a man, he looks a lot like dad's brother Creighton, and he knew things he shouldn't know. He is eerily gifted. So, he had to be a Blackthorne. At my request, a DNA test was done to confirm it. Doctors ran their tests to see if I could help." Rourke paused, shifting uncomfortably in his chair. He had the look of one contemplating a quandary. "We were a match. So he got his bone marrow transplant surgery. Edwin is presently recovering at home, and now I get this blasted limp as a side effect for a while. Annoying, but worth it. Sounds like he'll be fine."

"I'm glad to hear my only nephew is doing well at least." Rafe's comment was hesitant.

"That's not entirely accurate for I have five kids of my own," Bastion said. Reaching behind him, he lifted his shirt and pulled a paperback out. He tossed it on the table. "If you managed to locate this book series of Karisma's, then you know that."

"You found Karisma's novels? How?" Rafe asked.

"The how is a bit hard to explain. If you are already aware of these stories, how were you oblivious to my existence when I arrived? She explained within," Bastion said.

"Honestly, it was a recent discovery. We didn't get around to reading the ones covering the RavenCroft family yet. When I read the jackets they looked like she changed our names and was writing essentially the same stories, but with variations. So, we started reading the ones with our names in it first."

Bastion became thoughtful, noting how Rourke was being unusually silent. From what he observed so far the man tended to always have something to say on any given matter. "Interestingly, she gave me another kid I don't have. I have four boys and a girl, like you Rafe. Triplets and a set of twins which is in keeping with our family history, it would seem. But no Synedra, which is apparently a girl. I'm not sure why she did that."

Finding this odd, Rafe admitted, "She did that to me too. A daughter named Crisalya. I wonder why?"

Rourke hesitated, wondering at whether he wanted to say anything yet. In the end, he forged ahead. "Karisma gave us a sister we don't have. Additionally, one to our father as well. Rathbourne had only one living brother, named Creighton."

"Had?" Bastion interrupted, noting the past tense in the mention of their uncle this time.

"It is unclear whether he is alive or dead." Rourke gained Rafe's attention. The teapot whistled forcing him to tend to their drinks. "Dah, cannot find him and neither can I. We've done some extensive looking, too. Even hired a private detective at one point. He was a waste of time and money though. By the time we'd returned to Scotland all those years ago, he disappeared. Their brother Broden, of course, had died when they were young. What's interesting here, is Karisma had a family tree hanging on the wall of her office before I had it burned down. It listed a sister, Kirstine next to Creighton. Anyone like to venture a guess as to why she keeps giving everyone an extra child, a girl, that isn't real?"

"Did you say you burned Karisma's house down?" Bastion and Rafe both spoke in unison.

"That's what you got from that?" Rourke shook his head while getting up from his chair. "You took off with Karisma and left behind a mess, Rafe. It was very sloppy of you. I got there barely in time to deal with it. Someone had to before your so-called friend Henley arrived and could get his hands on it. She had notes everywhere," he said, with a flourish of his hands. "Binders filled with extremely detailed character charts, family trees. I was already aware you had children," he said offhandedly to Bastion, "There were dozens of flash drives, and a computer tower with a hard drive filled with copies of her stories in addition to more she started. She also had a laptop and tons of notebooks. There was too much for me to attempt to haul away in a short amount of time. So, I did the only thing that seemed reasonable at the time. I set it ablaze." Extending one arm in the air he whipped it around for effect.

"Not before taking off with the flash drives, laptop and hard drives, am I right?" Bastion asked smoothly.

"I'm not stupid like you simpering nitwits keep implying." Rourke picked up his cane from the floor and pointed it toward Rafe. "I had enough sense to know you needed help, so I hauled my arse overseas and tied up your lose ends. Or attempted to, at least."

"You were there in Indiana, Pennsylvania?" Rafe asked.

"And I'm the one deemed an idiot?" Rourke's eyes widened in dismay, his gaze falling on Rafe's sons. "My posterior is asleep, this awful chair is giving me kinks, and I'm quite parched. Shall we retire to the living room with our hot drinks for more comfortable seating and some privacy? We can discuss the matter of Karisma and her books there. And Dr. Some Thing Funny? I understand you're quite accomplished in the kitchen, do be a good man and make me a snack. Something with bread and cheese. Something with fruit maybe? Yes, something indeed." He turned and looked at ST who had begun to seethe angrily. A devilish smirk lined Rourke's features. "What is it, man? Is something wrong?

ST's face went livid. All three of his brothers-in-law had to hold him back as their snob of an uncle disappeared through the kitchen door into the living room, chuckling heartily all the way.

"I understand now why you haven't talked to him in years," Breydon said with a scowl, having difficulty keeping ST from racing after him.

"Calm down ST. He is intentionally bating you," Rafe warned, wondering at why Rourke had homed in on his son-in-law to torment. Had it really been because of his name alone? Somehow he had the feeling there was more to it. "Clearly he's been reading Karisma's books."

"How many do you think he's gotten through?" Bastion stared at the door, now swaying back and forth between the kitchen and living room. He wondered briefly how many she wrote and what was on the flash drives he now had. At his brother's prompting, he took a hot toddy mug in hand and sipped at it gratefully, making it a point to recall how Rafe had made it. The drink was very good.

"He's read more than we have. Particularly now that he has everything she's ever written in his possession."

Bastion nodded his agreement and followed after Rourke, already not liking or trusting the man.

"That seems too heavy an advantage, if you ask me," ST snarled angrily watching the walking dead man disappear into the living room. "And I'll get him a snack before I leave for the hospital all right. One he can choke on."

"Easy now," Rafe chided. "You have a Hippocratic Oath to consider. And don't go getting any ideas without checking with me first."

"Why?"

"Because if they're here for what I think they are, and your ideas are any good, I might want to use them myself." Rafe banged his way through the door, leaving his sons to eavesdrop from the kitchen.

Chapter 9

Blackthorne Horse Ranch
Kalispell, Montana

The three brothers retired to the living room, settling in around the fireplace with their drinks. Rafe indicated for Rourke to take the chair off to his right, so naturally, the man took the one on the left.

"No doubt Rourke thought he one-upped me," Rafe said as he took the seat he wanted in the first place. "He didn't. He's where I wanted him." With a satisfied smile, he relaxed against his chair and took a much-needed sip of his drink.

Bastion stretched out on the couch, not shy at all about kicking off his shoes and getting comfortable. He laughed over his brother's obvious animosity,

Rourke grunted in response, irritable over having been tricked and skeptical over the hot toddy concoction. He sniffed his glass hesitantly. Crossing his aching leg over his good one, he leaned against the cushion of his plush chair and tried the mixed drink. The warmed rum, lemony sweet flavors, and spices hit his tongue, sending a sensory response of unanticipated pleasure throughout him. Unwilling to give his brother the satisfaction in knowing he enjoyed his drink; he instead posed his first question.

"How is Karisma doing, Rafe?"

The genuine concern in his brother's Scottish brogue caught Rafe off guard. "She is inconsolable, disinclined to eat, prone to dark rooms, and easily upset over random reminders of them."

"For obvious reasons, she's bound to be grief-stricken over the loss of her children. Worry more, if she didn't grieve at all. " Rourke absently swirled his drink.

"How is she coping with losing her husband - Matthew is it?" Bastion asked.

Rafe narrowed his gaze between his two brothers. Why were they so interested in Karisma? He regarded Bastion suspiciously, avoiding the man's question.

"What have you read so far? And what prompted you to come here after all this time?" Rafe's attention shifted to the other brother. "What about you, Rourke? I'd like answers to those questions from you as well."

Bastion stood, unable to contain his agitation. Heaving an exasperated sigh he paced sock footed in front of the hearth. "I don't feel I can answer your question without knowing what of the six books are in your possession and which ones you have read."

"There are twelve," Rafe said.

"Wait, a dozen?"

"You're surprised?" Rafe asked.

"I'm only aware of half a dozen in the, An Unfortunate Lineage series, three of which tell of my family. The other three are tales of yours, Rafe. All are penned under Karisma's pseudonym. She advertised on her website a seventh novel to be released soon. When I discovered you brought her here, I came in-part to learn what stage the final book is in. I am awaiting information that may be within." Clasping his hands behind his back, Bastion shifted back and forth on the ball of his feet while he waited for Rourke's response to their brother's questions.

Rourke harrumphed softly. "Karisma wrote a second series of six books penned under Vortigern Black called Lineage. Between the two pseudonyms there are a total of twelve published works so far. The titles of both collections are oddly riddled with the words Karisma and Kayos. It didn't make sense why she did that until I discovered her given name by her adoptive parents."

"She started a new series about my family without completing our story in the other one?" Bastion asked, taking note of his brother's failure to answer Rafe's questions.

Rourke hedged. "Not exactly."

"I didn't read any of the Lineage series, but I read through the online and paperback descriptions." Rafe hated being at a disadvantage with Rourke. He wished he had taken time to delve into them, but too much had been going on.

"I wouldn't worry about digging into them too much. I don't believe anything in the Lineage series applies to what's happening now. The only thing they share is a similar plot to the series in your possession, Bastion. But they do lack the annoying Vortigern Black narrator who happens to be a character within the, An Unfortunate Lineage story." Rourke tried to gauge his brother's reaction to his dig. Not getting one, he continued. "The latter series includes a lot of what would appear to apply to the here and now."

"Hm, yes, the narrator. An unusual writing style for a fictional paranormal suspense romance series. Wouldn't you say?" Bastion asked, making the decision to keep silent on the matter of Vortigern Black. Aware of the true narrator's identity, he didn't feel he needed to bring his brothers into the loop on the situation.

"Normally, authors do not break the fourth wall in such books, but utilizing a narrator is not unheard of. The style did seem an odd choice to me. I didn't understand what the point was to having narration in the first place," Rafe said.

"You only read the volumes about your family. If you bothered to start the series from the beginning, you would know the reader's job is to figure out who this storyteller, Vortigern Black is within the tale. By doing so, you learn who took off with the laptop and flash drives belonging to the heroine, Angel Stryfe, in volume five who happens to be a writer," Rourke said.

"What is this Angel Stryfe character writing about in the story? Does it specify?" Rafe was beginning to see the connection between his and Bastion's books.

"Oh, yes. Angel writes about Bastion's family, but is oblivious to their existence until they go pick her up and bring her to their valley in Loveland, Colorado," Rourke said.

"That's the same story plot as Kayos Knows," Rafe said, eyeing his brother. He sensed the man was trying to tell him something.

"What are you talking about? The same? Where are these books of yours? Can I see them?" Bastion didn't like being out of the loop. The only one who seemed to have the full picture of current events was Rourke. The notion didn't sit right with him.

Rafe retrieved his copies of the twelve volumes and lay them on the coffee table.

Bastion skimmed the backs of the last two novels in both collections. He paid closer attention to the descriptions of volumes five and six of the, An Unfortunate Lineage series he received. His expression became more perplexed as he read.

"All four of these descriptions sound as though they have the same plot. In the two about your family, Rafe, the author within is given the name Ciara Biardon instead of Angel Stryfe as they are in mine."

Rourke shook his head, setting his half-empty mug down. "They are similar plots, but the stories themselves are different. The heroine's name starts as Ciara Biardon, but halfway through the book she's given a new name by Rafe who passes her off as another woman." Rourke said.

"Okay, what's the name?" Bastion asked.

"Inara RavenCroft," Rafe said slowly, struggling to wrap his head around what was happening. He sat with his elbows propped on his knees as he massaged his forehead.

Eyes shifting back and forth between Rourke and Rafe, Bastion got the distinct impression he was awaiting a time bomb going off. Flipping the books over, so he could read the back cover of each one again, it occurred to him what Rourke said was poignant.

"The Rafe within the story gives this author, Ciara Biardon, a new name. My late wife's name. Why would you do that? How would you come by the name in the first place? Did you know my wife Inara somehow?"

Rafe shifted in his chair while swirling the liquid of his hot toddy with a stirrer. The connection in his head was finally made. He never met Bastion's wife in person, but he recalled speaking with her via phone about her David Pearson books many times years before. He often wondered what happened to her. "Your late wife's name was Inara RavenCroft?"

"Yes. Her maiden name was King." Bastion said. "When we married she became Inara RavenCroft. And now in real life, Karisma Kayos will what? Return to her birth name which happens to be Inara Kingsley?" Laughing out loud he stared at the books in a kind of horrified awe. "In her own way, Karisma is foretelling the future in these stories, isn't she?" He turned to Rourke. "She's trying to pass on a message?"

"Yes, I believe so," Rourke said, sensing the man was finally getting to where he needed him to be in his head, regardless of whether the theory was accurate or not. With pleasure, he encouraged him along. "What do you think she is saying?"

"Karisma wrote in her story that you made her my wife, Rafe. Which lends credence to my suspicions and the other reason which brought me here. She foretold the union herself, Rafe. Karisma is meant to become the Angel of my tale. My wife. Our marriage is part of the prophecy that'll break our sons cursed state. She and I need to marry, or they'll never be free of the shadows."

Cracking his jaw, Rafe's insides went cold. This is what Rourke wants. To create animosity and confusion between him and Bastion.

"No, that's not how this story goes. Read it and you'll see. My late wife's prophecy is very clear. The woman with the name Inara is meant to become my wife. "

"I don't see how the supposed fact is clear at all," Bastion said.

"Rafe, the time frame has been upped. It would stand to reason, Lilyandhi's prophecy may well be a false one. Things have not transpired as either woman foresaw. Neither Lilyandhi nor our Karisma who sleeps upstairs." Rourke took great pleasure in seeing his brother squirm.

Fed up with where the conversation had gone, and refusing to believe their theory, Rafe stacked the books together, yanking the Blackthorne novels from Bastion's grasp. "Karisma is in my home, in my care, and under my protection. She will stay where she is for now as she heals from her loss. Who she marries, if anyone, will not be decided by either of you."

"She does not belong to you, Rafe, she's meant to be mine."

"No one will bother her, are we clear? No one will interfere or try to woo her. She is to be left alone for now. She needs time to recover from her losses. It will be given to her." Rafe's tone brooked no quarrel.

"That is not your decision to make," Bastion said.

"Bah, for the first time in his life he's actually right about something," Rourke said with irritation. He gave his long-lost brother a calculating look. "She is a very recent widow who lost her bairn. Two of them to be exact. She should be given time to mend. Thirty days seems most appropriate."

Not willing to allow Rourke's ludicrous assessment of what Karisma's grieving period should be pass, Rafe regarded his brother with pure disdain. "Right, because it only takes a month to recover from the loss of someone you love. They had to sedate and hospitalize her when she found out. I recall it took a whole year before I could breathe again after losing my wife. And you, Bastion, you want to schlepp her from here to your home with strangers, so she can, what? Mend there? I don't think so. Besides, according to the description here on the back of your story, the character name for the author is Angel, not Inara, regardless of it having been your late wife's real name."

His estranged brother exhaled, trying to maintain control. "As to names; the back of yours says, the character name of the author is Ciara, not Karisma. She can mend just as easily in my home in Loveland, Colorado."

"Absolutely not." Rafe refused to allow that to happen.

"The truth of the correct choice here is in your own story, Kayos Knows." Bastion said, watching as his brother adamantly shook his head. Exasperated, his tone became firm. "Rafe, you brought her to safety and are meant to give her over to me."

"How dare you! Such arrogance," Meg yelled from the hallway.

Bastion gaped at Meg as she charged into the living room at him. Her eyes flashed with anger as she raged at all three men. "You - all three of you - fighting over this woman as if she were an object; a prize to be won."

"Technically, I'm not," Rourke said as he swirled the remainder of his hot toddy in his mug. He glanced up in time to catch Meg's scathing eyes flicker in his direction.

"How could you, Dad? You act as though her fate is sealed, that she belongs to you somehow when she doesn't even fit the story. Get the picture?" Meg gave her father a hard look. Out of the corner of her eye, she noted her Uncle Rourke had cast an annoyed glance her way. "Think about what I said for a minute. Besides, no one has ownership of her, but Karisma herself. And you, Bastion," she spat, "you show up after thirty years, demanding this woman be handed over as if she's what, a concession for having been abandoned by your mother?" Rounding on Rourke, she fit him with a dark glare.

Unfettered by her outburst Rourke made the mistake of stoking her ire further. "Yes, my little warrior? Attempting peace talks are we?"

"Oh, you really should not have said that," her husband ST could be heard to say as he strolled into the foyer on his way out. "I'm on call at the hospital if I'm needed." Grabbing up one of the briefcases in the entrance, he slammed his way out the door.

Incensed over her uncles attempted dig at her Mandan Indian ancestry, Meg stalked across the room picked up Rourke's cane and smashed it down over his legs. He yelped in startled pain as she held him fast.

"And you, you pompous arrogant old windbag, you're the worst of them all. You came here for nothing but sport, didn't you? In the hopes of, what? Pitting one brother against the other? Have you become so bored living with Grandpa Rathbourne in your plush Scottish estate that you must cross an ocean to gain your entertainment?"

Wincing, Rourke glared at Meg, fisting his hands at his sides. His face reddened and his mouth pinched, as he struggled to keep from exploding.

"Go ahead. Hit me like you struck the mother of your unborn children. You can come here and tell your stories of how Grandpa Rathbourne was the monster and you were a mere victim all you want to. But that doesn't change the facts. Did you or did you not tell Sarah you would marry her?"

"Yes, I did, and I meant it!"

"That remains to be seen. Did you or did you not call off your secret engagement when you found out she was pregnant? You even went so far as slapping her and calling her a whore."

Becoming incensed Rourke sputtered. "You weren't there. You don't know what happened."

"Be careful how you answer Uncle Rourke, because Breydon's in the kitchen. He will know if you lie. Did you or did you not slap Sarah and dump her when you found out she was pregnant?"

"Fine, yes! Yes, I did. But there were circumstances you don't understand."

"Didn't you love her?" Meg shouted.

"Yes!"

"Then help me understand, Uncle Rourke." Meg snarled the familial reference as if it were a loathsome notion he were in any way related. "You say you loved her. You even asked her to marry you. But you bed her, impregnated her, then dumped her after hitting her, leaving her only one last course, but to tell her father she was expecting and hope he would help her. What did you think would happen? The way Dad talks James Croft was a horrible man who treated her poorly after her mum died. If you loved her so much and wanted to make her your wife, why turn her away? Why leave her to fend for herself? Why leave her defenseless, laden with child, and at your own father's mercy?"

"Because, I didn't think they were mine," Rourke shouted.

Rafe was astounded. "Who else's would they have been? The two of you were inseparable for six months."

"She told me she was pregnant and, oh, Sarah was so excited. She said she would never forget the night they were conceived. The night, mind you." The memory flooded painfully into Rourke's head increasing his sarcasm tenfold. "We were never intimate at night. Our encounters were always during the day." He cast an accusing glare toward Rafe. "I was so sure at the time the man who took her was you. We are identical after all. Who else could the doppelganger be, if not you?"

"I never touched her," Rafe said. "I swore to leave her alone as long as you promised to always treat her right and not allow the shadows to cause irreparable harm to her. Now, who failed in that bargain? Me, or you?"

"I did. I know I failed her." Rourke turned on Meg, grasping the cane from her hands. "I slapped the tramp, yes. Sarah cheated on me with another man, and she was so sure she became pregnant that night. So, yes," Rourke growled back. "I dumped her. I refused to marry a woman who would spread her legs for any man. Because clearly, I was any man to her if she couldn't tell the difference between me and someone else. Especially if he wasn't my brother." The shock of his words took a few seconds to sink in. "Now, if you're done, making me out to be a monster, because I see monsters, then I will gladly take your leave. I need a swim."

They watched him limp away, heading down toward the pool room.

"He shouldn't be here, Dad. Something isn't right. I can sense it, but I can't pinpoint what."

Rafe was uneasy. "I know."

"I sense it too, but I'm new to this familial environment so, my sensors might be off," Bastion said.

Meg snorted, then fixed both men with a dark glare. "The two of you, leave her alone. If a choice needs to be made, she will make it when she is ready. She has enough to deal with." She stalked away, still muttering under her breath. "A bunch of Neanderthals running around this house. Small wonder Dad stayed behind here instead of going back to Scotland. It's like we've reverted to the dark ages."

- - -

"Another?" Bastion lifted his empty mug indicating the need for more drink.

Rafe hedged, not inclined to accommodate him after the demands he made.

Sensing his reticence, one eyebrow rose, as amusement played across his features. "I can always find my way into your prized Scotch later. Or is it too presumptuous of me to assume I am welcome here until Karisma wakes?"

Thinking better of the idea to deny the man, Rafe took the mug from him, and they headed to the kitchen. "By all means, stay. We should talk more. I would like to understand how you came to end up in Colorado." He paused, staring at the third empty glass he picked up from the stand before heading to the kitchen. "I suppose I should make one for his highness too."

"Aye," Bastion joked, trying to imitate Rourke's Scottish accent. "I'm guessing he could use another. He took a mighty thrashing from Meg. A well-deserved one, if you ask me." It hadn't been lost on him that Rourke had been taking great pleasure in their argument.

"Maybe," Rafe hesitated. "I do not have my daughter's gift to discern emotions. That said, even I can't help but sense much heartache in him." He worried over his brother, knowing full well how he tended to respond when he was hurting. Experience taught him the hard way that he would lash out or make stupid decisions. Much like what had happened with Sarah.

"Rourke was in love. The way he spoke, made it pretty clear. Losing someone as he did and under such confusing circumstances; the pain is bound to run deep," Bastion agreed, paying close attention to Rafe's preparation of the hot toddies this time. He wanted to remember how they were made once he returned home. "The visions. What Karisma sees makes her tired?"

"It would appear so."

Bastion grimaced, coming to the bothersome conclusion he would not be heading back home to Colorado anytime soon. The need to speak with Karisma on multiple topics had become extremely important, so her need for sleep made him anxious.

"In the interest of peace, I will concede for now and not pester Karisma on the marriage issue, but I will be speaking with her when she wakes." If marrying again helped his son, Kalab then Bastion would do his part, though he preferred to avoid it, if he could.

Incensed, Rafe slammed the lemon he retrieved from the fridge onto the cutting board and began sawing it so hard he smashed the fruit. Obviously, his brother managed to discern his thoughts, and they had aggravated him.

"Calm down, Rafe. You're acting like a jealous lover. From what I gathered so far, you only recently met her yourself. Besides, you're not the only one dealing with drama within your home. It is essential I speak with her. I must find out if she has any more knowledge of my son's children and their whereabouts. We thought his ex-wife Eliza aborted them a couple of years back, but Karisma's story indicates otherwise. They may be in danger, and our efforts to locate anything on them came up empty so far."

"What sort of threat are we talking about here?" Dante wanted to know. He and his brothers were at the table, not bothering to hide the fact they were eavesdropping while they snacked. He popped a cheese curl in his mouth and shook the bag, awaiting his uncle's response.

The ringing of a phone prevented him from explaining further. There was a flurry of activity to check phones, which was ridiculous considering the ring tone repeated the phrase, 'Hulk smash.' There was only one person in the house with the ring tone on their cell.

"I am sorry. Hold that thought please, I must take this." Chagrined at having to put Bastion off at such inconvenient timing, Rafe reached for his cell from his pocket. He knew Drin was trying to reach him. The ringtone had been an internal joke among his sons ever since they watched the first Avengers movie together.

"Your son, Drin? The one trapped out of time?" Bastion received a nod in answer while his brother punched the talk button on his phone.

"What's up? Where are you now?"

"No place I want to be. I'm alone with two toddlers at a rest stop waiting on Veta. She gets motion sickness on long drives. Do we have to wait until we get to Chicago? Can't you send a plane here?"

"No, it doesn't work that way; and you be nice to her. You like this woman, right?"

"What's not to like? She's gorgeous and generous and sexy and sweet and geez! I thought I was going to lose it when I first saw her. My heart dropped to my gut, my nards hit the floor, and my head lost what little sense

I had when she opened the door. I can barely put two words together without stuttering."

"Drin, you are on speakerphone."

There was silence.

"Who's there?"

"All four of your brother's plus your Uncle Randulf who is not dead after all, but has been living in Loveland, Colorado all this time. He now goes by Bastion. He showed up along with your other Uncle Rourke who is cooling off in our pool as we speak."

"Uncle Randulf. He's there, like, near you?"

"Yes."

"You're seeing Uncle Randulf?"

"Yes, Drin."

"Uh, Dad, Uncle Randulf has been dead for forty-seven years and you're just now seeing his ghost? Are you high or something?

Bastion gave a hearty laugh. "You should wait to explain until he gets back."

"Good point," Rafe mouthed, then he spoke aloud. "Drin, focus. Just forget what I said. I'll explain when you arrive home."

"Hey, wait a minute. Who's this Bastion guy?"

Dart, Dante and Breydon started laughing as Rafe face palmed his hand. "Your Uncle."

"I have an Uncle named Bastion? When did that happen?" The voice coming through the speaker sounded like his mind had been blown.

Shaking his head in wonder, Bastion accepted the proffered drink from Rafe and took his leave. Indicating he would be outside for a bit, he stepped out on the patio to allow his brother a chance to deal with his son. He knew Drin to be one of the triplets which meant he must be nearly thirty years old. The man they were talking to just now, sure didn't sound like it.

Sitting in a patio chair near a table, he set his drink down after taking a long gulp. He recognized he needed to slow down on the hot toddies, but his need to relax overcame his heads good sense.

With a heavy sigh, Bastion pulled out his cell phone. He had a call of his own he needed to make, and he didn't look forward to it. No doubt, his son Kahner was tearing his hair out, waiting for answers about his children. The misunderstanding from five years before which led to his son's wife Eliza taking off with his three sons had come to light when he learned of Vortigern Black's existence. The potential truth of the matter was given some credence after speed reading Karisma's books. A little investigation of his own into the matter prompted more questions for the so-called mysterious Vortigern character. Between that and additional thorough research into the author Delaine Christine he was led to Karisma Kayos and by extension back to Montana.

His son Kalturek, the deputy Sheriff, assumed when Eliza came out of the abortion clinic that she already aborted their babies. It turned out, she changed her mind, but never said anything or tried contacting them again. They never would have known had the stories not arrived in the mail; addressed to Bastion RavenCroft. The last book in the series ended with Eliza showing up on their doorstep fourteen years after she had them. Since it appeared the time frame of potential future events had been upped by about ten years, that meant, his grandson's would be about four years old.

Bastion knew, if Eliza were out there alone with those boys, and they were starting to show signs of their abilities, then they were at risk of being discovered by the Phenom organization who hunted down gifted individuals. A Blackthorne didn't come fully into their gifts until the age of twelve, but they could still be experiencing aspects of their gifts. He had to find them before the people from Phenom did. He only hoped they weren't on their radar already.

Pausing before he placed the call, Bastion hunkered over the table cupping his mug in his hands. There had been no return address label on the package he received with the books in, but it had looked as though it had been overnighted from the United Kingdom. Rourke lived in Scotland. It occurred to him that his brother may be the one who sent the box with the paperbacks. Frowning while his gaze took in the Blackthorne horse ranch, he wondered what Rourke's agenda could be. His attempts to aggravate Rafe were obvious to him. The question was why? And to what end?

Taking one last drink before placing his call, he relaxed back against the patio deck chair. Afterwards, he intended on locating Rourke and demanding to see Karisma's laptop and notes. It might provide him answers a bit sooner, rather than having to wait until she woke up. Maybe he'd even check in on Karisma. It couldn't hurt. Besides, from the way things sounded, he needed to get used to the idea of her in his bed.

Kahner answered on the first ring. "Yeah, Dad. What's up? What did you find out?"

"Whoa, slow down, Son."

"I can't, Dad. I'm wearing holes in the floor. I've been out riding four times today and went running twice."

Bastion could hear the anxiety in his voice. "Karisma is here."

"Holy crap! Are you serious? She's there? You've met her? What did she say? Where are my kids? Are they okay?"

"Kahner!" Bastion shouted, trying to edge a word in between his son's rapid-fire questions. "I can't answer anything if you keep talking. I don't have any answers for you yet, but I can tell you what I do know. There was an auto accident. It forced my brother Rafe to bring Karisma here from her home in Indiana, Pennsylvania."

"Karisma is hurt?"

"Not the kind of hurt you're thinking. You need to have some patience here. She lost her husband and two children in the terrible tragedy."

There was a long pause.

"I can't even imagine what she must be going through. Is she even cognizant?"

"She is, to an extent. Like Angel in our stories though, she was unaware what she wrote about was real. Between her loss and learning of her gift, she is more than a little rattled. Her visions make her tired too. Presently, she's sleeping one off."

"I see, hence the no answers so far."

"That doesn't mean I can't try searching for clues while she sleeps. While your Uncle Rafe absconded with Karisma and hightailed her here to the Blackthorne ranch, your other Uncle Rourke managed to grab her laptop and notes from her home before it burned down."

"Her house burned down too? Wait a minute, Uncle Rourke is there? I thought you said your brothers don't speak to each other."

"They don't. A concession has been made for the moment. He arrived a few minutes before I did and somehow he knew I was alive."

"Are you thinking he sent those books?"

"I believe he did but cannot prove it yet. Now, hush, so I can explain what's going on."

"Okay, but can I ask one last question first?"

Bastion sighed in exasperation. "What is it?" No immediate response came. "Spit it out. What's the problem, Kahner?"

"Can I let the stupid narrator out now?"

"No."

"But Dad," Kahner said uneasily. "Vortigern's been in there since before you left."

"That backstabbing poor excuse for a son-in-law is not allowed out of the room until I have returned."

"When do you think you'll be back?"

"It'll take as long as it's going to take. My hands are tied by grief and the need for sleep." Bastion could hear his son's heavy sigh from the other end.

"I get it alright? The rest of us are as riled up as you are about the books, Dad, but you're not the one being tortured by her incessant crying. She hasn't stopped since you left."

Having become worked up Bastion had taken to his feet. He paced a hole into his brother's patio deck. Pausing he chanced another glance out over the Rocky Mountains; a view he didn't think he would ever see again until now. It was breathtaking and, for whatever the reason, had a calming effect on him.

"All right fine! If it looks like I'll be here longer than a couple days I will re-evaluate my decision on the matter at that time. Until then, what I told you stands. No one is allowed to see or let out our so-called elusive and mysterious Vortigern Black." Bastion sneered, unable to hide his contempt.

The idiot had thought it all a game; a means to get back at him, of all things! In truth, Vortigern Black and the commissioned novels had likely been the variable that cost Karisma her family and prompted current events to start playing out ten years sooner then what had been intended. He had no intentions of letting the news fall into his brother's hands anytime soon, though he suspected Rourke likely already knew.

Chapter 10

Lifting her baby from his stroller, Angel Stryfe stepped into the Ryans Private Investigations Agency while carrying Kalturek, straddle style against her slender hip. She dragged the now empty stroller along with her. Her eyes widened as she walked into Chase Ryans office space.

Vibrant royal blue curtains adorned the windows and the walls were painted a pale, but warm yellow. Contemporary hanging lights flooded the room with their luminescence and the matching decorative wall sconces had been turned on to remove any unnecessary shadows. Five brightly painted canvases with fun pictures of a little boy, playing at being a superhero, hung on the wall above a comfy looking sofa. They caught her attention. She laughed outright in delight, her hand clasping over her mouth as her bright blue eyes sparkled; the color of which seemed to shift with her tickled emotional state.

Hearing a noise behind her, she spun around. An attractive bald black man, just shy of six feet tall with a short-cropped goatee, entered through an office door. His molten brown eyes caught sight of her standing near the paintings. The easy smile he threw her way put her at ease for she recognized him instantly from her own description. As expected he wore blue jeans and a simple military green t-shirt.

She knew Wilton had been wrong.

From the moment the images began popping in her head, she sensed the people within them were real.

"I thought I heard someone out here. I hope you haven't been waiting long. Can I help you?" Chase Ryans gave the woman before him an appraising look. Short and petite, she had long silver-blonde hair that had been braided to keep the small child in her arms from grasping and tearing at it. The thick braid hung across her chest and down past her waist. But her eyes were what caught his attention.

"That is so clever!" Angel pointed toward the paintings, her voice rising with excitement. The baby cooed at her hip catching the man's eye. Grateful for the moment's reprieve from Chase's shrewd gaze, she suspected he, as Wilton would put it, sized her up, whatever that meant. She never understood the phrase when her husband attempted to explain it to her.

"I'm glad you like the painting. Most people do. My brother-in-law who painted the canvases sure knocked it out of the park."

Angel became confused. She tilted her head toward him, giving him an odd look. "Knocked it out of the park? I heard the expression before, but don't understand what the phrase means." She paused, searching her mind for the word she needed.

Her child-like response, caught Chase off guard. She appeared to be mid-thirties, but her presence and the way she spoke made him wonder if he estimated her age accurately.

"In this case, the expression saying he did a good job capturing the vision I had of the boy in the paintings."

"Oh, I see. That makes sense I guess. The world is so big with so much to learn, and so many ways of saying things. Wouldn't you agree?"

"I suppose it is." He couldn't quite figure it out, but something seemed a bit off about her and the way she acted. As though everything around her looked new and fascinating to her. Much like a five-year-old would, who discovered the world's many wonders around them for the first time. He sensed an innocence about her that put him at ease and made him want to protect her.

She stared back at him as though she'd drawn a blank.

"Did you need help with something?"

"Do you know me?"

Taken aback, he looked her up and down one more time. "No, I can't say as I do. Are you looking for someone?"

"I am indeed. Your Chase Ryans, an adept and crafty Private Investigator located in Loveland, Colorado, and I'm Angel Stryfe. I was Angel Doe until Wilton came and got me, but we said some words together in front of a guy and the last name they gave me changed just like that. Neat, right? So now people call me Mrs. Stryfe. But I prefer Angel because it's prettier, wouldn't you say?"

Her ramblings caught him off guard. She acted as if she didn't fully understand what getting married meant. She also appeared sure of the fact that he was Chase Ryans. "Yes, I agree, Angel is a nice name. It suits you too. I'm sorry, have we met? I feel certain I would remember meeting you if, if I had."

If possible, her face brightened more. Walking toward him, she reached out and took hold of his hand before he had the chance to extend his. She shook it hard several times, jerking at his arm as if she had no grasp of the need to be gentler.

"So sweet of you to say. People tell me that all the time, at first anyway, but then most people get confused when they talk to me. It's got something to do with me not acting my age or something."

Chase Ryans didn't know what to make of the woman before him. She had to be the mother of the child in her arms, because the little boy had the same pale silver-blonde hair, as well as her bright luminous blue eyes.

"What exactly can I help you with Mrs. Stryfe?"

"Oh, right. Of course, straight to business." She laughed; the sound reminiscent of a little girl. She swatted at him playfully, but her face squirreled into a troubled frown. She heaved a huge breath then exhaled while gently shaking the little boy straddling her hip to keep him calm.

"I know what Wilton keeps telling me; he says what I'm writing is just a fantasy. But after searching online, discovering you were real and meeting you, I'm positive now what is in my stories are also real. The thing is, events aren't playing out like they're meant to. Wilton disappeared on me a few days ago and hasn't been back. He wouldn't do that, because he knows I need him. It must mean something happened to him, and I'm pretty sure nothing is supposed to for another ten years or so."

"So, you're saying your husband has gone missing?" His shoulders slumped. Was this going to be a job about locating another dead-beat dad who took off on his wife and child? He hated those jobs. They never ended well.

"Mhm. We fought about my cooking, and how I ruined another meal. He said, me trying to learn to cook is getting too expensive for him." Her face fell as did her head, but her eyes shot back up toward him plaintively. "I couldn't help it. I didn't realize you're supposed to dump the water off the pasta. The instructions didn't specify. Anyway, he took off to replace what I ruined, but never came back from the store. He's been gone ever since, and he's never gone that long, because he knows I need him."

"How long has he been gone?"

"Three days."

"Did you report him missing at the Loveland Sheriff's Department?

"Now, why would I do that? No, silly! But he never came home that night, so I did report him missing where I live," she said proudly. "I grabbed up my son, a granola bar and a bottle of orange juice, because I don't drink milk," she shivered as if the notion frightened her, "and I walked on down to the Pocahontas, police station all by myself. I had to walk, because I can't drive. Wilton says it would be too dangerous for everyone else if I did, but walking is good for me."

Chase's eyes widened at her ramblings. "Pocahontas. Doesn't sound familiar. Is the town local?"

Angel laughed again. "You're funny! No silly. I'm from Pocahontas, Iowa."

"I'm sorry, I'm a little confused Mrs. Stryfe."

"Call me Angel, please? I never liked my last name." She covered her mouth with her free hand as she whispered the latter conspiratorially.

"Angel then, if you can't drive, how did you find your way here? And what are you wanting me to do? Does your local police think he's in Loveland? Is that why you're here?"

"Oh, no! They have no clue where he is or what happened to him. They only know he arrived at the store and bought what he needed, because the manager showed them a video, but he disappeared from the parking lot and never came home. Makes me wonder if he fell off the face of the earth." Her sad face brightened. "See, I learned an expression! That one doesn't make any sense to me either though, because the face of the earth is round."

"Mrs. Stryfe."

"Angel."

"Sorry, of course. Angel, what brings you to Loveland, Colorado, if he disappeared in Pocahontas, Iowa?" He gestured for her to step into his office and to take a seat.

Following his lead, she spoke as she sat down in a chair before his desk. "I'm here, because I found you online." Settling her son in her lap, she handed him a binky.

"You mean, you saw my website?" Though pleased to hear investing in the business web page hadn't been a complete waste of money, Chase couldn't help but feel they were going in circles with the conversation.

"Yup. See I wrote about you in my novels, but Wilton said you weren't real. He disappeared though, and I realized something had to of gone wrong. So, I thought to myself, who better to help me than a character from my own book; crafty Chase Ryans, Private Investigator of Loveland, Colorado."

"I'm sure you could find a PI's closer to home." Did he hear her right? He could swear she said she wrote him in as a character in her novel. Something was weird with this lady, and it was not the yellow floral printed dress, fuchsia pink leggings, jean jacket, and tennis shoe combination she wore, but he decided to play along.

Angel hedged. "Maybe, but I'm positive no one can help me the way you can."

"And why is that?"

She huffed in exasperation, as though he should know the answer to the question. "I'm not supposed to talk to anybody or tell anyone about what I'm capable of. Of all people, I figured you would understand. Cause it could be dangerous for me and my son, as well as other people too. Wilton has always said as much. Plus, I don't have all the stories written yet. Since the events occurring now aren't following with what I wrote, I figure I should find out where I'm at in the story first before rushing headlong to Bastion."

"Wait, did you say Bastion?"

"Yes. Bastion RavenCroft. You are his son-in-law, right? Didn't you marry his daughter Mackenzie? Or, did that not happen yet?"

Chase splayed his hands on his desk for support. What is going on here? "Let me get this straight. You're telling me you wrote stories about me and you intend on taking them to Bastion?"

"I'm not writing only about you."

"Of course, I wouldn't presume you were."

"I put Bastion in them too."

"You wrote about Bastion?" Alarm bells went off in his head. He knew Bastion wouldn't like that, no matter what kind of story she wrote.

"Oh yes. I'm telling stories about all the RavenCroft's and their potential mates."

Did she say, mates? He gaped at her.

The baby began to fuss, his lips puckering as he cried. "Oh, dear, little Kalturek is hungry."

Chase's eyes flew open in surprise. The boy's given name is the same as his brother-in-law, the one who happened to be Sheriff of Loveland County? An uneasy thought crept into his mind making him suspicious. "Is Wilton the boy's father?"

"What? Little Kal?" Angel peered down at her son with an affectionate smile. "Yes, well, I'm sure he was supposed to have another daddy, but Wilton has been good to him. I'd better take him back to the hotel, so I can feed him. I'm staying at the Travelodge so you can reach me there if you find anything out about my husband, and why the story isn't following along the right plot anymore. Or, maybe mention to Bastion I'm there." Her cheeks flooded with color, and she giggled nervously, the sound reminding him of tinkling bells.

"But maybe it would be a bad idea telling him since we don't know what's up with my current husband yet. Oh, S-t-r-y-f-e by the way. In case you aren't sure how to spell it. Took me a long time to learn that." Getting up from her seat she carried her son out to the stroller and locked him in place. He continued to whine as she popped the binky back in his mouth.

Chase followed her in a daze. Why had she gotten all goofy eyed and nervous every time she mentioned his father-in-law?

"I'd better head out before he starts wailing worse. It took a while to walk here." Taking hold of the stroller handles Angel prepared to exit the office when she suddenly stopped. "How silly of me. I almost forgot!"

Reaching into the sizable diaper bag, she pulled out a flash drive case and handed the leather pouch off to Chase. She grabbed the small laptop in the bottom of the stroller under the agitated boy and passed it off too.

"This was the whole point in coming here, and I almost forgot. That's everything."

He stared down at the flash drive case and IdeaPad in his hands, then looked back at her with a raised brow in confusion. "Everything?"

She frowned, misconstruing what he said. "I think so. Oh, wait!" Digging under the stroller again she hefted out several spiral notebooks and laid them on top of the laptop he held. "Now, that's everything."

"You're giving me your laptop?"

"Oh no, I'm gonna need that back at some point, because I do like to write. Putting all the words into a document helps clear the images out of my head so my IdeaPad is a loaner for now. I don't have everything saved on the flash drives yet because, well, hehe, I ran out of room on them, and Wilton didn't buy me more before disappearing. But you might need to reference everything within, so it's all yours for now. You can do with the story files as you see fit. Alright, there's some money in the spiral notebook for your trouble. Thanks again for taking this on. I sure appreciate it. Call me when you find anything out," she called sweetly as a piece of her fly-away silver-white hair caught on her lip. She hooked it with her left pinkie finger, pulled it from her face, and tucked it behind her ear. The child-like gesture made her look wide-eyed and innocent.

Spinning around, her skirts swirling about her pink knees, she took hold of the stroller and proceeded to maneuver the bulk contraption out the door with one hand as she propped it open with the other. Seconds later, she disappeared from view through his office windows.

Did that just happen?

He didn't normally become flustered with people, but what she said threw him. Her a genuine innocent quality was distracting, and her natural beautiful didn't help any either. She acted like she knew the RavenCroft's and him personally, but he was sure he never met her.

Chase stared out the empty window, then glanced down at what he held in his hands. He didn't agree to take her case and didn't have a clue what she expected him to do from Loveland, when her husband Wilton disappeared in Pocahontas. He also couldn't make sense of what she meant about the last part, how the story wasn't following the original plot anymore.

Carrying the stuff she left him into his office he laid them on his desk. Unzipping the flash drive case he noted thirteen USB's within. Each one had labels with a title; some with the word Kayos, others with Karisma in them. Opening the laptop he turned on the IdeaPad so it would boot up as he put the first flash drive marked book one in the drive. He leafed through the spiral notebooks finding two twenties lying between two pages. Lifting the bills from within, he rolled his eyes heavenward. It occurred to him he never got the chance to discuss monetary compensation. This wouldn't even cover an hour. Taking a close look at what she wrote, he became further alarmed by some scrawled notes. The handwriting was child-like, as though her penmanship were in the learning stages of writing letters and words, but he could still make out the names of the characters she listed on one of the first pages. Though occasionally misspelled, every single member of the RavenCroft family made the list. She also added his name and the Blackthorne brood in Montana, who were secretly related to the RavenCroft's.

Chase Ryans stomach churned. His eyes fixated on the screen as he began opening one document after another from the desktop as well as the first flash drive. Before long he found himself speed-reading through the stories, both in awe and terror as well.

The Angel who left his office wrote about them, and she knew things she shouldn't. Things he didn't known.

Until now.

- - -

Chase Ryans couldn't put Angels manuscripts down. His inability to do so didn't have anything to do with them being well written. On the contrary, her lack of punctuation and capitalization made them difficult to read, and he frequently came across misspelled words. The content within her stories had him absorbed.

After two days he pulled his head out of her laptop, deciding it was time to sit down with her again. A lot of questions roiled within his head after reading what equated to several novels. Chase tried contacting the hotel Angel said she would be staying at, but she checked out already, sighting the inability to afford the room any longer. He felt guilty, for not checking on her sooner. He scoured the local hotels but had been unable to locate her so far. Was it possible she went back to Iowa?

After three days and a lot more reading, he deduced she was likely still in town. If she went back to Pocahontas he suspected she would have retrieved her laptop from him. A little voice nagged at him, reminding him of what she said about endangering herself for speaking about what told him. So, her absence concerned him, since he didn't have a way of reaching her. Anticipating she would likely contact him again, he headed back to his office after checking in at the hospital and med clinic just to be sure. He figured it would be wise to read through more of her stories. Regardless of them being written at an elementary reading level, they had been very illuminating. The setting was in a time period about ten years from now, and they read like a road map of events to come. Some things she wrote already happened.

In the first story, listed as having occurred five years prior, his brother-in-law, Kahner divorced his wife Eliza because she aborted his child. His wife Mackenzie told him all about what Kahner went through after they were married, but he had no way to know for sure if events within the Blackthorne family tales happened until he did some investigating. When he delved into the second volume about the RavenCroft's, she managed to convince him she was the real deal.

In that one, Angel told about his other brother-in-law, Kalab, and how five years prior he was in an auto accident which took the life of the first and last woman he ever dated. Chase remembered the night in question. He witnessed firsthand how his Kalab lifted the vehicle and threw it like a Tonka toy.

He also understood better now what she meant about the story not following how it was supposed to. The third volume about the RavenCroft's, told how ten years from now her husband Wilton, would be killed by a couple of henchmen of a drug lord, by the name Kobi Radford. The events leading to those circumstances had not happened yet. His brother-in-law, Kahner had not returned home with a woman and children he found by way of his job.

With the RavenCroft's being gifted as they were, Chase knew anything was possible and couldn't help but wonder if there might be reason for concern. Did something happen to him ten years sooner than she expected? And if so, what prompted the change, and how many other people might be affected by it?

Learning what he had, left him both intrigued and overwhelmed, especially after doing some investigating of his own regarding her claims. He contacted the Pocahontas police department to verify Wilton Stryfe as a missing person and learned they had no new leads. When the Police heard Angel found her way to Loveland, Colorado they were curious how she managed it. The officer he spoke with stated she didn't seem terribly bright for a thirty-five-year-old. He'd also been concerned she left the state when there was an ongoing missing person case for a husband she claimed to have, of which they couldn't find a record for. The video recording of the man she said was Wilton Stryfe was the only proof he existed.

This news prompted Chase to dig into Angel's identity, but he couldn't find anything on her. Or at least, not until a year ago when an Angel Doe requested a marriage license in Grand County, Colorado listing Wilton Stryfe as the spouse. On the license request form, she put Angel Stryfe as her married name, but the papers were never filed. So, either the officiant failed to submit the document, or one of them forgot. Regardless of who was at fault, Angel and Wilton were not legally married.

After considering what the lack of marital status might mean, he searched the United States online vital records database for both of them. He located a Wilton Stryfe, but he was listed as deceased more than ten years ago. No record could be found on her.

The information did not bode well for Angel. He was starting to think the man she knew as Wilton Stryfe might be what he initially thought - a deadbeat dad on the run who may well have been living under an alias. But then he did a more thorough check into Angel Stryfe, or Doe as it had been her maiden name on the marriage license request.

There was no such person.

Leaning back in his chair, he crossed his legs on his desk. Making a face, he shook his head while pulling the laptop into his lap. Chase had a talent for being able to read people; it was why he got into the business of PI work in the first place. The way she talked and acted he could tell she thought they were married. Unsure what he was dealing with, he dug a little deeper into why he couldn't find a record - birth certificate or otherwise - for Angel Doe. But he couldn't find anything to explain her lack of documentation.

Switching gears, he opted to sift through the Blackthorne tales about his wife's cousins in Montana. He was not as concerned about reading them word for word though. They were more religious in nature, he didn't have the habit of reading Christian fiction, and he assumed their stories didn't apply. He was more curious about what she wrote of the RavenCroft's. He didn't normally speed read like his father-in-law, but he could when he needed to.

Getting back to reading the third novel about the RavenCroft's, Chase dropped his legs suddenly from the desk. Leaning forward, he set the laptop in front of him and leaned toward the screen, engrossed.

Was it possible?

From what he read so far; he had the impression Angel was saying her character - meaning her in real life - might be like the family he married into.

Gifted.

It made sense. Otherwise, how else could she know the things she did? Personal information no one outside of the family could be aware of. It would be presumptuous to assume the RavenCroft's and Blackthorne's were the only ones in existence with extraordinary abilities.

Making his way through the book he stood and began pacing his office, while carrying IdeaPad with him as he read.

Holy crap!

He stopped reading. His mind raced at the absurdity of him not having figured this out before.

Geez! Why didn't he see the signs before? It was so obvious now. Thinking back over the past couple of years it occurred to him, he should have picked up on Bastion's secret a long time ago.

No, no. It couldn't be.

But, if Bastion was what Angel claimed him to be, then his father-in-law could be his salvation with his most recent retrieval case he took on.

Years before when he was working toward his Criminal Law Degree to become a Private Investigator, Chase recognized the need to have a second income. He learned most licensed PI's often didn't have enough steady work to keep the bills paid. Wanting his other source to relate to his career choice, he took the appropriate measures to be licensed as a recovery agent within the state of Colorado. He applied for and received his permit for a concealed weapon and registered with NAFRA as a Fugitive Recovery Agent. So he was more than a PI, but a bounty hunter too.

Dropping the laptop back on his desk, he unlocked his filing cabinet, pulled out the top file drawer, and dug for the most recent case he received.

Hunter Grabill.

The man was more than a nuisance. Wanted for the murders of three men in two different states as well as bank robbery. The man somehow managed to bond out. It never made sense to him why the judge allowed it, for he was a clear flight risk. He suspected something shady had gone on with his Honor. If Chase were a betting man, he would wager, the judge had been paid off by someone. No sooner had the future felon been released when he took off to parts unknown and, as anticipated, disappeared. But Chase managed to finally locate him after a tip he received the same day Angel appeared in his office.

The problem was, Hunter Grabill crossed the border into Mexico. The country didn't have extradition laws, which meant he couldn't go bring the man back himself. He wanted to hire someone on a cash base to go pick him up. Then he could claim the fee for catching him. He couldn't employ just anyone for this case either. He needed a mercenary. The one he used, retired after his last job, and he was having difficulty finding someone he trusted.

And Chase wanted that bounty.

When he and Mackenzie married, Bastion imposed a stipulation. They had to live within the borders of their valley. At the time Chase didn't fully understand what that meant, so he agreed. The property in question was beautiful and there was plenty of space to allow for building their own home, regardless of the occasional nuisance of the blasted ravens. But to break ground he needed capitol. Currently, they lived at the RavenCroft ranch which was not okay with him on an indefinite basis. The bounty on Hunter Grabill would set him up to start construction on his own home and get them out from under Bastion's thumb.

Eyes gleaming, Chase smiled. He now had the solution to his problem, because he knew his father-in-law's secret. The rest of the world might think of Bastion RavenCroft as a devoted father and horse rancher, but according to Angel's stories, he was also a mercenary.

Chase was willing to bet his meager life's savings the rest of his family didn't have a clue. He needed to find out for sure if his father-in-law was what she said, but without involving Angel and her manuscripts. She entrusted him with the understanding he would be utilizing them to help find out what happened to her husband. Even though she didn't sign his non-disclosure agreement yet, he still felt the need to protect her privacy. The forty bucks she left him was by no means his normal retainer fee, but she had paid him and sounded anxious about Bastion learning what she wrote so far.

Now he knew why.

Thinking quickly, he powered down and pulled the flash drive, returning the USB to its case. Stacking the notebooks and flash drive case on top of Angel's laptop he carried them to the closet. Kneeling down on the floor in front of his safe, he opened the door and placed everything within. Getting the steel box installed in his office had been a pain and required Kalab's brute strength to set the large fireproof standing safe in place. At the time he regretted the purchase, for it wound up costing him a month's wages, but this was one time he was grateful to have invested in the larger one.

Closing the door and resetting the lock, he got up and kicked the door shut with his foot. Before he did anything, he needed to verify what she wrote. The best way to do that was to find Bastion's hidden room back at the ranch. The possibility it could really be there had him walking with a bit of a swagger.

When he met, fell in love with, and tied the knot with Mackenzie, he thought he had been the luckiest guy to walk the earth. The woman was beautiful, amazing, gifted, and because they were now married he was privy to information about her and her family no one else was aware of. So far, the past year and a half had been quite a ride. The things he learned boggled his mind and in some cases, seriously scared the crap out of him.

Chase had always known there was evil in the world. When one dealt with the dregs of mankind as he did, it was hard not to believe such a thing could exist. But when he found out demonic shadows were real he about lost his head. The discovery prompted the renovation of his office, and the need for light in every room anywhere he went.

After he learned the whole RavenCroft brood had abilities, the family night conversations started making so much more sense as well. With a mind reader, truth seer, clairvoyant, empath, aura reader and one who could see dark spirits or shadows at the dinner table, it made for some interesting evenings.

One thing was for sure, being part of the RavenCroft family had been entertaining. It was literally a whole new world to him and it often made him feel like he stepped into a movie or television series about people with paranormal abilities. From the moment he met them, he considered them to be good people. A bit messed up sometimes, but he thought of them as the law-abiding sort. Particularly with a Sheriff, Prosecuting attorney and a CIA agent in the family. Chase would never in his right mind have guessed Bastion had this secret.

Pulling out his cell phone he decided to text his wife first. It wouldn't do any good to drive all the way to the ranch to investigate, if the man was home. Plus, he needed to come up with a truthful excuse for being at the house during the day, because if Breydon, the lie detector of the family, showed up he would be outed. Deciding it best to start with a greeting, he texted her.

C: Hey, sexy! How's your day going?

He waited, hoping it was not one of those busy days in the office where she couldn't text right away. Fortunately, he didn't have long to wait. He received a smiley face first. He hated emoji, but then she texted more.

M: Okay, I guess. I'm a bit tired though and chilled. I wish I grabbed a sweater before leaving.

Chase smiled. She gave him the perfect excuse for heading back to the ranch. He needed to play it cool though and be extra careful not to lie in the process. He didn't like being dishonest, but sometimes she would ask questions about what he did during the day, and he couldn't always give her straight answers. Because of the nature of what he did for a living, he had to keep a lot of his daily routine from her. Taking a second to think it through, he responded back.

C: I have a work reason to be near the ranch here shortly.

It wasn't untrue, and if Bastion was a mercenary he wanted to hire him to haul Hunter Grabill back from Mexico. It would be in both their best interests. The man didn't talk much, nor did he complain about them being there, but he sensed he got tired of them being under his roof. Mackenzie didn't need to know that though.

C: Would you like me to bring you a sweater from the ranch? I could grab you a coffee on the way too.

He stopped, waiting for a response. She didn't respond right away. Did he mess this up by being unusually helpful or did a phone call interrupt her? Several minutes later his cell chimed.

M: If you're sure it won't be much trouble, that would be amazing!

Perfect. He breathed a sigh of relief. He managed to leap the first hurdle. Now he needed to find out where Bastion was, because if he was working out of the house today, then there was no point in bothering to go and look.

C: None at all. If I see your Dad, I'll tell him hi for you.

Chase had the sudden urge to bang his head on the wall. What possessed him to send that? But it was the best he could come up with, and not sound openly nosy. She responded right away this time.

M: Thanks, but Dad's gone for the day.

Gone, eh? Perfect, as long as he didn't return home unexpectedly. Her response gave him the opening he needed to be nosy. Because he thought he remembered Bastion mentioning other plans for today which would have him on his property right about now.

C: I thought he wanted to fix the tack barns?
M: He did. But the horn broke on his saddle, so he made a run to Colorado Springs.

Chase wondered what the heck Bastion did to break it. Not as versed with horse gear as the rest of the family, he did know enough to realize those couldn't easily be broken.

C: Why didn't he buy one from a shop in Loveland?
M: LOL, He's particular.
C: Right. See you soon sexy lady.

With that settled, Chase placed his phone in his right back pocket, and grabbed his wallet and weapon from the desk drawer. He tucked the wallet in his remaining back pocket and the Glock down the back of his jeans, being sure to cover it with his shirt. He kept the shoulder holster for the gun in his closet, but he rarely used it since it was too cumbersome under his arm. The gun in his ankle holster he always had on him from morning to night. Even though he was only thirty-four years old, he managed to anger quite a few people in his line of work already.

Turning off the lights on his way out, he flipped the Out on Business sign around and set the burglar alarm on his office door before locking it. Any calls would forward to his cell phone after three rings.

Settling into his Dodge Charger, he headed straight for the ranch. From work, he was only twenty or so minutes away dependent upon traffic. Passing by the motel Angel originally said she would be staying at he made a mental note to do a more thorough search for her whereabouts. Four days had gone by since she showed up at his business now, and her lack of contact with him was starting to concern him.

Chapter 11

RavenCroft Ranch Home
Loveland, Colorado

Arriving at the ranch a few minutes later because of traffic, he let himself into the house, past a patio deck and yard full of ravens. The black buggers usually didn't disturb him, but for some reason they felt more menacing today. The Raven King, perch near the steps, spread his wings wide and cawed at him when he entered the house. He didn't intimidate easily, but the creatures movements and beady black eyes spooked him.

"Blasted bird," he said aloud as he hesitated. "Leave me be, I'm just entering my own dang home."

"Talking to birds are we?"

Startled by the unexpected voice, Chase whipped his head around and peered through the partially open door. Kalab stood in the entryway holding a large telescopic box.

"Ah, Kalab. I didn't expect to see you there."

"So I gathered. Hold the door will you?"

"Sure thing. You're heading out?" He noted Kalab marked fragile in larger print than necessary on the side of the box he carried through the door. "I take it you're making a delivery to the museum? You need any help?"

"Nope, I'm good. Meant to be out of here sooner. The museum called two days from now wanting the paintings yesterday, if I was able. So, I need to motor or I'm going to be twelve hours late instead of three." Kalab paused at the top of the porch steps, standing a few feet away from the Raven King without a thought to his proximity to the bird or what he had said. He looked back at Chase absently. "What are you doing here this early?"

"Picking up a sweater for Mack." It occurred to him, Kalab did it again with the time thing and wondered how frequently he said that sort of thing in public. He used to say weird stuff like that to him when he dated Mackenzie, which always confused him. Knowing what he did now, it didn't faze him, but he figured he better say something to Bastion about it. "I was in the area on business when she texted she was cold and short on steam."

"Steam?"

"I'm bringing her a coffee."

"Oh, right. Yeah, I'll just bet she is tired." Kalab started down the steps as he spoke. "She wouldn't be so sleepy if the two of you would slow down on the nocturnal activities and sleep instead. Be sure to lock up. I'm out of here."

At his brother-in-law's last words he banged his head against the door frame before he closed the door.

"I gotta get Mack and me out of here."

Closing the door behind him, he locked it straight away then peeked through the window curtains next to the door in the direction of the garage. Kalab closed the back end of his truck, having secured his paintings and hefted himself up into the driver's seat. Chase released the curtain when the engine revved. Expelling the breath he held with a loud whoosh, he headed straight for the pantry, turned on the light and stepped inside. On either side of him long rows of shelves stretched the length of the walk-in pantry. The way Angel explained the entrance in her book there would be a trap door under the carpet. Staring at the floor Chase became disheartened at seeing no carpeting. Had the trip been a waste of time?

Walking the length of the pantry he came to a dead-end and looked on either side of him, then back down at the floor. Crouching down he ran his hands along the floor, trying to find any kind of cracks or crevices that might indicate a passageway. Not finding anything he stood.

The wood flooring replaced the original when the kitchen had been renovated after their wedding. Bastion did the work himself while they were away on their honeymoon. He glanced around him then poked and prodded among the shelves. Unable to locate any kind of lever or push-button for a door of any kind he became frustrated. Resting one arm over the other across his chest he leaned against the wall without shelves at the end of the pantry to rest and think.

The wall shifted.

Standing erect Chase turned and stared at the wall. When it moved, it made a soft swooshing click noise. He stared at the blank wall again. He didn't see any nicks, cracks, crooks, or crannies. Could the wall itself be the door? Laying his left hand against the plaster on one side he added pressure. The wall moved on him again, making the same noise as before. The sound was more obvious to him this time since he listened for it.

If leaning against the drywall meant it depressed and opened, then this time he closed it. Pressing against the wall one more time, he could feel movement and heard the same noise once again. Noticing this time that one corner now appeared to have created a long slit from floor to ceiling he became excited. Placing both hands on the plaster, he tried moving the wall further open with his left hand. The wall pivoted creating a two-and-a-half-foot opening. Peering within and down, he caught sight of a hanging light switch and a set of narrow steps with a steep decline leading down.

Holy crap! There really is a secret room.

Hesitating only a second, he switched on the light and traversed down the carpeted steps, ducking his head, so he didn't hit the ceiling on his way down. His feet found a carpeted floor when he entered the pitch-black room. He barely made out a few shapes within. He had the vague impression of a table; some cupboards maybe along with a microwave and a toaster oven. Was that a counter and sink?

A kitchenette maybe?

Searching along the wall for a light switch he managed to find one and flicked it on. The room was bathed in a bright light which extended from the kitchenette into the next room. Wandering into the massive room next to the kitchenette Chase stopped in his tracks and gawked.

Angel's description hardly touched upon what he found. A half a dozen massive security monitor screens hung along the wall to his left. Some showed varying views of the exterior of the ranch and its surrounding property. Others showed rooms in the interior of the house. A long wooden desk sat below the screen with alcoves, shelving, and drawers stretching the full length of the room. It wrapped around the connecting wall creating an L shaped desk ending at the edge of the trim of a door. Wide-eyed, overwhelmed by what he discovered, and more than a little curious he pulled out his lock pick and moments later opened the door. Peeking in, he found another room which likely extended to the front of the house. It was filled with shelving, file drawers, gun cabinets, a knife display and weapon racks, as well as an array of ammunition in varying sizes. Everything was well organized and accessible. With a quick perusal of Bastion's weapons cabinets, he discovered them filled with various guns, rifles, shotguns, crossbows and sniper rifles. No doubt some items were illegal, if they weren't they should be.

His father-in-law had a whole other side to him, so he figured, if the man discovered him here he would likely to kill him before bothering to ask questions. Exiting the room he made sure to shut and lock the door behind him. Before he left, he noted a wall opposite the screens with a map. It took up the entire space, for the RavenCroft valley as well as much of the surrounding area had been charted in detail on it. The map included a secluded airport hangar too. Chase expelled an appreciative whistle.

The man had every entry point into their valley highlighted in yellow. From what he could see, at one time there had been a dozen ways of getting in and out, though four were now crossed out in red. He was only aware of the one highlighted in orange. A green line haphazardly circled the whole of the valley which made up the RavenCroft property line. It looked as though his father-in-law managed to map the exterior which meant he knew where people who were not like them would start getting confused or turned around.

That's the explanation he received anyway. No one located the valley and entered its boundaries unless they were a RavenCroft by blood, married to one, or gifted like them. Even then, there was no guarantee a gifted person wandering into the area, wouldn't wind up getting besieged by the ravens who called it their sanctuary. Either way, once they left they would forget having found the place.

The RavenCroft family, or Croft family as their ancestors before them were named, found the raven sanctuary several hundred years ago while fleeing from people who intended them harm. Discovering the unique quality about the valley shocked Chase to his core, for time flowed slowly within the grounds of the sanctuary. One day within the valley equated to three days to the rest of the world. Those who lived within its borders appeared so much younger than their actual age because of the slowed time, and it also explained why Kalab said certain weird things.

In the entryway sat a special clock one of their ancestors made many years before which the entire household ran on. When they needed to exit its grounds for work, shopping, and grocery runs they would be able to do so without running late. They all set their clocks and watches to it on a daily basis for that reason. Except for Kalab. Born with an internal clock of his own, he always seemed conscious of the time in either place. Chase often wondered if his uncanny ability to tell time resulted from being capable of seeing the shadows.

"Wow"

He spoke aloud, his voice sounding foreign to him as his eyes shifted about the room once more. Computers, monitors, gadgets, and gear took up the whole of the desk with one small area left for writing. A half a dozen or more towers of varying shapes and sizes cluttered the space, the largest of which sat on the floor, some of which had working or flashing lights on. One machine kicked on suddenly, startling him, its soft whirring noise reverberating within the once silent room.

"Geez, Bastion, I don't think I want to know what all you do down here."

Catching sight of a post-it note pad he grabbed up the nearby pen and scribbled something across the pad. Pulling the top yellow post-it off, he tacked the yellow square to the monitor he suspected Bastion would see first thing when he entered his room. He guessed the man hid here in the evenings when he claimed he headed to his room for the night.

"Let's see how long it takes you to find that."

Taking one last cursory look about the room he turned off the lights and exited the way he came, being careful to make sure the wall closed up behind him. Filching a bag of chips from the shelf he headed to his bedroom, grabbed a sweater for Mackenzie, locked up and set the security alarm, then headed back to his vehicle. He whistled while smothering a grin as he drove out of the raven sanctuary unaware he was being followed by the raven king.

Chase had to handle the situation carefully with Bastion. If the man's collection of weaponry was any indication of his skill set, then he suspected he had some pretty dangerous abilities beyond his gift of knowing.

Heading toward town he decided to grab a black and white coffee from Mackenzie's favorite coffee house before dropping off her sweater at her office. She would be able to sense his conflicting mood; both giddy yet apprehensive. If she asked him about it, he would tell her the truth. He had some unexpected developments on a case that could be beneficial for them. He only hoped Bastion didn't already know about his newfound knowledge. After all, the man did have the gift of Knowing.

- - -

Arriving home in time for dinner, Bastion RavenCroft dropped his new saddle off at the stables and headed up to the house. Mackenzie promised to deal with dinner tonight, and he hoped she didn't burn the food this time, because he felt like he hardly ate all day. Take-out food never seemed to sustain him the way home-cooked meals did and that's what he relied on for lunch. His distrust over the possible state of their dinner stemmed from her tendency to flambe certain things.

Entering the house he smelled rolls baking in the oven and roast beef cooking. Earlier that morning he observed the crockpot had been set up, and he suspected the beef slow cooked in there all day. Somewhat relieved, he made his way toward the kitchen.

"Hey, Dad. Dinner's almost ready."

"Roast beef?"

Mackenzie chuckled. That nose of his. "Swiss steak to be more specific, but I prepared the meat the way you like it with the gravy?"

"Ah, yes." Bastion inhaled the aroma of the meat, set on low now to keep it warm, as he lifted the lid. Most of the juices had been drained to make the gravy. He placed the lid back on the crock. There was a small pan on the stove with more gravy and another medium-sized pan with mashed potatoes. Two more pans covered the back burners on the stove. He grimaced. It looked promising, but...

"You do realize Kalab will be home tonight? Are you sure you made enough?"

Mackenzie snorted and rolled her eyes as she set the table. "I'm not stupid."

Bastion gave her a quizzical look.

She chuckled, half in disgust, and gestured toward the end of the counter while grabbing hot pads as the buzzer went off. "The other crock is down there, along with the first batch of everything else. That said, I'm tired of having to make two full meals every night just to make sure there's enough for everyone."

Bastion exhaled, nodding in agreement. "I'm aware. I intend to do something about that. Give me a little time."

Conceding with a shrug, she pulled the giant pan of rolls from the oven and set them on the counter.

With another appreciative whiff of the freshly baked yeast rolls, he turned and headed toward the stairs, suspecting she'd defrosted the premade dough from the freezer. "I'm going to wash up. I'll be down in a minute to finish helping you with dinner. Where's Chase?" he asked as he walked away.

"He texted and said he might be a bit late. Something about a case he's on."

"All right. I'll be down."

- - -

Chase arrived mid-way through dinner with a laptop and flash drive case in hand. Setting down at the dinner table he thanked his wife for the food before partaking of the plate she set before him.

"I manhandled that away from Kalab for you," Mackenzie said, indicating his plate.

He glanced over at Kalab who suddenly found the ceiling very interesting. "I'm sorry, Honey. You're the best though; thanks for saving a plate for me." Inhaling his dinner, he finished before anyone else. Wiping his mouth with a napkin, he stood, taking up the laptop and flash-drive case and excused himself.

Mackenzie set a frozen apple crumb pie she baked on the table as he was leaving. "You don't want dessert?"

"Maybe later. Save me a piece if you can." Seeing her frown, and Bastion's curious look his way he shook the laptop before him in his hand. "I have some reading I need to catch up on for a case I'm working. I'm having a little trouble locating someone and I'm hoping what's on here will help me find them."

"If you have too much trouble you could get with the Sheriff," Bastion said while pulling a piece of pie from the pan in front of him. "I'm sure Kalturek could help you out if you find you need it."

Chase tilted his head, giving Bastion a head-on look. His eyes gleamed with repressed humor and his mouth twitched as though holding back a laugh. "I imagine he could. I might have to involve him at some point, but I'm hoping to avoid needing to as it's a sensitive situation."

"Oh? Why's that?" Licking pie filling off her fingers, Mackenzie turned toward her husband with a mischievous glint in her eye.

Chase liked the game she played. He chuckled. Sexy vixen. The moment he thought it, his eyes shifted toward

Bastion. His father-in-law gave him a stormy look. Yeah, okay. He heard his thoughts all right.

"I have a lady I'm working for who thinks she's married. Turns out she's not. The guy isn't who he says he is. Why do you suppose a man would perpetrate a falsehood like that; pretend he's someone he's not?" Even as he spoke, Chase sang the big mac song in his head. He discovered in his research Bastion could read minds. He didn't know that before and doubted his father-in-law's own kids were aware either, which included his wife. Angel's notes indicated singing songs in one's head, could sometimes prevent them from catching what a person thought.

Bastion's expression changed. His eyes squinted at his son-in-law, suspicious of his line of questioning. He sat up in his chair, his arms propped on the edge of the table with knife and fork in hand.

"As with any man, I imagine he had his reasons whether good or not."

Head bobbing thoughtfully, Chase ruffled his wife's hair, tenderly kissed her on the forehead, and moved to escape up the stairs. He needed to keep his distance from the man. "True. Could be any number of reasons. But it makes a body wonder; to lie to someone you claim to love... Well, I'll see you upstairs, Honey?"

"I'll be up in a bit."

Bastion stared after the man as he disappeared up the stairs. Why in the world was he singing old fast-food commercial songs in his head?

- - -

After dinner and dessert, Bastion announced he was heading to his room then ducked into the pantry when his daughter's back turned. Shutting the pantry door behind him, he slipped off his boots, picked them up, and padded sock footed to the end of the pantry. Letting himself into his passageway, he shut the wall behind him as he began stepping down the stairs while carrying his boots. The moment his foot hit the carpeted floor he knew something wasn't right. He pivoted on the ball of his feet, before turning on the lights.

He had excellent vision in the dark, but he couldn't tell if anything appeared to be out of place. Slowly moving into what he affectionately called his "war room," he allowed his gaze to search for anything out of the ordinary. The room seemed off to him. Noticing his pen had been moved from his writing area his gaze homed in on the post-it note stuck on one of the computer screens.

That is new.

His insides churned; his body and mind coming alert to potential danger for this meant someone found out his secret. As he switched on the light, he realized what tipped him off. A scent lingered in the air. Foreign to the room maybe, but not to him. Recognizing the after-shave before he snatched up the post-it to read, he growled angrily, deep within his throat. The message read simply:

We need to talk.

His son-in-law's signature was scrawled below the message. Swearing, he crumpled the post-it note within his fist and chucked it across the room. It waffled in the air and dropped to the floor. The weapons room door loomed before him ominously, causing his eyes to widen at the notion that popped in his head.

He scowled, becoming even angrier. Knowing full well what his son-in-law did for a living, and his capabilities, he suspected when the snoop discovered the room, he picked the lock. Kicking himself for not having secured the room with a keypad entry rather than a simple key lock, he made a mental note to fix that in the near future.

Shoving his boots back on, he unlocked, swung the door open, and pushed his way through. The scent of after-shave lingered in this room too. The question now was, how the heck Chase discovered his secret, and what did he intend to do with the information. Did he find the entrance by accident? And did he learn everything somehow, or is he making false assumptions?

Not willing to take any chances he grabbed the first handgun nearest to him which happened to be his Glock. Confirming the gun had ammunition, he tucked it into his right boot. Placing a hand on his belt to reassure himself he had on the one with the knife hidden in its buckle, he exited his weapons room, re-locking the door behind him, and moved toward the monitors on the wall. Where is the piss-ant little pain in his butt now?

In the interest of privacy, he didn't allow for the camera's within his kids rooms to be viewable at any given time, but there were some there for this sort of situation. Not seeing him in any of the public rooms he turned on the camera in his daughter's bedroom. Chase sat on the love seat near their bed with his feet propped on the coffee table while reading from the laptop he brought home. Bastion snarled in disgust. He wanted to talk, did he? The PI didn't know it yet, but he was about to get what could be the last conversation of his life. Now he understood why the man had inhaled his dinner and disappeared without dessert. Chase loved pie, whether from scratch or baked from frozen.

Making a mental note of the location of everyone in the house he decided on how he wanted to handle things. Heading back the way he came, he secured his war room before exiting the pantry and took the stairwell in a few long quick strides.

Mackenzie stood washing the pots and pans in the kitchen which meant her back was to him. His son Kalab was in the art studio above the garage, likely trying to paint away the shadows from his mind and vision.

Bastion's sure-footed steps took him straight to his daughter's bedroom. Thrusting the bedroom door open without knocking he nearly punched a hole in the wall behind with the doors handle. Chase's eyes met his across the room as though he expected him.

"Follow."

It was an order, one that didn't allow for argument.

His son-in-law stood, placing the laptop under the bed; the secretive movement giving Bastion cause to wonder at it now, whereas before he wouldn't have thought anything of it. He left his face impassive, not allowing any trace of emotion one way or the other as Chase met him at the door. Neither one had taken their eyes off the other.

Chase exited his room being sure to stay face to face until they reached the hallway. They paused on the landing, neither one inclined to allow for the other to descend from behind.

From the moment Bastion entered his bedroom, Chase began singing show tunes in his head. He stopped suddenly, allowing for a thought to cross his mind, unimpeded.

'Side-by-side then?'

Bastion didn't respond one way or another, intentionally schooling his features and emotions into a mask of indifference, but his heart rate escalated. Somehow the man discovered he could read minds. Again he wondered how. Not even his children knew. Making a silent agreement, they descended the stairs, walking side-by-side until they reached the bottom of the stairwell.

Taking hold of Chase's left arm in a vise grip, he steered his son-in-law to the left, past the spare bedrooms and down the hallway toward his study. Not slowing down, he watched the confusion cross the man's face as he led him to the patio door within his study. Unlocking and opening the door, he shoved him outside, taking pleasure in the look of alarm that crossed his face.

Heading toward the path that led into the woods he continued to forge ahead in silence, fully expecting him to follow his lead. Once they reached the fork in the path Bastion took hold of the front of Chase's shirt with his other hand, fisting the fabric within his grip, and got right into his face.

"What are you doing?" His voice was cold; lethal.

"Bastion."

"Who do you think you are, barging in where you don't belong? I wanna know how you learned about it, how you found it, and what possessed you to think I'm okay with you going through my private things? And I wanna know now." He shoved Chase away as he spat at him, his anger surfacing past the cool facade. His demeanor became darker, more dangerous, his stance that of a predator stalking its prey. The shadows in the forest darkened with every moment they stood at the fork in the path as the sun extinguished the last light of the darkening sky. "Be sure you don't make presumptuous conclusions about what you saw."

Refusing to allow Bastion to intimidate him Chase had to admit to a little unease. When his father-in-law grabbed him and took him to his study he expected they'd stop there, but instead he shoved him out of the house and dragged him a distance into the forest before they stopped. Had it been for privacy? Or should he be worried the man had other plans?

Bastion snorted in disgust as he seethed. "Don't be worried. Be afraid, be very afraid." He heard what his son-in-law thought and sensed he figured out that he knew too.

Taking a defensive stance, Chase put his hands between them, keeping his palms toward the man in a submissive gesture. "Now hold on, Bastion, I'm not trying to out you or anything."

"Then what are you trying to do? You still didn't answer me; how did you find out in the first place, and how long have you known?"

Chase dropped his hands, his shoulders drooping a bit in exasperation. "I came home to pick up a sweater for Mackenzie. She texted she was cold. I happened to be working in the area. I got hungry and decided to grab a snack first from the pantry. That's when I discovered your room."

"Yes?"

"The wall shifted when I leaned against it."

Bastion's eyes rolled in his head, yet he never completely took them off his son-in-law. He sensed the man still kept something from him. "What exactly do you think you have on me?"

Chase took a chance, but was cautious in how he questioned him. "Would it be fair to assume what I found down there means you're a mercenary?" At his question, his father-in-law didn't flinch, but he thought he saw something change in his eyes. The pale crystal blue, normally luminous when in darkened rooms, appeared to have darkened unnaturally. It sent a chill up his spine.

"What do you intend to do with the information you think you have?"

"I didn't plan to do anything," he said quickly, trying hard not to take several steps backwards, for Bastion had most definitely gotten up into his personal space. He had the distinct impression he was on dangerous ground.

Bastion didn't say a word, but he shoved his face within inches of his own. One eyebrow shifted upward making it clear in his cold impassive expression, he didn't believe a word he said.

"I mean it, I didn't plan to say anything, but two things occurred to me when I found it, which left me thinking it'd be a good idea to make you aware of that."

His father-in-law didn't move an inch, but his expression had changed, giving him a calculating look as if to say continue. So he did.

"You have the whole place set up to be watched. It occurred to me that might include your room down there. If you happened to go back through footage and discovered I found it. I figured, if I didn't at least say something to you about discovering the space you'd be more upset."

Not confirming one way or another whether there was any such footage, Bastion said. "You would be correct. And?"

"Sorry?"

His father-in-law placed two fingers in front of his face. "You said two."

"Right. A little space here would be great, Bastion. When you're up in my face like this it makes it hard to think." Chase didn't like having to concede the man's manner toward him intimidated him, but his eyes had clouded in a way he'd never seen before and it scared the crap out of him. Sensing the man had no intentions of moving, he took a few steps back of his own volition as he spoke. "As I said, I don't intend to out you."

Bastion took two aggressive steps toward him and was back in his face. He snarled at him. "But?"

"It occurred to me you might be able to help with a problem I have." He raised his arms between them once again.

A barking laugh escaped Bastion's lips, but the mirth didn't reach his eyes. He circled Chase while looking him up and down as though he deemed him wanting in some way.

"Let me get this straight. You entered my space without my knowledge or consent. You investigated my rooms and went through my things, knowing full well you had no business being there in the first place. Now you want my help?"

He didn't respond right away. When Bastion put it that way he sort of couldn't blame him for being upset. Trying hard to think of a response, while at the same time singing show tunes in his head was getting to be a challenge.

"It's this bounty I've been hired to retrieve."

"Oh, I see. You want me to do your job for you? Is that it? Find your bounty and bring him in for you? You got a lot of nerve asking me that after what you pulled."

Becoming a bit angry himself, Chase responded without thinking, forgetting to curb his tone. "I didn't ask anything of you yet, and I already found the guy. I know where he is."

"Then what's the problem? Go grab him yourself."

"I can't."

"Why?"

"He's in Mexico. There are no extradition laws there which means my hands are tied. I can't go get him and claim the sizable bounty on him. But I could hire you."

"Stop." Bastion chucked, disgusted with the man and his gall. "So this is all about the money? What made you think I would do this for you? You invaded my private space."

"It's in both our best interests, for you to help me out."

Seething, the RavenCroft patriarch couldn't help but laugh for real this time at his son-in-law's sheer audacity. "Oh, really? How do you figure?"

"Because you want me and Mackenzie out of the house just as much as we want to move out. But you tied our hands when you made living in the valley a condition of my being able to marry her. As it stands now, I'm not in the position to build a house anytime soon. But this bounty, even after paying you for the job, there would still be plenty to begin construction on a house."

"You sure about that? I might ask more than you're willing to pay after this."

His mind racing now, Chase wondered if he screwed up in how he handled this. He figured the man would be just as anxious as him to have them out of the house.

"How much would you want for a job." Pain wracked his jaw, reverberating up his cheek and thundered through the rest of his head as he lost his balance and crashed to the forest floor. The metallic taste of blood seeped into his mouth. His head spun, trying to make sense of what just happened when he heard an angry voice near his ear.

"Keep your mouth shut and figure it out yourself." Thoroughly incensed, Bastion left Chase spread eagle among the brush on the forest floor. He began to walk away, ignoring him when he called out to him. The next time he called out, the idiot's words stopped him in his tracks.

"Kalab's doing it again. The whole-time thing."

This time he did glance back, a mixture of confusion and disgust spread across his face. The man was a paradox. He still lay with his face in the dirt after being knocked down because he crossed a line, yet he still took the time to warn him about his son.

"I'll deal with him."

He strode away without looking back, his feet finding their way back to the house without having to think about where he was going. Reaching the patio door of his study, he went inside and locked the door behind him. He never felt the need to put cameras in his war room before. The secret entrance had been effective enough until now. Adding that to his mental to-do list, along with installing the keypad lock to his weapons room, and having yet another talk with his cursed son, he headed back to the pantry. On his way, he ran into Mackenzie.

"Have you seen Chase? I can't find him anywhere."

"I think I saw him head out for a walk," he said, still heading in the direction of the kitchen and pantry.

"At this time of night?"

He shrugged as he called back to her. "Got the impression he has a lot on his mind."

"Oh, well, where are you going? I thought you headed up for the night."

"Snack." He pointed toward the pantry a couple of feet away. He knew she wouldn't think anything of it, even if they had just finished dinner not an hour ago. Snacking before and after meals was something they all had in common. RavenCroft's were notorious for their have high metabolisms.

Sensing something was up with her father, but too tired to care, Mackenzie decided to wait and bug him about it in the morning. "Okay, well, if you see Chase, let him know I went up to bed?"

He didn't respond, but nodded his head as though in assent as she moved down the hall. She did seem tired tonight and for a brief moment wondered if he should have given Chase such a hard to time. The man was not entirely wrong. He had limited their options when he insisted on the arrangement he made with them, but he thought it best for all involved. Mackenzie and the rest of the family's gifts needed to be kept secret, but it was not the only reason. His daughter had married a PI who moonlighted at times as a bounty hunter. When he did a thorough background check on the man, Bastion learned Chase was very good at what he did. Which meant he also developed a lot of enemies as a result.

He waited until she stepped around the stairwell and head up, before entering the pantry as he heaved a troubled sigh. He needed a drink, but that would have to wait. There had been enough screwing around for one night. It was time to get to work.

- - -

In the forest at the fork in the path, Chase struggled to sit up. His head spun and his heart thundered in his chest. He didn't intimidate easy, but Bastion took him down with one punch; he turned fifty not but two weeks prior. He also managed to take him by surprise which not only had scared the crap out of him, but infuriated him as well.

What he proposed would benefit them both, and he offered to pay him. He understood Bastion's anger over him finding out his secret and locating his room. He disregarded not just his need though, but Mackenzie's as well.

The man had tied his hands.

So be it; he was about to tie his.

And he had more than enough leverage to do it.

Getting to his feet he walked back to the house becoming more aggravated when he discovered the jerk had locked the study door, preventing him from re-entry there. Trekking around the house to the front door he became even more upset to discover he locked him out of the house for the night. His blood began to simmer.

Noticing a light still on in the art studio above the garage, he made his way toward it. Kalab could let him in, and then he would grab the laptop from under the bed. So far he hadn't found Angel, but she told him when she gave the stories to him to do with them as he saw fit. At the moment, he needed to use them as a means to an end. Finding a ghostwriter to fix them up and ready them for publication shouldn't be too hard. If Bastion wanted to be difficult, then he was about to become a major pain.

Chapter 12

Chase knew he was a dead man from the moment he opened his messenger and clicked the links the ghostwriter sent him. He began to sweat.

The plan had been to prepare the novels of Angel's, so they looked like they were ready to be published. In their previous form, they appeared to be written by a ten or eleven-year-old and wouldn't be taken serious by his father-in-law. If Bastion didn't concede in going after Hunter Grabill for him, then he would threaten to go public with them. He hired a guy to track him from a distance which was why he was sure his bounty still hid in Mexico. The snitch watched Hunter's movements, but the individual didn't have the skills, nor the connections to bring him back.

That might be a moot point now.

Clicking on the first link, his heart almost stopped beating when he saw the author's page on amazon.

She published them.

The ghostwriter published every last one of Angel's stories.

Or did she?

Only seeing five of them, he noted an arrow to the right of the fifth book. Thinking he got an ever so slight reprieve, he clicked on the arrow, only to be sorely disappointed. The sixth one was listed too, the screen only allowed for five to be viewed at a time.

A strangled sound of horror escaped his throat.

She was never supposed to publish them!

Sure, for the past two and a half months they worked on revising the manuscripts, arguing frequently on how much he needed to narrate them; especially the Blackthorne stories. But once they were ready he thought the ghostwriter understood returning the stories to him. He intended to present them to his father-in-law who wanted answers to how he found out Bastion could read minds. Each time he broached the subject, Mackenzie or Kalab interrupted them. The accidental discovery of his secret room had been one thing, but it didn't explain how Chase became aware of his additional gift.

Oh, geez!

Panic-stricken his fingers flew across the keyboard, hastily sending off a message to the ghostwriter within his Facebook messenger.

C: These links aren't live, are they?

Impatiently tapping his fingers on the keyboard he awaited her response.

DC: Are you stupid or something? Of course, they're live. Why? What's the problem?

He about choked on his own spit. If the meeting with his father-in-law in the woods indicated the sort of swift punishment the man inflicted, then he wouldn't bother with a warning this time, let alone a preemptive strike. He would attack and be done with it. Yup, Bastion would murder him.

C: You weren't supposed to publish them!!!

DC: Seriously? Why wouldn't we?

C: I didn't want them online.

DC: Dude, if you didn't intend to publish them then what was the point of the last two and a half months? Why are you even wasting my time having me make book covers? Does this mean you don't want me to upload the last one?

What did the author mean by, the last one? He went back into the author page and recounted the book covers on the screen. A finale had been listed, minus cover art. A seventh book?

C: I thought there were only six stories. Where did this finale come from?

DC: Geez, where have YOU been? The story is already started on one of the flash drives, and there are tons of notes. I finished it from that.

The ending is unconventional, if you ask me,
but hey, whatever makes you happy.

DC: So what are you saying here? You want
me to pull the stories?

Chase banged his head on his desk. He didn't know how he could make his request any clearer. He played them off as fictional paranormal romance stories with the ghostwriter, so hopefully no one took them seriously if they saw them.

C: YES! Yes, yes, yes and double yes! Pull them
like yesterday. How long have they been up?

DC: Don't get your panties in a bunch, I'll pull
them, but you better pay me for having my time
wasted like this. They've only been up for the
past three days or so.

C: Paid? Yes, yes, anything. Just pull them, they
can't be online for people to view.

DC: Not sure why you're freaking out. They're
fictional novels. The characters and plot aren't
real. So what gives?

Hysterical laughter fit the moment, yet it sounded unnatural coming from him. His panic was two-fold.

One, because being murdered by his father-in-law didn't sound like a lot of fun; and two, after reading through the stories again, he understood better the danger all the RavenCroft's and Blackthorne's could be in should the wrong person get their hands on them. Namely, this Jericho Henley character.

He missed a lot the first time around. Because of that, when he finally located Angel and her son at the local Women's shelter, he bought one-way bus tickets for them to Georgia, so they could stay with his sister until he sorted out their situation. The way her books read, he figured he better keep her away from Loveland for a while until he determined what happened to her husband. Considering she unwittingly wrote a reverse harem sort of story where three out of the four RavenCroft siblings attempted to "woo" her, he didn't want to risk any of them running into her by accident just yet. Especially after reading the last chapter and finding out who she wound up with.

C: Did you pull them? Are they down yet?

DC: Keep your pants on, I'm dealing with it.
Man, you are certifiable. Who writes full-length novels and novellas they don't want to be published?

C: I never gave you permission to publish. I paid you to fix them not publish them. SO IS IT DONE YET!?

No response.

Antsy, he erupted from his chair, covered his bald head with his hands, and paced the room. He would be ripping his hair out right about now, if he had any.

The computer chimed; another message. He raced to the desk, nearly tripping over the chair wheels before sitting down.

DC: YES ITS DONE! I unpublished everything. Even the revision of the last RavenCroft novel with the missing chapter. (I'm glad I found it, because I totally didn't see that ending coming. The missing chapter makes for a much better cliffhanger.) Keep in mind, it may take up to 24 hours for the eBooks to disappear.

DC: And I can't do anything about the books already purchased or downloaded.

C: Wait, someone bought them?

DC: Yup, every last one has been purchased in both paperback and eBook multiple times each. It's why I think you're nuts. Most self-published authors don't sell anything right away. Looks like you have a story people want.

C: Somehow I doubt it.

DC: You're weird. I'm done.

Chase heaved a huge sigh of relief until he reread the last several messages the ghostwriter sent. She changed the ending to the last RavenCroft story?

C: Wait! You found a missing chapter? I need to see it. Now. And you said you finished the finale?

DC: I wrote the seventh volume but didn't edit the manuscript yet.

C: I need that too. Send them both to me. In fact,

return everything to me. I need to figure some things out before going any further with this.

DC: Give me a minute. I'll send the files shortly. Do me a favor and don't message me again with ridiculous stories you're going to refuse to publish.

DC: And on a final note, I want my payment in my PayPal account now.

Chase started to send the message he would send what he owed right away. Deleting the missive off the screen before he could send it, he changed his mind. Too afraid the person wouldn't return everything to him if he paid them off now, he countered with a different offer.

C: I'll pay you half our agreed-upon rate now. The other half, plus a fifteen percent bonus if you overnight everything to me, will be deposited into your PayPal account once I receive the package.

DC: Fine.

The prompt response pleased him. He figured the bonus would get their attention and appease them a bit for their efforts. The person edited and added his narrations, they didn't need to do a lot of actual writing, but the speed in which they worked impressed Chase.

Promptly sending the payment in question, the ghostwriter confirmed receipt and promised to send off the package within the hour. Hearing his computer chime again, he checked his email. Seeing the manuscripts for the revision and the finale, he eagerly opened the first document and arrowed down. His document file for volume six stopped at chapter eighteen. He didn't have the nineteenth she spoke of. Before reading, it a thought occurred to him which gave him reason to send off one last message to the ghostwriter.

C: Where did you find the missing chapter and what prompted you to add it in?

DC: Found the file on the flash drive with the finale, marked as belonging to the third Raven-Croft story. The chapter felt more like an end to that book than a beginning to the last one, so I added it.

Thinking the chapter being separated odd, he began reading. Before long, he found himself leaning back against his desk chair in shock. Kahner's ex-wife did not abort his child. She went through with the pregnancy, delivered, and raised not one, but three boys - triplets. According to what he read, ten years from now Eliza would show back up on Kahner's doorstep with his teenage sons. Chase sat in stunned silence for the longest time.

His brother-in-law fathered triplets, but didn't know, all because of a mistake made by his identical twin brother, Sheriff Kalturek. This meant Eliza was out there somewhere trying to raise three gifted little boys on her own. They would be about four years old.

Sick to his stomach at the discovery, Chase started at the sound of his phone ringing. Glancing at his cell, he chose to let his voicemail take the call, for at the moment he couldn't think.

Chase needed to tell Bastion. Everything. Kahner worked undercover for the CIA, so he didn't have a way to reach him, but his father-in-law could. His brother-in-law had a right to know he was a father, plus it was imperative they find Eliza and her boys right away. If the last two novels were any indication, they were all likely in great danger.

Gifted people were being hunted by Jericho Henley and the Phenom organization he worked for. According to Angel's story's, they wanted to possess those individuals and harness their abilities for their own purposes. They would even kill people to get them. From what he read, Bastion had been delving into the inner workings of Phenom for some time now.

Or was he?

Angel wrote much of the setting of her stories in a time period ten years from now. Future Bastion had been aware of Phenom and Jericho Henley's affiliation with them. But did present-day Bastion know? The stories never specified when he discovered Phenom's existence.

It occurred to Chase he could find out if Bastion knew by confirming what Angel wrote his father-in-law hid in his study. The little nugget of information didn't make it into the novels, but she scrawled the secret in her notes a couple of times. When not in use, he locked his study door, but Chase suspected he could find the key.

Resigned to the inevitable beating once he found the key and item Angel talked about, Chase decided to wait until tomorrow. Saying anything wouldn't do any good until he received the ghostwriter's package. He needed the proof in hand when he told Bastion. Everything would arrive tomorrow, but by then would it be too late?

- - -

The Next Day
RavenCroft Ranch Home
Loveland, Colorado

"I'll be in the study if anyone needs me."

Grabbing his mug of spiced hot cider from the counter, Bastion took a sip of the steaming brew as he moved toward the hallway. The drink needed one more ingredient; Scotch. He would add the alcohol from his secret stash in his study, but before he could put a foot into the hallway, his son halted him.

"Your package is on the credenza near the door. It came with the mail I picked up in Loveland." Kalab absently pointed to the foyer as he leaned back in his chair.

"I didn't order anything. Are you sure the package is mine?" It wouldn't be the first time his son got mail mixed up.

"Your name on the box."

Curious, Bastion carried his drink to the foyer and set the mug on the credenza next to the parcel. Noting it listed his name, he pulled his pocketknife out, slit the tape, and opened the package.

Books.

Lifting a few from the box, he peered inside at the rest of them. He didn't recognize the titles nor did he recall having ordered them. Shuffling two of the books he pulled out from his left hand to the stack in his right, he closed the lid briefly, peering at the return address. The return address and company name listed on the box didn't look familiar, and it came from the United Kingdom. Further perplexed, he dropped the books back in the box. He would investigate them and the sender more thoroughly in his study. Tucking the package under his left arm he picked up his mug and headed down the hall to his study.

Shifting the box under the opposite arm holding the mug, he steadied both while pulling the key from his pocket, only to discover the door unlocked. Did he forget to lock the door the last time he left his study?

No, he remembered locking it. Cautiously opening the door, he peered inside only to come up short at the sight of his son-in-law, Chase Ryans, standing behind his desk near the window. The cabinet door near his desk stood open, and in the man's shaking hand, tilted toward his lips with his mouth parted, was a bottle of his prized Scotch. His son-in-law's hesitant gaze found his across the room and their eyes locked. Chase looked more than a little inebriated which made sense considering the bottle was now almost empty. When last Bastion poured a glass, the bottle had been two-thirds full.

Incensed to his core, he glared at the presumptuous PI. His hand fisted tightly around the handle of his mug as his jaw clenched and his body went rigid. What was with this guy lately?

"How in the world did you get in here, and what possessed you to think I'd be okay with you drinking my prized Scotch from my own personal stash?"

Chase licked his lips nervously. He closed his deep brown eyes then slowly opened them, preparing himself for what happened next. For the past two and a half months he called himself Vortigern Black within the stories he and the ghostwriter edited but, in truth, he was just Chase Ryans, private investigator and bounty hunter. He only wished he were someone else and that he was somewhere else.

When he drove to the ranch to learn if Bastion had heard of the Phenom organization yet, he somehow had a feeling current events would play out as they were. There would be subtle differences since things were happening ten years sooner than expected, but they would be similar.

Angel's version made it sound like he published the stories intentionally, but he would never do that. Ever. He loved his wife and respected the individuals within the family he married into way too much to betray their trust. As far as the ghostwriter was concerned, she believed the stories were fictional, not real.

With a heavy sigh, Chase gave in to the inevitable. An hour ago he read the very end of the last Blackthorne story, Kayos Knows, so he was aware of what would happen before it occurred. So, the no longer reclusive, and by no means mysterious, Vortigern Black, produced the key he found hidden in the door frame.

"K-key," he stammered with a terrified slurring stutter. "In the door frame."

Wide-eyed, Bastion jerked his head back toward the entrance of the door, dumped the package and his drink on his desk, then checked the hiding spot near the hinge. Seeing a small slit of a hole where the key used to be, his face registered shock. No one could know about the hidden key unless they were told.

"How did you?"

Words escaped Bastion as Chase pointed toward the laptop, flash drive case, and stack of notebooks on the desk with one hand while offering up the bottle of Scotch to his father-in-law with the other.

"Trus' me. You're g-gonna wanna be d-drunk fer this, Bastion."

Slamming the door shut, Bastion locked it behind him as he seethed within.

His son-in-law jumped at the loud noise, then hiccuped. "N-now hold on a sec ... J-jus' one sec, befo' you beat me to a pulp. I hafta'... gotta tell ya somethin'. Is impotent."

"I'm about to make you impotent for sure." Bastion raged across the room. Fisting Chase's shirt in his hand, he lifted him off the floor, bringing him within spitting distance of his face. This was the second time his son-in-law had gone where he didn't belong, and this time he got caught. "Nothing you say will keep me from beating you within an inch of your life."

"Y-you're a grandfather, Bastion."

"I don't have grandchildren."

"Eliza gave birth to t-tiples, I mean triplets." Chase was struggling to stay conscious. He got drunk on purpose, not wanting to be lucid during what he was certain was to follow. "Over foe' years ago," he said, raising four fingers of his hand near his father-in-law's face for emphasis, he then repeated himself all the while slurring his words. "Four. K-Kalturek messed up. Eliza ch-changed her mind."

Stunned, Bastion pulled back momentarily, trying to determine if the man was trying to pull one over on him, so he could sneak away. "How do you know this? Or about the hidden key in the door frame?"

Awkwardly shifting his four-fingered hand and arm toward the desk, the inebriated PI once again pointed out the laptop, notebooks, and flash drive case for Bastion's benefit. "It's all there. Everything she wrote is how I know."

Shoving Chase roughly against his bookshelves, he lifted a notebook. Skimming the first few pages within, his eyes narrowed in confusion upon seeing a character list of names with his entire family, including his brother, nephews, and niece in Montana, listed on the first several pages. Turning his attention to the laptop screen he saw a document was open on the screen.

"What is this?"

"Stories." Chase slumped into the chair in front of the desk near the box. "Six of em'. Or rather seven ta' be exact. Course I haven't gotten through all seven, or rather I have, but not really cause we're livin' the story. So I don't have a clue what happens after this moment because, well, we're in the middle of it, but I've a sneakin' suspicion where the plots a goin' afta' this. That said all this a happenin' ten years sooner than 'spected so story could deviate." He laughed bitterly. "Who am I kiddin'. It did change. Everything has changed! 'Specially since I suspect her 'usband died ten years sooner which is likely what prompted the here and now to be different, though I don' know how or why, and have no way of proving that yet."

Bastion stared at his son-in-law, struggling to make sense of what he heard as he tried to decipher what he had in front of him. Was this a manuscript for a novel he was looking at?

Catching sight of the box Bastion dumped on the desk, Chase leaned toward the package, his curiosity getting the better of him, regardless of his precarious situation.

"Whatcha got? Books?"

Reaching in he grabbed one out with his free hand. He read off the first title aloud. "Terrible Karisma." His drooping slits for eyes widened in alarm. Dropping the Scotch bottle on the desk he stood on wobbling legs and dug in the box, yanking one book after another out, gaining his father-in-law's attention. "You ordered them? Of course, you're aware of the books, and me being Vortigern Black. You know everything with the future thing you do."

Flopping back in the chair, his head lolled as he reached for the Scotch bottle from the desk in the hopes of nursing it a bit more. The second his fingers brushed against the glass; it was hoisted out of his reach. He stared up at the bottle now being waved before his face. The remaining liquid sloshed back and forth within enticingly.

Bastion teased his poor excuse for a son-in-law with the Scotch bottle all the while his eyes glimmered with barely repressed rage. He didn't fully understand what was going on yet, but he knew one thing for sure. He would not like it one bit.

"Sum it up, Chase, before I clobber you for finding your way into my office and my Scotch. I received a box of books I didn't order - which you seem awful familiar with - and a laptop, a bunch of flash drives and several notebooks filled with my family's names. Explain and make your explanation brief. How does any of this relate to Kahner and Eliza having kids."

Chase took a deep breath, trying to think how best to relay the information, all the while knowing Bastion was bound to misunderstand, regardless of what he said. It was how it was written after all.

"All that," He pointed at the desk, then indicated the box of books, "and all those are the same."

Bastion prompted him, to help keep him on track. "Okay."

"One vast story." This time Chase put one finger in the air as his head wobbled precariously. "Two gifted families." Another finger rose slowly. He stared at the appendage intently as though willing it to join the other extended finger. "Both differ in their origin beliefs regard...(hiccup)...regardless of th-the book. All are linked by the same lineage, the same prophecy, and hunted by the same group of people."

One skeptical eyebrow quirked in irritation. Now the drunken lush was going on about prophecies? An uneasiness pooled into his gut. The last bit he said raised warning signals in his head.

"There are six, no s-seven books. All are about the Blackthorne's; including you's, the Raven... (hiccup) ...RavenCroft's. All written by a g-gifted author who has no clue they have abilities. So they're g-gifted like you guys, see? I found out everything, because of the stories she wrote. Some of them tell the p-past from five years ago." Chase lifted two more fingers. Realizing his count was off he sniggered and raised one more causing Bastion to seek the heavens in exasperation. "The rest is set ten years in the future. Some events are happening now, but the story is off course. S-something happened; went terribly wrong."

Making the mistake of leaning forward and placing a flattened hand on his father-in-law's arm, Chase howled in pain when the adept mercenary deftly maneuvered away, twisting the offending appendage into a brief submissive hold before releasing him to lounge back in his chair.

"Who wrote all this?" Bastion growled, losing patience.

"The author, or well, ghostwriter." Chase began to ramble nonsensically, having recovered from his ordeal, while scratching the back of his neck in a daze.

Grabbing one of the books from the box, Bastion waved it in front of his son-in-law to gain his attention.

"Are you saying the same person who wrote this novel, also wrote what's on the laptop, and that they're saying Kahner fathered three boys?"

"Who?" Chase looked as confused as his father-in-law for a moment. Then his thoughts suddenly cleared. "Delaine Christine - Karisma Kayos," Chase swayed back and forth as he wavered in his response. The RavenCroft patriarch could tell he would pass out soon. Snapping his fingers in front of the man's face several times, he kept his distance because his breath reeked of alcohol.

Startled back to attention, Chase said loudly. "Angel's! (hiccup) Angel's what done it in the end. He's a daddy all right."

The way Chase made things sound, the authors were guardian angels or something, when they were actually a liability and a danger to his family, as far as Bastion was concerned.

"Is' too bad though." Lost in his own muddled thoughts, the drunken PI shook his head back and forth then peered up at his father-in-law as he paced before him.

Bastion stopped, his chest squeezing in on itself. "What's too bad?"

"I'm p-pretty sure they're in some s-serious trouble. The need to locate them fast is the only reason I'm allowing myself to go through this now. Cause you need to know. You need to find them."

"What kind of trouble?"

"They're being hunted of course."

"By whom?"

"Same people what's hunts all the Blackthorne's and RavenCroft's, of course. The ones who did in Inara. Phenom is what they call themselves, according to her notes."

Not normally prone to being taken off guard by anyone, Bastion RavenCroft inhaled sharply. His expressive crystal-clear blue eyes became enormous as he gazed at his son-in-law without really seeing him. No. He couldn't mean them. No one was aware of what happened to his wife all those years ago. They were the reason he become a mercenary in the first place.

With clear malicious intent, the horse rancher turned merc gripped the armrests on either side of Chase, pinning him to the chair. The PI shrank back further. Chest heaving as he breathed heavily, Bastion's clouding and darkening eyes burned holes into the man's soul as pure unadulterated rage coiled within him. His voice dropped three octaves when he spoke.

"You are on dangerous ground. To whom are you referring to exactly."

"I am not your enemy, Bastion, nor am I a part of Phenom."

Bastion growled. The name of the organization he swore to bring down from the moment his wife died slipped from his son-in-law's lips. The same man he entrusted with the heart of his daughter.

"But Jericho Henley is," Chase said, further enraging the man. Even in his drunken stupor, he could tell his father-in-law could no longer see reason, nor would he listen. He foraged on though, knowing he had to get it out before it was too late. "They hired him, see? Jericho Henley; to hunt down anyone who's gifted. He's been after them now for the p-past couple years. I s-suspect it's why the author gave me w-what she wrote, cause now the tale is a d-different story. Something has changed."

He might have known the first punch was coming, but he sure didn't see it. The brute of a man was fast regardless of his immense size. Chase's feeble attempts at defending himself gave way to the inevitable beating he suspected he only partly deserved. The problem was, his father-in-law still only had part of the story.

The moment he mentioned the name of Bastion's late wife within the same couple sentences as the Phenom organization, he knew he added salt to a wound that had become septic over time. But he had to at least try to warn him though, for all their sakes.

As Chase lost consciousness from being decked in the face for the fourth time, he only hoped he managed to tell him enough.

Kicking the door of his study open, breaking the lock, Bastion dragged Chase down the hall toward the dining room. The noise from the fight in the study drew attention from those within the house which meant witnesses to his blustering rage.

Gasping at the sight of her battered and bleeding husband being dragged to the dining room, Mackenzie froze in place at the bottom of the stairs. Sidling up beside her, Kalab hauled her back against him when she tried to run after their dad and to her husband's aid.

"Let me go, I have to stop him," she shouted while struggling against her brother to no avail.

"Thought you'd defy me?" Bastion thundered as he passed them. "I gave you one rule when you married my daughter, and it is law in this house. You betray one of us, you betray us all."

Watching their father disappear with Chase in tow around the corner into the dining room, they both followed quickly after him in a state of confusion with Kalab in the lead. They heard a scraping whooshing noise before they reached the doorway. Stepping into the room they watched in stunned silence as their father opened a wall, exposing a room with sleek metal walls.

A panic room?

In all the time they lived at the ranch they didn't know the room was there.

Mackenzie became further horrified as her dad disappeared within the room, dragging her husband behind him. She chased after him in a panic, worried about what he intended to do, and wondering what provoked her father's angry state.

Startled at discovering a secret passage in the dining room, Kalab didn't catch his sister in time before she attempted to go after their dad and her husband again.

"Dad, stop! What are you doing? Why are you doing this?"

"He betrayed you. He betrayed me. He betrayed us all!" Shoving Chase on the floor within his panic room, Bastion grabbed his daughter around the waist before she could step in after him. He hauled her out of the doorway entrance, putting her in Kalab's capable hands and shoved the wall back in place; closing the idiot in.

"No, no, no! Don't do this. What are you doing?" Mackenzie clawed at the wall, trying desperately to figure out how her father opened the secret passage. Unable to open it, she chased after her dad, who stalked to the kitchen and opened the freezer. "Open the door. Let me in now. He's my husband!"

"Husband or not, he stays where he is for now."

"Why? What did he do? You can't leave him alone in the room." Racing toward him, Mackenzie grabbed his arm trying to pull him toward her, so she could see him. He planted his feet and refused to move. "Please, Dad! He's hurt, he's bleeding! I need to help him. Whatever he did, I'm sure he's sorry."

"Sorry?" Bastion roared, flabbergasted by her meek assertion. "He hasn't begun to comprehend what sorry means, because I'm not done with him yet. That is merely a way station for him."

Mackenzie gasped, her hands flying to her mouth.

"Dad?" Kalab spoke up, not liking the implication he was making. The cold look of steel in his father's eyes had him searching the ceiling for the shadows of which he suspected had used whatever this situation was to bate his dad further.

"We've been found out by an outsider and from the sounds of things, it's because of him. He stays where he's at until I find out how severe this danger may be." Shoving the freezer door closed after taking out an ice pack, he placed it on his fist then stepped down the hall. "Call everyone home. Now. No excuses and no delays. I'll be in my study until they all arrive, trying to sift through the damage Chase caused, and attempting to locate Eliza and your brother's three sons."

Stunned into silence, Mackenzie stared after their father. Through her tears, she tried to make sense of what he said. "Did he say what I think he did?"

"Kahner is a father," Kalab confirmed, his shrewd eyes following in his father's wake. He noted the shadows were skittering about and cackling over their triumph.

"But how? I thought Kalturek said Eliza aborted them," Mackenzie said.

"As did I."

"I don't understand. What does Kahner being a father have to do with my husband?" Mackenzie began to cry. "And why did he say Chase betrayed me? He would never do that. Never."

"You know as much as I do."

"He's hurt. Kalab, can you please?"

"No." His response was firm and as unyielding as her father. "Until we find out more of what's going on, he stays. Honestly, he might be safer in the panic room and out of his sight. Dad wouldn't put him in there, if he didn't feel he had cause."

"But Kalab."

"Did you see his face? Dad was scared, Mack. I only ever saw that look in his eye once, and it was back when mom died."

Mackenzie's face crumpled in distress, her insides roiling with her own emotions as well as the stark terror and rage she felt from her father. Tears swam in her eyes and fell down her cheeks in waves. She wouldn't believe - couldn't believe - Chase, her husband, the man who loved her more than life itself, would ever betray their secret to anyone.

"We need to get everyone home as he said. Something's happened. Something bad too, or he wouldn't be acting like this. Where's your phone? I'll grab your cell so you can call Drayke."

Nodding sadly, Mackenzie's gaze shifted into the dining room worrying about the extent of her husband's injuries. His face looked like his nose had been broken. "My room," she said finally.

Steering his sister toward the kitchen he set her down at the table, started a pot of tea then headed upstairs. After retrieving the phones he came back down only to find she moved into the dining room and curled up in front of the wall. One hand pressed against the drywall as she rested her head against it.

Resigning himself to calling everyone himself, he placed his first call to Kalturek, figuring it might be wise to have the Sheriff around. He suspected his father would be calling Kahner, for he imagined he wanted to break the news to him on his own.

Chapter 13

Present Day
Blackthorne Horse Ranch
Kalispell, Montana

After hanging up with his son, Bastion returned to the house to find Rafe doing the same with his own. Their eyes met across the kitchen, each sensing questions needing answered. In silent agreement, they walked down the hall toward the pool area in search of the man they suspected had the knowledge they both sought.

Arriving at the pool doors, they discovered their brother was skinny dipping and being none too shy about it.

"You can't be swimming in the pool without a bathing suit," Rafe yelled, feeling a sudden need to empty the pool to add new water and chemicals.

"Oh, posh. Stop your blathering about. I haven't swum in a long time; I'd like to enjoy it." Rourke called as he turned in the pool and began swimming back the opposite direction. "Incidentally, the clothes used for swimming in are called swim trunks, you uneducated yank. Besides, as you might recall, I've never had the use for them." Feeling the need to be difficult he suddenly switched to the butterfly kick as he swam on his back.

"Geez, Rourke. Must you put it all out there like that?" Bastion glowered, not terribly inclined toward being on the receiving end of the view.

Rourke grinned devilishly in response. "What? If the sight is so displeasing, then do be sure to not look in the mirror anytime soon."

"Have you no shame whatsoever?" Rafe averted his gaze as his brother continued swimming laps in that way, splashing about more than what was really necessary. He didn't appreciate the jibe any more than Bastion had and suspected he knew it. Trying to keep his head and not let the wretched excuse for a brother get to him, he tried to appeal to what little morality he might have left. "There are impressionable young children in this house."

"Apparently, we have children in here who can't handle a little nudity." Turning in the water once again Rourke sighed loudly and switched back to a scissor kick. "Oh, bollocks. You have a fair point. Next time I shall wear swim trunks." There was a mischievous gleam in his eye as he continued with a jeer. "No worries Rafe, I'll be sure to borrow yours."

"You will not. You'll buy your own dang swimsuit. I won't have you wearing mine. Take care, Rourke, I've no qualms about kicking you out, and I'm still in good enough shape to forcibly do it myself."

With a smirk and a shrug toward Bastion, his brother reverted fully to a slow breaststroke as Rafe filled him in on what he'd learned from his son.

"According to Drinian, the reason they didn't fly back was because he saw a snobbish looking old man with a cane and an expensive-looking car paying off my pilot at the airfield there in Maryland when they arrived. Absurdly, he seemed to think the man was familiar to him somehow. I don't suppose you know anything about that?"

Rourke scowled, thinking his brother's son should learn some respect for his elders, and he needed to get his eyes checked if he couldn't recognize a man who looked exactly like his own father. He paused briefly to tread water. "You had an issue you were unaware of; I fixed it. I'm sorry if my presence inconvenienced them, but surely this will give them more of a chance to get to know each other. I have returned with your plane by the way." His voice echoed around the pool room.

Not wanting the two men spiraling off on another argument, Bastion confronted Rourke about the books he received anonymously. For a split-second, he could have sworn he saw a faint smile attempting to spread across his face before he blustered his response.

"Of course it was me. Who else would it be? Certainly not our father, Rathbourne. He hasn't a clue. He's still wallowing in self-pity that mum hid you away for nearly forty-seven years. I came across the books after his heart attack. It's a good thing I had the forethought to purchase multiple copies, because I noticed they were unpublished within a couple days of having ordered them. Interestingly, the book descriptions were deleted too. My first thought was you had something to do with that, but then I realized you wouldn't have gotten them in time. That's when I followed the IP addresses and discovered what was really going on."

"And what, pray tell, is really going on?" Bastion imitated his brother's Scottish accent just to irritate him. He suspected the man was enjoying being difficult.

Rourke laughed heartily, his eyes giving way to his glee at knowing what they didn't. "You have a snake in your midst, a snitch, a rattler, an idiot of sorts. I'm glad to know, or suspect anyway, that it's not you. It would be awful disappointing to learn my long-lost brother was the dunderhead who blundered it up, though I'd wager you're not all there if you allowed such an idiot to marry into your midst."

Bastion groaned. The man knew.

"Who is Vortigern Black, my dear brother? I take it you've sussed it out, and its why you're here. If I had to guess at the reason for your sudden presence here, it would be because you received the books and you're looking to glean some information on your long-lost grandchildren. Bit of irony there, I'd wager. The long-lost son having missing grandchildren." Rourke gave his brother a smarmy grin. "I sent the books off, once I located you. It's smart to have all mail sent to a post office box, rather than your real address to protect the location of your raven sanctuary there in Loveland."

"Is he always this slimy and stuck up?" Bastion asked.

"Usually worse. This is mild for him. Either age is catching up to him or he's hiding something," Rafe said.

Both men looked at Rourke when he began singing heartily while staring up at the ceiling as he swam. He clearly intended to ignore them.

"He's hiding something," they agreed in unison.

"By the way, Rafe, you can tell that dolt of a son of yours - Drinian, I believe is the name - to rest easy. I have Veta's divorce papers, signed and all. All she has to do is place her own signature on it when she arrives, and then have Breydon file them for her. The happy little love birds can have their happy little bairns straight away.

"How did you get her divorce papers and get that sick freak to sign them?"

"Paid him off, of course. At least, he thinks he's been paid off." Rourke laughed uproariously, enjoying his own internal joke. He tucked something highly illegal into the packet of money he gave Mitch, which didn't get discover until he attempted to go through an airport security check for a flight. Dogs sniffed him out, and he was being arrested even as they spoke.

Rafe gave his brother a look; one-part frown, the other half, impressed appreciation for the man's ability to hoodwink, for he shared what he did with a thought. Bastion, started laughing along with them, having gleaned the information as well.

"It won't come back on me," Rourke called, having caught what Rafe had been thinking.

"How do you figure?"

"I passed myself off as her lawyer."

"But we're identical," His brother's blasé attitude left Rafe to believe he hadn't fully thought his plan through.

"Didn't say he wasn't an idiot too. He saw a man with a cane, stash'n beard, glasses and a Scottish accent to boot. Probably figured I was a bleeding doppelganger. Who knows? Anyway, I tracked him all the way to the border, where I have it on good authority, he's been detained and is in the process of being arrested."

"Tell me truthfully. Do you think he's in league with this Henley person?" Bastion wanted to know.

"The thought occurred to me. I think we'll have to watch the situation closely. People's lives can sometimes overlap in peculiar ways. In some cases, allowing for the whole Karma thing to come back and bight 'em in the arse, as I expect it needed to in his case."

"Agreed. Though, I'd say it was because he was the evil man who sought only rebellion, and you were the cruel man sent against him."

Bastion snorted and looked to Rourke who rolled his eyes heavenward. "Leave it to you to repeat what I've said in your own ridiculously religious way, Rafe."

"It's not my way, it's God's," Rafe said. "It says as much in Proverbs chapter seventeen verse eleven, or have you not bothered to crack a Bible in the past century?"

The two men exchanged another look, then spoke in unison. "It's the same thing."

"I suppose now you're going to tell me our gifts aren't from God," Rafe said, both stunned and exasperated. Were they both atheists?

Bastion laughed outright. "If there's a God he's got a cruel sense of humor passing on some of these so-called gifts. Personally, I've always preferred believing they were a product of nature alone."

"Nature? I suppose you're one of those science people, who thinks our abilities have developed over the past three millennia to what they are now; like how man supposedly developed from the ape," Rourke said.

"You're only half right," Bastion conceded. "Our gifts are genetic, no doubt, but it never developed over time. It didn't have the need to. Every last one of our ancestors, going as far back as three thousand years ago, have all always been gifted in some way."

"Hhmm, yes. On that point, I think we all should agree, wouldn't you say, Rafe? Though I daresay your theories, Bastion, on how, are baseless."

"Have either of you come across anyone gifted like us or our children, who didn't stem from somewhere in the Weir-deVere line?" Bastion asked.

Having returned to his swim during their discussion, Rourke paused once again, throwing a suspicious look his brother's way. He was pretty sure the remark alone gave him the answer he needed. "I have to concede your point. Any and all individuals I've come across, who have had any kind of minute ability of sorts, has been a distant cousin or relative of some sort. Doesn't mean nature alone has a part in the gift letting among our family's, whether close or distantly obscure." Rourke gestured his head toward Rafe. "What about you? Have you met any?"

"There have been two."

"Really? And you're certain they have no connection to the Weir-deVere line in even a small way?" Bastion asked.

Rafe sighed. "Anything is possible, but I've looked into them both and for as far back as I was able to go, I could never connect either one in any way."

"Who were they?" Bastion asked.

"My wife, Lilyandhi."

"I see, and?" Rourke asked.

"Karisma," Rafe said. "Or, I guess we should be calling her Inara now."

"I'd prefer you not call her that," Bastion said.

Rafe shrugged, wondering why it bothered his brother so much. "It was her given name originally. What would you have me call her?"

"Angel," Bastion said firmly. "Certainly not Karisma and most definitely not Inara for that was my wife's name."

"An angel she is for sure, but I'm afraid Angel could never be her true name." Rourke crawled up the steps and out of the pool.

Rafe quickly threw him a towel, smacking him in the face with it intentionally. "How do you figure?"

Rourke frowned at him. "Because there is not enough strife within her."

Rafe gave his brother a calculating look, suspecting he had a theory and wasn't simply toying with them. "What are you on about Rourke?"

"Consider their names, brother, and you'll discover her correct place."

"Is it my imagination or is he talking in riddles again?" Bastion asked.

"He has been living with our father and grandfather all this time, its small wonder he'd become the Riddler."

Instantly thrown off subject, Rourke said hastily, "I was never the Riddler."

"No?"

"No."

"As I recall, you were the Punisher, Rafe, and I was Iron Man. I honestly don't remember which one Rourke was," Bastion said.

"You're remembering it wrong. I was Superman, you were the Punisher, Bastion. He was Iron Man," Rafe said.

"Bah, you're both wrong," Rourke said.

Rafe was skeptical. "Rourke doesn't really know. He just wants to be right."

"I am right, you idiot. Rafe was Iron Man, because he wanted to fly without having to wear, as he called it, a gay frilly skirt as a cape, Bastion was Batman cause you kept flinging ma's nail filer and peeling knives from her manicure set across the yard like they were bat blades, and I was Superman."

Rafe laughed suddenly at the notion of his brother playing at being a superhero rather than a villain.

Accurately construing his laughter as being at his expense, Rourke responded harshly. "Yes, that's right, I wore the bloody gay frelling skirt as a cape. If you recall though, we designated Ma the avenging angel and Da was appropriately nicknamed the frelling Punisher, not me. Don't think I didn't notice the two of you getting it all mixed up. Just as Karisma did. You Bastion, you started it when you gave your son Kahner the name Toni Starck as an alias, I suspect just to be difficult, and you Rafe, when you mistakenly gave your son Dante the name Franc Kastle. It was likely also done, because you could. You both knew full well they'd receive heck for it."

Both men made noises of agreement and smiled mischievously, fondly remembering the moment when they were playing as superheroes at the river forty-seven years before.

"Frelling?" Bastion finally said amid the silence. He noticed Rourke's tendency to quote one of his all-time favorite television series. It also hadn't been lost on him that Rourke referenced the stories as having been written by Karisma. As he expected, it meant she was the one Chase received the stories from.

"Noticed that too, did you?" Rafe said with a grin.

"Yes, yes, we all seem to have the same Farscape fetish. We are identical triplets after all. We're bound to have a few minute things in common." Rourke groused as they both grinned at him. "I believe we've gotten thrown off subject here."

"Was there really one subject to begin with?" Bastion grinned.

"Yes, the main point, the one you both came out here for in the first place which is the biggest of them all and has nothing to do with pilots, swim trunks, and who played at what hero before your supposed demise." Rourke flicked the towel at Bastion before finally wrapping it around his waist.

"Which is?" The two brothers prompted in unison.

"The books speak of three women, not two: Angel Stryfe, Ciara Biardon, and Inara RavenCroft. Presently a Karisma Kayos is asleep in the study. The dilemma we face here with her gentlemen is this. Which one is she really? Or, the more disturbing possibility, is she a compilation of all three? If that be the case then who is she meant to end up with? For if we do not figure it out straight away, and accurately, then chances are, no one will be finding peace from those blasted accursed shadows and the prophecy will never be fulfilled."

- - -

Present Day
RavenCroft Ranch Home
Loveland, Colorado

"I'm done waiting on them." Kahner RavenCroft was agitated. He rapidly paced the kitchen floor all the while clenching his hands into fists in frustration.

Sheriff Kalturek RavenCroft winced, more so for the ice pack he was holding to his left eye than from his identical twin's proclamation. "There will be hell to pay from Dad if he discovers you let the snitch out before you were supposed to."

"Don't you mean, Vortigern Black? And I have to agree, I'm not sure it's a good idea." Kalab took the melting ice pack from his brother and placed it back in the freezer. Grabbing him a new one, he tossed it to him. He couldn't fault Kahner for having decked him when he first arrived home. Kalturek was the reason why his brother's ex-wife Eliza had disappeared nearly five years before while still pregnant with his triplets. All because he misunderstood what really happened when she was trying to leave the clinic.

"Are we men or five-year-old's who take orders from Daddy?" Kahner sneered, certain his intended course of action was the right one. Disappearing from their view he traversed the short distance from the kitchen, crossed the hallway, and stalked into the dining room. He knew the entrance was here. They told him as much. If that wasn't enough, the fact his sister was still huddled on the floor next to the wall was clue enough for him. Her head shot up as he approached, her eyes beseeching him to help her figure out how to get in.

"It's not true, Kahner. Chase loves me, he would never betray us."

Cupping her cheek with his hand, he gently rubbed her tears away with his thumb.

"A man can love a woman with all his heart and still make a terrible mistake without intending to. Trust me, I speak from experience." Releasing her, he stepped back thoroughly inspecting the wall, eventually homing in on what looked like a tiny notch in a knot of the wooden paneling. He attempted to grab it with his fingers, but they were a little too thick and big to slide into the notch.

"Geez, Dad. If I didn't already know it was warranted, I'd call you paranoid." Helping his sister up from the floor, he took out the pocketknife he always carried, slid it into the notch in the knot, and gently pushed, then pulled forward. A soft swooshing noise came from behind the wall. "Did any of you bother trying to open this?"

"I looked. I tried. But I didn't see that," Mackenzie said anxiously, becoming excited.

Not sure what he was going to find, Kahner hesitated. "Give me a minute with him first."

"He's my husband. You've no right to keep him from me. Neither does Dad." Anger coursed through Mackenzie's veins.

Giving in to the inevitable, he pulled on the paneling. A section of the wall swung open to reveal a hidden metal room the size of an elevator shaft. The floor was solid wooden oak and the walls were a sleek metal as was the door he held. By the light from the hallway, he could see it was empty but for a small metal box in the corner of the room, and Chase who was zip-tied to a chair laying on the floor in the center. His back was to him. His brother-in-law's body jerked with the noise and his head rose weakly, trying to look around to see who was there as his eyes squinted from the welcome light.

Kahner stoically stood with his arms crossed. He frowned down at him.

"Hello, Kahner." Mouth dry from lack of water, Chase's voice came out as a craggy croak.

Mackenzie raced over to him, frantic to see him released from his prison.

"Vortigern Black, I presume or, so I'm told. Sounds like you deserve this." It seemed odd to Kahner, how his brother-in-law was always able to tell the difference between him and his identical twin brother Kalturek. Even now with his vision impaired by the swollen eye, it didn't faze him.

"No, he doesn't," Mackenzie snapped.

"What do you say, Chase?" Kahner asked.

"Before hearing the tape I'd have said, maybe a little. But now." He sniffed miserably. His face twisted in pain at the movement. He was sure his nose was broken.

Having gotten down on her hands and knees to investigate his injuries, Mackenzie sat back on her heels and gave her husband a hard look. "What are you saying?"

"I'm saying I screwed up, Mack. B-Bastion told me when we got married." He banged his head against the floor. The anger he felt over his part in what had happened built to a point he could no longer withhold. He cried out in frustration, barely able to choke back a hoarse sob.

Clasping her hands over her mouth in shock Mackenzie's pale eyes shimmered with renewed tears. "Are you saying you told someone? About us?"

"Yes. No. Sort of, but not really. Then again, yeah?" Chase coughed, his body wracked with pain.

"What is it: yes, no, maybe? You're not filling me with any desire to help you. Not before telling me where Eliza and my children are." Kahner's movements were slow as he crept further into the room and rounded on his brother-in-law, leaving the door propped open, so they had light from the dining room to see.

Chase continued to cough violently causing his wife to shout for her other two brothers to assist in releasing him from his bindings. They came quickly into the room, glancing around them curiously as they entered, then stopped abruptly at the sight of their sister's husband on the floor.

"Don't just stand there, help me get him out of here," Mackenzie pleaded. Hurt by her husband's betrayal, she was more concerned with how bad he looked. Blood was spattered across his face and had dripped down the front of his mouth and nose. It had dried, crusting over the angry welts on his cheek. The left side of his face was badly bruised and the flesh around his eye had blackened. The white of his eye had turned red from a broken blood vessel.

Both men looked to their elder brother.

"I have a question first before you take him out. Dad says you don't know where Eliza and the kids are."

"I don't. I swear to you on my life, on the life of your sister, if I knew I'd tell you."

"Explain to me how you knew about them at all. These books Dad spoke of, I don't understand what it all means. How did you come by this information in the first place? And why would you consider publishing them?" He signaled to his other two brothers, letting them know it was okay to unbind him and at least let him up. "What tape are you talking about?"

"What has B-Bastion t-told you?" Chase asked as Kalturek and Drinian helped him off the floor of the panic room and dragged him out to the kitchen. The mid-afternoon light blinded him until his one good eye adjusted enough to allow him to see. He still clutched the recorder in his hand. "Where is he? Did he tell you to let me out?"

"He's out of town. I'm releasing you of my own volition."

"Put me back."

"You can't be serious," Kalturek said at the same time as his sister.

Mackenzie huffed. "Why would you want to go back in there?"

"I don't, but I need to, because if he finds out." Letting off a startled yelp as Kahner snatched the recorder from his hand, Chase lunged for it unsuccessfully.

"What is this?" Kahner turned the recorder over in his hands. He pulled the small unlabeled tape out then put it back in. The whole time Chase kept attempting to grab it back unsuccessfully. "Is this from an answering machine? No one uses those anymore."

"Give it back!" Chase was frantic. The stark terror in his eyes giving away his fear.

Kahner ignored him, as his brothers held him back and shoved him in a chair.

"Didn't Dad have one in his study until about four or five years ago?" Kalab took hold of Chase's arms, easily holding him in his seat yet unsuccessfully doing so without causing him pain. It was becoming clear the man's arm had been popped out of its socket. "Stop moving or it's going to keep hurting."

"No! Don't play that. You shouldn't have let me out. B-Bastion would have never wanted this to be heard by any of you." The PI's eyes were wild. He wriggled in his seat, all the while calling out in pain.

"What's on it?" Mackenzie asked. "You tell me right now, Chase."

"I can't." He could see the wounded look in her eye. "He'd kill me," he said desperately trying to make her understand. He struggled to keep humming one commercial after another in his head, knowing pretty soon his efforts would be futile. He was so tired and weak already.

Setting the recorder on the counter Kahner gave his brother-in-law a calculating look. "I can't glean anything from him. He's figured out how to keep me from reading his thoughts. That's okay though. The easiest way to find out is to play it."

"No!" With a fierce yell, Chase bent down and bit Kalab on the arm. Momentarily caught off guard, his brother-in-law released him in order to tend to his injury.

"He bit me. He actually bit me and left a mark! Who does that anymore?"

Surging across the kitchen, Chase grabbed for the recorder on the counter, narrowly missing it. Kahner reached over, snatched it up, and punched him across the face in the other eye.

Mackenzie squealed in dismay as her husband dropped to the floor in a heap. Racing to his side she saw he'd been knocked unconscious. "Dad's already beaten him to a bloody pulp! Was that really necessary?"

"He betrayed our trust and is still trying to keep information from us. So yeah, it was. We need to hear what's on this tape. It might be something about Eliza and my kids." Punching the rewind button then play, they were all startled by the voice they heard when it started. As they listened to the recording their expressions changed, each one of the siblings responding differently to what they heard. By the time the recording stopped, the RavenCroft children were in shock and Mackenzie was crying.

"Was that who I think it was?" A voice spoke from the doorway of the kitchen. No one noticed or heard when Drayke entered the house. He planted himself against the door frame as he listened quietly, only now speaking. He peered at each one of his siblings in turn.

"It sure sounded like her. I don't think it's been altered." Kalturek glanced down at Chase who was still in a heap on the floor.

"How do you suppose he managed to get the tape?" Kalab asked.

"A better question would be, how long has Dad known?" Drayke asked.

"He's right. Chase said Dad would never want this heard by any of us." Kahner quoted loosely. "And I happen to know what dear old Dad has been up to behind our backs for the past five years. Learning this explains a lot."

- - -

Twenty-Four Hours Earlier
When Bastion and Chase Last Spoke

Propping Chase up in a chair in the middle of the panic room, Bastion zip-tied him to it by both his wrists and ankles. Hefting the bucket of water above the still unconscious form he tipped it, sending water pouring over his head and down his front, drenching him.

Not surprisingly, Chase finally stirred. His eyes struggled to make sense of his surroundings. The small room he found himself in was dark and unfamiliar which meant he was likely in the panic room he'd read about. It took, but an instant to realize he wasn't alone as he attempted to blink the water from his eyes.

Illuminated by a couple of glow sticks tossed on the wood floor, Bastion circled his son-in-law preparing to question him about the books he'd received and the author who wrote them. He'd been researching the author who wrote the, An Unfortunate Lineage Series ever since he knocked Chase out and locked him in the room. He rifled briefly through the child-like versions on the laptop and flash drives, but summarily disregarded them when he realized they were the same story as the paperback books he received. Unconcerned with the three novels covering his brothers family in Montana, he concentrated instead on the three that might give him the answers he sought about the grandchildren of his Chase spoke of.

Upset to see his family's names within a novel, Bastion had been more furious to discover Chase had given himself an extra part within the stories as well. The man's narrations had been illuminating, but it was the content and story plot that had gained his attention the most. If the author was to be believed, they were all part of a prophecy where if his children met the right individuals, married, and had children of their own with them then his son Kalab might somehow find a reprieve from the shadows which haunted him. If there was any truth to it than he would definitely be looking into it, but for now he had more immediate concerns, the biggest of which was locating his former daughter-in-law Eliza and her three children before Jericho Henley of the Phenom organization found them.

"Why hello, Vortigern Black," Bastion spat.

Chase jerked in his chair, unnerved by the ominous tone of so few words. "Listen, Bastion."

"I found your author."

"My author?" Disoriented and confused, Chase tried to wrap his mind around what was going on. His face felt as though it had been pummeled with a meat mallet and his head throbbed.

"Yes, the one who wrote An Unfortunate Lineage. The book series where Vortigern Black spouts off at the mouth about things he has no right to."

Worried about the safety of the ghostwriter he hired, he hurried to correct his father-in-law's thinking. "S'not like that B-Bastion. It's a f-fictional story. She doesn't know it's real. I never told her anything."

Bastion creeped close to Chase's ear, causing him to flinch as he spoke. "I know who she really is."

Confused by the statement he began to think Bastion was talking about Angel rather than the ghostwriter. "I was never able to figure that out."

"I have resources you don't."

Chase nodded weakly in agreement. What more could he say? It was true.

"I know what I must do."

"You do? Are you going to go get her?"

"Hm. That depends on you."

"I don't understand."

"Tell me where Eliza is."

"Eliza? I don't know."

"Tell me where she is!" Bastion thundered.

"You know what I know; what's in the laptop and notes."

His dark, disgusted laughter echoed in the small room. "I don't have the time to read through all that prattle. What has the author told you? Tell me what you know."

Thinking fast Chase struggled to understand what was going on. "I don't know anything. All I know is Eliza is out there, and she had Kahner's triplets. The notes said they're gifted and could be in danger of being caught by Jericho Henley and..."

"And?"

"She's the one who wrote them, not me. I don't know any more than what she's written. If you want to learn more, than you need to go get her; ask her. Maybe she knows something that will help."

"I can't go get her," Bastion admitted finally.

"Why?"

"She's no longer there."

"What?" Chase became frantic. Did Angel leave his sister's place in Georgia? He told her to stay there until he could come to get her or send Bastion to get her.

"It would seem he got to her first."

"Are you saying the 'Milkman' got her first?" Panic-stricken, Chase strained at his ropes.

"Milkman. What are you going on about milk for?"

"That's what she calls him. The Milkman."

"Why would the author call my brother a Milkman?" Bastion paced the short distance of the room, perplexed by what he heard.

"Your brother?"

"Yes."

"Your brother found the author?"

"He sure did. Apparently, it's all written in the stars too." He shook the books in the air while speaking sarcastically. "Or in these books anyway."

Chase tried to think through the throbbing pain his head was experiencing. "I don't understand. Why would your brother, a man you've never spoken to, go and pick up your Angel?"

Bastion became unhinged by what he deemed unnecessary confusion. "This is what comes of disobeying me. I told you not to break the cardinal rule of this house, and what did you do?"

"But I didn't. I never told the author you were real when she gave me the stories."

"Stories based on reality; with knowledge of potential future events and also our real names you idiot!" He cracked him across the jaw. "I have it on good authority a man from Phenom went after the author. How my brother became aware of her potential danger is unknown to me as yet. Perhaps he too discovered her stories. I won't know until I get there and attempt to bring her back."

Blinking several times, Chase's head lolled for once from something other than being drunk. Unfortunately, it had been a short reprieve for he was no longer intoxicated. "I'm sorry Bastion."

"You're sorry? Do you have any idea of the danger you've placed not just my family in, but the Blackthorne's of Montana as well as the ones in Scotland? You have no idea the reach of these monsters in that organization. I hardly even know. I've barely scratched the surface so far."

Chase stifled a whimper, his face contorting in anguish over the damage his actions may have caused for so many people. In his misery, a tear streaked down his cheek. "I didn't understand."

"No you really didn't," Bastion said coldly. He slowly reached into his pocket and pulled a small old tape recorder from within. Adjusting the sound to high, he started the tape as he spoke one last time and placed it in his son-in-law's hand. "This is what happened to the last person who defied the Phenom organization."

A garbled female voice began to play through the recorder.

"Hello? Hello! Are you there?" came the desperate voice of a woman.

"Oh, please, please, please pick up!" The voice became more frightened; panic-stricken. The sound of an engine revving, as well as distant traffic noises, could be heard in the background.

"I wish you were there, Bastion, I need you. I needed to talk to you. Something terrible has happened, and I made a mistake. I'm so very sorry." The woman sobbed and began to cry. "I didn't know. Honestly. I didn't understand. When I started writing the stories for them, they said it was for an experiment. I didn't know they'd be used to find people gifted like our children." She shuddered the sound carrying through the phone, making the action unmistakable. Hysteria was building within her. "I didn't know what they were doing to the people they found. When we discovered their plan we tried to save them," a sob culminating to a high-pitched squeal caused chills to run the length of his spine. "But we were too late," the voice whispered close to the phone. There was a troubling pause in the recording as sounds in the background, engines revving and tires squealing, became more prevalent and the woman's breathing became erratic.

"I'm on my way to you now, but they found me out. Someone from Phenom is after me. If I don't make it -- oh, no! What was I thinking? What have I done? I have to lead them away. They can't know. I can't let them find our home in the raven haven."

Chase met Bastion's gaze, suddenly realizing who the individual on the recording must be. Her voice abruptly changed, becoming stronger, braver. "I think they've been listening in on my calls, so I need you to listen to me now. There's a...a package I need you to pick up for me. I was supposed to, but I can't now. This is really important. You have to find my partner Flynn Hunter, get it from him."

Squealing crunching noises from a crash could be heard through the recorder. The metal grinding and crunching together came to a sudden stop. For one horrible moment, they heard nothing. The silence within the panic room was so thick it made him feel like it was swallowing him whole. The sound of footsteps cut through the emptiness of the room, echoing and becoming louder with every step.

"B-Bastion." The weak breathy voice whispered softly, urgently. It was clear the woman was in severe pain. "P-package. Y-you mu-must save the w-white raven f-from..."

A soft whining sound silenced her, then the footsteps could be heard running away. An engine revved in the background and tires could be heard squealing away. Eventually, the recording stopped.

The pallor of Chase's complexion turned ashen and his throat clogged with emotion. "It wasn't the car crash that killed your wife."

"It was made to look like one."

"Do they know?" Both men knew to whom he referred, Bastion's children.

"No, and I intend to keep it that way."

"But the coroner. Wouldn't he have noticed?"

"A bullet wound?" Bastion laughed harshly. The sound was grating and a bit scary. "Not when it melts after tunneling through an ear."

Chase didn't know what to say, so he wisely stayed silent. He'd never heard of such a thing.

"Never could find her partner Flynn Hunter, nor the package she referred to. I suspect they met the same end as my wife."

Bastion took the recorder from Chase, rewound it and set it on pause as he spoke. "I found the books my wife referred to in this recording though. She'd written a whole series of paranormal stories, penned under the name David Pearson. They're based on our own children."

Chase's eyes widened as understanding finally dawned on him. The fifth book of the, An Unfortunate

Lineage series, Deadly Karisma, began with one of the characters within finding a box filled with novels in the attic written by someone named David Pearson. One of the characters, Sable Kryder, had read some stories.

"They used her work." The painful memory was making it difficult for Bastion to maintain his cool facade. "They're still using them to this day to find gifted people and bring them in. They track the sales, see? Locate those who purchase them and then investigate to see if they're gifted. People with abilities are prone toward reading this type of story so, once they start they can't stop reading them."

Bastion hovered within an inch of his son-in-law, placing the recorder within his hand. "Close your eyes, Vortigern." He snarled, his voice so low, so cold the hairs on the back of Chase's neck prickled from fear and his heart pounded wildly in his chest.

He did as he was told as his body shook in the chair, wondering if Mackenzie knew where he was and whether she was even worried about him. Chase could feel the small plastic recorder being clasped into his hand; his finger being poised directly over the play button.

"Now I want you to listen to it again, very closely," Bastion whispered darkly into Chase's ear then depressed the button, allowing the recording to play again. His own face crumpled at the sound of his wife, calling out to him, recalling vividly the helplessness he'd felt when he'd heard it for the first time, after it had already been too late. "Listen to it again. Only imagine this time that it's my daughter -- your wife."

Chase shuddered, the shock of his words pummeling his heart with such force he couldn't hold back his fear, or his tears.

"Because of you I now have to do the one thing I swore I'd never do, go back home. If anything, and I mean anything happens to my family, because of what you've done." Stepping back, Bastion walked away and left the room, closing Chase in alone as he was forced to listen to the recording once again, unable to keep from imagining the woman speaking was the love of his own life.

He sobbed. If there was a God.

There had to be. Angel claimed as much within her stories. Anger, sorrow, regret, fear and most importantly love had him bowing his head in a not so silent prayer. He didn't ask for help or forgiveness for himself, but for his wife and her family of whom he had grown to love, regardless of Bastion's most recent treatment. It had been well-deserved because he screwed up.

They needed a miracle.

"Dear God, I beg of you, if you're truly real. If you're out there somewhere listening, watching, then please, protect the RavenCroft family, as well as the Blackthorne family. I give you all of me. I'm yours to take, to use, to bend to whatever will you have planned."

The recording continued to play, the terrified voice of Rafe's late wife Inara instilling within him a fear he never knew before. Forced to listen, he tried desperately to turn the recording off. Unable to contort his fingers to get at the buttons properly all he managed to do was knock it to the floor near his feet. Straining in frustration, Inara RavenCroft's words repeated and echoed in his head. He cried out desperately while trying to shift and move his chair in the hopes of knocking it over.

"I think someone from Phenom's after me."

All Chase could see in his mind was the image of his own wife, Mackenzie lying broken in a pool of her own blood as a gloved hand pressed a Glock with a silencer to her ear while she begged for help. Anger surged within him at the thought of his sweet, sensitive, and giving lover being subjected to such a cruel end. He couldn't listen to the rest. He couldn't bear to hear it again.

Putting everything he had left into it, he struggled fiercely to tip the chair. Finally, managing to get it to wobble he kicked even harder with his feet. The landing, once he fell to the floor, was loud, jarring, and had him crying out in pain, but he didn't care. The desperate need to turn it off before it finished playing, before it got to its end had him wriggling about on the floor in order to reach the recorder.

"Y-you mu-must save the w-white raven f-from..."

He gasped as the wine of a silencer silenced her. Compressing his eyes closed as tightly as he could in an effort to dispel the images playing out within his tortured mind, Chase sobbed uncontrollably, unable to stem the flow nor the panic within.

"Ah, God! Oh, God, no! Please, Jesus, you have to send an angel. Only an angel can keep them all safe. I know they're there. I know they're real. If they weren't she wouldn't be writing about them, would she? Bastion's Angel that is. She knew. She knows."

Choking on his own words, he gasped for air as a thought wriggled its way into his mind. The conversation he had with his father-in-law moments before was replaying in his head. Had Bastion been referring to Angel in the end? Was he going after her like he needed to? She was the one with all the answers. That's not what he said he was going to do though. No. He said he was going where he'd promised he'd never go again.

Back home.

His mind raced as the revelation came to him.

Bastion didn't fully understand.

"No, Bastion, you're going after the wrong woman! Not the ghostwriter, you need Angel! You need an Angel, not a ghostwriter."

His own craggy voice trailed off as he banged his head against the wooden floor. Tears dripped down his face as he cried shamelessly. The man was going the wrong way and once again, it was all his fault.

"Please God, if you're there if you're real, send Bastion an angel," he begged hoarsely. He needed water, but at the moment he didn't care. "Be it Maleeka, Whoreash, or Rohn." A bitter laugh soon turned to hysterical giggles. "Shoot, send him Angel herself for all I care. One way or another, you have to send him an angel, Lord, please. One that'll help him find Eliza and her kids before something happens to them. Cause he's going the wrong way."

Chapter 14

A Miracle
Rawlins, Wyoming

She was so tired of running.

This time Eliza Dushku didn't know where she was going either. She'd been driving for the past four and a half hours, ever since their hasty departure from the small two-bedroom apartment in Sidney, Nebraska, where they'd lived for the past three months. She'd hoped it would be longer, but it wasn't to be.

The moment her son began singing the 'Safe Place' song at the breakfast table, she and his brothers knew they had to leave. They learned over the past couple years whenever he began singing it, if they didn't leave quickly then bad things would happen or bad people would come and try to take her boys away from her. She didn't know who they were, but she was certain she knew why they were after them.

Frantic to get away before they were found, Eliza insisted they leave without even finishing breakfast. Only taking what they absolutely needed, she packed a couple of bags and grabbed her fire safe lockbox while the boys had helped each other get locked into their car seats. In less than ten minutes they'd abandoned their home and taken off.

Glancing at the dashboard of her GMC Savana passenger van, she noticed it was past eleven-thirty. So far she'd managed to entertain her four-year-old sons with music, books, and a movie on her old laptop, but she knew they were tired of driving. She'd been heading west on interstate eighty for a while now, but figured to stop at the travel center. Taking a left onto Higley Boulevard, she called back to her boys.

"We're stopping for a bit guys, so we can stretch our legs."

"And for a potty break. Yes, mommy."

"You're right, but please don't interrupt me, Peter. It's rude."

"Sorry."

She turned right into the parking lot, peering back at Gabriel as she did so. Her son's knowing eyes caught hers after he'd taken in their surroundings with a glance.

"Good place to stop. Looks safe."

She released a weighty sigh, somehow knowing he'd direct her one way or another. If people knew she took direction from her son they'd likely lock her up and take away her kids. Experience had taught her though, to trust his instincts ever since he'd been able to start talking which had been earlier than his brother's. They all acted and sounded older than their age, Gabriel in particular. She suspected it was because they were gifted.

After herding them all to the restroom, purchasing a new phone charging cord, because she'd left her other one behind, they all wandered over to the sub shop within the travel center. After ordering two-foot-long sub sandwiches, waters, and grabbing a large bag of chips to share, they headed back out to the vehicle to eat there. She divided one of the foot long's up, then realized she would still have a six-inch left over after she ate. Leaning into the vehicle while holding the bag with the foot-long in her hand, she stared down at it, thoroughly mystified.

"Now why did I do that?"

"Cause Angel's hungry too."

"Peter, who are you talking about?"

"The angel," Andrew answered for his brother.

James gave his mother a knowing look. "She needs."

"A ride, Mama," Peter said, finishing his brother's sentence. They did it so much now Eliza finally learned to stop telling them not to interrupt. It was just the way her identical triplets were.

"She can't walk, " Andrew said.

"The whole way," James continued.

"After all," Peter finished.

She stared at her boys in utter confusion.

Gabriel pointed out the window. She looked in the direction he was shaking his little arm. A woman with a child in her arms stood at the corner of the building where the sub shop was located. Her long silver-blonde hair hung to nearly her hips and it appeared to be falling out of its braid. The woman was frazzled, clearly distressed, and appeared a bit lost as she attempted to shush her crying child.

"Are you talking about her?" Her son nodded and kept pointing. She pushed his arm down, chiding him softly for continuing to point when it wasn't necessary anymore. "Stay here and locked in. Go ahead and eat. I'll be right back."

Closing the sliding door, she locked the vehicle and kept it in her line of sight as she stepped cautiously over to greet the woman.

"Are you alright? Can I help you somehow?"

"I went the wrong way." The strain in the woman's unusual eyes was all too familiar to Eliza. They looked troubled; as though she'd endured much hardship already.

"Are you lost?"

"Yes. No. Maybe a little." Angel said while patting the one-year-old's bottom.

What little hair the boy had was as pale as the woman who held him and his eyes were similarly unusual in coloring as his mothers. Eliza couldn't quite make out the color for it flashed between blues and silver as he cried.

"I took the bus to get to Georgia as he said to, but as soon as I got off I knew I was in the wrong place. So I bought a new ticket and headed this way. But they just said inside there that I can't get where I need to go from here cause no buses run that way."

The woman was jittery as though having been unsettled or frightened by something or someone.

"Where are you trying to get to?"

"Flathead Valley," she said shyly, her expression turning sad.

"Where is that?"

"It's in Montana, silly."

Angel acted as though Eliza should know for some reason. "Oh, I see." She chuckled at being chided by her.

They stared at each other for a minute, both trying to gauge if the other was trustworthy.

"Are you like me?" Angel finally said in a loud whisper with one hand cupped around her mouth. "Because you seem like you might be a little like me."

"How do you mean?"

Angel hesitated, but only briefly. The nice woman had stopped and asked her if she was okay. She couldn't be all bad. Not seeing any other options, but what was before her she inhaled a shaky breath and took a chance. "At wits end, in need of direction, and looking for a place to keep our children safe."

Normally Eliza's first instinct would have been to run as far away as possible from someone making statements like that. She had her own problems to deal with and her own boys to consider but the woman didn't seem to give off any kind of negative vibe at all. If anything, the way she stood in her fluorescent green flip-flops with her long hair all messed up, her face and flowered dress smudged with dirt and a little boy stuck awkwardly in her arms, it made Eliza feel the need to be protective of her. She was frumpy in her current state, for the dress was too big, but she was very pretty and seemed so darn sweet, as well as a bit slow. She suspected the slowness had likely caused her to get taken advantage of a lot.

"What's your name?"

"They call me Angel and this here is my son Kal." The way she spoke and acted made her seem younger than she looked.

Eliza's eyes went wide upon hearing her name. She whipped around, gazing back at her van. She could see her boys still strapped into their car seats through the windows awaiting her return as they watched her from the vehicle. Marveling at how her sons were capable of doing that, knowing things without knowing why, she resigned herself to the possibility she was meant to help Angel get to her destination for some reason. Having dealt with the gift herself when she was pregnant with her son's, she knew better than to ignore the signs.

"Angel, my name is Eliza. Would it be safe to assume you haven't the money to get there by any other means?" She asked tentatively, trying not to embarrass her.

The woman's pale face flushed crimson and her eyes began to tear up. That was answer enough. Praying to the heavens she was making the right choice, she offered her a ride, hoping Flathead Valley might be a good place to settle for her own children. Opening the back end of her GMC, she explained the seating situation with her vehicle.

"When I bought this van it was used, and the third row of seats was missing. Technically, I shouldn't let you sit back here with your son like this, but if you stay down and out of sight we should be okay."

"Oh, this is perfect," Angel said happily. "I can still set him in his carrier - he'll be safe in there - and I can nap next to him on the floor. I'm so tired. I couldn't sleep sitting up in the big giant bus. There were so many people."

After purchasing some water and formula for Angel and her child who was becoming increasingly fussy, Eliza gave her some cereal she packed for her own kids as well as the other half of her sandwich.

"Thank you so much," Angel took a blanket from the stroller and laid it out on the floor of the vehicle, folding it over a bit so it looked like a makeshift sleeping bag. Situating her son's carrier on the floor in the back end she tucked herself and her son in. Getting help from Eliza to mix up a bottle, the boy soon quieted and was content to munch on his cereal in intervals.

"I don't know how, but someday, I will repay you for all of this. You're being so kind to me, Eliza, and you don't even know me. Some people haven't been so nice on this trip. It's making what I have to do so much harder. I wasn't supposed to have to come find him, see? He was supposed to come to me."

The comment struck Eliza as being odd. Deciding not to pry, she moved the bags she had in the back end, up in front of her boy's seat and the passenger seat. It suddenly occurred to her she hadn't seen Angel with any luggage.

"Do you not have any bags?"

Angel's head bowed sadly as her lip trembled. She looked upset. "I'm so stupid. I grabbed the stroller but never thought once to grab my bags. If Wilton were here, he would have reminded me. It's a good thing my laptop and flash drives weren't in there. Chase still has those," she said as if Eliza should know who that was. "And my pad of paper is in little Kal's bag, so thankfully I didn't lose that. My friend would have been so mad if I lost that."

Eliza cringed, knowing full well how the loss of her things was likely affecting Angel. She was more than familiar with having to start over from scratch herself. She had to do it many times in the past four years.

"Oh, my. Well, hopefully, your friend will be able to help you out a bit once you get there. Maybe he can help you get your things back."

"Who?"

"You do have someone you're meeting in this Flathead Valley place, right?"

"Yes. He left his home to go back to his birth home. He should be there. I think he's meant to be a real good friend one day," she said shyly.

"I see. I need to gas up before we leave. You'll have to direct me so I know where to go."

"Okay." Angel's voice was small giving Eliza a moment's pause.

Shutting the door of the back end she got in the vehicle and pulled it up to the pump. Once the vehicle was fueled up, she hopped in and turned in her seat, so she could look back at her boys and Angel.

"You boys all set?" They all nodded. "I think you already know Angel, but her son's name is..."

"Kal," Andrew said.

Eliza sighed. "Right. Angel, meet my son's; Peter, Andrew, Jacob and Gabriel. How are you doing back there? Are you going to be okay?"

"Yes, thank you." She mumbled in response around mouthfuls of her sandwich.

"So, where am I going?"

"Um, not sure exactly, but I can get us there regardless."

"Okaaay. What does that mean?"

"Kalispell. I know we need to go to Kalispell, Montana," Angel said softly as she popped her head up over the seat. Her large beautiful shimmering blue eyes had swirls of a silvery light shining out from them. "Between you and me, I know things, see? And I know where we need to go but won't know exactly how to get there until we get there. Does that make sense?"

Eliza stared back at the woman, wondering how it was she kept running into people within her lifetime who was gifted like this and why? First, it had been her boy's father, Kahner. Then their father's family; the

RavenCrofts. When she was pregnant with them, she began to appreciate for the first time what it must have been like for their daddy growing up, for she'd experienced their gifts while she'd carried them. Now they were developing the gifts she'd experienced and here was Angel, with similar abilities. It made her wonder if the woman was related maybe in some way. She couldn't see how though. The woman's hair was a pale silver-blonde rather than black like her own four boys and their father; and Angel's eyes, though blue, were not the pale blue like the RavenCroft's and by extension her boys.

"Will you still be able to figure out how to get us there knowing only that we need to go to Kalispell, Montana in order to find your friends home?"

"I think so." She took up her cell phone and pulled up maps. She had the nagging feeling she heard of this Kalispell before, but couldn't figure out why it sounded familiar. "I can put the city and state in here and it should direct me to the city's border. You'll be able to tell me more once we get there?"

"Yes, I should be able to." Angel continued to munch hungrily on her sandwich. Seeing her eating made Eliza's own belly growl. She plugged in her destination, thinking she'd wait to try to eat until they were on their way. It was important to her that they made as much distance as possible between them and Nebraska. She didn't want anyone to catch up to them. It was why she was using cash for now. Eventually, she'd have to use her credit cards though. She wouldn't have any choice.

"From the looks of it, this will be a thirteen-and-a-half-hour drive. We'll have to stop somewhere part of the way for the night. But we'll work that out later."

"Okay. Eliza?"

"Yes?"

"Thank you for saving me."

Unsure how to respond, she smiled and said, "How could I possibly say no to an angel?"

The woman giggled secretively and gave her an impish grin back.

- - -

Blackthorne Horse Ranch
Kalispell Montana

"Is this where we need to turn?"

Eliza was at her wits end. Angel had been struggling to stay awake in order to give her directions and it was the fourth time she'd had to prompt her to stay awake.

Yawning loudly, Angel's eyelashes fluttered slowly closed then shot open again. She looked sleepily around through the windows as though trying to recognize landmarks.

None of them had slept well the night before. Owing to the need to keep expenses at the minimum they all shared a double queen-sized bedroom when they stopped in Pocatello, Idaho. Eliza slept in a rollaway she requested, and her boys took up the queen-sized bed next to her. Angel and her son took the other one.

She would have thought it would have been little Kal, as Angel called him, who would have kept them up, but instead it had been Angel for she kept waking from bad dreams. The last time she woke had been as the sun was rising. The woman cried out about someone she called a Milkman who was after them. Terrified and unable to be appeased, Eliza grudgingly got her boys up, so they could continue on to Fathead Valley at Angel's insistence.

"Angel?" Eliza prompted her again, feeling just as drowsy and a bit irritable. "I know you're tired but if you could stay alert for a little longer."

The woman's head popped up. She shook her head to clear it. "Yes, of course. Sorry." Angel blinked trying to clear her eyes, so she could focus.

"Am I going the right way?" Eliza asked, wondering for the tenth time in the past hour what in the world she'd been thinking when she picked her up. It felt like they were driving around in circles.

"There's an entrance, I assure you. It's hard to find. Not easy to see by your everyday person."

"Yes?"

"There!" Angel shouted while pointing wildly off to her right.

Squinting in the direction she was pointing; Eliza heaved a relieved sigh. "You mean that spot there? Between those two pillars of field stone? Is that a driveway?" It looked like at one time a wooden signage had been erected up from and over the field stone pillars, connecting them in order to create a crude archway. She wondered briefly if the name of the ranch had once marked the entrance of the driveway.

Nodding tiredly, Angel gave a half-smile, then settled back to the floor of the vehicle as she called out to her. "If you keep following this unmarked road it'll take you all the way up to the main house of the ranch. It's long and deep into this part of the mountainous valley, but that's part of what makes it so safe. Oh, and don't be alarmed by the funny sensation you get as you drive through it."

The woman had the habit of saying odd things like that. Choosing to ignore it, Eliza continued along the partially paved road. They were surrounded by trees and brush on all sides. Sunlight was barely finding its way through the densely packed trees. It made it seem darker out then what it should be for the time of day.

She found herself experiencing a bit of déjà vu as she tunneled a path through the forest, thinking it odd a ranch would be tucked away within a forest rather than out on open plains. For some reason, it reminded her a bit of the entrance to where she once lived with Kahner in Loveland. Minus the creepy ravens, of course. At least this road was partially paved, so she wasn't too worried about getting lost yet. The one to the RavenCroft ranch home had barely been a dirt road.

Taking another look around her, she looked back through the rear windshield. The road didn't appear as obvious from this angle. It seemed to blend in with the environment well. After what felt like nearly twenty minutes of driving, but was probably more like fifteen, the canopy of trees opened to a clearing. The sprawling ranch and its main house came into view, startling her at its size. She'd never seen such a large ranch before, though it did look like it might have been added onto at one point. It had a beautiful wrap around porch which appeared to extend all the way around the house and the lilac bushes near the porch entrance were lush and gorgeous. She expected they smelled wonderful.

Parking near the sidewalk that turned into a path leading all the way up to the porch, she let loose a loud yawn, unable to squelch it. Glancing back in her rear-view mirror she noticed everyone had fallen asleep. All four of her boy's heads were lolled to one side or the other and their mouths were partially open.

She loved watching them sleep; they looked so peaceful. Making a few attempts to call back to Angel to wake her without getting a response, Eliza got out of her vehicle and walked around to the back end. Peering in through the window she noticed the woman was out like a light. Grimacing at the inconvenience, she stood with her hands on her hips gazing about her. It was such a glorious view even from where she stood. She could see the Rocky Mountains from any direction she turned. It looked as though the vast ranch were nestled within a valley of sorts.

Again with the déjà vu.

Trying to shrug it off, she opened the back end and made several attempts to wake Angel to no avail. Frustrated, and unwilling to be hindered any further from finding a place to stay for her own kids for the night, she closed the door and headed up the walkway to the front of the house to get Angel's friend to help. All seemed quiet from the exterior, so she hoped he was home. It occurred to her suddenly as she reached the porch, Angel never gave her their last name, nor told her what her friend's name was. Figuring whoever lived here would likely know the name Angel either way if they were friends, she didn't let it stop her from moving forward.

Stepping up onto the porch she admired the porch swings and all the flowers in their planter boxes as she knocked on the door. After a minute of waiting, she noticed there was a doorbell. Feeling silly it occurred to her no one had likely heard her knocking if they were in the back of this enormous house, so she rang the doorbell a couple of times. Rocking back and forth on her worn tennis shoes she turned and glanced back at her vehicle to check and make sure her boys hadn't woken up yet. Hearing the door swing open behind her she spun back around then stopped dead in her tracks.

The man in the doorway gazed back at her looking both alarmed and confused. His brow suddenly furrowed. "How did you find this house?"

The question threw her as did the man himself; if this was Angel's friend, he wasn't exactly what she imagined. She assumed when the woman had spoken of him that she was referring to her son's father. From the looks of him though, she couldn't see how that was possible.

"My friend helped me find it," she said by way of explanation. "Or, I guess she's more your friend than mine. I just met her yesterday and gave her a lift here."

ST stared back at the woman on the Blackthorne porch with a blank expression. To his knowledge, no one had ever found their way onto Rafe's property without the assistance of a Blackthorne or without being one themselves. He was almost positive she wasn't a family member which left him wondering who she was and if Rafe was aware she was on his property yet. The woman was slender and small, but tall at about five foot eight, and she wore her straight black hair cut short above her shoulders. The dark color seemed a bit unnatural against her skin tone, but she had some of the most amazing soft amber eyes he'd ever seen. They were almost cat-like in nature.

Deciding to play along to find out who she was, ST leaned casually against the door frame. "If you gave my friend a lift, then where are they?"

"She's in the back end of my van. I'm having trouble waking her though."

"You say she is in that van there?" ST pointed toward the unfamiliar black GMC parked in the driveway.

Eliza nodded, thinking the man's response had been a bit odd.

"Tell you what, I'm sure I can help wake her up. The name's Dr. ST Wong, by the way, in case she didn't mention it. And yours?" He stepped out of the house, closing the door behind him then, walked beside her to her vehicle.

"Oh, right. Sorry. My name's Eliza." Missing seeing him raise an eyebrow down at her as they walked amicably, she gestured toward the back end. "She's in there with her son. The stroller is on the side next to my son's. I'm afraid she has no luggage."

"No bags at all?"

Eliza gazed up at the man as she moved to open the back door of her van. "She accidentally left it on the bus when they dumped her off in Rawlins."

"I see, and that would be Rawlins, where?"

"Wyoming." Eliza hesitated at opening the door. "I'm sorry, were you not expecting Angel?"

"Did you say, Angel?" He sounded alarmed.

"Yes."

"There's a woman by the name of Angel in your van, and she has her son with her?"

"Uh, yes?" Suddenly anxious, she gaped at him as he began to laugh.

ST pulled his cell phone from his pocket with one hand as the other gently clamped over hers on the door handle. "Wait, please. Just wait," he said while texting frantically. He snorted as though he found something highly amusing; an internal joke of sorts of which she was not privy to. "Don't open it up yet. Hold on; all will be explained, I assure you. There's someone I need to bring out here first before we wake her."

Eliza stamped her foot, unwilling to be a party to whatever game the guy was playing. "From the looks of her, Angel has been through hell trying to get here to you. She found herself broke, stuck in Rawlins, Wyoming after having already taken a bus all the way from Georgia. I gathered she came from somewhere else in an attempt to get there and both trips had not been easy until I met up with her. People were mean to her, and I have the impression at one point someone ripped her off."

"Wait, Angel was in Georgia?" ST asked suddenly, pocketing his phone. That most definitely didn't fit with the stories. He wondered briefly how she'd come to be in Georgia as he leaned casually against the back end, struggling to keep from peering into the window. He was terribly curious, but figured the Blackthorne men should see her first, though he was anxious to gauge their reactions.

Taking a couple of steps back, Eliza unhooked her keys from her belt loop. Grasping the biggest key in her hand so it pointed toward him, she threw him a hard look. "I'm getting the distinct impression you don't know this woman at all."

Seeing he'd spooked her, he continued to lean against the back end, but raised his arms in a defensive posture. "There's no cause for alarm, I assure you. Trust me, I expect Angel will be treated as well as she's been named, but there's a lot going on in this house right now."

"Dr. Sum Ting Wong, what is the meaning of this message you sent?" Rourke shouted crossly, as he stepped down from the porch and walked hastily along the sidewalk, assisted by his cane. Following close behind him was Rafe with Bastion taking up the rear.

"We have a visitor," ST called from the vehicle while scowling darkly at Rourke. From his vantage, he could see the three men easily enough, but Eliza's vision was obscured by the tall vehicle as well as his presence next to her.

All three of the Blackthorne men stopped in their tracks on the walkway. Rafe gaped at the unfamiliar vehicle in his driveway in dismay, his face going ashen. "Did you say, we have a visitor?"

"Yes."

Rafe was frozen in place.

"How?" Rourke demanded, knowing full well why his brother was so disturbed.

"I take it you have your place set up to alert you to unwanted visitors too?" Bastion asked his brother quietly.

"Come, come! You need to see," ST called, enjoying a little too much that he finally knew something everyone else did not. He knew full well they'd have questions for the woman who brought her, on how she managed to locate and get onto the property, but he suspected he already knew the answer to that.

All three men moved quickly toward the vehicle, not missing the fact there were children sleeping in car seats inside. Waving Eliza back, so he could open the door, she hastened toward the driver's seat, more than willing to speed off if she needed to. She hadn't been able to get a good look at the three men yet.

"Gentlemen, meet the monkey in your wrench," ST swung the door open, exposing the sleeping woman and child to their view. The woman called Angel was curled in a corner on the floor of the van while leaning against the back of the seat in front of her. Her long silver-blonde hair flowed freely down the length of her in soft waves, cascading over her arms and legs having been taken out of its braid earlier in the day. She slept peacefully while holding her napping son close in the curve of her side. Her bare feet poked out from under the blanket she'd used from the day before, and her face was flush from the heat within the van.

All three men stared in shock.

"This is Angel. Angel Stryfe, I do believe. I am correct on that or am I not?" ST asked the woman who stood anxiously by the driver's side door.

"I couldn't say for sure on the last name. Come to think of it, she never actually said." Eliza's eyes went wide. All three of the Blackthorne men had stepped around the van to see who ST was talking to. She looked from one familiar face to the next, with her enlarged eyes finally settling on the last man to have stepped around the vehicle.

"Bastion?" She asked incredulously, thoroughly in shock to see her former father-in-law with two other men who looked almost identical to him, but for their facial hair or lack thereof. He'd hardly aged a bit since she'd last seen him. "Bastion RavenCroft? How? Who are they?" Completely tongue-tied, she watched him step cautiously toward her as his gaze shifted through the windows then back at her. His expression was so hard to read.

Reaching out to her, he took hold of a piece of her hair then gazed back into her face, recognition now clear within his eyes. "Eliza? Why did you cut and dye your beautiful blonde hair?" There was genuine concern in his tone as he gazed into her eyes, searching for what she wasn't sure. "And how have you come to be here?"

This was the last thing Eliza expected to find upon arriving in Montana. Her heart was in her throat as she gazed in distress up at him. She was slowly starting to remember some history Kahner told her about the Blackthorne's from which the RavenCroft's were descended from. Could it be she somehow found her way to the Blackthorne ranch and family he'd spoke of? Casting a shrewd glance toward the men who could be none other than his brothers she wondered at why Bastion was even here. She recalled vaguely he never bothered having any contact with them. What happened to change that?

Taking a shaky relieved breath, Bastion startled her further by reaching out and engulfing her tightly in his arms. He rested his forehead against hers. "Eliza, Honey, I'm so, so very sorry. Kahner and I have been desperately looking for you, for the past several days. Thank the Gods and all the heavens that you found your way safely here. You can stop running from them now. Your safe with us."

"Running? How do you know?"

Releasing her from his unexpected bear hug, Bastion stepped back, raising a hand to gain her attention.

"All will be explained in due course. Long story short, we didn't know, Honey. Kahner had no idea you changed your mind and carried them to full term."

Cross and confused, Eliza gave him a disgusted unbelieving look. "That's impossible. I told Kalturek."

"I know. I get it. There's been a huge and horrible misunderstanding of which I suspect the shadows played a major part. Before we get into all of this, Eliza, if you would please. Can I meet my three grandchildren?" Bastion asked hopefully, knowing full well he had another potential issue to deal with in the back end of the van.

"Three?" Eliza laughed. For the first time in days, a genuine smile stretched across her face, brightening her normally dulled expression. "I didn't have triplets, Bastion."

ST stood erect, glancing inside the van as the three Blackthorne men exchanged perplexed expressions.

"But there are..."

"Four car seats with toddlers, yes. I had quadruplets." She could tell she shocked him to his core. With a weary sigh, she leaned her shoulder against the van for support. She was so tired and beyond annoyed by his news. If what he said was true, it meant she'd spent the last four and a half years running from dangerous men for no reason, when she could have been living safely within the grounds of the RavenCroft ranch. "Wait until you see what Gabriel can do." She said with a slow secretive smile. "That boy is the reason Angel is with me, and why we're here now."

Surprised, Bastion took several steps toward the back end of the van and glanced within at all the car seats then down at the sleeping form. The woman he saw slumped on the floor with her boy looked so peaceful in this state.

"Like an Angel," he said, not realizing he spoke aloud. His eyes crinkled as a half-smile played at his lips. Could she truly be the Angel Stryfe of his story?

"Bastion." Rafe laid a hand on his brother's shoulder, attempting to gain his attention. He could see his brother was lost in his thoughts and suspected he knew why.

"Hhmm. Yes?"

"Let's get everyone inside. At the very least, she'll be more comfortable on a couch then the floor of a van,"

Rourke said quietly before Rafe could. "The children can play with Alaina's kids while we sort things out." Contemplating what her presence meant, Rourke was certain of one thing. Her arrival changed everything.

Chapter 15

Blackthorne Horse Ranch
Kalispell, Montana

"It's time to let him out."

There was a long pause on the other end of the phone. Bastion knew his son disobeyed.

"You let him out, didn't you?"

"Yes, but with good reason." Kahner said from the other end.

Swearing, Bastion paced the theater room as he watched over Angel and her sleeping child. Sensing she wouldn't wake soon, he wandered out into the hallway and headed down to the playroom.

"Your reason would be?" Bastion asked.

"I figured he might have answers you hadn't beaten out of him yet about where to find Eliza."

"She's here."

"What?" Confused, it took a second before Kahner realized what his father meant. "The author? I know.

You told me Karisma was there when we talked last time."

"I'm not talking about her."

"Then who?"

"Eliza." Bastion's answer was met with silence.

"Are you saying Eliza is there with you? Now?"

His son sounded incredulous. He couldn't blame him. "Yes."

"How? When? What?"

"Breathe Kahner."

"Are you frelling kidding me?"

"No."

"You're telling me to breathe after informing me Eliza is there with you? How did you find her? How did you get her there?"

"Rapid-fire questions won't get the answers you seek any faster than shutting your mouth and letting me speak," Bastion said.

"Then speak."

"She found me."

"In Montana? But how?" Kahner asked,

"It'll take a bit to explain and I don't have all the answers yet. I figured to put your mind at ease in regard to her and your children's whereabouts. You could say she arrived with more than one surprise."

"Why? Is she okay? Are all three of my kids all right?" Kahner started to panic.

"Eliza's fine, and they're all safe now. She's tired for sure, in need of a good meal, and desperate for a full night's rest. And she didn't have triplets."

"I see." Disappointment clouded Kahner's voice.

"She had quadruplets." Bastion grinned, still tickled by the news.

More silence.

"Did you hear what I said?"

"I'm the father of four children?" Becoming choked up, Kahner wiped at his eyes, his heart constricting in his chest as a weight seemed to lift from his shoulders. Anger surged within him at having lost four years with his kids. He resented not having been able to be present at their birth. "What do I have? I mean, boys, girls?"

"All four are boys." Bastion said proudly, though admittedly wishing at least one had been a girl. "Technically she did have triplets. They're identical too. All of them have black hair and our eyes, of course. Gabriel resembles them a lot, but he's bigger."

"I have a son named Gabriel!" Kahner was incredulous. He laughed with pure joy. "And the others? What did she name them?" He couldn't help be jealous and resentful of not being a party to naming them.

"Peter, Andrew, and James; all good strong names. It's the order in which they were born too, but Gabriel came first. It took a lot out of her, so she can't have any more kids."

Kahner laughed again. There were tears in his eyes. "I don't care. I have four boys, Dad!"

Grinning from ear to ear, he watched the children he was now speaking of play with Alaina's kids while their mother took a well-deserved rest. "Now that the news is out of the way, tell me why you let our mysterious Vortigern Black out?"

"Because I was impatient." Kahner's mood shifted, the memory of the recording and what it meant came back to smack him in the face. His mother's panicked voice haunted him even now. "It's a good thing I interrogated him, or we never would have learned about Angel."

That got Bastion's attention. He hadn't said anything to any of them about her yet, nor had he left behind the novels for them to investigate.

"Angel, you say?"

"Yes, Angel Stryfe. I know you're mad, but if it hadn't been for Chase we never would have known about Eliza and the boys. We also wouldn't have found out about this woman, and how she might be able to help Kalab. She's the real author of the stories, Dad. Karisma was only the ghostwriter Chase hired to fix them. You're in the wrong place. Angel is in Georgia, and she's in danger. But, I guess it was good you were there in Montana or you wouldn't have been there when Eliza arrived."

"Kahner stop."

"What?"

"Angel is here," Bastion said.

"Wait, what? I could have sworn you said Angel was there too."

"I did, and she is."

"How?" Kahner asked in surprise.

"She arrived with Eliza in her van. She and her son fell asleep by the time they arrived. They still are sleeping, for that matter." Bastion grumbled, rolling his eyes heavenward at the inconvenience of it all. He could hear a faint whine in the background on the other end of the call. It sounded like he was speaking to him from within a vacuum. Hearing his son dictating directions to someone else, he became suspicious, his attention alerted to the fact something wasn't right.

"Where are you right now?"

"We were on our way to Georgia to pick up Angel, but I turned us around. We're on our way to you now.

Why is everyone who can give us answers always asleep? That's very inconvenient."

"Yes, more so than you know. Now, who is we, why would you think Angel was in Georgia, and how are you traveling here?"

"Dad, rapid-fire questions won't get you the answers you seek any faster than shutting your mouth and letting me speak." Kahner couldn't help taking a little pleasure in getting to throw his father's words back at him. He grinned openly as he heard him groan from the other end.

"Touché. Speak."

"We include me, Mackenzie, Drayke, and Chase. How we're coming is by way of your second personal jet you hid in your secret hanger."

Bastion swore fiercely into the phone, in the process letting it slip that a certain narrator would soon be a dead man.

"Hold on, before you get all riled up. There's a lot you don't know and more we won't know until speaking to Karisma. Angel too, for that matter. I'll tell you how I found your, well, everything later, and it was not by way of Chase. We need to talk more, but I'm flying now and need to get off in a minute."

"All right fine. Where are Kalturek and Kalab? Tell me they're still at the house," he said hopefully.

"They're on their way elsewhere right now." Recalibrating his course, Kahner checked to be sure there was enough fuel to make it to Kalispell, Montana instead of Georgia. Seeing there should be plenty he relaxed back into his seat.

"Where exactly? I have a distinct impression now is not the time to be out in the open."

"Kalturek is helping Kalab pick up Ariana in Massachusetts."

Bastion expelled an exasperated sigh while running a hand through his hair, having the feeling he should know that name. Had he read it in one of Karisma's stories?

"Who is Ariana again?"

Another familiar voice could be heard through the phone which meant he was annoyingly on speakerphone. "Ariana Davis is the one being stalked in Dalton, Massachusetts. Kalab and Kalturek went to stop it. They're hoping to convince her to come with them. I take it you haven't learned anything from the writer so far?"

"Vortigern, your lips are so loose, even if Angel wasn't still asleep, I wouldn't tell you a thing. Kahner, get me off speakerphone, now."

Snarling, Chase grabbed Kahner's phone and shoved his mouth close to the speaker.

"Right back at you, you selfish self-absorbed prick. I was referring to Karisma, the ghostwriter, not Angel, the author. Since you seem to like being spiteful, I think I'll reciprocate said behavior. All you get is a name. Wilton Stryfe."

"Who the hell is that?"

"No more answers. Do what I did; read. You're so smart and all-knowing, so you figure it out." With his good arm, he slammed Kahner's phone against the wall, cracking the glass, then threw it on the ground and smashed it with his boot.

"I needed that phone," Kahner yelled.

"He needs a kick in the head more than you'll ever need that blasted phone," Chase hollered. He was still sore at his brother-in-law for having punched him out and taken the recorder off of him. "Anyone pulls their phone out like they're going to text or call Bastion, and I'll do the same to their phone too."

Punching at the air angrily, Chase whirled about, stomped toward the back end of the plane, and took a seat, looking away from everyone as he brooded.

- - -

Staring down at his phone, Bastion glowered. "Wilton Stryfe? What's he talking about?" It occurred to him the last name was the same as Angel's.

"Wilton Stryfe, eh?" Rourke said unexpectedly from behind him. They were standing in the hallway between the pool room and dining room. "By chance was that the elusive and mysterious Vortigern Black you were speaking to?"

Disinclined to respond to the eavesdropper, he stayed silent, shoving his phone in his back pocket.

"Ah, yes, still sore is he at being bested and beaten down by you, a fifty-year-old man and his father-in-law? Or is it that he found out you went after the escaped felon in Mexico and gave away his bounty out of spite."

Scowling, Bastion planted his hands on his hips and glared at his brother. He didn't like being around someone who always seemed to know everything all the time. He wondered if this was what it always felt like for Chase, living around him and his family as he did.

"And it's not eavesdropping when I'm sitting in the dining room drinking my tea while you're wandering the halls speaking into your phone."

Before getting the chance to respond, both men were alerted to the arrival of Drinian, Veta, and her children who finally made it from the airport. They could both hear the awe in the woman's voice over the chandelier in the foyer as they entered the house.

"That chandelier gets them every time." Rourke took a few steps to where he could peer around the corner, not bothering to use his cane. "Ah, even more lovely then I imagined. It's so unfair for a man as daft as him to wind up with such a gem."

Bastion snorted then stepped around him, so he could see for himself. He whistled. "Angel's description pales in comparison. That's one very lucky man."

"Aye, if she'll still have him after discovering what a man-child he is."

"Oh, I don't know. There's something endearing about the ignorance of an innocent. It could be mighty refreshing being around someone you don't have to try so hard with all the time. They're likely to be much more accepting of a person's faults."

Giving his brother a curious look, Rourke replied quietly, "One can only hope." With a troubled furrow of his brow, he walked away without much assistance from his cane. "Hhmm, Wilton Stryfe. It's getting crowded in this house with all these children. I wonder at whether Karisma is going to be able to handle this. Read Bastion, read," he added as though an afterthought. "Your narrator isn't wrong, there is still stuff you need to know that you have missed. I suspect Rafe is upstairs with Karisma by now. Best I go stop him from making a complete fool of himself."

Bastion watched his brother go, wondering at what it must be like to be him. He didn't act as though the shadows affected him the way they did his son, or for that matter Drinian, but he wondered.

For the first time since arriving, it occurred to him the prophecy within the, An Unfortunate Lineage series might well have a positive effect on Rourke as well, were it to be fulfilled.

Rafe told him in confidence that the man had been affable most days, even with being able to see the shadows. Now, he was pompous, bitter, and cantankerous. Bastion hoped their own sons wouldn't wind up with the same fate though he imagined, from the way Rafe talked, living with Alestair and Rathbourne for the past thirty-seven years had likely not been a positive influence for him.

Shaking off his thoughts, Bastion checked in on Angel once again, confirming she was still sleeping, then headed back to the playroom before wandering to the downstairs library to see if Eliza was awake and felt like talking. He needed to prepare her for Kahner's arrival. There was much about him she didn't know. He wanted to be sure she had all the information this time, before deciding what she wanted to do.

- - -

In the upstairs library, Karisma woke to Rafe at her side with a tall mug in his hand. She could see the steam billowing forth from the top of the cup.

"Another hot toddy? Are you sure that's wise?" She yawned then stretched and rubbed at her eyes.

"With them here setting my nerves on edge, I've no choice. It helps me relax," Rafe said with a slow sardonic smile. "Sort of."

Karisma chuckled, curled around her pillow and watched as he drank. "I wonder what one tastes like."

"You're welcome to try mine."

Her calico and white cat, Haven, got up from his perch at her feet and leaped down to the floor, ready to wander the house again. He always found his way back to her when she needed him. She scratched at his ears, and he purred, licking her fingers. Then he bounded away. She chuckled again.

"That sounds nice, but I suspect the visitor we're about to have will likely not appreciate you giving me alcohol."

Rafe paused mid-sip. "You're aware of Eliza and Angel's arrival?"

She sighed, her face becoming more drawn. "I am, yes, but that's not of whom I speak."

"You wouldn't be trying to tempt the lady with spirits would you, brother?" Bastion stood in the doorway, lazily twirling his cane. For a moment he stared at the cane then down at his leg and back up again. Not waiting for an answer he continued. "What do you put in the water here?"

"We don't add anything to the water. Why do you ask? And I only offered her a sip to try. She says she's never had a toddy before."

"Really?"

"It's true. Ask her yourself."

"Not that, you nitwit. I trust what you say. I'm speaking of the water. You don't add anything special? A particular ratio of chlorine to cyanuric acid, perhaps?"

Rourke paused at seeing his brother shaking his head, noting he set his hot toddy down as though to stay for a while. His eyes narrowed upon him. "The pool has been quite invigorating. Dare I say, healing? This darned leg had been giving me a load of trouble since the surgery. One dip in your pool, and it would appear to be having a kind of restorative effect."

"Interesting. It might have been simply the need for a bit of weightlessness on the limb itself. You could ask ST to check it out for you."

Rourke waived the notion of doing that away with his hand as though it were an appalling suggestion. "I don't need that poor excuse for a doctor touching my limbs."

"What is your problem with him? He's done nothing to you. You're not prejudiced are you?" Rafe asked.

Stepping further into the room, Rourke leaned in conspiratorially. "I've nothing against a doctor of color or any man of color for that matter. It's the name, I tell you. There's just something wrong with a doctor by the name of Sum Ting Wong. Think about it. Imagine the conversation during an exam. 'What is it, doctor? Is something wrong, Dr. Wong? Did you find something?' It'd be like being within a perpetual comedy routine that never ends. One would never know when to take the man seriously."

Rafe couldn't help himself. He chuckled. "He's not Wong, now is he?"

Stifling a giggle of her own within her pillow, Karisma's eyes twinkled.

Reaching over, Rafe tickled her side causing her to laugh. She stopped the moment Rourke knocked his arm away with his knobby cane.

"No need to be getting fresh with her now." Rourke took a seat in the chair next to the sofa bed on the opposite side of his brother. "I am glad to see you're awake, Karisma. I gather you're feeling a bit more rested?"

"A little better, yes. Thanks for asking." She yawned and glanced at her family picture Rafe left on the stand near her bed.

"Good then. Do you feel up to having a talk with me?"

Rafe planted his legs, one across the other, on the side of the sofa bed, as if to say he wasn't budging from the room.

"Fine then. With him as well." Rourke said, acknowledging his brother with first his thumb than his middle finger.

"I see we've reverted to the behavior of a ten-year-old," she said bluntly.

"What can I say? He brings it out in me."

"That's not it and you know it. You pick at him, provoking his ire because you're insecure. You're worried your brothers are going to once again have the one thing you've always wanted, but never got the chance to have, because pure chance, poor decisions, the shadows, and an unforgiving nature prevented you from having it. Rourke Blackthorne, you are afraid of getting the shaft again."

"You don't hold anything back do you?"

"Nope."

"Just let it all out there."

"Yup."

"Knife to heart sort of thing, is it?" Rourke asked.

"What can I say? It comes with not having an off switch in my head. You know?"

"Oh, yeah, I know all about it." Rourke sat forward in his chair, unnecessarily holding his cane in his hand as though ready to take flight at any moment. "You didn't have many friends, like ever, did you?"

"Hardly a one. And before that one died, he always tried to explain it away as being a product of my accident I had before my thirteenth birthday, but truth be told, I'm pretty sure I was born this way. I've never been able to control it."

"I see."

"Do you?" she asked as Bastion appeared in the doorway. He moved further into the room, not bothering to wait for their approval.

Rourke gave her a questioning look as both Bastion and Rafe looked on in awe.

"What are you even doing here, Rourke?" Karisma asked suspiciously.

"I'm here to..."

"To what? Save a son, set the record straight, bust some balls, pee in somebody's pool, and, I don't know, Rourke, maybe steal somebody else's oven?"

"What are you talking about ovens for?"

Bastion laughed, having caught her analogy right away. A second later Rafe was exclaiming in dismay.

Blustering in embarrassment for having taken so long to realize her meaning, Rourke gave Karisma a look of pure bewilderment. "Steal somebody else's?"

"D-d-did I stutter?" Karisma asked Rafe before glancing over at Bastion whose eyes were full of mirth. "I'm pretty sure I didn't."

Laying his free hand on her knee to gain her attention, Rafe patted it before pulling the hand away. "If I may, I think he - we - have been and are confused, because of the stories you wrote."

"My stories."

"Yes, the An Unfortunate Lineage series you published." Bastion's torso shifted forward, anxiously awaiting her response. He suspected the answer had been given to him ten minutes ago.

"I may have published them, but I sure didn't write those. That was all Angel. I only know what she wrote in those stories, because I edited and proofread them for her. Well, okay, I guess it was for Vortigern Black, which I gather is the Private Investigator slash bounty hunter your daughter married." Karisma directed her gaze at Bastion as her mouth thinned irritably. "Yeah, I'll be having words with him when he gets here. What he had me doing borders on plagiarism. I have a reputation to uphold as a reputable ghostwriter, and he put it at risk."

"The Vortigern Black character is your son-in-law?" Rafe paused mid-sip, groaning internally at learning they were about to have more visitors.

"Catch up, Honey," Karisma urged Rafe. "Cause the story is gonna fly from here on. If you get too far behind in your thinking you're going to be lost by the end."

"Did she also write the series called Lineage?" Bastion wondered aloud.

"I'm afraid that mess is mine." Pulling her legs up against her chest, she rolled her eyes self-consciously. Shoving her face into the blankets at her knees, she ever so slightly peeked out from behind them. Her face grew hot with embarrassment. "Angel is a much better writer then I'll ever be."

"But you're a ghostwriter." Rourke stood, peering down at her. "I've looked you up. You've assisted with many authors works and made a decent living doing it from what I gather."

Throwing her head back, Karisma snorted as she laughed. "No, no, no. You see, that's different. People give me outlines and descriptions of the stories they want to create and pay me to write them up for them. Me trying to formulate my own idea, create a timeline, put it all in order, and write it up so it makes sense is a whole other story. Angel's only problem, is she can't write above an elementary school level yet, mostly from what I gather, because she's still in the process of relearning everything. Me? My gift is all messed up."

"Why do you say your gift is messed up?" Rafe asked.

Scrunching her eyes closed, Karisma tried hard to think straight, wanting to make sure she wasn't telling it wrong. "I might be talking out of my butt here, but from what I understand, I think all three of the writers in the stories are supposed to have the same type of ability in real life, kind of like you guys, you know? To know things without knowing why. But I think we're also supposed to be able to write out what we're visualizing in our heads as the potential real-life stories come to us."

"To see what choices affect the surrounding lives? In order to better direct what's to come," Rafe offered.

"Could be."

"That's not a stupid theory," Rourke said grudgingly, eliciting a disgusted growl from Rafe.

"This Angel and the Ciara author are capable of visualizing it all in neat order. I'm not. Mine comes in bits and pieces at random intervals, so I wind up with a lot of chaos. Because of it, I have to piece the chaos together like a puzzle in my head, but even then it comes out looking and sounding chaotic. It's also why I have three different completed versions of volume five. As opposed to the little personality quirk I have, the injury I sustained to my head in the accident when I was twelve is the probable cause of my writing issue. So any stories I tried to write of my own, turned into a jumbled, confusing mess. Often times, the names aren't even right. Particularly when I was writing the books in my Lineage series."

"I'm trying to understand, but you're not making this easy," Rourke said, trying hard to be nice, but quickly regretting it.

"A bit slow, are you?"

"Focus, Karisma. Where does that leave us?" Rafe asked, unsure if he was entirely following her himself.

"What's the line between right and wrong, good and evil, order and chaos?"

"Balance," Rourke said

"Hope," Rafe countered.

"Your both right. If the stories of Angel's had progressed as they were meant to, one would need a light in dark times."

"I see. According to Angel's story at that point, Rafe needed hope."

"One of you would need a sign that a good or benevolent force was present and trying to aid them."

Rafe and Rourke didn't even blink as they both turned in unison toward Bastion.

"And one needed a bit of chaos to brighten their otherwise dreary days."

Rourke made a noise in his throat, "You definitely breed chaos."

Karisma shrugged, unable to deny it. "Out of the three of you, you are the one most familiar with Angel's stories, Rourke. What do you think happened?"

"A variable changed the course of time," he said.

"Between Angel's stories and notes, that's what I'm gathering, yes," she agreed.

Bastion's gaze shifted between Rourke and Karisma, then from her to Rafe. "So now?"

"Now it's a different story." Rourke said in understanding. "For some of us, our needs are different at this moment in time then what they would have been ten years from now if that variable hadn't changed."

Karisma pointed at him then lifted the same index finger to her nose as if to say he'd gotten it right. "Here's what I don't understand, and maybe Angel will be able to answer it for all of us, since she's the one who wrote it in the first place. So far, all the stories before were about Angel and Ciara and written by them, not me. I've never been mentioned in any of those, and it always felt like a piece of the story was missing."

"Your question is, what piece is missing?" Bastion asked.

"Yes, and what variable affected this outcome?" Karisma asked urgently, becoming choked up. She wanted to know what caused her to lose her children and husband. Yawning, she patted at her mouth as her eyelids began to droop. "I know the answer is in my head, but for some reason, I can't get to it."

All three men watched the grieving woman before them with sympathy, their shrewd gazes taking in her tired state. She plumped her pillow then punched it in the center with a fist and nestled her head in the hole she created.

Rourke leaned down toward her. "I have one last question for you before you sleep."

"Ask the stupid question already," she grumbled into the pillow.

Rafe chuckled, sharing a smile with Bastion who appeared to be troubled and mumbling something under his breath.

"This accident you had. When did it occur, and how did it affect you?"

"Mmm. As I said, it was right before my thirteenth birthday. My adoptive parents were killed in it. I was badly injured; my head, as you know."

"I see."

"They had to perform a hysterectomy," she said as though an afterthought. "I woke up in a hospital room on my thirteenth birthday. The insensitive lout of a doctor I had was kind enough to inform me that I'd not only lost both my adoptive parents, but the ability to ever be able to have a family of my own. Happy frelling birthday to me."

"So your children weren't biologically yours?"

"Nope. Adopted." Karisma finished with a sad sigh. She gazed sadly at her family picture Rafe brought from her parents' home. Tears swam in her eyes as she began to cry into her pillow. A soft meow came from the doorway as Haven raced forward and leaped up onto the bed next to Karisma. The cat curled up next to her head, licked at the tears on her cheek and began purring. It rested its head within the crook of her neck.

Grimacing, Rourke bent and kissed her forehead then petted her cat. "It looks like Haven's here to comfort you. Be at peace."

Raising up to his full height he exchanged looks with Rafe who also bent down and gave her a kiss on the cheek.

"Trying to one-up me, are you?" Rourke groused.

Rafe raised one eyebrow. All three men exited the library, turning off the lights and closing the door before they left. Wandering down the hall, they convened near the top of the stairwell leading down to the kitchen.

After a moment of contemplative silence, Bastion spoke first. "I'm betting I know what the variable was."

Rourke nodded in agreement while tapping his cane on the floor lightly. "Hm, I'm guessing your thinking it has something to do with Wilton Stryfe's untimely disappearance, perchance?"

"Stryfe," Rafe said thoughtfully. "Would that be Angel's husband?"

"Late husband. Or so we believe?" Rourke said as though questioning Bastion to confirm his theory.

"Agreed. I'm betting Wilton died ten years sooner than what he was supposed to. I can't confirm that until my family arrives or Angel wakes up. I hope their presence here won't be a problem?" Bastion ran his forefinger and thumb down the line on either side of his short goatee, smoothing it out as he rubbed it down. "I'd have asked first, but they were in flight when I found out they were on their way."

"Not a problem, and it's to be expected." Rafe put his brother at ease. "I imagine Kahner is anxious to meet his four children."

Rourke's eyes widened. "Four. There have never before been four. In Angel's story, she listed only three arriving at your doorstep ten years from now."

"Interesting. There must be significance," Rafe said.

Bastion nodded his agreement. "In every story Angel wrote, she kept giving each of us a child we don't have. Now Eliza has an extra one our little writer never mentioned. I have to agree."

"I have a theory; a suspicion. Let me run with it and I'll get back with the two of you." Rourke rapped his brother on the leg to gain his attention for he could see he was deep in thought. "Bastion, how soon will your family arrive?"

"I am unclear. They were on their way to Georgia to pick up Angel when they learned she arrived here with Eliza, so they turned around."

"Isn't that what Eliza said; that Angel had come from Georgia? Why was she coming from there in the first place, do you suppose? I thought she resided in Pocahontas, Iowa in the story," Rourke said.

Bastion answered. "I suspect Chase sent her there for some reason. He has a sister who lives near Atlanta. I won't know why until he arrives."

"Read and I suspect you will find out," Rourke assured him with a mischievous grin. "I believe chapter sixteen of Deadly Karisma, in particular, will be most enlightening. Rafe, I need you to use your connections for me to help me find what's missing. I'd do it myself, but my contacts are across an ocean."

"Let me guess, you're thinking what's missing is the third author."

"Ciara Biardon." Both men finished in unison.

"Only she might not be a Biardon right now. Remember, it's ten years sooner," Bastion reminded them.

"Right, ten years," Rafe agreed, appearing thoughtful. "It could mean she is between supposed marriages right now."

"Supposed marriage?" Bastion was confused.

"You should really read the Blackthorne stories. It would help you connect the dots," Rourke urged.

"Maybe once I've finished my own. Speed reading them wasn't sufficient."

"I'll see what I can find. It shouldn't be too much trouble."

"Yes, yes." Rourke was becoming increasingly uneasy. "Do it. My gut is telling me we are running out of time. Oh, and Bastion."

"Yes?"

"I want the Blackthorne and Weir-deVere book of lineage returned to me at the earliest convenience."

"Ah, figured it out did you?"

"Give me some credit. I'm not a blathering idiot."

Furious at this news, Rafe yelled. "You mean to tell me it's been with you, Bastion, all this time?"

"We'll deal with that when time allows."

"Yes. I must away," Rourke said hastily, as upset over the missing book as his brother.

Thoroughly annoyed, Rafe disappeared into his study. Bastion rounded the corner to the front stairwell, taking the steps down to the front study. Rourke moved to follow then hanged direction.

He needed to see it.

Taking a few steps down the hall as though heading to the other side of the house he stopped, reached up, and pulled on the chain dangling from the ceiling. The folding steps for the attic slid down. Taking the stairs one at a time, he shook off the unsettling sensation creeping in on him as the room seemed to darken and the light he turned on flickered ominously.

He growled deep within his throat.

Fed up, he was. He was so beyond fed up with dealing with them.

"Go away you blasted shadows. Fifty years is way too long to be stuck with the lot of you pestering me, you blasted troublesome three."

- - -

It was right where Rourke read it would be.

The exact location of the secret passage in the attic took little effort to determine. Rourke entered Rafe's secret room through the short narrow door, knocking his head on the frame. There was no doubt in his mind upon viewing the room for the first time, his brother was extremely talented.

"How does he do this? I can barely paint stick figures."

He marveled at what he saw, all the while mumbling under his breath and roaming around the many canvases propped up on easels around the room. He moved toward the back of the art room where he could see a life-size portrait was being obscured from view by a long curtain hanging on the wall. A portion of a woman's face poked out from between the fabric.

Setting his cane against a cabinet, he reached up and pulled open the curtains the rest of the way. Pushing his spectacles further up his nose, he gazed upon the woman known as Ciara Biardon in the sixth volume of Angel's book series.

She was beautiful.

Rafe had done an excellent job, though his brow furrowed in confusion when he saw she was, in fact, wearing Lilyandhi's wedding dress as Angel had written.

"Why would you paint her this way?"

Exclaiming suddenly, he cut himself off with a delighted laugh when he noticed it. His hand reached out toward the background of the painting where a figure stood, barely discernible among the trees near the main barn. He wondered if his dolt of a brother noticed it before or if he were too intent upon the focus of the portrait to realize what he painted.

Ciara was not alone in the portrait.

Angel's original story about the woman in the wedding dress was very touching. Rourke now knew it was never meant to progress that way regardless, for the wrong woman had been the focus of it. He understood what the angel at the end of volume two of the, An Unfortunate Lineage series meant. The angel Woreash asked where the war bedraggled bunch of angels had come from when they abruptly arrived after Astraia and Dante were wed. The responding guardian angel stated he should, 'ask not from where, but from when.'

The angel's words made sense now.

Delicately tracing the line of the woman's cheek in the painting with his forefinger, he chuckled. His gaze traveled the length of Ciara to the bottom right corner where his brother signed the painting, noting the date listed there. He paused, his mind processing the oddity of what he was seeing.

The signature did not match the date.

Rafe's name was slanted to the right, but the date was straight up and down. If the date had been painted all in numbers then Rourke might not have thought anything of it, but the month was written out in the same straight print as the numerals of the day and year.

Curious.

Getting down on his hands and knees, he investigated the corner with the date. A small fingerprint had been used to create the comma after the day. A pinkie maybe? Rourke lay his own finger against the canvas. There was no way it could have been his brothers. He had large hands, like himself. The pinkie print was too small.

"Huh, I wonder." He pulled at the frame to see if the portrait was hung or not. Discovering he was able to pull the portrait away from the wall, he tucked the curtain up, over, and behind it, so he could see the back of the painting.

"Blimey, what is that?"

Heart racing, Rourke swallowed hard, his breath rapid with excitement. Something was written on the back of the portrait. There had never been any mention of this in Angel's stories or notes. Forcefully pulling on the frame, he dragged it further away from the wall. Then he turned it over so he could see the back.

"Well, I'll be. Lilyandhi Blackthorne, you little minx."

Rourke never had the chance to meet Rafe's late wife, but he sure wished he had the chance now. On the back of the portrait was the very poem discovered in his nephew's diary in volume six of Angel's story, but with a very important and telling missing excerpt at the end.

A prophecy was made this day
a healing path is on the way.
Two of mirror image there will be
crossing their paths in time you'll see.
A choice to make, one right one wrong.
We will know for sure before long.
Two years from now it must begin
or the millennium will see much sin.

Fifteen years we must then wait.
If not start by then twill be too late.

Through waxen hair no gift doth breed
for surely lacking the strength of seed.
Another shall come on the last of day.
A writer's word shows another way.
For through fiery hair of silver and gold,

and eyes of night filled with silver mists of old.
A seed shall lie within her womb;
three times blessed we can presume.

Not a borrower nor lender she'll be;
her gift to know, her child's to see.

A dove brought forth shall burst to fly
when she sends a gift through the nigh'
For during a time of memory
its gift of peace shall set her free.
But lo' beware the shadows will call,
tear her apart and make her fall
For within her lies a fragile heart
but without her, we'll all be torn apart.

- - -

And among the Haven and Hollow there'll be;
a moment out of time when they won't see.
For a decision made by one to kill
will soon mean for another much ill will.
The chaos effect forces one to take,
which will cause them all to soon forsake
In order to fix time's delicate strand,
earlier out of time she'll have to land.
Another decision will have to be made.
If it's made wrong, then to rest she will be laid.

-Lilyandhi Blackthorne

Pulling out his cell phone, Rourke took several pictures of the poem, which was painted in large letters with the same hand as the one who painted the date underneath Rafe's signature. He had no idea when his brother painted the portrait, though he suspected it had been sometime before he married Lilyandhi. What he was certain of, was Lilyandhi found the painting hidden behind the curtain on their wedding day. Upon seeing the portrait she had a vision of one potential future and had been inspired to write the poem. Not having one of her books accessible to write in, she did the next best thing. She turned the painting around and painted it on the back of the portrait in order to help commit it to her memory.

The problem came when she ran out of room at the bottom in order to date it, as was her habit within her journals. So she added the date of her prophetic poem underneath her husband's signature on the front, then failed to list the last excerpt of the poem in her journal when she wrote it down later on. The question now was whether Rafe had known all along it was on the back of the portrait. Thinking back over his time at the ranch so far; Rourke would bet a full years' salary the giant pain in his arse always knew.

"Bah! Sneaky blighter. Should have realized. The voyeuristic perv has a house full of secrets what with hidden rooms tucked away everywhere; like Bastion. Two peas in a pod, they are."

Turning the portrait back around he wrestled it back in place. Tromping back through the not-so-secret art room, he exited the way he came without bothering to look back or close its door. The missing portion was important indeed. It meant they needed to locate Ciara quickly. But first, he needed to make a couple of phone calls as he waited on his brothers to do their part. Neither of which he was looking forward to.

- - -

Locking the door behind him, Rafe turned around and headed straight for the portrait of his late wife Lilyandhi. Taking out his pocketknife he slid it into the notch on the left side of the portrait at about waist level. Pulling at the frame, he opened the portrait door which uncovered a vault as tall and as wide as the portrait itself. Entering the key code and placing his fingerprint on the keypad, he opened the vault door. Reaching within, past the stash of weapons he kept inside, he took hold of a cell phone and turned it on. Sending off a short text, he set the phone on his desk, hoping to hear from his contact soon. He didn't want to use this one, for doing so meant he could never utilize him again, but it couldn't be helped. There was little time to waste.

The individual he contacted was in so deep, not even his son Dante was aware of him. He also knew if anyone would have the answers he was seeking, this man would.

Wanting to be clear-headed when he spoke to him, Rafe closed the vault door without pulling out the Scotch bottle he kept within. Instead, he turned toward the computer screen on the opposite wall. He was sifting through his most recent emails when the cell phone rang. Spinning around, he faced the desk and picked up the phone.

"Now's no bueno, Senor."

The voice on the other end sounded harassed, his Spanish accent becoming more pronounced as a result. He knew his contact didn't normally speak Spanish unless he was feeling stressed.

"I need to know what you know."

The other party paused, then spoke on a sigh. "You understand what this means if I tell you everything, David."

"I do, yes," Rafe said, struggling to get used to his alias again. It had been awhile since anyone called him David.

There was a slight pause, before the contact began. "Phenom had a recruit slip through their fingers."

"How recently, who, where, and how did they find this person?" Rafe asked.

"A few days ago. It was a woman from Indiana, Pennsylvania. They found her, because they've been tracking any and all purchases of a book series called Phenomena supposedly written by you, Mr. David Pearson," Pegueros said mockingly. "This woman purchased a majority of the series online. They tasked our illustrious double-dealing Agent Henley on it."

The woman Agent Pegueros spoke of was, Karisma who was safely sleeping in the room next door. It bothered Rafe a great deal to learn the Phenom organization was following the sales of that blasted collection of books of Inara's. Wanting to know if Agent Jericho Henley was running solo on the job, he queried his contact further.

"Was he rogue?"

"No. He hired it out initially which was a mistake on his part."

He made a non-committal noise in his throat. Mistake or not, he was grateful for it. If Henley hadn't hired it out, Karisma wouldn't be with them now.

"Who?"

"Man by the name of Hunter. Sounded like Henley used him many times before, but the guy was retired; wanted to be done with it. I got the feeling he was being hired for three jobs. One right after another. It's probably why he made the mistake."

Though gearing away from the subject matter he was trying for, Rafe's interest was piqued. "You say this Hunter guy made a mistake. Was the woman a target or recruit?"

"Recruit. There was only one target on the job; her spouse. Henley wanted the kids for leverage."

"This Hunter misunderstood?"

"No, he screwed up, big time. Phenom told Henley to clean up the mess. Henley's on his last leg with them, so he's been desperate to find a replacement for the last couple women he's lost, and it looks like he's got one."

"He's lost more than one, and is already after another recruit? Do we know who?" Rafe's gut clenched uneasily.

Pegueros went silent, then sighed heavily. "I can't speak to the first woman he lost. It happened about five years ago so, I don't know what happened there, but I've been following the progress of their tracking system closely after what happened to the family of the last one. No doubt Henley's secretary is making the connection now and is about to take it to him. If you're going after this one, I want in on it."

"Not a good idea."

"They called the kids collateral damage, David," Pegueros shouted, causing Rafe to have to pull the phone away from his ear. "The mercenary murdered the father on Phenom's orders, accidentally killing two little kids in the process then was shot for his trouble by Henley in a fit of rage. The woman that got away from him couldn't even have kids. Imagine what he's gonna do to one who can."

"You in a position to help?"

"I can be an hour away by helicopter when you need me, but I'd advise to do this soon. Henley won't wait on Phenom approval to go after her. No one deserves to be 'recruited' by Phenom, but after finding out what this woman's been through in the last four years, she shouldn't have to go through this too."

"Why? Who is it?"

"She was married to my estranged half-sister's husband."

"Did you say, ex-husband?"

"No, David, her husband. They're still married in Mexico and have been for eight years now. The guy left to make a living here in the United States for them and married again when he got here in order to gain citizenship, so he could bring them over the border. But this Ciara Marketti didn't know any of this until four months ago. She tried to leave to go to the police, and he put her in the hospital. Three and a half years they were married and it was all a lie."

Raising up from his seat the moment he heard the name, Rafe's insides went numb. Was it possible the woman they were speaking of was the same one he was looking for?

"So her name's Ciara Marketti? Where is she? I need everything you got on her."

"Way ahead of you. Just sent it."

Spinning around, Rafe sat and opened Agent Pegueros email, regaining his feet when he saw a picture of the woman in question. She was listed as a strawberry blonde with blue eyes, but the photos from the emergency room he was viewing had her with black hair, sporting bruises on her face. He continued to peruse her information as he spoke.

"I see she lives in Mishawaka, Indiana," Rafe said.

"Yeah, but she works out of South Bend, Indiana at a hotel. Dependent upon time of day, pick up might need to happen there."

"Got it. I'll be en route to your location."

"You personally?" Pegueros sounded surprised.

"Yes. Let's say we've both got something invested in this one and leave it at that," Rafe said.

"Deal."

- - -

While muddling over what he learned so far, Bastion made himself at home by filching water bottles from the fridge, an apple from the counter, and a bag of chips from the pantry. Tucking the bottles under his arm, he walked down the hall toward the theater room, munching on barbecue chips along the way.

Angel had slept for a while, so he figured he better check on her and the little boy too. He didn't want to wake her, but knew it might become necessary soon. His family would be arriving within the next few hours, which meant they would want answers.

Rafe and Rourke intended to reference the seventh novel Karisma finished writing, for the answers they sought. As with the fifth volume in the, An Unfortunate Lineage series, the laptop and briefcase Rourke arrived with had been stolen by someone within the house the day before.

No one would admit to taking it.

Bastion wouldn't put it past his Scottish rogue of a brother to be less than honest about its whereabouts, but the man appeared genuinely distressed to discover it went missing. He claimed he didn't recall seeing a seventh finalized novel among her files. The missing laptop and flash drives meant piecing their answers together from a grieving woman and a sleeping Angel. It was proving to be a challenge since they both endured stressful experiences, and tired easily as the result of their gifts.

Making his way into the theater room he noted Angel was no longer lying on the couch where he left her. Hearing the soft snuffle of a child he turned to his right. She was not only awake, but sitting on the end of the couch nursing her son. Though she smiled back at him, she didn't move to cover her chest where her son was feeding hungrily.

He envied the boy.

"Hello, Bastion, I'm Angel. Wanna meet my son?" She patted the seat next to her on the couch shyly. One thing was clear; she knew who he was.

Hesitantly walking toward her, his eyes skimmed the room as well as the windows, making sure no one was watching her like this. He took a seat next to her and peered down at the boy, his eyes softening upon him.

"Nice to meet you, little guy."

"As you may know, his name's Kalturek, but Wilton and I always call him little Kal. He never liked the name I chose."

"Good to know."

"Does it bother you to see him feeding like this? I usually use a bottle with formula to feed him now that he's over a year old, because Wilton says I should, but I'm not sure where his diaper bag went."

The way she talked, she sounded very young which was a bit disconcerting considering the view he was getting. Taking a moment to formulate his answer he responded gently.

"No, it doesn't bother me, but others within the house might become uncomfortable if they were to walk in on you like this."

Her beautiful bluish-gray eyes widened, giving her an innocent quality. With the long silver-blonde hair and pale skin with a pinkish hew, Bastion imagined she couldn't be over thirty years old.

"Of course, sometimes I forget the whole, oh, what did Wilton always call it, public indecency thing." If it were possible her cheeks flushed an even more flattering shade of rouge.

Taking a small crocheted afghan from a nearby chair, Bastion lifted it before her. "May I," he asked, indicating his willingness to cover her and her son for modesty's sake as he fed. At her agreeable nod, he placed it loosely over her shoulders and settled back in next to her, as she thanked him. "For future reference, I do know where the bag went. I can grab it for you, if you'd like."

"Please. He's likely to need a change and to be burped. All his bibs are in there."

Leaving to grab the bag, he returned in short order, setting the back at her feet after getting a bib and burp rag out for her.

Angel rested her head against the back of the couch. Her eyes drifted shut then she opened them again. She looked tired and drawn even after having napped the afternoon away. Feeling guilty for wanting to question her, he cleared his throat before speaking.

"Listen, uh, Angel."

"Where were you Bastion?" Her soft query took him by surprise. Her eyes peered up at him, beseeching him for answers even as her lips quivered.

"Where was I? What do you mean?" Confused, he became uneasy at her question. The way she asked it, gave him the impression he was supposed to know of her somehow.

"He said Inara told him you'd come for me when it was safe." She spoke softly her face becoming crestfallen. "But you never came."

He could tell she was on the verge of crying. "Who told you this?"

"Wilton."

"Your husband?" Bastion asked.

"Yes. Oh, but at the time he wasn't my husband when I first wandered away. His name was Flynn when he found me in the woods back then."

The moment she said the name, things began to click in his head. Stunned, Bastion finally understood. "Flynn Hunter, my wife's former CIA partner, is Wilton Stryfe, your husband?"

"He was anyway. I think he died, because he didn't come home." There was a catch to her voice. "He always came home, no matter how mad he'd get at me for not understanding or burning things. Cause he knew I needed him. But he got a phone call and went to the store."

"He received a phone call before he disappeared?" Bastion asked. "Chase never said anything about that. Do you know who he was talking to?"

Angel shook her head in answer as she cringed. "I think I forgot to mention it to Chase. And I couldn't say what the person's name was. He said he was the 'Milkman' and I always had to be very, very quiet when he called."

He noted she shivered when she spoke of him. "Did you happen to hear anything?"

"No, all he said, was the 'Milkman' might have a job for him. He was mad at me for burning dinner, and said he was heading for the store, but never came back."

She did it again; a slight shiver caused her whole body to shake the moment the caller's nickname was mentioned. When he asked her about it, she said because the 'Milkman' scared her. She couldn't explain how or why, because she had no memory of her life before Wilton found her in the Colorado Rocky Mountains where his wife left her.

"I'm afraid of actual milk too. Wilton always said it was stupid to be afraid of a liquid, but I can't help it." She further explained she couldn't drink it or be near it, because she would get scared and start shaking like crazy.

Bastion had heard of the phobia once before long ago. He recalled it was called Galaphobia, but he never met anyone who was afraid of it. He couldn't help but wonder if her fear was linked to the man her husband called the 'Milkman.'

Turning her head away from him, Angel gazed out the window at the glorious mountains which surrounded the Blackthorne Estate and encompassed the whole of the valley in which they lived. She marveled aloud at how peaceful and beautiful it was, then her face twisted and crumpled as though she were about to cry.

"Why didn't you come for me when you were supposed to?" she asked again. She stifled a sob and became choked up. A tear escaped down her cheek.

Bastion heaved a troubled sigh, unsure how to respond. He didn't like seeing her cry. "I don't know, Honey, I'm sorry. You say Hunter found five years ago? Do you recall what month it was?"

"It was April."

316

Bastion swore, finally another piece of her puzzle. He winced and kissed her on her forehead.

"My wife Inara died five years ago the very same month, Angel," he said against her ear. The action caused her to shiver. He chuckled knowingly and pulled back a bit, not wanting to disturb the child as he ate any more than necessary. "In April. It was a very bad time for me for I learned..."

"That Inara had been killed by someone from Phenom. The recording, of course." Angel's brow knit together. He could see she was trying hard to be understanding, yet her lip puckered out in a pout, nonetheless.

"Was your time with him so bad? He didn't hurt you did he?" He asked in a joking manner, but when he saw her heave a troubled sigh, bite her lip, and look away, he became worried. "Angel, did Wilton hurt you?"

She nodded in distress and her eyes teared up even more. "He said I owed him, because he was protecting me and keeping me safe from the 'Milkman.' He told me I should try to p-please him in bed at night, especially since he married me to keep me safe. I didn't understand what it meant at the time. I only wanted to make him happy cause he was helping me. But he h-hurt me when he p-put my son in me." She sobbed, unable to control her tears anymore. The look she threw his way was of a wounded child, one unable to comprehend why people would hurt each other at all. "And he hurt my heart c-cause he p-promised to n-never hurt me. It was so painful when I had Kal at home," she wailed. "He said it wasn't safe to take me to a hospital to deliver and that it would go away after a while, but he lied. It took so very long for it to stop. It was m-months before I h-healed," she said.

Bastion visibly winced, realizing what her statement implied. From the way it sounded, she'd been a virgin and an innocent to the ways of men and women in addition to the world in general, because of her lack of memory. He wondered what caused her to lose not just her memory, but any knowledge she gained from the world around her from the moment she'd been born. Hunter knew this about her and took advantage of her. Anger surged within him.

The woman next to him was extremely beautiful. Her unique hair coloring and unusual eyes were entrancing. It seemed a contradiction, but there was an abundance of wisdom within her eyes because of her gift, regardless of her elementary mentality. Knowing Wilton Stryfe was once known as Flynn Hunter, his late wife's supposed CIA partner, Bastion now understood Angel had been the package his wife had been referring to as the white raven.

His late wife said in her recording she was trying to bring her to safety and that he should locate Flynn and get the white raven from him. It was her last request before Phenom murdered her, so he tried to locate him after discovering the message. No matter how far and wide he searched, he could never find him. But he knew Flynn knew how to reach him, for he'd known Kalturek was a Deputy Sheriff at the time. It was why he came to the incorrect conclusion Flynn Hunter had been discovered and silenced too.

Learning the man failed to bring her to him, and took Angel as his wife, Bastion was left to wonder if Flynn duped Inara into helping him gain her as his prize, and she died for it.

The rage within threatened to spill forth. Unwilling to allow Angel to see that side of him, he suppressed it as best he could. If the man weren't already dead he'd torture and kill him himself.

With a shaking hand and arm, he reached around Angel and pulled her to him. She rested her head on his shoulder and cried, the stress of trying to find her way to him without getting caught had taken its toll.

"I can't do anything about the past, Honey. But I can assure you from here on out, I will do everything in my power to keep you and little Kal safe. You have my word on that and a Blackthorne's word is everything."

"But Rafe, isn't your last name RavenCroft?"

"I may have been given the name RavenCroft by my adoptive parents, but I have been and always will be a Blackthorne, regardless of the name I carry."

The sound of his phone chiming interrupted their talk. Regretting having to reach for his phone, another chime came through as he was pulling up his messaging screen.

Swearing, a soft growl escaped his lips. He could feel Angel moving next to him. Slipping the spaghetti strap of her dress back up onto her shoulder, she threw the burp cloth over it, tucked the bib about her son's neck, and held him against her chest. She patted little Kal's back to try to burp him. He gurgled while smiling up at him. The boy's eyes, so much like his mother's, seemed to know what he was thinking.

"I'm sorry, Angel, I'm gonna have to go."

"Rafe discovered where Ciara is, and you're all running out of time cause the 'Milkman' is after her." Angel said on a sad sigh. "You'd better hurry, because he's become desperate. As Wilton used to say, 'desperate equates to dangerous' or some silly thing like that. I don't remember completely. Oh, and I'm betting your son landed at the airport sooner than expected."

Looking between her and his phone, Bastion shook his head. The woman was amazing. A rare white raven indeed.

Chapter 16

"Come in."

The sharp knock on the office door interrupted Agent Jericho Henley's agitated pacing before his desk. A woman with a small pale face, round-rimmed glasses and dark brown hair popped her head through the door. There was a pleased expression plastered on her face.

"You have something for me." It was more of a statement than a question. In the span of three years since he hired her as his secretary, he'd come to know the woman's looks well, happy or otherwise.

"I got another hit on those books," she said.

Henley's interest was instant. "Who? Male or female? How old?"

Stepping into his office, she extended the file in her hand to him for his perusal. "It's all in there. Her name's Ciara Eve Marketti."

"A woman. Good, very good."

"Yes. She's thirty years old, recently divorced, and lives in Mishawaka, Indiana."

Intrigued, Henley attempted to temper his excitement.

Pushing her glasses back up her nose, she sucked on the inside of her lip, waiting for the question he always asked of their candidates. She couldn't wait to tell him.

Noting his secretary was practically bursting at the seams he chuckled. "Okay, I give. How many has she purchased so far?"

"All of David Pearson's Phenomena collection for children, youth, and adults."

His mouth plunged in disbelief before quickly becoming cross. "She bought them all? How did you miss her?"

"They were all purchased within less than two weeks, by way of two different amazon accounts. It took me a while before I realized it was only one individual purchasing them, not two."

A slow smile crept across his features as he perused the stats lying before him. "Get him on the phone."

Accustomed to his demanding requests she didn't think much of his curt dismissal of her, and she knew to whom he referred.

"Right away, Sir."

"So many in such a short time," he mumbled to himself. Instinct told him the woman's gift was likely as strong if not more powerful than the last woman they'd attempted to procure. He stared at the woman's Bureau of Motor Vehicle picture. She was a strawberry blonde with freckles and blue eyes, but he wondered.

"Ciara Marketti. I'm looking forward to meeting you." The woman seemed familiar to him, but he couldn't place why, and his memory for people was normally quite good.

The intercom system buzzed. "Lord Dugald Roideach is on line one, Sir."

He reached for his phone, reclining back in his swivel chair as he spoke. "I've got another one."

Dugald Roideach's aging voice sounded anything, but pleased. "It's about time. How is it you keep missing these people?"

"They are gifted after all. It tends to give them an advantage."

"These books were supposed to prevent that from being an issue." Dugald was being understandably testy. Their last recruit had gotten away. "Are you sure about this one?"

"She ordered over a dozen novels in less than two weeks. So, yeah. I'd say she's a prime candidate. As to the books; you've seen yourself over the years how they've proven to be most beneficial. They were well worth the cost it took to procure them."

"So you say. Inara RavenCroft was a huge asset," Dugald said.

"One that became a liability." Not interested in rehashing the past, Henley changed the subject. "If I'm right, this woman may be of great significance to us."

"How so?"

"The candidates I'm attempting to locate now are not your average person with abilities like what we've acquired in the past. Those people were only distant descendants. We're talking about an entire family of individuals who are directly linked to the Weir-deVere's. This means we may have found what others have been looking for, for centuries. If this woman's gift is as strong as I suspect, then she could very well lead us right to them." What Henley didn't tell him was he found one before, but because of Inara, the individual had escaped the facility and had eluded him for years.

On the other end of the line, Dugald's eyebrows rose, his shrewd charcoal eyes sparking with something other than cold indifference for once. "Are you telling me you're aware of actual descendants of Maxwell Blackthorne? The bastard son of that incestuous relationship between Major Thomas Weir and his sister Jean Weir from nearly four hundred years ago?" Dugald knew other's thought Maxwell Blackthorne's existence was nothing but a rumor; a fantastical story made up around the year 1620 by an angry servant bent on destroying Thomas and Jean Weir for having cut out her tongue. He, along with a few others within the council, knew otherwise.

"The very same."

"Are you certain?" There was an edge of excitement to his cautious tone. "We must be careful. There are many among the council who no longer believes. They think they're nothing but legends. Tales of folklore; children's stories, and the like. If we're wrong it would be very embarrassing for you."

"For both of us."

Dugald didn't say a thing, leaving Henley to believe if things fell through, the man would happily allow him to take the fall, particularly after his last bit of misfortune. A bit anxious he took another swig of his milk carton, discovering he emptied the last of it already. He'd been particularly thirsty this morning. It was his third one since breakfast and it was only nine-thirty in the morning.

"What reason are we giving for bringing her in?" Dugald wanted to know.

"This one has been tied up in a pretty little ribbon for us." Henley's smile widened as he continued reading through the file while talking.

"Oh, how so?" The man's disbelief was unmistakable.

"Ms. Marketti was recently divorced from an illegal immigrant." Henley could almost hear Lord Roideach smiling on the other end.

"Perfect. Any Progeny?"

"None."

Lord Roideach laughed coldly. "Not yet anyway."

Grunting at the response on the other end of the line Henley's lip curved into a thin smile.

"I'll know more in a bit. Get back with you then." Replacing the handset on the receiver, Henley rested his elbows on his desk, steepling his hands together. "What are you capable of Ms. Marketti, and was your ex-husband aware of your gift?"

Unceremoniously stacking the papers back within the folder, he tucked them under his arm and left his office. Striding past his secretary's desk he called back to her as he went.

"Nice job Emma. I'm gonna be gone for the rest of the day. Let my pilot know I'm on my way." Stopping near the elevator, Henley paused and turned back after hitting the button to go up. She'd come to him with the file after bringing him his morning milk. "Anyone else aware of this?"

"I brought it straight to you. You did tell me not to say anything to Agent Pegueros."

Henley nodded his approval as the elevator door opened, and he stepped within. This one would be in-house by the end of the day, whether she wanted to be or not.

- - -

Same Day
Chicago, Illinois

After arriving at the Chicago O'Hare airport by way of a small charter plane, Rafe and Rourke took a shuttle bus to the Schaumburg Municipal Helistop. They were about five minutes away from meeting Agent Pegueros who would be piloting their helicopter flight to South Bend when it first hit Rourke. The surrounding air pulsed unexpectedly, then froze in place, giving a feeling of unreality to the interior of the shuttle they were sitting in. Sometimes his visions were disjointed, but this one was as clear as day.

He could see the woman they were attempting to save was seated at a desk, eating her lunch as she read a book. Getting a glimpse of the cover, Rourke noted it was written by David Pearson. Becoming rigid in his seat, he was vaguely aware his brother next to him was similarly indisposed. Unable to move and with a vacant expression on his own face Rourke watched as the woman set the book down and continued to eat only to be interrupted. Appearing displeased and annoyed at her boss, he watched her exit the office with the manila envelopes.

Ciara walked through an upscale hotel lobby with wall-to-wall windows and exited through its front doors. She stopped suddenly upon seeing two black vehicles race forward and stop near the steps in front of her. Two men exited the vehicle, one of which quickly singled her out and identified himself as Agent Jericho Henley. The second man managed to box her in, so she had no escape route.

326

"I'm going to need you to come with us, Ms. Marketti."

"What? But why? I don't understand, what have I done?" The uneasy look on her face had Rourke's heart racing and his blood boiling in his ears. He wanted to reach through the vision and tear the man's eyes out for the lies he knew he was about to spew. Instead, he was forced to watch it play out.

Taking a firm hold of her, Henley forcefully guided Ciara down the remainder of the steps and toward the vehicle's open door.

"No need to worry, Ms. Marketti, we only have a few questions for you about your marriage and recent divorce from an illegal immigrant. There's an additional issue of bigamy we need to discuss as well."

"But I'm the victim here. I didn't know he already had a wife, and I can't just leave, especially without saying anything. I'm supposed to be taking my bosses mail to the post office."

Taking the manila envelopes from her as he pushed her into the SUV. He handed off the envelopes to the other man who was now back in the driver's seat. Henley crawled in next to Ciara, forcing her to scoot over in the seat.

"My comrade will take care of the mail for you, won't you there, Clint?" The driver gave him a curt nod in response as Henley continued. "See now. We'll have you back to work in no time there, Ms. Marketti."

The way he kept saying her name put Rourke on edge.

The driver put the vehicle in gear and after finding an opening pulled back into traffic. There was sheer panic in Ciara's expression as the vehicle drove away and it had Rourke fighting mad. Her face paled, becoming stricken and helpless as tears threatened at the corners of her eyes. Jaw clenching he turned toward his brother in the seat before stepping out of the shuttle. Their identical determined visages could mean only one thing. They had the same vision.

Rafe took hold of the bag his brother was shoving into his hand. "We need to hurry."

"Agreed. We still have time to keep it from happening."

Exiting the vehicle both their phones could be heard chiming in unison.

"I'd lay odds that's Bastion."

Rourke glanced at his phone. "Yes, it seems it was a shared vision by all. He also says he's landing in Elkhart as we speak."

The two men exchanged concerned glances. Bastion was flying his private plane solo as he had the vision. They knew full well how dangerous it could be. A thought popped suddenly into Rourke's head. Encouraged by it, he sent a quick response back then pocketed his phone. The request would distract his brother until they arrived and in the long run, would help him as well.

Guiding Rourke in the direction they needed to go, Rafe began telling him what he intended to do in order to pull her out safely. He was well aware of his brothers plan to repel down to her, by way of the helicopter. He intended to snatch Ciara up to safety before Henley could grab her.

Rourke humored him as they walked toward the man standing on the helipad with his back to them. Their voices carried, gaining Agent Pegueros's attention, causing him to turn around. Doing a double take, his body jerked as though he'd been jolted by a bolt of lightning.

Pegueros stared openly at the stuffy looking gentleman who, aside from his clothes and facial hair, looked identical to the other man next to him of whom he knew as David Pearson. They were complete opposites in every way.

"I don't know why you bothered packing for this. We're not going to be within time long enough for you to need it." Tired of carrying his brothers bag and feeling like his porter, Rafe forced him to take it by shoving it toward him.

"I didn't know you had a twin brother, David." Pegueros regained his senses quickly. "What's he doing here anyway?"

"He's here because he thinks he needs to be present for every step of this operation. He mistakenly believes he has a vested interest in it," Rafe said, then turned on his brother. "How are you planning to get from here to Elkhart, Indiana to meet Bastion in time anyway? You never did explain that. If it were me, I'd do a hot drop into the Elkhart Municipal airport."

Rourke scowled and shoved his cane at his brother to hold as he slipped off his shoes and set them on the ground. "I knew you were slow; I didn't realize you were stupid. I'll be getting there the same way you are. By helicopter."

"That's absurd and I'm not giving you my shoes. Why do I need to give you my shoes?"

"We don't have time for this." Rourke turned between the two men. "I'm here, because I'll be the one repelling from the helicopter to grab her up."

Stunned, Rafe laughed out loud. "You are, are you? Says the man walking with a cane."

"No, says the man carrying the cane. Use your eyes man."

"My eyes are telling me you're not capable of or equipped to handle this situation."

Rourke grumbled. "Shows how much you know. You never did bother to ask what I've been doing since I left now have you? And I don't need the cane to walk anymore. I carry it, because I've found it has other uses. Now give me your blasted shoes. It never occurred to me I'd need any, so I never packed any when I left Scotland."

Watching as the two brothers argued, Pegueros eyes couldn't have gotten any wider as he cut in on their argument. "Man, you gotta have experience for what he's about to do. No offense intended, but you look like you've come from a board room."

"Looks can be deceiving, Man." Rourke mocked. "You look like you came here in the back end of a truck, but I don't hold it against you. Besides, I'm more than capable." Rourke walked toward the nearby building fully aware he insulted the agent.

"So you're telling me you can repel down from a moving helicopter while you're in a harness, grab up Ciara, and then hoist the two of you back up into the helicopter?" Rafe shouted while trying to keep up with his brother who was already at the building's door. He was suddenly surprisingly quick on his feet. "And where do you think you're going? The helicopter is back there."

"There's this wee thing called a water closet. You might know it as a bathroom. People go in, tinkle, plop a few turds, wash if they're of the mind, then exit to places unknown." Sticking two fingers in the air he made them airwalk for effect. "Sometimes they even change clothes and do things like, I don't know, shaving," he exclaimed with animation while jiggling his bag. "And of course I'm capable of what you ask. I am MI6 after all." The latter he whispered close to Rafe's face as he shoved his forefinger before his own lips and shushed his brother as if to say, don't tell. Eyes twinkling at the shock effect he landed on him; Rourke opened the door to the building and spoke as he entered. "I would have shaved before I left, but you didn't give me much time. I'll want those shoes when I've returned."

Rafe was still staring at the door when Pegueros caught up with him.

"Where'd he go? And if he's your brother how is it he's got a Scottish accent?"

Without thinking, Rafe responded. "My father is Scottish; he normally lives with him." Realizing what he said, he changed the subject quickly. "Bathroom; he needed a shave."

"Now? Aren't we on a timetable here?"

Inhaling deeply Rafe blinked and shook his head to clear it. "We are, but he's right, he needs to shave. If he really intends to go in after her, and he happens to run into or be seen by Henley then he needs to look like I do now."

Pegueros gave him a perplexed look. "Why does it matter?"

"Because Henley has seen me within this past week. There's no way this face could grow much of a beard in such a short time." Seeing understanding in the man's eyes, Rafe leaned in a little closer. "You understand, no one, and I mean no one, knows about him. It's extremely important it stays that way."

Becoming anxious at the look he was being given, Pegueros squirmed uneasily. "It's all good. No one is gonna hear it from me. I'm gone after this anyway, remember?"

Less than ten minutes later Rourke was hurrying sock footed to the helipad sporting a freshly shaven face, a black pair of jeans, and a black t-shirt while carrying the duffel bag.

"I'll have those shoes now."

"What took you so long? And where did you get those clothes?" Rafe asked suspiciously.

"If you must know it took an extra minute or two to convince myself that removing my stash and beard would be worth it. I've maintained them for almost thirty years now. Having to lose my identity in order to become you rates right up there to never wanting to drink from a urinal. As for the clothes, I got them from your laundry."

"You're wearing clothes from my dirty laundry basket?" Rafe's disgust was obvious.

Offended by the mere notion of what he accused, Rourke lashed out as he grabbed for the tennis shoes his brother unwillingly offered up. "Of course not, you nitwit. I got them from the clean laundry basket. I must say though; I've never tried briefs before. They're a bit roomier than I expected."

Pegueros could be heard smirking from the pilot seat of the helicopter as Rafe groaned with disgust.

"No worries, dear boy." Rourke smacked his brother on the shoulder as he stepped into the harness. "I'll be sure to return your articles the moment we get back."

Already in his own harness, Rafe hopped up into the helicopter. He fumed while hollering above the noise of the rotor blades. "Burn them. I don't want them back."

Laughing openly now, Pegueros prepared them all for their imminent take-off.

- - -

Elkhart Municipal airport
Elkhart, Indiana

"He told you to do what?"

Having been more pushed then dropped off at the Elkhart Municipal airport seconds before, Rafe went into a blind panic upon discovering Bastion wasn't at the plane when he arrived. A minute later, the man came tearing into the airport by way of the borrowed jeep of the guy he'd bribed in the tower.

"To get Chinese take-out for his highness. Something about it being a Scot thing, and I wouldn't understand. As he put it, apparently he requires food after a caper." Bastion halted mid-step while lugging a large box filled to the brim with food cartons and a bag. "What does he even mean by that anyway? When has that man ever been involved with anything other than a round of golf and why are you even here? What is he thinking? He's never going to be able to pull this off."

"The way he tells it, he'd have us believe he was MI6," Rafe whispered loudly.

"That man is an MI6 agent?" Bastion's disbelief was apparent.

"If you can believe anything that comes out of his mouth." Rafe rolled his eyes heavenward. "This is the same man who had no qualms whatsoever of shoving me out of the helicopter after having told me he agreed it'd be best that a pro went after her. I didn't even see it coming, so I wound up with my face planted in dirt. I was lucky the pilot wasn't dropping me over the asphalt."

"You're serious." Bastion stared at his brother, unsure what to make of this. Was it possible Rourke was

MI6? If it were true, why would he bother admitting it to them?

"Does this look like the face of a man who wasn't being serious?" Rafe shouted while grabbing the bag of 2-liters and cups from the seat of the jeep. They both raced toward the plane.

"You might not want to shake those 2-liters so much. They're liable to explode."

"Let them explode up his arse for all I care!"

"And here I thought you were a Christian."

Lips pursing angrily, Rafe snarled and halted at the top of the steps of the private jet, preventing Bastion from getting through to his cockpit. He needed to get his jet going and now. It didn't take long by helicopter to go from Elkhart to South Bend and back.

"Contrary to what you might think, Christians are human and therefore as emotional as everyone else," Rafe countered, tired of getting that thrown in his face. "And besides, even God had his angry moments." Seeing his brother was highly skeptical of his outburst, he ground out. "Think Noah."

"Can't say I'm all that up on the Bible or anything, but I thought there was more disappointment in mankind then anger that prompted that event." Both men ducked through the opening of the plane and set the food and drinks down.

"If mankind back then, is anything like Rourke is now, I wouldn't be surprised if it was both. Where did you get all this from anyway?" Rafe indicated the large box laden with food containers and the big bag sitting next to it. He had to admit, the aroma was heavenly.

Bastion moved toward the cockpit as he spoke. "A place down the road called Lucky's. It's more Thai food then it is Chinese, but I figured it'd do for his highness in a pinch. I was a little skeptical at first. It looks like they moved into an old Dunkin Donuts shop, but they were packed and the eggrolls are absolutely fantastic."

"How would you know?"

Bastion laughed as he started the plane. From the open door, his keen ears could hear a helicopter in the distance. He knew he needed to get in position quickly. Hopefully, their idiot brother hadn't screwed up, and they'd have an additional passenger getting on with them shortly.

"I ate four of them on my drive back here," he yelled as he put his headgear on. "They're quite addictive."

"-Ecko to Raven, I say, Gecko to Raven, I'm inbound."

"ETA?" Bastion waved his hand in the air in order to get Rafe's attention.

"Any second now. And Raven, you tell David we got a problem."

- - -

Doubletree by Hilton Hotel
South Bend, Indiana

Lips moving soundlessly, Ciara Marketti's eyes flew across the page, barely catching the words before moving on to the next sentence, the next paragraph. Completing the last segment, she turned the page.

It was the last book she had in the Phenomena series, but she couldn't seem to help herself. She was speed reading. David Pearson was her favorite author. His capacity to show her what he was trying to say without telling too much had her hooked from his first book. The fact the stories were about everyday people with supernatural abilities was merely a bonus. She didn't know why, but she'd always been drawn to that sort of story.

Within fifteen minutes of her thirty-minute lunch break, she was about to finish reading the three-hundred and ninety-eight-page novel she started the evening before. She fervently continued to read, excited for the ending.

Ciara couldn't help it, she much preferred living among the pages of the books she read. The stories were so much better than her reality; the one where she hated her job, had lost her house, been forced into bankruptcy, and was recently divorced from a bigamist after over three and a half years of supposed marriage. Learning of her ex's betrayal and subterfuge had hurt her deeply, worse than most around her probably realized. To add insult to injury, she'd had to not only use up all her savings and vacation time between the hospital visit and the court days, but dip heavily into her retirement savings as well, so she wouldn't be able to take the trip to Montana this year as she hoped either. The realization served to both infuriate and depress her. She'd been saving for the trip for the past five years.

With a sad discontented sigh, she closed the book she finished and placed it on her desk next to her. If only novels could be real, the people within them too. If she were an author that's what she'd write; stories about people who were real and unaware they were gifted. Now that, in her mind, would make a fascinating story. She'd typed up a short outline of the idea a while back, but never did anything with it.

Leaning her head against the headrest of her chair, she gazed toward the ceiling with a far-off look wishing she was anywhere but where she was. Her heart ached within her chest and the vivid dreams from the night before were making it even harder to concentrate on her work today. The second her lunch break had come around she dove back into her book and to a world where happily ever after's actually existed, because they sure didn't exist in the real world.

Ciara propped her feet up on her desk and continued eating. She peered at the time on her monitor. It was eighteen past noon. She grumbled in disappointment. With only twelve minutes left, she knew she wouldn't have time to run to the used bookstore down the street from the hotel where she worked. This last story had her synapses sparking and whirring in her head, leaving her with the desperate need for more stories on the same subject. She was anxious to see if they had anything new. She needed some books to tide her over until she could find herself a new series to read.

"Can you not do that?"

Turning her head toward her bosses office, Ciara grimaced. What now? She wasn't even finished with her lunch and the devil woman was already looking for her? The Director of Sales Manager gave her a look of both disapproval and condescension all in one. She marveled briefly at the woman's ability to convey multiple emotions in one look.

"What am I doing wrong this time?"

"Your feet, Ciara." The woman huffed. "Get them off the desk and let's try to be more professional, shall we?"

Acquiescing she set her feet back on the floor. Okay, so the woman wasn't entirely wrong. This time.

"Sorry, I was trying to relax. I'm on my lunch."

"That's another thing. No more eating at your desk."

Ciara gaped at the woman. Was she serious? "Where else am I going to eat?"

"I don't care, just do it elsewhere. Use housekeeping's break room." The woman shoved several manila envelopes toward her. "I need you to get these mailed right away."

Taking the addressed manila envelopes from her boss she slid them in her outbox for the end of the day. She'd already been demoted from a Managers position to clerical work, she wasn't about to return to eating in the housekeepers break room. That's where she had started. She worked too long and hard to get out from there to allow it to happen.

"What are you doing?"

Ciara hedged, wondering at what she did to warrant being snapped at. "I put it in the outbox until after lunch."

"Now. I want them mailed now."

Glancing at the clock she noted it wasn't twelve-thirty yet. "I still have ten minutes, and I haven't finished eating."

"You know how I hate to repeat myself," her boss said waspishly, giving her a look that dared her to argue.

"Fine." With an exasperated sigh, she gazed longingly at her half-eaten spaghetti Bolognese, grabbed the manila envelopes out of the in-box with one hand, opened her desk drawer, and pulled out her purse. Pulling open the glass paned office door to exit out into the lobby entrance, she was halted by her bosses words.

"And Ciara, you're attitude lately has been duly noted and will be going into your next review. Be sure to return with a receipt this time."

Lips pursing her temper flared. What a witch. "I returned with receipts the last five times you've sent me on mail runs, during my lunchtime, mind you. It's not my fault if you keep losing them."

She left the office without looking back, mumbling about where broomsticks could go. As she walked through the hotel lobby entrance Ciara started experiencing an uneasy sensation in her chest. Taking a deep breath she exhaled, trying to alleviate her anxiety. The emotion-charged sensation didn't make sense. She'd argued with the Director of Sales Manager many times before. This time wasn't any different. She wasn't worried about what she said about her review, because she was already looking for employment elsewhere.

Reaching the front door of the lobby, she waived halfheartedly at the porter who stood at his post. He smiled back at her, his eyes laughing. "Giving you a hard time again, is she?"

Ciara sighed. "Always. This morning it was her coffee being too cold. She asked for an iced coffee. Hello! What did she expect? The fact I opted for a pantsuit and dress boots rather than a skirt today, was apparently a no-no too. Now it's the mail during my lunch, again."

"Chin up, love. You never know when fair winds will swoop in and lift your spirits away."

She stopped at the door and turned to face the man. For some reason, his words seemed poignant somehow. Her heart fluttered in her chest as the pit of her stomach lurched uneasily. Maybe the pasta wasn't sitting well with her.

"Thanks. Guess I'm on a mail run for now." She gave a halfhearted laugh as she joked. "Who knows, maybe I won't come back."

The porter frowned.

Not giving him a chance to respond, she flipped her black hair over her shoulder, pushed through the door, and walked out onto the sidewalk. The hotel was in the heart of downtown South Bend and her car was located in the parking garage attached to the building.

The hotel garage.

Well crap. Without thinking, she went the wrong way. She would have to head back inside and take the elevator to the parking garage. Rolling her eyes heavenward at her own stupidity Ciara was about to turn around when she noticed a couple of black vehicles speeding toward the building.

At the sight of them, she experienced an all-consuming wave of fear for some reason. Her heart raced as the vehicles came to a stop in front of the building, somehow knowing they were there for her.

The same moment the door of the vehicle opened, she felt winds whip up around her and heard the sound of a helicopter above her. Her head spun around as a man dropped from the sky next to her.

"Ciara Marketti, I presume?"

She stared at the man in wide-eyed shock. It wasn't what the man wore, the fact he dropped from a helicopter, or that he somehow knew her name that had her tongue-tied. It was more about him being extremely handsome as well as familiar to her. If she didn't know better, she'd swear he was the man in the painting she rendered years before. Minus the scar on his brow. It was the spitting image of him otherwise, right down to the crystal-clear color of his eyes. Well, almost anyway. One thing was missing.

"How do you know me?" Not so dumbstruck to forget the vehicles which frightened her only moments before, she panned from him to the black man now stepping from within the vehicle. He looked angry and ready to kill as he reached for something at his waist.

"No time. Talk later. Must go."

Attempting to pull her hair out of her face, she was barely aware they had gained the attention of passersby on the sidewalk and in the streets. Suddenly, finding herself engulfed and pinned within the man's strong arms, she gave a startled cry. He yelled something loudly that sounded a lot like "Go, go, go." She gasped as her feet lost their footing on the ground. The manila envelopes dropped from her hands the moment the weightless sensation hit her. She screamed and reached around him, grasping his waist tightly in terror of being dropped. Where seconds before she was walking on the ground, now she was flying through the air.

Was this really happening?

Crushed against him, she plastered her head to his chest as her horrified screams caught in her throat. They were whizzing up and away, dangling from the helicopter by a chord. Unable to handle the sight of the buildings and people getting smaller as they flew up and away she squeezed her eyes shut tight. She dug her face into the man's chest, not caring she had no real clue who he was, why he was whisking her away, or where they were going.

Her chest constricted with fear, her breathing coming in erratic spurts as she shouted loudly above the noise. "Don't let go! Please, please God don't let me go!"

The deep rumbling voice, muffled by the rotor blades and gusting winds, was nonetheless unmistakable in its response as his lips brushed against her ear.

"You've my word, love, I'll never let you go."

- - -

South Bend, Indiana

The woman had been ripped from his clutches before his very eyes; torn away by David Pearson, the same man who escaped with the last recruit they'd attempted to bring in.

Losing his temper, Agent Jericho Henley shot multiple times at the retreating figures, before ceasing and falling back to the vehicle to give chase. Calling in the identification number on the tail of the Bell UH-1 Huey helicopter, to his headquarters, he learned it was scheduled to stop at the Goshen Municipal airport.

"We're attempting to track it. Goshen police are en route and will detain."

Henley pulled into the airport when they learned the officers missed the helicopter. It landed briefly then took off again. No occupants were said to have exited during the stop and a careful search of the airport showed no signs of the individuals he sought. Hoping the stop had been a ruse, he called headquarters to request the pilot and couple to be detained upon arriving back in Chicago.

Henley's insides were churning anxiously when they pulled into the Schaumberg Helistop, only to discover the agents detained the pilot, but that there had been no occupants. Further interrogation of the man led to the discovery he was not the original pilot. The one who flew it back from Goshen had been hired to return the helicopter, which meant Agent Henley had spent the better part of his day wasting time.

In a fit of rage, Henley shoved the paperwork and computer screen from a nearby desk to the floor and proceeded to deck his own man for good measure. This time, he didn't have anyone to blame for the fiasco, but himself and, therefore, had no one to shoot in order to vent his anger.

Worse yet, he knew Dugald Roideach would be less than pleased.

Hands shaking visibly from a mixture of pure rage and fear of reprisal for allowing them to escape, Henley unsteadily exited the airport. Pulling a cigarette from his pocket, he lit it with his favorite milk carton lighter. His determination to locate and subjugate the gifted individuals among the Blackthorne and Weir-deVere lineage hadn't abated. If anything, this incident had lit a fire within him. One way or another he would find them. When he did, not even David Pearson would be able to stop him.

- - -

Elkhart, Indiana

Rourke tumbled to the grass with Ciara at the Elkhart Municipal Airport after having jumped with her from the helicopter. The winds from the blades whipped her hair up into his face as they rolled to a stop. Hoping she fared okay when he dropped to the ground, he turned her, so he could see her face. She was still catatonic and had been that way from the moment he pulled her up into the helicopter.

He had to get her quickly to Bastion's private jet since it was ready and waiting on the runway. He pulled her arm up over him and hefted her onto his shoulders. Grasping her on one side by her arms and on the opposite side by her legs, he proceeded to carry her fireman style to the awaiting jet. Barreling up the stairs, he slid her off his shoulders and carried her over to a seat. Rafe pulled the steps up and closed the door even as Bastion began taxing down the runway.

"Help me get her locked in."

Agitated and uncharacteristically shaky, Rourke eased Ciara into the gray leather chairs as Rafe reached across and clicked her seat belt in place.

"What's wrong with her? Has she gone into shock?" Rafe locked himself into the chair across from her when his brother stole the seat next to her before he could.

"Aye, it would seem she's afraid of heights." Still recovering, Rourke snuck a glance out the window as he took a steadying breath. It had been a few years since he had an operation like this one. It rattled him a bit more than expected. The sensation of her heart racing against his chest while he held her, left him more than a little unsettled as well.

Noticing they'd achieved lift-off and were gaining in altitude, he checked to see how she was doing. Her eyes were still glazed, and she was unresponsive when he snapped his fingers before her face.

"How's she doing?" Bastion called back from the pilot seat, having seen his brother carrying the woman as he ran. "Is she all right? What happened?"

Not answering, Rourke hollered irritably back at him instead. "How soon can I take this blasted seat belt off?"

"Give me another minute. I want to get a little higher first."

"You're staying off radar, right?"

"Have faith, Rafe. This isn't my first joy ride."

Rourke didn't bother stifling his reaction. "Clearly."

Sensing something happened, Rafe tried to get him to talk. "You going to tell me?"

"What? Tell you what happened?" Rourke shifted uncomfortably in his seat all the while scoffing at his brother in disgust. The nosy bugger wasn't giving him a chance to recover before trying to pepper him with questions. He was fifty years old now. It wasn't like he'd been doing this sort of thing on a regular basis anymore unless he had to.

"Rourke."

"She's gone into shock. I want to get a blasted blanket around her, then we'll talk." His voice sharper then he'd intended, he took another steadying breath. As he inhaled he could smell the tantalizing aroma of the food he'd requested. "And I need something in me."

At his brother's questioning look he said, "To eat. There's food. I distinctly smell Chinese food."

"It's Thai, but yes, there's food."

"Good. That'll do." His brother gave him an odd look.

The moment Bastion informed them it was safe to move, Rourke was out of his seat. Finding a blanket first, he wrapped it around Ciara, tucking it around her arms and legs for good measure.

Kneeling before her, he peered up into the face from his brother's portrait which was now framed by a wildly messy black mass of waves. "I'm not getting anything from her."

"Neither am I, and I must admit I wasn't expecting to see her hair that way. I wonder when she dyed it black."

"I'm betting she did it when she found out about her ex." Grabbing the contact case from his pocket Rourke removed the brown colored contacts that were driving him crazy. Accepting his eyeglasses case and eye drops from his brother, he put a drop in each eye and placed his spectacles on his head.

"Much better. The blasted things were drying out my eyes. I hate wearing those things." Picking up the box of food, he sat it on the floor between them. For the moment there was nothing they could do, but wait and see how she fared. He wanted to avoid having to give her a sedative unless they had to, but if it came to that, he would.

Finding plates and plastic silverware in the box, he pulled out the food cartons and began divvying large portions of Governor's chicken, lo mein and fried rice onto one of the plates. Filching a couple of eggrolls from the bag, he took a bite of one and groaned. "Oh, that's good." Unaware of the hand reaching out for the bag, he peered inside worriedly. "That's not going to be enough eggrolls. You should have placed at least two orders, Bastion."

"It is two orders. There's twenty-six in there; more like twenty now. I might have eaten a few on the way back to the helipad."

"I thought you said you ate three?" Rafe's back was turned to Rourke as he spoke with his brother who was in the pilot seat.

Bastion grinned at him. "I might have also fibbed a little. I meant it when I said they were addictive."

Suddenly the bag was gone from Rourke's hands; snatched away by the woman next to him, nearly tearing the bag in the process. The noise of the crackling bag and his brother's startled yelp had Rafe turning around to see what was going on. Both men gaped at her openly as she eagerly reached inside, took out an eggroll, then held the bag protectively against her chest. Without saying a word and while staring at the two men in wide-eyed fascination, she bit into the eggroll and chewed. A contented sigh escaped her lips, and her eyes fluttered closed then back open.

"Hhmm. Lucky's, I thought so," Ciara said, maintaining her cautious perusal of them. She'd been listening in shocked silence over what was happening to her, since she'd been hauled onto the private jet, until she learned there were eggrolls. She thought she recognized the delicious aroma as it assaulted her when carried onto the plane. Her olfactory senses hadn't been wrong.

Both men stared, unsure what to say.

Cradling her hand around the top of the bag Ciara narrowed her gaze upon them. Her legs came up off the floor, and she tucked them close to her chest, but not completely, creating a protective cave for the bag to hide within.

"Mine."

Rafe exchanged looks with Rourke.

"I haven't had one yet," Rafe said hesitantly.

She gave him an impudent glare, as though daring him to try to take one. The fire in her eyes told both men in no uncertain terms that none of them would be getting any.

"Lucky's eggrolls."

That was all she said at first. Returning to their seats, the two men ate slowly from their respective plates as they watched her warily, wondering how she knew where the food came from.

"On a plane."

"Technically it's a private jet," Bastion called from the cockpit. Turning in his seat, he glanced back at her to where she could see his face. Inhaling sharply, her eyes widened at the sight of him. But for his goatee, the pilot looked exactly like the other two men.

Ciara pointed at him with an index finger while holding the partially eaten eggroll in her other hand.

Periodically she'd take additional small bites and chew, then swallow. "A private jet to."

There was an abbreviated pause as she waited for an answer to a question she hadn't asked yet.

Rafe leaned back in his chair, propping one leg up on his other knee as he held his plate and ate. "Montana," he said between bites. "Near Kalispell, Montana to be specific." Her eyes widened even further.

She started rambling. They made a mutual silent agreement among them to stay quiet unless a response to anything she said became necessary. Recognizing her need to process and wrap her mind around what was happening, they wanted to give her the space she needed.

"Lucky's eggrolls. In a jet. Heading to Montana. This has got to be a dream. Of course, it's a dream. It is the sort of ridiculous delusion I'd come up with.

-Or am I imagining it? Have I finally cracked? Going crazy was bound to happen."

Rigorously shaking her head back and forth, she blinked several times then stared at them. "That has to be it or I wouldn't be seeing three identical gorgeous men alone with me on this jet otherwise."

Rourke grinned as his brothers chuckled.

She continued to ramble as she pointed at each one of them in turn. "And those eyes. Oof, absolutely amazing! I can say that out loud, see? Without being embarrassed. After all, this is all in my head cause no man in his right mind would ever snatch me up and fly me away like this.

-Oh, my gosh! I must have gone absolutely mental; like the mouse that got into my energy drink two weeks ago."

Bastion guffawed loudly as she slapped her forehead with her free hand and began rubbing it in circles with the palm of her hand.

"I need to seriously consider committing myself after this whole kidnapping part of my delusion is over."

Rafe paused mid-bite, taking exception to her last assumption. "I assure you; you're not being kidnapped."

"Hhhmm. Funny. Did I know I was going with you?" She turned to look at the identical man opposite the one who spoke.

Rourke's mouth quirked up on one side as he shook his head.

Did you ask if I wanted to go with you?"

The uncomfortable silence led her to believe the answer was no, which was funny cause she already knew that.

"Was I forcefully removed from the steps in front of the hotel where I work and suspended mid-air by helicopter?"

Rourke adjusted in his seat and blew air from between his lips while thinking how best to respond. They hadn't talked about how they were going to explain this to her. His mind went blank. Why was he allowing her to get him all tongue-tied and flustered?

"Let me ask you this. If I were to request to be let off this plane?"

"-jet."

"Jet, sorry. If I told you I wanted off this jet now, this instant; you're saying you'd let me go?"

"We're in the air right now," Rafe said.

"So, that's a no. Gee, guys, I don't know. This pretty well sums up the definition of being kidnapped. Although, if the three of you are kidnapping me, so I can be the focus of a reverse harem sort of deal, then..."

"Reverse harem? What fool thing are you going on about?" Rourke sounded confused, disgusted, and amused all in one. His fork full of governor's chicken was poised in the air near his mouth.

"Did someone hire you to kill me or something? My ex maybe? I assure you I'm not worth the bullet, or shovel, or gas to fly the plane you're about to throw me off of." Her expressive face mouthed the word 'Wow' as she inhaled deeply. Her black hair appeared unnatural, tousled about her pale, drawn face. "Boy, I hope you guys got paid first before hauling my butt on this plane because my ex is broker than broke. I don't know what he promised you, but it couldn't be worth it."

"Jet," all three men said in unison. "It's a private jet, not a plane."

"Right, right. Private jet. Why exactly does that distinction matter again? One way or another it's still an aircraft." Her head shifted around the interior, taking it all in.

It appeared to be an eight-seater for there were four more chairs situated behind her with a narrow aisle to allow people to reach them. At least half of the seats, including the ones she and the man next to her were seated in, allowed for the passengers to see into the cockpit and watch the pilot as he flew. From where she sat she could see out of the windshield. Peering around, she noted there were circular windows on either side and much of the interior was done up in white and pale gray. The vessel appeared to be built with both comfort and practical use in mind.

Snagging another eggroll from the bag without thinking, Ciara crunched down on it hungrily, then attempted to talk between bites. Her hand had begun shaking slightly. "Course now, if you're planning to throw me off, will you do me a favor and please knock me out first? God help me, I wouldn't want to be awake for it."

"No one here wants to kill you," Rourke assured her, becoming alarmed by where her head was going. "What could we possibly gain from murdering you?"

"Ah, okay, now we're getting somewhere. You snagged me up and got me here, but have suddenly realized you've mistaken me for someone that matters."

This statement got her a plane full of silence.

"Ciara Marketti," Rourke said sharply, instantly gaining her attention. He hadn't liked the way she said that at all. It gave him the impression she didn't think herself worthy of anything. "I 'snagged you up' as you put it, in order to prevent you from winding up at the mercy of the monster who was trying to pull you into his vehicle."

"Henley was there then?" Rafe realized how close they must have come to losing her. He understood now why Rourke had appeared so shaken when they'd first arrived.

"Oh, yes. He shot at us too. Dang near hit his mark." Rourke lifted his arm, exposing a tear in his shirt.

Ciara started humming. From her appearance, she looked as though she were trapped in her own little world in her head. Unabashedly reaching for a plate, she snatched some plastic silverware and opened the lid to the sweet and sour chicken.

"Mind if I have some of this?"

"By all means." Rafe gestured toward the food containers at large, surprised she was of the mood to eat. With disappointment, he noticed she'd set the bag of eggrolls next to her left hip in her lap where he couldn't reach it.

"You guys be sure to save me some," Bastion called from the pilot's seat.

"I'll get you a plate momentarily. A little of everything, I'm guessing?" Rafe asked.

"Everything, but the eggrolls," Ciara yelled, then began grumbling. "I figure it's the least you can do, feed a girl a last meal of her favorite food from her favorite restaurant, before she winds up in some twisted reverse harem dream-scaping sort of... I don't know what this is. But if I'm going to be so unlucky as to die today, of all days, then I'm sure as heck gonna die with a belly full of Lucky's."

Shaking, with tears in her eyes, she began ravenously eating the overly full plate of food as if her life depended on it. Tears swam in her eyes, and she could feel her heart thundering rapidly in her chest. Her situation was only now starting to sink in. She was alone on a private jet with three attractive men she didn't know who kidnapped her. Regardless of whether they seemed familiar to her somehow or not, she knew those sorts of situations never tended to end well for a woman.

Heat suffused her face as she struggled to choke down the bite of sweet and sour chicken threatening to catch in her throat. Her eyes darted frantically around her as she ate. What in the world was going on?

Becoming alarmed by what appeared to be the onset of a break-down, Rourke set his plate in his chair and shooed Rafe from his seat. Leaning toward her, he took the plate from her, set it down, and clasped her small hands between his own overly large ones. He noted she still held her spork propped between two fingers of her hand. Tears were no longer threatening, but now spilling forth from her eyes.

"You're safe with us, Ciara. Always will be. No one here is ever going to hurt you, but if we'd left you there, with the men in the black vehicles; then it'd be a whole other story right now."

"Why is that?" She demanded to know. "I don't understand. Why me? First Bruce, then my ex, and now... Why does stuff like this keep happening to me? What did I do to deserve this?

"You did absolutely nothing wrong," Rourke assured her, starting to realize she truly didn't have a clue what was going on. His gaze shifted briefly up to Rafe, who exchanged looks with Bastion.

"She hasn't a clue does she?" Bastion said quietly from the pilot's seat. They hadn't anticipated that. The Ciara in the sixth volume of the, An Unfortunate Lineage series had been like Angel, seemingly all-knowing of everything Blackthorne family related.

Rafe paced the small expanse of the plane. Everything was happening ten years sooner than expected. In the books, Ciara had been aware of them, but hadn't started writing about them until after remarrying and having her children. So when he came for her in the story she already knew.

"Rourke."

"Yes, I've managed to suss it out as well. This changes things a bit."

"What? Changes what?" Ciara cried out as a sudden wave of anxiety hit her.

Rourke shushed her. "Try to calm yourself."

"Calm myself?" She laughed, near hysterics. "I've been hoisted in the air and flown across a county without knowing who was grabbing me, for what purpose I was being taken, and where I was going. I still don't know who you are."

"I know none of this makes any sense at the moment but it will soon. Take deep breaths if you need to. That's right, there you go. Now, let's start over. My name is Rourke Blackthorne, this git here is my brother Rafe," he said winning himself an irritated frown from his brother, "and the pilot is my other brother Bastion RavenCroft. In time, we will explain everything, but for now, know this. You are safe, and we have no intentions of harming you. Okay?"

Ciara's head bobbed up and down as she took another deep breath and exhaled slowly. "Okay," she said absently while reaching for and pulling out another eggroll.

"Good then. Rest now. It'll all be better when you wake." Rourke tapped the syringe of sedative he snuck from his bag against her hip as he reached for the eggroll bag and the one in her hand.

"Rest? Are you kidding me? Hey, wait, those are my eggrolls." Ciara's head drooped suddenly against her chest and the chair.

Rafe scowled as he growled. "Was that necessary?"

Shaking the bag before his brother's face, he finished off the last of the eggroll he filched from her hand. Rourke reached in and took out two more.

"It is if you want any eggrolls."

Chapter 17

Blackthorne Horse Ranch
Kalispell, Montana

"Get the doors, will you?"

Rafe scowled. "First it was your bag at the airport, now it's 'get the doors?' Who do you think I am, Rourke, your butler?"

Bastion groaned loudly, tired of his brother's incessant bickering. They'd been at it ever since they arrived at the airport and all because of a woman.

"Don't be ridiculous. I've too much respect for my butler to ever consider you worthy of such a position." Rourke released his seat belt and opened the car door. "Besides, he gives much better Christmas presents then you do."

"How would you know? I haven't given you a gift for over thirty years."

Bastion leaned across the seat toward Rafe before getting out. "I think that was his point," he said in a low voice. He hated to encourage it, but there were times when it was highly amusing to watch them regardless of the irritation factor. This was one of those moments.

Exiting the vehicle himself, he shut the door. Bending down, he peered in through the window of the back seat at Ciara who appeared to be still unconscious. A hand not so gently shoved him out of the way.

"Move it," Rourke said imperiously, without bothering with a please or thank you. "And I only asked you to carry my bag, Rafe, because I needed to carry her."

"Never would have needed to, if you hadn't knocked her out," Rafe said.

Rourke pulled the woman from the vehicle and was lifting her in his arms as he spoke. "To clarify, I didn't 'knock her out' as you so erroneously put it. I sedated her, because she was rightfully becoming hysterical under the circumstances. There was no way we could have known she wasn't already aware of us. In hindsight, we should have taken it into consideration. But we're long past all that now."

Bastion couldn't help noticing his brother smile down at her before picking her up which made him wonder if he was enjoying himself.

"And anyway, you never would have gotten any eggrolls if I hadn't."

"Not the point, Rourke." Rafe stepped forward and attempted to take the woman from his brother's arms. "You already carried her from the airport. I can take her from here; it is my house after all." Before he could take hold of her, Rourke took a step back and hefted her more securely in his arms. Ciara's head lolled for a moment then rested against his chest.

Bastion frowned. For a second he could have sworn he saw her peeking out at him with one eye. That's when he realized the woman wasn't asleep at all, but faking it. He smothered a laugh, wondering how long she intended to play this out.

"I don't think so; I already have her. Now, get the bloody doors."

Incensed, Rafe threw down the bag and walked away along the sidewalk.

Glancing from his bag to Rafe, then Ciara, and over to Bastion, Rourke gave him a pleading look.

"Would you mind terribly?"

Bastion couldn't help it, he goaded him. "What's the magic word?"

Rourke's brows lifted then narrowed. "All of you can suck it for all I care." He began kicking at the bag as he walked.

Laughing, Bastion chased after him, grabbing up the bag before his next kick.

"Don't do me any favors. I wouldn't want you to break your neck."

Arriving at the porch they found the doors were not only closed, but locked. "He's a bloody child, that one is; and with her out here in my arms and everything. I'd wager he didn't think this one through. Small wonder where Drinian gets it from."

"It's no big deal." Bastion pulled the lock pick kit from his back pocket. "I saw this one coming."

"So, you've known all this time it would play out this way, did you?"

Managing to pick the lock on the door, Bastion pushed it open so his brother could carry her inside. "Only this moment at Rafe's front door. I had a brief vision of it on my way here the first time. I figured

357

karma was bound to bite me in the butt after having locked Chase out of my own home not long ago, so I've made it a point to be prepared."

"Hm, indeed."

The same moment they entered; they could see Rafe was barreling back to the foyer from down the hall that led past the kitchen. He stopped suddenly at the sight of them standing in his entryway with the doors wide open and gawked.

"Told you, Bastion. Didn't think it through, did you, Rafe? What a git. Locked her out too and everything."

"Most men don't think."

The small voice had come from the woman in Rourke's arms, and yet she hadn't moved. The foyer went silent, but for the footsteps of other household occupants padding their way.

Rourke scowled. "How long have you been awake?"

Covering her smirking mouth, Ciara yawned sleepily and attempted to stretch in his arms. "Since we landed."

"You've been awake this whole time?" Rourke thundered irritably, "Then why am I carrying you?"

"Who am I to say no to a free ride?"

His mouth dropped and so did she. Out of spite he let her go.

She gasped and gave a startled cry as she fell. "So much for not hurting me," she grumbled. Rolling onto her hands and knees she moved to lift up and rub at her backside when she caught sight of the two women who stepped in the entryway from the living room. "Ooaahh! Such beautiful hair," she exclaimed, startling everyone. Waddling over to the women while still on her knees, she reached up reverently within a hair's breadth of touching Meg and Angel's long locks.

"Distracts easily, doesn't she?" Bastion smiled.

"Is she mad crazy?" Angel asked aloud.

Meg giggled, then her mouth drooped sadly. "She just misses her own hair. It used to be down to your waist and strawberry blonde before everything with the ex, didn't it, Ciara?" A sudden influx of emotion hit her, rendering her speechless. Unable to control herself, and much to everyone's surprise, a loud sob escaped Meg's lips and tears welled in her eyes. Her head was spinning, envisioning the day Ciara dyed and chopped her hair all over again. Now she understood. She wondered when they picked up Karisma, why she hadn't looked like the woman in the portrait and her prophetic dreams. Now she knew why. The last few dreams, the ones with the accident had been of Karisma, but in the rest of them, she'd been seeing Ciara. The whole time she'd been dreaming and having visions of two women, not just one.

Meg's face wrenched, and she began to cry, unable to control it or hold it in any longer. She peered down in horror at Ciara who was idly playing with swatches of both Angel's and her hair together for she couldn't get herself under control. The pain in her heart wrenched deeply.

Next to her, Angel bent down a little, giving the woman a quizzical look as she absently braided the black and silver-white hair together while mumbling incoherently. Ciara was completely disregarding the reaction Meg was having.

"Your heart hurts awful bad, doesn't it, Ciara? You didn't even know why you were getting all worked up these past few months, did you? Poor thing. Knew something worse was coming, but had no clue. No worries though, you're safe now and you'll understand soon." Wrapping her in a hug, Angel gave her a motherly kiss on the head then rubbed Meg's shoulders in the hopes of easing the emotional pain she was experiencing from their new guest.

"No worries gentlemen, we've got her from here." Angel gave Rourke and Rafe meaningful looks.

The three men in the entrance continued to hover. "I'm not sure you understand," Rafe said.

"Yes, I do. More so than most of you. Now go. She doesn't dare be around any of you Blackthorne's right now."

"We need to talk to her," Rourke said. "She doesn't know anything."

"Of course she doesn't. Everything's happening ten years sooner." Angel gave Meg an apologetic look. "I'm so sorry, I should have prepared you for her emotional state when she arrived. It never occurred to me."

Ciara stopped braiding Meg and Angel's hair together and wandered the entryway, gazing in wonder at the chandelier above her. Each time she stopped, her hand would go to her chest and flex there as her face became increasingly drawn and blank, her eyes not entirely focusing on any given point. Every time that happened, Meg would receive a new onslaught of emotion.

"In my defense everything has changed, so I'm trying to catch up like the rest of you," Angel said to Meg. "You should go, stay away from her for a while until she's able to shield it off again."

Understanding finally dawned in Rourke and Rafe's eyes.

"She's a..."

"Bloody shield. Of course."

Confused, Bastion took both men by the shoulders and guided them toward the kitchen. "How about you two explain to me what a shield is, while we get something to eat and drink?"

Ciara spun about, stopped suddenly, and pointed at the men accusingly as they disappeared. The expression on her face was openly hostile.

"They ate my eggrolls!"

- - -

For the next three days out of time, which was equivalent to about nine days within time, the three men explained to Ciara what was going on. They did it in small doses periodically during the day, trying hard not to overwhelm her with too much information. Sensing what they were doing and that they were keeping things from her, she put a pause on what they were telling her on the fourth day, insisting on clarification of a few things.

"Let me get this straight. The three of you came after me, because of this series of books written by Angel the Elf. A collection which was ghost-written for her by Karisma the snark lady, because the people within, you all and, well, I guess even me, are real. Have I got that right so far?"

"Yes, for the most part. Though I'd appreciate it if you'd stop using those nicknames."

"Ciara, please."

"Oh, fine!"

Lifting one of the books from the pile of paperbacks they brought out and set on the kitchen table for her to see as proof of what they were saying, she read the back description. Setting it aside she grabbed another, then another, continuing to read each one until she got to book six. Starting on the back cover, she read the excerpt of the last book. Her eyes widened at seeing her name in print, but then she frowned. The whole time she'd been reading she mumbled incoherently.

Because she was a shield, Rafe was unable to discern what was going on in her mind, nor could he understand what she was saying. Reaching out, he lay his hand over the book when she opened it as though getting ready to read.

"What is it?"

"What?"

"You're mumbling."

"Oh, sorry." She sighed, creases appearing between her eyebrows. She looked confused. "Something about the stories seems familiar to me for some reason. It's like I've read them before."

He pointed at the book in her hands. "According to this one, you would eventually have written a version of the stories as well, because you're gifted. That might be why they seem familiar."

She tilted her head at him. "It's funny you should say that. About a week ago I got the idea to write a story about a writer who was writing about real people. I made an outline and everything, but that's not what I mean. I feel like I've actually read a series of books something similar to these before. Wild huh?" As she said it, she experienced a weird sense of déjà vu. In her mind, she could see her hands opening a book to a marked page. The moment the image came to her it was gone. But she distinctly recalled seeing something about a Thorne on the page.

Shrugging it off, she skimmed the first few pages of the novel. It wasn't the first time over the years she'd gotten images in her head. Suddenly, she shoved her face into the book. "I supposedly marry again? Fat chance of that!" She snorted loudly. Her voice was saying one thing, but Rourke could see both pain and a look of longing in her eyes.

"Wait, this says here I'm going to have three kids. Twin boys and a girl."

Rourke took a deep breath, exchanged looks with Rafe, then dove in headfirst. "It was one possible future."

"You said 'was.' That's very telling. Why is it, 'was,' pray tell?"

Rafe re-iterated about what happened so far; the discovery of Karisma's stories, finding out about the accident that killed her kids, realizing she was in danger, and how they'd gone to get Karisma to bring her to safety within the grounds of the Blackthorne ranch as they had done for her.

"So, she was, what? Having visions of what could happen in the future?"

"Sort of. As I said, Karisma ghostwrote them; Angel was the one who actually wrote them. Her gift is a bit messed up for some reason compared to Angels. We believe it's because of the accident she was in before she turned thirteen."

Ciara remembered they told her Karisma lost her husband and children recently, and that the kids weren't supposed to have died before. She couldn't even imagine being in that position. Losing a child at any age must be horrible. She momentarily pulled her hand away from the books as though uneasy. Could there be truth to it all? There must be some anyway, otherwise, how could Angel have known about her and her ex. As far as she was concerned, it was all the more reason to call her an elf.

"It would appear that way."

Ciara stared at the novels stacked at her feet. Her eyes were blinking rapidly, as though she were attempting to process and file the information away in a neat order within her mind.

"Let's say I believe you, though I'm still a bit skeptical even after seeing all this and meeting everyone. What happened to change the course of events, that were meant to come?"

Bastion sat down in a spare chair next to them while cradling a large coffee mug in his hand.

"At the same time Rafe learned about Karisma and was going after her, I was being informed by good ol' Vortigern Black himself that I had grandchildren I didn't know I had. They were in danger of being caught by the very men who tried to take off with you a few days ago."

"Who's Vortigern Black again?"

"Ah, sorry. He's the narrator of those stories and also his son-in-law. Chase Ryans; he's a private investigator," Rourke offered up while pointing to Bastion.

"Huh?" It was all very confusing and there were too many names to keep up with. "You mean the bald black guy who keeps wandering around here with a Scotch bottle in his hand? You're saying he's this Vortigern Black and Chase Ryans, PI all rolled into one?"

"Yes, that's the gist of it. Is it really necessary to be so rude, Ciara?" Rafe asked.

"What? The whole color thing? Geez, Rafe, is he a bald black man?" She flung her arms palms up onto the table.

"Well, yes." Flustered, Rafe's face became pinched as he turned red.

"Tell me, how is it rude to call a bald black man what he is? You're a black-haired white man. Now did I offend you? No. Cause you're a black-haired white man. Or, I guess, you're really more tanned I suppose."

"We're getting off subject again here." Rafe couldn't figure the woman out. Her personality was maddening. Sometimes she was really quite amiable to talk to and be around, like Angel. Other days she was all over the place and talking like Karisma. It was like she was a mix of the two women, only for some reason she kept sounding like she was trying to talk with Rourke's Scottish accent.

Chuckling Rourke thumped the table lightly to get her attention. "He's not wrong, Ciara, now listen up."

She saluted him awkwardly, then giggled. "Yes, Sir."

Rourke smiled openly. They kept getting off subject, because she kept putting Rafe in his place every time he opened his mouth. It was most amusing to him. Picking up the fifth volume he shook it in the air.

"About two and a half to three months ago. Angel Stryfe, from this book, showed up in Loveland, Colorado looking for Chase. Her husband Wilton disappeared on her and had been gone for three days. She'd written all these stories and suspected the people within them were real, so she looked Chase up, because he's a private investigator, among other things. I gather she was hoping he might be able to shed some light on why Wilton disappeared on her now, when he wasn't supposed to die for another ten years."

"That's got to be horrible," Ciara said sadly, her face paling. "Imagine knowing when someone you love is going to die like that."

"In some ways, I'm sure she was disappointed by the knowledge, but I get the feeling his absence now isn't a huge loss," Bastion said.

"Ah, he must have been as bad as my ex."

"Possibly. Regardless, she felt she needed answers and in general, knew she needed help, so she left the stories with Chase. He read through them, discovered a few of my secrets and approached me with a proposition of sorts. I declined in, shall we say, an aggressive fashion, so he got mad and hired someone to fix them up. It turns out Karisma happens to be a part of this story as well." Bastion pointed at the sixth volume she still held in her hand.

Ciara's frown deepened.

"Angel's stories were written at an elementary level." Bastion went on to explain. "He had Karisma, who's a ghostwriter, update and prepare them for publishing in the hopes I'd take him more seriously when he approached me with them and his proposal once again. Unfortunately, she jumped the gun and self-published them for him without his consent, which was something he'd never intended to do. That's when he came to me and told me what happened and about my grandchildren. As Also that same day, the novels in paperback form arrived at my door from him." Bastion deferred his head toward Rourke.

"You were aware of the books?"

"Yes. Around three months ago my father, late grandfather, and I had all been having visions of the same auto accident. It never deviated until the day Alestair, our grandfather, died which meant something happened to change the course of events. That same day our father discovered Bastion here was still alive for he pulled a woman from the car wreck in the vision." Rourke pushed his glasses back up on the bridge of his nose. With the same finger, he indicated his brother with the goatee and giant coffee mug.

"You were supposed to be dead?"

Bastion snorted uncomfortably, "Long story short, my father tried to drown me as a child and thought he succeeded, because my mother never told him she'd managed to revive me. She sent me to live with, and be adopted by, the RavenCroft's near Loveland, Colorado where I still reside. Hence, my current name."

"Why in the world did your father try to kill you?" This cockamamie story of theirs was getting increasingly complicated and messed up. What kind of parent did that to their own son?

All three men exchanged looks. Rourke responded slowly. "That is, as yet, unclear to us. The point is, after discovering he was alive, I began searching for him after our father's heart attack. I came across the books, and upon reviewing them sent copies on to Bastion when I learned of his location. It seemed prudent to me, he should be made aware of what was going on in them. I suspected at the time something this Vortigern Black character in the stories had done, changed the course of events."

"I see."

"Now, I believe otherwise," Rourke said.

"Wilton?" Bastion offered as the reason.

"Yes."

"Sorry, there's so much here. Wilton is who again?" Ciara asked, randomly picking up and discarding another book.

"The husband of Angel," Bastion said.

"The one that disappeared. Got it." Ciara said, starting to finally follow things a bit. "I still don't get why his disappearance would have affected everyone though."

"I believe it has to do with him having been my late wife's old partner, Flynn Hunter," Bastion said, taking a sip of his coffee.

"Wait a minute, did you say Hunter?" Rafe asked, finally making the connection as he recalled what Agent Ricardo Pegueros told him. "That's the name of the mercenary Jericho Henley hired to take out Karisma's husband and bring her and her children in, but Hunter messed up and her kids died too. According to my guy, Henley shot and killed him for it."

"So, Wilton Stryfe is dead and all of this started, because of a poor decision he made?" Bastion ran his hands through his hair in aggravation. How was he going to tell Angel this, and was Karisma aware yet that Wilton was the reason why her kids died?

"Hm. I'm betting the man was never originally supposed to take the job," Rourke said thoughtfully. "We'll likely never know why he did. That one choice affected everything, creating a chaos effect."

"I'm glad whatever it is you didn't realize before has now been brought to light, but I'm still confused over here." Her whole face screwed up into a comical sort of perplexed state.

"What is it we've managed to confuse you with?" Rafe knew they'd thrown a lot at her in the past several days. So far, she seemed to be taking things pretty well, but because of her tendency to distract easily, she'd get things turned around.

"From the looks of it, the first four books of this series are about yours and Bastion's kids and their, for the lack of a better way of putting it, love stories? All because of a prophecy your late wife made." An eyebrow rose at this as though disbelieving anyone was capable of such a thing. "A prophecy is somehow supposed to save

Kalab and, help me out here, there are way too many names."

"Drinian."

"Right, Drinian. It'll save them from being tortured by the shadows, or demons as you called them Rafe. I'm still trying to wrap my mind around that little revelation, by the way." Her gaze shifted suspiciously to Rourke, wondering at whether he would gain some peace by the fulfillment of the prophecy as well. He'd told her the day before he could see them as well, only from what she could tell, he appeared to handle it a bit better than Kalab and Drinian. She wondered why that was.

Rafe nodded. The concept of shadowy demons being real was always hard to accept by everyone. No one ever wanted to believe they could be real.

"The last two books start out like they are about each of your third sons, but then you find out they're your romances, not theirs. Have I got that right?" Ciara smirked, thinking it was a funny turn to the stories. She liked the way Angel wrote.

"Essentially. Though, that one does cover Dartanian's a bit. Or rather, it gets ironed out in the end." Rafe turned to his brother. "I take it yours doesn't though, Bastion, for your third son?"

"No, but then he hasn't met this Stephanie lady yet."

"From what I gathered, that's a good thing," Rourke said.

"Regardless, if I'm to believe all of this, what you're saying is there's more than one thing going on here. Both sets of triplets are having to meet their lady friends earlier or to fulfill this prophecy of Lilyandhi's, because Wilton chose to what? Accept a job he originally never took? While all that's going on, there is an organization of people who are avidly searching for gifted people like you on a regular basis, and that's why they came after me."

"That's correct."

She gave him a disbelieving look. "For the moment I'm gonna ignore the fact you all think I'm supposedly gifted somehow. Even if it were true, how would they discover I have these abilities when I didn't even know I was? And for what purpose are they wanting these people?"

"Been reading any good books lately?" Bastion asked knowingly, disregarding her last question for the moment.

Her mind instantly went to the last series she read. It was about people with special abilities. "I've been reading a lot of David Pearson's novels lately."

"My late wife wrote those. That's how they find people," Bastion said.

"They track the sales of these," Rafe explained while tapping his pencil on the table. "They add you to a watch list the more you purchase of them. Then they investigate you. How many have you read?"

"All of them. I just finished the last one. Wait a minute, your wife is the author, David Pearson? Boy, that's a bit disappointing. I pictured someone a bit different." She began mumbling incoherently about tall men with broad shoulders.

The three men exchanged looks, all thinking the same thing. Henley was bound to be in a fit of rage for losing her. They learned from both Karisma and Angel that they only read about half of them. If she read them all, it meant she had the potential of being highly gifted.

"So, I supposedly have an ability, because I've read these books?"

"No, a person is gifted, because they're naturally predisposed to it." Rourke suspected the woman seated next to him had more than one ability from what he read and saw so far.

"Huh, okaaay." She inhaled then exhaled quickly, all the while her eyes were the size of saucers, her mind suddenly switched gears on her as she stared at the book covers for volumes five and six. "Let me get this straight, according to book five, Angel is meant to wind up with you Bastion. This Ciara character from the last book though." Hesitant, her eyes shifted with anxious suspicion between Rafe and Rourke. What they were telling her sounded absolutely insane, yet for some reason she found herself believing them.

"Yes?" Rafe prompted. He had the look of a man who was completely unfazed by the fact they were discussing a future marriage between the two of them, when they didn't even know each other. She didn't like the idea of her life being predetermined by anyone.

A bit anxious, she heaved an exasperated sigh and dropped the sixth book on the table. "I guess, I don't understand where Karisma fits in. Who is she? What's she doing at your house, Rafe, waiting to be relocated somewhere safe? And if you're meant to be with the, uh, Ciara of the book, then why did Rourke come and get her? Me. Oh, this is too insane." Her eyes shifted with renewed suspicion to the man with the glasses whose face had become stubbly over the last three days. He was trying to grow back the beard and mustache he shaved off when he came to get her. It was odd, but she had no problems imagining him with a beard for some reason.

Looking uncomfortable, Bastion got up from his chair. "I'm gonna eavesdrop from over there."

Bastion and Rourke exchanged looks once again. There was a mysterious half-smile playing at Rourke's lips.

"I guess it's because Karisma is Inara." Rafe appeared confused. "Which explains why she doesn't look like the woman in the portrait," he said carefully while scratching at his head. He knew he should have been the one to pick her up, but Rourke had been absolutely insistent on the matter.

"That didn't really answer my question, and what portrait are you on about? How could Karisma be Inara? Isn't Inara supposed to be Ciara in the story? You said, and I quote, volume six starts with Ciara Biardon and ends with her becoming Inara. There's no mention of a Karisma in the stories."

Rourke tried to explain. "Rafe painted a full-length portrait of a woman many years ago. It's a painting of you, with Karisma in the background."

"Karisma is not in the background," Rafe said.

"Oh, but she is." Pulling his cell phone out, he laid it on the table, so they could all see the picture he took of the portrait. Shocked to see herself in a painting with the strawberry blonde hair she used to have, before she left her ex and dyed it black, Ciara gasped. Rourke enlarged the picture, so they could each distinctly see an image of a woman far in the background among some trees."

"My word, she is in the portrait. How could I have missed seeing that?" Rafe asked in dismay. "Or recall I painted her in there, for that matter."

"I still don't see how she's Inara if her name is Karisma," Ciara said absently.

This time Rafe explained. "Karisma was adopted. When she was born, the name she was given was Inara Kingsley."

"Ah," she said as though finally understanding, then suddenly she looked confused again. "Huh, no, still don't get it."

"Why? What's so confusing?"

She huffed as though the reason for her bewilderment should be obvious. "It seems to me like there are too many names, is all. Too many women, get me? I mean, it's not like you can end up with two women there, Rafe. That would be bigamy. Been there - albeit unknowingly - and done that, not doing it again. There's an Inara, Ciara, and now there is a Karisma? Think about it. Why give the same woman in a story two different names, when in real life there are two women with those names?"

"It almost feels like the same thing is happening all over again here in real life, cause this Inara is being called Karisma. I just wonder why. That's all. Three names, three ladies? Makes a body wonder." Ciara's voice trailed off as she pulled out books five and six from the pile. Absently laying the fifth book next to the sixth book, she found herself covering the first word of book five and the last word of book six as she yawned.

"Karisma Kayos," she read aloud not seeing the looks of the three men were shooting toward each other. "See now, if it were me, I'd make that a character, you know?" she sighed heavily, leaning forward in her seat to pick up the other four books. Shifting them around on her lap, she periodically covered words here and there as she yawned again suddenly feeling tired and sensing she was experiencing another bout of déjà vu.

"Deadly Karisma Kayos, Karisma Kayos Knows, Total Karisma Kayos... Look at that, it's almost like an anagram of words." She laughed, thinking the titles were awfully clever; completely oblivious to the fact Bastion had returned from his table near the patio door and was staring down at his brothers. She glanced up and wondered briefly why they were just staring at each other as though in silent conversation. It occurred to her, after glancing back and forth between the men and the books, that they might well be.

The women in the stories were writing stories about people they weren't supposed to know, and yet somehow did, who were all gifted in some way. One book had a telepath, another talked of visions of future events, and all three of the men were talking about how Angel seemed to know things.

Ciara's head was spinning. Licking her lips, she realized she was thirsty. Taking a few sips of the fruit smoothie she'd been given earlier, she set it down and leaned back only to realize she couldn't rest her head on thin air. It occurred to her for the tenth time in the past couple days that a sane person probably wouldn't do what she was doing. Living amicably within a vast house among three men who had kidnapped her three days prior.

Or saved her?

Hhmm. She was still debating on that part.

But she already established she was crazy, and she'd become so very tired after messing with the books. It was as if something suddenly drained her of all energy.

Regardless of whether what they were saying was true or not she couldn't help but feel excited about being in Montana once again. She'd always wanted to come back here after her first trip nearly ten years before. Now she was finally here.

Peering out the patio door, she noticed the birds were all over the lawn again. Her eyes narrowed irritably, wishing they weren't out there obscuring her view of the lush grass and taking away from the mountain view. Why did there have to be so many ravens? Curiously among them, she noticed a dove. It lifted up from the ground and flew over to the porch, dropping something near the sliding glass door. Taking flight once again, it seemed to hover briefly, then flew away.

Her curiosity getting the better of her, Ciara got up from her chair and padded toward the door in her sock-clad feet. As the men watched her in varying perplexed states, she opened the door and peered down at her feet. Bending down she picked up the pale blue crayon and held it in her hand. A faint memory filtered into the back of her mind causing her to gasp in surprise. She recalled a poem book she wrote as a child about a horse named redemption and a rider, as well as a crayon drawing of a two-sided portrait. The pale blue crayon was the same color she used for the eyes.

"What do you have there, Ciara?" Rafe called across the kitchen.

Whirling about Ciara's face suffused with color as she tucked her hand with the crayon behind her back. Her face went slack. In a daze, she shifted her head a bit as though in denial over something. Quickly glancing between Rafe and Rourke, she suddenly raced from the room.

Chapter 18

Three days later

Blackthorne Horse Ranch
Kalispell, Montana

"Karisma, I need you to wake up. I need you to tell me your name."

Groggy and irritated at being awakened, Karisma rolled over, sat up and rubbed at her eyes while yawning. Sunlight spilled in from the open window drapes in the library where she was attempting to nap. Her face fell. He always opened them when he expected her to get up.

"What are you on about, Rafe? Can't whatever it is wait a few hours?"

Taking her chin gently in one hand, he tilted her head up, so he could see her face as they talked.

"Your given name at birth was Inara Kingsley, but your parents re-named you Karisma Kayos, like in the title of the books. Is that right?"

"Mmm, yup. The name wound up being an ironic sort of tongue in cheek joke, if you think about it. You know, cause of the lack of filter thing I have going on. It may not be spelled like the word charisma, but it's pronounced the same." She eyed him through heavily lidded lashes. Flinging her arms wide in exasperation, she moaned miserably. "Is this really what you woke me for? More questions? I'm tired, Rafe, let me sleep." She fell back into the comfort of the pull-out bed, with the royal plush mattress topper on it. She snuggled into her pillow while attempting to burrow under her blankets. All she wanted was to fall into nothingness.

Rafe sat down next to her, his weight causing her to shift where she lay. He tried first to gently shake her a bit to gain her attention and keep her awake. "I know all you want to do is sleep right now. I promise, if I'm able, I won't disturb you for long."

She groaned into her pillow and waved him away with one hand.

Patience waning, but knowing he needed to tread carefully, he gently nudged her again.

"I'm sorry, Karisma, but we need to talk to you. It truly is important." Rafe hated to disturb her, but he and his brothers had been trying for the past week to get Angel, Karisma, and Ciara all together in the same room for once. They needed to gain answers to some of their questions and hash out a theory they had. All the women had developed odd sleeping schedules for different reasons, so at any given time at least one of them was asleep when the other two were awake.

"Fine!" Flustered and angry, Karisma threw her blanket off and sat up. Becoming a bit dizzy at first for getting up too quickly, she blinked while stretching her arms out on either side of her for balance. She focused on the bookshelves in front of her that extended all along the wall and around the room.

"If you've been sleeping the whole time I've been down at the corrals, then why are you so tired?" He assisted in steadying her and she fell into him. Rafe automatically wrapped his arms about her waist, a habit he'd been getting into whenever they were alone recently. She peered beseechingly up at him through heavily lidded eyes.

"I haven't been sleeping well, because there are too many people in this house now, Rafe, and they wouldn't leave me alone." Her head turned to the clock on the mantle, and she whimpered. "I've only been down for barely an hour." She leaned heavily against his chest.

He couldn't help, but chuckle. "Who wouldn't leave you alone?"

"Bastion's brats," she pouted. For a brief moment, her mannerism was reminiscent of a child's. It quickly disappeared and was replaced with a very tired angry woman. "Specifically Kahner, but Mackenzie was at it too. They kept badgering me for answers today for Kalturek about his 'woman' from his story." She air quoted giving him more reason to chuckle. "At least Chase was kind enough to disappear into your front study with a bottle of your Scotch again today."

Rafe growled deep in his throat at the news. The man had been going through his Scotch like it was water. He'd have to have a talk with him about it.

"But after Mackenzie and Kahner skyped with Kalturek this morning after breakfast, from then on they wouldn't leave me alone."

"What do they want to know?"

She summarized the extent of it, telling him how Kalab had managed to catch the stalker who had been after, Ariana, the woman from his own story, since she was a preteen. Between him and Kalturek, they convinced her to leave Dalton, Massachusetts and come home with them for a change of scenery. Apparently, the happy couple had been getting along great and, because of the success with the two of them, Kalturek wanted to know about his lady."

"According to what I've read, he's better off without her," Rafe said.

"Kalturek's not looking for Stephanie. He wants to know if there's someone else. Who it might be, and all kinds of other questions I have no answer or clue of. I don't know why he doesn't just let it happen naturally as Drayke did. Either way, I kept telling them they needed to talk to Angel, because the bits and pieces of what I know always come to me in a mess of a puzzle. I could steer them wrong."

"I take it they didn't listen?"

She shrugged. "I guess they tried, but every time they did she ran away from them. Angel's very cagey with people. The RavenCroft's especially, except for Bastion of course." Tickled by a thought, Karisma laughed, the sound ending with an unladylike snort. She covered her mouth in embarrassment. "It might have something to do with the stories she wrote and how they would have gone. One of them tries to seduce her and another attempts to drug her with tea. No wait, the one who drugged her is that chic of Kalturek's, not Mackenzie."

"Focus please." Rafe smiled affectionately, noting how pretty she was, even in her tired and rumpled state. "I know you're not going to want to, but I need you downstairs."

She gave him a suspicious look. "Why?"

Explaining the dilemma of needing to question all three together, he asked again if she would come down and talk with everyone awhile. Grudgingly agreeing after forcing a promise to let her sleep undisturbed afterward, they walked out of the library and down the hall.

"When did you learn you were adopted?" Rafe asked as they reached the landing.

"I was nine, going on ten. My original adoptive parents sat me down after church one day and told me the truth as they knew it." At his questioning glance, she continued. "According to them, I was either lost, abandoned, or wandered from my real parents at the age of four somewhere here in Montana. A man found me and turned me in to social services when he was unable to locate them with the aid of local police. Being only four years old at the time all I was able to tell anyone was that my name was Inara Kingsley. I was eventually adopted, and they moved me shortly after to Indiana, Pennsylvania for work, before getting killed in the accident nine years later."

"No one knows who your real parents are?"

Karisma shook her head, staying unusually quiet on the subject.

"Your first adoptive parents, they're the ones who gave you the name Karisma?"

"No. I went by Inara Kingsley up until the accident that killed my parents. Dan and Janet Miller renamed me at my request."

"Why?"

"Ah, see, I was never an easy child, but I became frightfully more challenging after the accident. I didn't feel like myself anymore. It was as though something was missing, or a part of me died. I don't know how else to explain it without sounding any weirder than it already does. Dan and Janet were the foster parents who took me in after the accident. When they asked about adopting me, I told them I would agree as long as I could choose a new name. One that fit."

Rafe laughed, "So you chose the name Karisma?" he asked as they reached the bottom of the stairs and stepped into the living room. Rourke and Ciara were already seated in separate chairs across from each other near the fireplace. It appeared as though they had interrupted a pleasant conversation when they entered.

Rafe sat down on the couch that butted up next to Ciara's chair which seemed to annoy Rourke, and Karisma followed suit by plopping down at the other end. She yawned loudly, scooted halfway down the couch, and rested her head against the cushion after throwing her feet on Rafe's lap, deliberately trying to irritate him.

She succeeded.

"Is that true, you chose the name Karisma when you were thirteen?" Ciara asked curiously, having overheard. The more she'd talked with Rourke while they were waiting for Rafe and Bastion to bring the other two women, the more perplexed she was by the one who laid down next to Rafe.

"Yup, I did. My father, Dan always used to say I was a bundle of chaos, I had no charisma, I was out of balance, and that I needed to fix it. Since I was such a paradox, I figured I should have a name to suit. My last name would change to K-a-y-o-s once I was officially adopted, which of course sounds like the word chaos. So, I chose Charisma and had them spell it with a K," she explained as Bastion entered the living room with Angel. Lifting her head up, she gazed at Angel's waist-length hair longingly, wishing she still had hers. While playing with a lock of her shorter black hair, out of the corner of her eye, she caught Rourke watching her closely and became self-conscious. She flushed and dropped the bit of hair. "Your hair is beautiful, Angel, it reminds me of my own, before I cut and chopped it."

Angel brightened at Karisma's compliment. "Oh thank you!" She stepped up on the couch on the opposite side of the room from Rafe and Karisma, turned around to face everyone, and playfully dropped with a giggle down into the cushion, sitting Indian style. Patting the empty space beside her hopefully, Bastion smiled and took the spot next to her. She was getting a rare moment when her son wasn't attached to her hip, since he was napping, and she planned to take advantage of it fully by spending time with Bastion.

Rourke leaned sideways in his chair. "If I may clarify Angel, did you title the novels you wrote or was that Karisma?"

"I didn't give them those titles. I had them listed as volumes one, two, three, etcetera, etcetera. If you ask me it's much easier to keep track of the order that way."

Everyone turned and looked at Karisma.

She blinked sleepily. "What?"

"They're wanting to know why you chose the book titles you did," Rafe said next to her. "Why did you put a part of your name, Karisma or Kayos in every one?"

Karisma was silent for a bit, scratching at her neck as she yawned again loudly. "I don't know. There was an Angel, Ciara, and an Inara in the stories. Though Ciara and Inara were supposedly the same person in book six, which of course they aren't. That part never seemed accurate to me, so I guess in my head, it always felt like someone was missing. A sort of omniscient outside source who was really telling the story," she said with a smile before noticing they all were staring at her blankly. Knowing they wouldn't understand, she exhaled sadly unable to explain what she meant.

"I don't know, maybe I was trying to be funny? Or maybe subconsciously I knew it wasn't Vortigern Black's story at all." Karisma imagined she looked as guilty as she felt for having edited and published Angel's stories without really having her permission. "By the way Angel, I am sorry about putting your stories out there. That wasn't my place. Nor was it our disreputable Vortigern Black's place either."

"It's okay. They looked wonderful the way you did them. All professional like." Angel giggled, smiling happily. "It makes me feel like a real author."

"You said, it felt like someone was missing?" Bastion asked, trying to keep the women on subject. "And how did you come by the spelling for your name? It's unusual."

"What part of, I don't know, do you not get?" Agitated Karisma rolled onto her back and stared at the ceiling with her hands tucked behind her head for support. She exhaled heavily. "And spelling it with a K just looked right. The other way didn't, as though it wasn't meant to be that way."

The three men exchanged looks, something they seemed to do a lot when they were talking to each other without speaking aloud.

Rafe was the first to speak after a curt nod from Rourke. "We think it might be prudent for you to return to your given name, Inara Kingsley."

Karisma's eyes drooped sleepily. Blinking several times to stay awake, she turned her head toward Rafe. "I guess it wouldn't bother me to return to Inara, in a way it would be a relief, but can I ask why the change?

"Because we think there is a woman out there by the name of Karisma," Rourke said in answer.

Wide awake now, Karisma sat up. She looked back and forth between the two women in the room, gauging their reaction to the news. She suspected she had the same look of wonder on her face as they had on theirs.

"You know what? I think you might be onto something there."

"Do you know who this Karisma is then?" Rourke asked.

"Heck if I know. What makes you think I know that?" She could see his lips compress and his jaw tighten; clear signs he'd become irritated with her. That was typical.

"Do you know anything, Angel? About a woman with that name," Bastion asked quickly, hoping to curtail further friction.

Angel shook her head. "I never had any Karisma in my books. The stories always came to me as though someone were telling them."

"That would probably be the woman who is meant for your brother," Chase interrupted, loudly banging his way through the door from the kitchen. Behind him in the doorway, his wife Mackenzie mouthed an apology for his intrusion as her eyes threw daggers at his back.

The three brothers looked at each other and then at the three women seated with them.

"Still haven't figured it out, have you?" Chase glowered at Bastion, his contempt and animosity with the man in no way were being hidden. He held a half-empty bottle of Scotch in his hand as he joined them. Sitting in an oversized chair at the back of the living room near the entryway, he announced, "Sapphire wasn't the only one who hid a child."

"What are you talking about? Where are you getting this information from?" Bastion asked.

Chase leaned back against the cushion and kicked one bent leg up, propping it on his other while still holding the bottle by its neck in his left hand. "The seventh novel; the one Inara wrote from Angel's notes. I have it, and I've read it in full. You really should have let me finish explaining everything before you proceeded to beat the crap out of me, Bastion. I could have saved you all some trouble over this past week. Poor Angel there, in particular. That novel is how I knew I needed to come with Kahner to the Blackthorne ranch, and how I knew I'd need to be in here right now." He indicated the living room with a circular motion of his hand. "Oh, and by the way, ST is the one who took off with your bag with the laptop and flash drives Rourke. I don't think he took kindly to your snobbery when you first arrived."

"That little thief." Rourke fumed.

"A seventh volume I wrote?" Karisma pressed a hand to her chest anxiously. She didn't care about the whole ST thing. She figured out he took the bag days ago. What bothered her was not being able to remember having written the volume he spoke of.

Chase tilted his head at her curiously. "Do you even remember what you wrote?" He knew the truth of where the story came from, but was aware she couldn't remember.

"I really don't. Honestly, I'm drawing a blank on the whole week before I sent it to you. You're sure I wrote it?"

"Hhhmm, yes, the seventh volume has most certainly come to us by way of you." Out of the corner of his eye, Chase could see both Angel and Rourke had given him a curious look. Blast it all, he'd nearly blown it. "Er, you stated as such when you messaged me through Facebook." He played with the cover on the arm of his chair with his right hand, gloating internally at, for once, knowing something that the 'all-knowing' RavenCroft's didn't; that Bastion, in particular, didn't.

"How can you be so sure?" Rourke wanted to know. He had a sneaky suspicion he already knew how.

"Because, what she wrote, we are currently living through right now, this very minute, as we speak." He could tell Bastion didn't believe him.

"You joke."

"I don't. In fact, this very conversation we are having right now is in the manuscript on the flash drive I have."

Met with silence, one eyebrow quirked in amusement then he frowned. "I promise to leave it for you to peruse on your own when I'm done here. I won't tell you beyond what I'm supposed to right now, because I do not want anything more to change that shouldn't.

The thing is, this is actually the end of this story; of all your stories, Blackthorne and RavenCroft alike. What needs to transpire in order to affect the outcome of the prophecy of Rafe's late wife has, for the most part, come to pass already. Those who need to meet, have met each other, except one, but I anticipate that'll be happening soon."

"No, there's two," Bastion argued. "You're forgetting Drayke."

"Haven't been keeping up on family matters have you Bastion? Drayke met Laynie yesterday at the opening of her Pizza Emporium restaurant." Chase took a drink of his Scotch, catching Rafe's cross look. "Oh, no worries I went out and bought some of my own. I'm finding I really like Scotch. Plan to keep drinking it regardless of getting cut off by you."

Thumping his cane on the floor to gain their attention, Rourke insisted they stay on topic, wanting clarification of what had been said. "You mean, for their children to have met the people they're destined to spend their lives with." He indicated both of his brothers with the cane. "And eventually have the children they're meant to have which will complete out her second prophecy. There were two if you recall. One with a bunch of numbers and symbols which indicated those births, the other a poem."

"I know." Chase made a face that was indiscernible and laughed at his own internal joke. "And you're sort of right, but not quite." He took a drink of his Scotch then looked to his right toward the kitchen door to see if his wife was still standing there. As expected she already left. Expelling the breath he held, he finally continued.

Clearing his throat he began. "Angel, you gave Bastion, Rafe and Alestair a sixth child they don't have. Do you know why?"

Cringing in her seat for having been put on the spot, Angel bit at her lip nervously and nodded.

Already knowing the answer to his next question, for Chase read he asked it of her in the finale, he asked it quietly anyway. "Would you rather I tell them for you?"

She nodded silently again.

"All right then. Rourke, before you all left to get Ciara, you asked Bastion, Rafe, your father, and Misham, the man who took in your Sarah, all the same questions. You wanted to know how many children, alive or dead, their wives had given birth to. Is that right?"

"Yes, I did."

"Alive, or dead?" Ciara asked, unsure she'd heard him right.

"Yes," Rourke said.

Pleased to hear the responses were going as anticipated so far, Chase continued. "What were their answers?"

"Rathbourne, our father, said there were three; me, Rafe, and Bastion. Misham said Sarah gave birth to twin girls and the boy, Edwin. Rafe said..."

"There were four," Rafe answered for Rourke, shocking everyone but Ciara.

"Aha! Of course," Ciara cried suddenly as clarity came to her out of the blue. She didn't know how, but somehow she knew where Chase was going with his line of questioning. Noticing everyone was staring at her though, she became embarrassed by her outburst and withdrew back into her seat. She waved at him to continue.

Agitated, Rafe sighed heavily. "I never told Lilyandhi. The birthing process was so very difficult on her already and there were complications with Drinian with the umbilical cord. I think she assumed it was afterbirth anyways." Becoming worked up at the memory he struggled to maintain his composure. "The fourth baby, she was so very tiny and stillborn."

"A fourth child," Karisma said with a glance toward Ciara who was nodding feverishly. "She would have been Drin's twin, I'm betting? His gift wasn't split at all. She would have had the ability to see the angels."

Chase pointed toward her then back at his own nose. "That would be correct. Bastion?"

Leaning back against the couch, Bastion threw his arms back, one arm unconsciously curling a bit around Angel as he spoke. "There was a fourth baby as well. She lived only a few hours and was also quite small. My wife was aware though. Inara took the loss very hard. Even the slightest of mention and she fell into tears. We both needed her to be strong for our three sons we still had, so I suggested we not say anything when they came of age. At the time, I didn't want one of them mentioning it by accident and causing her to fall into depression."

Ciara snapped her fingers, having come to the same conclusion Karisma did. "Kalab would have had a twin as well. One who would have been able to see the bright lights Drayke sees."

"They're angels," Rafe corrected.

"That's debatable," Bastion disagreed, eyeing his brother meaningfully. They each frowned at each other than leaned forward in the chairs, their posture and positioning identical.

Rafe scowled. "I suppose next you'll be telling me the maid who saved our ancestor was casting a spell over Maxwell of Blackthorne near the blackthorn tree and not saying a prayer?"

"Makes more sense than saying a prayer to a God that isn't there."

"Enough you two, debate this later," Rourke demanded. "Chase, this is admittedly all very illuminating, but what is the point of this? If you know something then spill it."

"The point is, there is always a fourth child."

"There wasn't in Sarah's case; nor with us." He indicated himself as well as Rafe and Bastion.

"There's no shame in them knowing; now spill it, Rourke." Chase couldn't help but take pleasure in throwing the man's words back at him. "When you donated your bone marrow to your son nearly two months ago, they some tests. Tell everyone what they found."

It took a moment before he comprehended what the man was trying to get him to admit to. "Ah, of course. I'm not ashamed of my son. That's not why I haven't said anything. It simply never occurred to me. Two in one, of course."

"He's a chimera," Ciara piped in, having caught on quickly. "Your son is a chimera, isn't he?"

Tickled she figured it out, Rourke bobbed his head as he smiled and pointed at her with his cane.

"He's a fire breathing monster?" Angel's eyes widened in alarm.

"No, of course not." Rourke rolled his eyes and tossed his head, though was surprisingly patient in his explanation for Angel. "It means he has two genetically distinct types of cells. It seems his twin died in gestation and his body absorbed the twins genetic material."

"You mean he's literally two people in one?" Angel looked like her mind had been blown.

"Yes, Honey, we'll talk more on that later." Bastion put a halt to the inevitable tirade of questions she was bound to have before posing a question of his own. "If all three of us had four, and seeing as Eliza also had four children, the first, it would seem to survive. Rourke, do you think this could mean Father lied?"

"We would have had another sibling," Rourke said angrily. His face twitched as he looked across the room at Chase for confirmation.

"You have another sibling." Chase's emphasis on present tense caused a ripple effect reaction around the living room. While nursing his Scotch, he further explained they had a brother rather than a sister. He watched as all three of the elder Blackthorne brothers stood suddenly in varying states of emotional duress and confusion.

"Are you saying he lives? He's alive now?" Bastion asked urgently.

"Not only is he alive, but he's the reason why your father nearly killed you when you were three. It's probably why, though still affected by the shadows, you Rourke, do not suffer quite as deeply as their sons for your brother did not die, but was separated from you. Drayke and Breydon don't see the bright lights or angels because of Kalab and Drinian's gift being split; they see them because it's a part of their own ability to know the truth."

"But why? It doesn't make sense. Why would Rathbourne try to kill me, because of our brother?"

Chase's resentment toward the man surged. He could personally think of many reasons why someone might want to kill him now. But as a child? Tempted to leave Bastion hanging, he played with the rim of his Scotch bottle before finally relenting.

"He wasn't really trying to kill you, although personally, I wouldn't have blamed him if he had been." That comment won him a death glare from his father-in-law. "Truth be told he only wanted to shut you up. You started describing a boy - your brother - whom Rathbourne gave away. Your gifts don't present themselves fully until your twelfth year, but you all tend to have aspects of or show signs of what they will be prior to then. He knew you had a vision of his fourth son when you described his green eyes and silver-blonde hair; a lot like Eliza's son Gabriel."

"Silver blonde hair? A Blackthorne?" Rourke said in surprise.

"But Gabriel's hair is black. Isn't it?" Bastion asked Angel, since Eliza wasn't present. He hoped she might know.

Angel shook her head, her expression uneasy. "No, that's not his natural color. She told me in the van on the way here that she dyes his hair black every few weeks, because the dye won't stay in otherwise, even if it's a permanent hair dye. She uses the same in her own so people don't ask questions about their father."

"But why?" Bastion wondered aloud. "And why didn't Eliza say anything?"

"Ask her yourself. She's in the kitchen." Angel said with a knowing smile. Calling for her with an excited squeal, Eliza popped her head through the kitchen door with a water bottle and bag of chips in hand.

"You needed me?" Eliza asked.

"Gabriel's hair isn't black?" Bastion asked.

Eliza hedged at first, then with a resigned sigh explained. "His hair is a lot like Angel's, only paler. It's more of a silver-white than blonde. It shouldn't be possible considering our genes which is why I haven't mentioned it yet, because I wasn't sure how to bring it up without you and Kahner thinking he wasn't his. People start asking lots of questions if I don't dye it.

One person who asked about it two years ago was particularly scary. He wanted to know if I knew whether their father was a descendant of the Weir-deVere's and Blackthorne's of Scotland. Knowing how carefully you all have guarded that secret through the years, having a man standing in front of me, asking me about it frightened me. And Gabriel's reaction to him was more than a little unsettling."

Every Blackthorne in the room whether RavenCroft or not inhaled sharply at the news. No one was supposed to be aware of their link to the family.

"I remember it so well," Eliza continued, "because he was very scary, Bastion, and he's why we've been running ever since. He pulled out his cigarette pack and started smoking right there in front of the kids in the restaurant." She began shaking her hand in the air as if she were indicating a small item within it. "Gabriel must have seen the little milk carton lighter he used to light it with, because he started chanting about the milkman and singing this song he sings when he senses danger."

Screeching loudly, Angel erupted from the couch, a look of stark terror on her face. She would have run from the room had Bastion not caught her in his arms.

"No, no, not the milkman. B-bad, bad milk from the milkman!"

Her cries startled and alarmed everyone present.

"H-hate the milk, h-horrible milk, No milkman!" Her screams of terror seemed to escalate, increasing in volume and hysteria.

"Keep it away, keep it away! Milk h-hurts, it hurts," she cried, her tear-streaked eyes were soaked in a pool of fear.

Taking Angel to the couch, Bastion sat with her on his lap, cradling her in his arms as she sobbed fearfully. Alarmed by her behavior, he peered up at his brothers then Chase, finally understanding for the first time what it was she was so afraid of when she talked about the Milkman.

"The man with the lighter. Eliza's referring to Jericho Henley, isn't she?" Bastion asked his son-in-law darkly while attempting to calm Angel as best he could.

Chase's affirming answer was obvious in his expression, and he appeared more than a little troubled as he watched his father-in-law struggle with Angel.

Bastion's features visibly darkened. "I want to see this story."

Promising him, he would get the chance to read it, Chase told him he'd have to wait until Rourke saw it first. Heading off Bastion's inevitable argument, he made sure he understood his reasons for it had nothing to do with their dispute and everything to do with the belief it was imperative Rourke had a look at it before they did.

Rafe didn't like the terms Chase was giving them. "What do you know that we don't?"

Chase stood. Pulling at his lip with his thumb and forefinger he sighed heavily, having come to a decision as he paced the middle of the living room. "A fourth child with silver hair born of the Weir-deVere line has been a well-kept secret ever since the birth of Maxwell of Blackthorne's sons. So, when Rathbourne saw the boy, he freaked, thinking either the child was an abnormality or Sapphire had cheated on him, which she, of course, hadn't. So, he gave the child away and didn't tell her. As far as he was concerned the boy could never be a Blackthorne and the possibility she might have been unfaithful plagued him ever since."

On the verge of tears, Karisma banged on the cushion of the couch arm angrily. Having lost her own kids, for obvious reasons the subject of getting rid of children was hitting her very hard.

"But why? He was just a child, and he was being tossed away, because of the lack of color in his hair? How could anyone do that?" Karisma asked in distress.

Chase halted her words with his hands, needing everyone to be silent, so he could tell them what they needed to know. "You all know the story, better than probably even me about the very first Blackthorne. The maid who was present on the day of Maxwell of Blackthorne's birth from Jean Weir knew he was the product of incest with her older brother, Major Thomas Weir of Lanarkshire, then later Edinburgh, Scotland.

In an attempt to cover up their misdeeds, Thomas sent the maid to toss the child in the woods to die. Instead, she found her way to a parish not far from the Blackwood Estates and left the baby at the base of a nearby Blackthorn tree. That's where she made her wish, or prayer, or cast her spell - whichever version you believe." Chase paused there, casting a furtive glance toward Ciara, then around the living room. His gaze settled on Karisma, suspecting that hearing another story like this so soon after learning of what Rathbourne had done, was likely going to bother her a lot.

"Because of her actions that day, the boy survived for he was found by the parish priest and raised by him. Since then, it's always been said, every Blackthorne would always be born with 'eyes as pale, bright and blue as the blackthorn tree's abundant sloe berries,' and 'hair as black as the bark of the blackthorn tree.' But this fourth child of Rathbourne's wasn't born that way. He had the palest of silver-blonde hair and green eyes so your dad took him to a shelter, claiming he'd found the baby, and abandoned him there, not understanding the damage he'd be inflicting on you Rourke by separating the two of you. Had you been raised together growing up you, well, you likely would have fared better."

"All of this is in the final book?" Rourke wanted to know when Chase finally paused.

"All that and more."

"Karisma, am I to understand, the finale is the only volume that did not get published?" Rafe asked.

"My memory from that day isn't so good, I guess, because I don't really even remember writing it. But I think maybe I'd just finished it when he emailed me about pulling the stories, so no. It never saw the internet."

"I'd say we dodged a bullet there," Bastion said.

"I would agree, because as I said, there's more," Chase said.

"We really do have another brother then?" Rafe interrupted, sounding as stunned as he looked. "One with silver hair and green eyes?"

"Yes, and his name is Black Thorne."

Chapter 19

"Blackthorne, you say?"

The shadows playing in the corners of the living room were of little interest to Rourke. His intense gaze focused instead upon the fire he requested Rafe to start in the hearth, for a chill had taken root within him. What Chase said didn't make sense.

"If our poor excuse for a father abandoned him, how did he end up with the family name?"

Chase reclaimed the seat he vacated moments before. "You misunderstand. His first name is Black, his last name is Thorne."

"That can't be a coincidence," Rourke said.

"Does he know about us, and who he really is?" Bastion asked.

"I think it's safe to say Black knows everything." Chase recounted how Sapphire found her son when he was about to turn ten years of age and shared how, unbeknownst to the boy's adoptive parents, she went to visit him at the playground near his house where he used to play. She wanted to reassure herself that he was okay, to explain what happened, and how he'd found his new home. Her visit was unnecessary for he already knew. Claiming he was all right, even within his present household of recently divorced parents, Black asked to see the book of lineage he knew the Blackthorne's had.

"She lifted the book from Rathbourne's study and took it to him the next time she visited. They arranged over the summer for her to come every other Friday for nearly three months in a row, so he could have the time to get to read through it and learn about his other family."

Rafe was stunned. "I can't believe she removed it from the house, and so frequently without Dad knowing."

"It wasn't the first time," Rourke said. "Actually, it probably was the first time. The second time was when mum sent it to you, Bastion, out of spite over what happened to Sarah."

"Kalturek will be bringing the book when he comes, by the way." Bastion said, smiling warmly. "You'll have it soon after he arrives. There is something I need to fix within it first."

"It's been too long since I've seen it," Rourke said gratefully. He looked as though a weight had been lifted from his shoulders. "Many thanks."

"I still don't understand what the significance is to the silver-blonde hair." Karisma frowned and glanced at Angel in confusion.

"Isn't obvious," Ciara said. As an outsider looking in, she had a unique perspective on the matter since she had now read the stories. She'd spent a lot of time in the past couple of years reading and researching about the history of man's origins, a favorite pastime of hers.

Having read a lot of fiction as well, she was also familiar with the many twists authors enjoyed throwing in, so she understood what the significance could be of a gifted child with silver-blonde hair coming from such an extensive lineage. "Any chance we could see Gabriel for a minute?" Ciara asked Bastion.

Not seeing any harm in it, the RavenCroft patriarch got up to go get him when the boy wandered in from the kitchen with a Popsicle in hand.

"You wanted to see me, Grandpa?" The boy smiled at Ciara, his green eyes sparkling with a silvery light as he passed by her. "Figured it out, have you? You are the wisest of the three, makes sense."

"Gabriel, may I see them?" The excitement in Ciara's voice was unmistakable. Before the boy's comment, her curiosity had been based on a guess.

The boy gave her a lopsided grin as he sucked on his Popsicle. Lifting his hair out of the way with his free hand, he showed her his ears. She covered her mouth with a soft gasp, then encouraged him to show his grandfather.

Though most of the ear was rounded like any normal child, there was a distinct point near the top of the ear, as though it were trying to form a pointed ear. Rourke turned to Ciara in astonishment when he saw them, his mind quickly wrapping around what the appearance of Gabriel's ears meant.

"Think about it," Ciara went on to explain her theory. "Your lineage, according to what I've read so far, and this is without having seen the book yet, goes back over probably, what? Three thousand years or more? Potentially linked without deviation to Princess Scota and the High Elves of Ireland via the Fairy Princess Plantina which means, there's both Elven and dragon

DNA within your veins as a result. It's why you have the abilities you have; not because of some wish the maid may have made, which I question, because I thought Major Thomas Weir cut her tongue out."

"What?" Rafe asked.

"Cut her tongue out." Rourke said.

"Where did you read that?" Bastion asked.

The three men shared the same confounded expression at her revelation, the sight of which tickled her.

"Now I really need to see that book again. I don't recall the parish priest making any mention of that. Are you sure that's right?" Rourke asked.

"Hhhmm, I suppose I could be wrong, but I'm sure that's the case. It's why the maid disobeyed Thomas and left his son where he could be found beneath the Blackthorn tree near the parish. She was mad over the loss of speech and wanted them to get caught."

Glancing across the living room at Ciara, it occurred to Rourke that her abilities were becoming increasingly stronger the more time she spent among them. Angel's halfhearted laugh carried across the living room, bringing him from his reverie. From all appearances, she was recovering from her scare, though there was still a catch in her breathing.

"Of course, yes! Ciara's r-right. It's coming to you in w-waves now, isn't it? You're finally among p-people who can relate to you so there's no need to shield yourself anymore," Angel said.

"I say hinky." Karisma got up and took a closer look at the boy's ears, fascinated by them. They really did look like they could almost be Elvin ears. "Regardless of whether that's where their abilities derive, if Thomas cut out her tongue then how was she able to say the prayer, or wish, or spell - whichever it was?"

"She didn't say it," Ciara said.

"Then where did the poem come from that's written within the Blackthorne and Weir-deVere book of Lineage?" Karisma asked.

"I only said she didn't say it; I never said she didn't think it." Becoming distracted by an onset of hunger pangs, Ciara wrapped an arm across her belly and stared into the kitchen, thinking a chicken quesadilla sounded amazing at the moment. It was getting close to dinner time.

Bastion's face lit up with understanding. "That would mean the parish priest..."

"Discerned what she was thinking?" Rafe asked, finishing his brother's thought without meaning to.

Rourke's confusion was short-lived. "But how?"

"The parish priest was a Weir-deVere descendant too," Ciara said. She pressed at her growling belly self-consciously, suddenly realizing everyone had gone silent. She looked up.

"What? You didn't really think you were the only ones out there, did you? Where else are the men from the Phenom organization getting all the other gifted people from? I'm betting the men from Phenom are looking to pair a person descended from the Blackthorne line that has silver-blonde hair, with another of the same. They had Angel but needed a male.

Your wife, Bastion, discovered what they were trying to do and was killed when she tried to bring her to safety. Imagine, a child so strong in gift and blood, raised and molded by them, and mated with another of the same."

"What would be the point of doing that?" Bastion was horrified. He shooed his grandson away to the playroom, thinking it best he wasn't present anymore. The boy shrugged and waved at them as he went.

Ciara's head raced with possibilities, but only one made the most sense. "Because they're trying to bring elves back into the world," she said, shocking everyone. "Or, depending on what you believe, angels. There are many cultures who believe elves and angels are the same. One theory is the elves were the angels who didn't take sides between God and Lucifer. That they are, what is often termed as, the 'Watchers,' who separated and went to live on earth."

"Bring them back? Nah, I'd say they're trying to find them, because they're still here," Karisma said, causing everyone to turn toward her and stare.

"I doubt that's possible. If there were still elves on earth, I'm sure we'd know about it by now." Rafe hesitated, then glanced toward his brother with a questioning look. "Rourke?"

Casting a sly glance over toward the woman in his brothers arms, Rourke returned Rafe's intent gaze with slitted eyes. "It is not as common anymore, but at one time people in Scotland believed elves were magically powerful people living, usually invisibly, alongside everyday human communities. They were also thought to be the cause of illness, and associated with magic, beauty and seduction."

"If that's the case, and they were or are real still then they cannot possibly be angels," Rafe said darkly, not caring for the direction the conversation had gone.

"Why not?" Angel asked from her perch on Bastion's lap. She wiped her wet eyelashes then rested her head on his shoulder. Her long silver blonde hair cascaded down, nearly touching the floor.

"Because angels are benevolent beings, messengers of God. They wouldn't behave in such a manner," Rafe answered.

"Lucifer is said to be an angel," Bastion reminded his brother, starting to wonder himself if Ciara's theory might be true. "Who's to say these, we'll call them 'Watcher's for now, didn't get bored?"

"Get bored. Are you mad?" Rafe was incredulous. "So what we're saying here is that what we call elves are actually 'Watcher' angels who live invisibly among us creating chaos out of boredom, because they, what, don't have anything better to do with their time on earth?"

"It makes sense to me." Karisma piped in, winning herself another disgusted look from Rafe. "Think about it. They aren't good, they aren't evil, they're in between. They're the balance, if you will, between the battle that wages between God and Lucifer. Problem is, their presence in the past thousand years or so has been seriously lacking. Where once they were known, seen, and felt by everyone, now they're barely a bedtime story about a fairy tale."

"Right, that's where I was trying to go with this." Ciara gestured toward Karisma with an appreciative smile.

"Are you serious with this?" Rafe asked.

Karisma nodded fervently. "Elves were wingless angels with no other purpose than to watch. They were bound to get bored. But their absence bled chaos into order, leaving mankind in charge, and look where that got us," Karisma said.

"Can't argue that," Angel said sullenly next to Bastion.

Rafe rolled his eyes, wondering at Chase s silence as he stared at his nearly empty Scotch bottle. "If what you're saying is true. Then why in the world would anyone want to bring them back or find them if they're truly still here?"

"Why else?" Ciara couldn't help, but think it was obvious. "Kind of like Rourke said. Elves were thought to be magical, immortal, supernaturally spiritual beings with varying abilities, the capacity to heal, and knowledge of things mankind had no grasp of. With the technology we have today and access to Elven DNA within the Blackthorne line, the people of Phenom could potentially bring magic back to the world - if you believe that sort of thing - become immortal, have the ability to heal, and maybe even get the answer to the one question mankind has sought since the beginning of time."

"What question would that be?" Bastion asked.

"I'd think that would be obvious." Rourke said quietly as he stood. Not really needing the cane, he used it anyway to aid him in stepping closer to the fire, for the chill was growing within his bones. He refused to acknowledge the shadows currently attempting to plague him. Closing his eyes, he thanked the heavens they'd managed to get to Ciara in time. "Elves or angels, angels or elves; either way they're spiritual beings. If any being ever could, they would know whether there is a God, or Gods. If the men of Phenom were to capture and have control over such a being, imagine the power they'd wield."

- - -

"May I join you?"

The gentle voice and whispered words brought Rourke out of his reverie. He'd been staring at the fire for some time now. He was thinking about what he learned earlier in the day and from the flash drive now attached to his laptop in his lap. Glancing up from where he sat on the couch since after dinner, he smiled when he saw a second steaming mug in Ciara's other hand.

"But of course. Please." Pleasantly surprised she sought him out, he closed the lid of the laptop and set it aside on the lamp stand. Moving his legs from where he stretched them out on the couch, he sat up as she offered the second mug to him, hoping it was what he thought it was.

"Hot toddy?" Ciara caught the appreciative light sparking in his eyes.

Accepting the steaming cup gratefully, he thanked her and took a sip of the spicy brew after inhaling, what was for him, a calming scent.

"Bah, this has bourbon in it." His disappointment was unmistakable.

Ciara laughed. "I told Rafe you liked it better his way, but he seemed adamant about making it with the bourbon this time. Something about wanting to make sure you got what you asked for when you first arrived."

Disgusted, he took another sip, made a face and set the mug down. "I'd wager the git did it to prove his point."

"Which would be?"

"That his recipe's better," they both said in unison.

Rourke laughed this time, his eyes lighting up along with his face in the wake of it. His cheeks, visible through the week's growth of stubble, were coloring from embarrassment at being found out. He pressed two fingers to his lips and shushed her.

"But don't tell him I said that. He'll never let me live it down."

"My lips are sealed." She settled in next to him, leaving a little space between them.

Turning in his seat, he stretched his arm across the back of the couch behind her, mostly for comfort. It was so much easier to talk facing her then it was to stare straight ahead, he rationalized, and besides, Ciara was easy to look at. Especially since Angel helped her dye her hair back to her favored strawberry-blonde that afternoon. The change had been a good one.

"Feeling more yourself are we?" Without thinking, he reached over to play with a strand of her hair, then pulled back awkwardly. Pretending the action meant nothing, he picked up his mug took another sip, then opted to hold it indefinitely.

She sighed and her sad eyes found his. "Aye, a bit."

His own eyes crinkled with amusement. The woman was a sponge and a mimic; that's what he and his brothers had determined. Which meant she truly couldn't help herself. She picked up on other people's responses, mannerisms and behaviors and imitate them, the same way a child might unknowingly mimic an older sibling they admired. It also meant people in pain would be drawn to her which was likely why so many within the household had been seeking her out to 'talk' every day since she arrived. The poor woman hadn't had a moment of peace, nor had he the chance to speak to her alone.

"Two pence for your thoughts?" she asked.

Rourke chuckled at her Scottish idiom, yawned, and rubbed a hand across his forehead. "My thoughts are worth more than one pence? Aren't you generous?" He sighed as though weighted down by the world, the muscles in his face tensing once again. "I am trying hard not to think."

"I get that. It's a lot to take in. Learning of a brother you didn't know you had after fifty years must be difficult too."

"Aye, there is that." They both took another sip of their hot toddies. Rourke winced and set his down on the stand, wondering at when his tastes had changed. At her gesture and request, he took her mug from her and set it next to his own. "Mostly, I'm thinking our story has played out."

"Oh? Has it now?" One of her eyebrows rose skeptically.

He made an affirming noise in his throat. "I tend to agree with Chase. There are things we each need to iron out on our own, but in the end, I think we all know who is meant for whom at this point. The only challenge now is in choosing whether we're willing to accept the gift we've been given here." At her questioning look, he clarified what he meant. "At the end of volume two of Angel's story, a group of battle-worn angels arrived at the day Dante and Astraia were to be wed. When one of the angels already present asked from where they had come, the one named Rokon responded by saying he should not ask from where, but from when. I believe strongly that it was Angel's way of saying some force, whether angels or not, has been fighting fiercely for us and for quite some time now."

Ciara bumped his shoulder playfully. "The Watchers maybe?"

Rourke rolled his eyes heavenward and responded grudgingly. "Maybe."

"But why? To what end?" She asked, thoroughly fascinated by the possibility.

"Isn't it obvious? To give us all the chance to not only fulfill the prophecies, but to prevent us from having to endure so much hardship, to give us more time, to have a better love story, to find ourselves with the correct partner, to affect their own desired end of course," Rourke paused mid-thought, his haunted eyes becoming distant. They shifted away from her and instead, gazed into the fire, before he continued speaking. His answer was both serious and joking all rolled into one. "And for one individual, to give them the chance to know love, when they might not otherwise have had the chance before."

Ciara could tell his mind had wandered to the past, likely wondering what might have been had he and his Sarah not been torn apart as they were. She knew he blamed himself for what happened, but that burden didn't sit on his shoulders alone. Thinking it best not to let him dwell too long on the past, she gently touched his forearm, running her fingers down the length of it to his hand in order to gain his attention.

"If that's true, and some entity is fighting for us, wouldn't that give one cause to believe there might truly be a God?"

"I know Bastion feels there isn't, though I'd wager that has more to do with the way his wife died. Personally, I've never questioned it, regardless of how I carry on, and what I've been forced to see all my life."

"I don't understand. I thought you were agnostic."

"At one time in my life, I was, yes. But I see the demons which plague us all on a daily basis, Ciara, which means I've seen the demons failures as well as their successes in the destruction of people's lives. So, how could I not believe? The only thing I've ever questioned was why it had to be me? Why, out of the three of us - or I guess it's four now, must I endure seeing them, and if I have to be the one, for whatever the reason, then why does Rafe get to hear God's voice when I can't?" His troubled gaze shifted about the room, his voice filling with raw emotion as he spoke.

"I can see how it might seem unfair."

Clearing his throat, he wondered at why he'd said anything. He never spoke of such things to anyone. "Yes, well, regardless of whether I'm right or Bastion is, either way, it seems clear to me there is a positive force at work one way or another, and it's working overtime to affect a less traumatic outcome for everyone. Pain affects the heart in ways we cannot fathom until it's too late."

"I can attest to that." Absently, Ciara's hand rested between her breasts, curling loosely as they lay near her heart. "Such betrayal wounds in a way many who haven't experienced it can't grasp. People say we shouldn't give the individuals who hurt us so deeply that kind of power over us by allowing it to fester and eat at us. There may be something to that, but I can't agree with it entirely. I always try so hard not to dwell on it, and I most certainly don't want to give my ex power over me. But sometimes, it's a little thing - a random thing that someone says or does - and my mind will unwittingly revert to a moment in time; a memory of him. It makes me pause, it makes me wonder where it came from, and it makes me angry all over again, because I don't want to remember. And no matter how hard I might try; it sticks with me for a while until something comes up to occupy that space in my mind."

"Time helps." Rourke offered kindly, wanting to ease her mind. Bumping her shoulder playfully back, he stole a drink from her mug. Making a face, and a gagging noise he got her to laugh which helped to break the tension. "So does allowing yourself to be open to new possibilities you might not have considered otherwise. Just look at Dart who found his Lylia."

"Oh, yes, that will be interesting on Sunday; meeting her for the first time. Have you menfolk figured out how to explain away me and my likeness to her yet?" Ciara asked.

"There is one variant between the two of you. She is a blonde."

"Yes, and I'm a red head, yet underneath the hair color we still have the same hair. So, in other words, not yet?"

"No, but we'll get there. I was hoping the answer to why you and Lylia look so much alike would be in the final volume, but it doesn't appear to be there."

Ciara thought about what that might mean before she spoke again. "I'd say, there are some things we're not meant to have all the answers to. Who knows? Maybe we'll find the explanation within another story." She winked at him, only partially meaning it as a joke.

"Agreed." A half-smile played at Rourke's lips, making him appear roguish. The weeks' worth of stubble was quickly turning into the short-boxed beard he'd had before. "Bastion's son Kahner would be an excellent example of things we may never know. In the first volume Angel wrote that ten years from now, he meets the Radford woman, brings her home to safety along with her children, and falls in love. He was never reunited with his ex. It begs the question, why was it so important for that to change?"

"True, but Eliza does show up again after Bastion married Angel in that story if you recall."

Rourke frowned, "Yes, and she was frantic too but Angel never says why. It leaves one to wonder now with Eliza's return, will he ever meet Kalysta Radford?"

Ciara held her tongue. She knew Angel had told Kahner the reasons why Eliza returned at that point in the story. Angel had come to her asking advice on the subject for she hadn't known what to do with the information she had, whether it would be better to tell him, or not to. So they'd sat down together with him before he left to take his kids and Eliza back to Loveland. They explained to him why, in Angel's story, the mother of his children had been forced to return with them ten years from now. At that point in the tale, Eliza was dying from cancer and had little time left. She was tired of running and wanted to make sure their children would be safe. It had been hard to break the news to Kahner and for obvious reasons he had not taken it well. Ciara hoped by telling him, they might be able to catch the cancer sooner and prevent it from spreading.

As to the other potential second woman in Kahner's life, she knew Bastion was looking into that, for the woman's spouse had also died earlier than expected. His death had occurred as it was written in volume two for he had still been killed by Astraia's husband who also died. It was how Astraia and her small children - of whom she had had earlier than anticipated - had come to be with Dante so much sooner as well. Ciara opted instead to change the subject, knowing Kahner, as well as Dante, had requested privacy on those matters.

"Anything is possible. Either way, it would appear time is on our side - for the moment anyway. After all, ST and Meg had already found each other when this all started."

"Mmhmm. It's odd Angel switched the names though. According to her stories, Chase was originally a doctor who was married to Meg Blackthorne and ST was also, oddly, a doctor who was married to Mackenzie"

"Aye. She may know a lot, but she is not all-knowing. She still has a long way to go in the learning department. It's not surprising she'd get a few things messed up."

"True. I get the feeling Rafe will be getting married soon."

Ciara grimaced with concern. "I'm betting Karisma is going to need a lot more than a week to recover, regardless of her fondness for him. Bastion and Angel on the other hand, I could see their engagement coming even sooner from the way they sound and act together."

"You could be right. Bah, what do I know? The last relationship I was in was thirty years ago. As you are aware, it did not end well." Agitated over the subject matter, he removed his glasses long enough to rub at the corners of his eyes with a shaky hand.

Giving him a sympathetic look she didn't respond, sensing his need for silence on the matter rather than comment. "I do believe Rafe will be good for Karisma in the interim," she said a bit too brightly, overcompensating for the awkwardness.

"Indeed. I'm sure Rafe will eventually find a way to get past Karisma's grating personality."

"Oh, stop!" Ciara laughed in spite of herself. "No doubt a reader might wonder why they end up together especially what with my name being in Karisma's story, but what Angel wrote was only one possible future, and in a couple of cases, like mine, inaccurate at best. If you think about it, she did almost the same thing with me and Karisma as she did with Chase and ST."

"Look at it this way, at least Angel didn't mix you up with Meg. You might have wound up as Mrs. Ciara Wong rather than Mrs. Ciara Blackthorne." Rourke winced internally as soon as he said it, wondering if he was being too presumptuous. Bless the woman, she was kind enough to put him at ease.

"It would have been so wrong to be a Wong, but funny?" She gave a nervous laugh, her eyes dimming sadly at the sharp pang within her chest. She could so easily have ended up with the wrong man and not even realized it, had things gone differently. If angels were real, as she suspected they were, then she was grateful to them for bringing Karisma out of time ten years sooner. Too high a price had been paid to make it happen though.

"That's all of us, except for one." A bit anxious, Rourke took a deep breath. "Last but not least, there's me and ... well ..."

And there it was, the elephant in the room.

She sighed. "You might as well say it."

Licking his lips nervously he took a chance. "Ciara, from the looks of what I was reading, I need to be heading back home soon."

"Oh?" Startled by the news, she glanced worriedly back at him, sounding disappointed. "H-how soon?"

"I'd say in the next day or two, and I likely won't be back for some time. Rather than waiting until then, I don't suppose you'd consider..."

"Yes."

"Yes? You don't know what I was going to ask."

Ciara reached around him for her mug. Her chest accidentally brushed against his when she pulled back. They both shivered lightly.

"W-weren't you asking me to marry you?" She took a small sip of her mug for courage. From the outside, she knew she might appear calm and sure of herself, but her insides were quaking from the slight brush against him.

"Err, Yes, I was going to."

"Then, yes."

"Just like that."

"Yup, just like that."

Rourke swayed between being both tickled and appalled. "You don't even know me; don't know a blasted thing about me."

"I know enough."

Flabbergasted, he found himself arguing without knowing why. "You just met me."

"Are you trying to advocate for yourself, because if you are you're not doing a very good job. Right now, it sounds like you're attempting to get out of our engagement."

"Engagement? I just proposed. Err, sort of I guess." She was throwing Rourke off balance with her confusing and perfunctory responses. It was making him crazy.

"Then yes. I did already say I'd marry you, didn't I?"

His eyes narrowed upon her. If he didn't know better, he'd say she was messing with him. "Why are you making this so difficult?"

"You were the one in the middle of asking, when I interrupted and agreed before you even asked, because I knew that was what you were asking. So it's more like, why do you have to make this so difficult?" she asked innocently.

Rourke was completely flustered. "Because you don't know me. Is this how you make all your decisions?"

"No, only this one. You want to know why?"

"By all means, please enlighten me."

"The first thing my ex did when he met me was open his mouth and lie. About everything. Starting with, 'hi, my name is.' But you, a fifty-year-old man, with - okay, maaaybe a few personality quirks - you flew across Montana, South Dakota, Iowa and Illinois then against your very nature pretended to be your brother in order to take a helicopter into South Bend, Indiana so you could repel down, from what equates to a bungee cord, snatch me up, pull me up into a helicopter and then carry me onto a plane filled with Lucky's Thai food, my ultimate favorite food by the way; all to bring me to safety and away from Jericho Henley and the Phenom organization."

He tried to interrupt, but she shushed him with a wave of her finger.

Grabbing up the book on the coffee table that she'd seen Meg reading earlier in the day, she took a quick look at it then held it out to him. "If I were to say to you, 'Rourke, this woman in this book Janet Evanovich has written is real. Her name's Stephanie Plum, and she's in danger. We've got to go get her, because someone wants to hurt her. You have to go get her and bring her to safety. What would you say to that?"

"Bah, first I'd say you're off your rocker. Then I'd tell you to piss off. What do I care about some lass I don't know?"

"Wow, that's awfully telling about your personality there, uh, Rourke, but uh, okay. Either way, you've made my point."

"How's that?"

"Why was it different with me?" Ciara asked eagerly, desperate for the truth in his answer.

Rourke fidgeted silently; either unable or unwilling to respond.

Disappointed, but unwilling to give up, she continued to push. "I was just some random character in a book, Rourke." Leaning forward she grabbed up volume six from the table where all the books had been abandoned earlier in the day and shook it. "This book. Why was I worth going after, when Stephanie Plum isn't?" Her voice was soft, barely above a whisper as she reached up to touch the short stubble growing on his face. "You shaved off your thirty-year-old beard in order to save me. If I was truly nothing more than a random character from a book then you never would have done that. That action alone is so very telling as well, and therefore worth my time to see this through, because if that's not some kind of love then I don't know what love is."

Cupping the back of her head with both hands, Rourke pulled her to him and kissed her; ravishing her perfect lips with an unquenchable hunger he couldn't seem to satisfy. Placing her hand to his chest where his heart thundered at a rapid pace, he hoped she'd understand that the small gesture was his answer.

Slow and reluctant, he pulled away moments later as they both trembled uncontrollably. Breathing heavily, their noses nearly touching, they took the time to enjoy the aftermath of their first of many kisses.

"Easy cowboy," Ciara said between breaths.

"I'm no cowboy, I'm a Highlander," he said gruffly, wanting to make sure that was clear. There was no way he was staying in Montana. He enjoyed the freedom of his Estate in Scotland too much. Besides, one day soon, he suspected it would be his.

Shuddering at the sound of his deep gravelly voice only a hair's breadth from her left ear, she let off a strangled sort of giggling laugh as pure pleasure coursed through her veins. With a giddy lopsided smile, she told him exactly what she thought of that.

"Highlander works for me."

- - -

Two Years Later
Kalispell, Montana

"Are you awake?"

"No." Karisma was in denial.

The man next to her chuckled and whispered playfully against her neck. "Are you sure?"

"I'm positive." Her voice was lethargic and muffled by her pillow. She sounded annoyed.

Propping up on one elbow Rafe Blackthorne smiled down at his new bride. They'd been married for about a month now, and they both were happier for it.

"When did you come to bed anyway? You weren't writing all night again, were you?"

Groaning, she rolled so she faced him. Peaking up through her tousled hair and sleep matted eyelashes she struggled to clear the fog from her vision. "I was so tired; I couldn't keep my eyes open. So, I crawled into bed at ten."

He gave her a speculative look, having noticed the dark circles under her eyes. "You look and sound like you've hardly slept an hour. Are you sure it was that early?"

She hedged. It felt like she'd had this conversation once before. What was that sensation called again? Oh, right. Déjà vu.

"Yes, I'm sure."

"It's time to get up. Are you going to be okay to go to the book signing today?" Concern etched his features into a frown. "Karisma, honey, is everything all right?"

Face drawn; her sad eyes shifted away from his toward the patio door. The sun already peaked through the drapes. She needed to get moving, but she was struggling to get up. Lost in thought over her most recent dream, she missed his last words.

"Sorry, I was just thinking. I dreamed about them again last night."

"It's bound to happen. No one expects you to forget. Your children and husband were a large part of your life. Their memories will always be with you." Rafe understood. As anyone would, Karisma had taken the deaths of her children and late husband hard. The first few weeks after the accident had been made worse by the drama of having to locate Angel and Ciara. The hasty wedding preparations before Rourke and Ciara's departure for Scotland hadn't helped any either. It had prompted all the RavenCroft's to converge on the Blackthorne Estate for the wedding. With all the family around, the wedding nuptials, and seeing Ciara in his late wife's wedding dress, Karisma wound up secluded in the library next to his room during the small reception.

It had really hit her hard to realize she'd never get to see either of her children grow up and get married one day. Seeing her now, troubled by her dreams, made him wonder again if they should have waited a little longer to get married. He'd waited nearly two years. Another one wouldn't have killed him.

"No, now don't do that. I know what you're thinking. It's got nothing to do with us tying the knot." The truth was, being married to him had helped. She missed her children dearly. Some days so much so it felt like her heart was breaking all over again, and she'd loved her husband unconditionally. But having someone to hold at night, and be held by, somehow made the heartache bearable.

While playing with a ribbon of her silvery golden hair she peered up at her husband. She could tell he was unconvinced.

"I'm okay. I am. And I'll be okay today too. I promise."

He searched her face, not seeing any artifice in her expression. "All right, if you're sure. Now come here." He pulled her into him. Wrapping his arms around her, he trailed his hands down her shoulder to the small of her back.

Shivering at his touch, a wry half-smile played at her lips. "I thought you said it was time to get up."

"It is." He grinned at her. His goofy expression lit a sparkle of mischief in his eye. "It won't hurt anything if you're a little late."

She laughed. Yanking the pillow from under her head, she tried pummeling him in the face with it to no avail. Putting an immediate halt to it, Rafe yanked it from her hands and threw her pillow across the room. She gave a startled cry as he spun her about, pinning her back to the bed.

"Now you're gonna be really late." He grinned down at her again as she smiled, only halfheartedly attempting to regain her position.

"I can't! All those people are counting on me to be there to scribble in their books."

With a barking laugh he shook his head. "It's called a signature. They want the awful fake author name of yours scrawled across your masterpiece."

She pushed at his chest angrily, knowing full well he was trying to goad her. She hadn't missed his not so veiled sarcasm either. "It's not awful. It makes sense. It's the perfect name really."

"How do you figure?" He had no intentions of moving from his position of dominance above her,

"Think about it. This way I still get to keep my own name only in a roundabout sort of way. Besides, it kind of fits me, don't you think?" Eyes narrowing to slits, she gave him a look of pure impudence. She liked being difficult. It was fun. Especially when her new husband was the target. "Either way, it's too late. It's on the book cover already which means it's everywhere now."

"Yeah, about that. I really wish you would have conferred with me on the title before submitting it for publishing."

Karisma's eyes enlarged, wide with innocence.

Rafe knew full well she was in no way blameless. Even if the idea for the book came from Angel. "It was one thing to use Bedlam Charm for your new pen name, but did you have to title the book Vortigern Black's Elven Angel Justice League? And sending Bastion an advance copy for a wedding present was so not the way of telling him about this."

She'd been trying so hard, but she just couldn't do it. The snort erupted from within her. Clasping her hands over her mouth as her body convulsed from uncontrollable giggles, she kicked at the white down comforter with her feet.

Her husband scowled down at her.

"What? I've never sold a book of my own before in my life! How was I supposed to know it'd become an overnight success and by extension a New York Times Best Seller?"

Burrowing his face in the pillow next to her head, Rafe groaned. "Bastion said you put a Ken Doll with pointed ears dressed as Vortigern Black in with the book along with a Batman action figure. Then wrapped it in what looked like Vortigern Black wrapping paper. Is that true?"

She snorted again, not bothering to disguise her laughter any longer. She'd done the same with Rourke's copy. Only she'd put a Superman Action figure in with his. Not surprisingly, they'd received a similar reaction from him.

"What can I say? I thought they'd appreciate being able to act out the scenes."

Lifting his head from the pillow, he stared down at her with a blank expression. "Please tell me there isn't going to be a sequel."

The moment her face lit up Rafe knew he was screwed.

"Oh, baby, this is just the beginning! The fans on both Twitter and Facebook have been begging for more, and I aim to please. I'm already half-way through the next one. I'm calling it Vortigern Black's Elven Angel Justice League and the Halloween Capers. I'll give you one guess when I plan to publish that one."

"Gee, let me think. October?" Rafe couldn't help but be part horrified, part amused. He knew full well he was never going to hear the end of this from his brothers. Especially Bastion.

Taking advantage of the distraction she created, Karisma scooted out from under him and leaped from the bed. There was no way he was going to make her late for her very own book signing.

"Where are you going?"

A surge of pure giddiness raced within her as she smiled sweetly. "Sorry Babe. I gotta go. You wouldn't want Bedlam Charm, to disappoint all her adoring fans, now would you?"

Rafe eyed her from under his arm. "I take it back. Bedlam Charm is the perfect pen name for a paradox like you, Karisma Kayos-Blackthorne."

She giggled, her eyes twinkling mischievously as she dashed for the bathroom. Today she was gonna be Karisma, maybe tomorrow she'd let out Inara, for as it turned out, Rourke's son wasn't the only chimera in the family.

An ending isn't an ending
but a beginning
whether it be old or new.

A NOTE FROM THE AUTHOR

Dear Reader,

Thank you so very much for taking the time to read this story. I hope you enjoyed every bit of the Blackthorne's saga as much as I did when I wrote it. I never imagined when I started writing that it would become such a spider web of events!

If you enjoyed the story then please be sure to leave a review of Karisma Kayos: Out of Time at amazon.com. I'd love to hear from you! Additionally, it would be great to learn whether or not any of my readers managed to figure out who the mysterious narrator, Vortigern Black was.

I'd also like to express appreciation to the readers who attempted to foray through all of the first six stories as well as the finale, for there were many characters to keep track of. In the finale alone, there were approximately forty-eight names. My apologies for any confusion, but to finish the Blackthorne tale in its entirety, it required combining the two family's into one story. Rest assured, in future works (other unrelated stories) there will be nowhere near as many!

If this is the first you've read of this unfortunate tale of lineage and you would like to check out three or more of the first six in this collection then you can purchase them through Amazon.com. Truly, there is so much more enjoyment to be had in the discovery of all that came before this. Or is it after this? Hmmm. Guess you'll have to read on to see.

For me, the An Unfortunate Lineage series was a labor of love, too many hours to keep track of, and a long time in the making. In preparation for the finale, extensive research was done which brought me to the story of Major Thomas Weir and his sister Jean Weir of Lanarkshire, Scotland (UK) then later Edinburgh. These two unfortunate individuals admitted to, and therefore were tried, convicted, and executed, for witchcraft and sorcery in 1670. Though I have created a fictional

A NOTE FROM THE AUTHOR

lovechild from their documented incestuous relationship, there was actually no child born of that union. I mention this to dispel any potential confusion for those familiar with their story.

Thank you again, and I hope you enjoyed the An Unfortunate Lineage!

Delaine Christine

For more about the series
and the author

vortigernblack.com

smashwords.com/profile/view
/DelaineChristine

Or to Contact the Author:
delainechristine15@gmail.com

Character List Of Suspects

CHARACTER LIST AND CULPRIT

Karisma Kayos – Born Inara Kingsley, she was adopted as a toddler and eventually changed her name. A ghostwriter by trade, she also writes supernatural fiction on the side.

Dr. Sum Ting (S.T.) Wong – He is married to Meg (Blackthorne) Wong and is an ER doctor at the local hospital in Kalispell, Montana.

Meg {Megorah Blackthorne} Wong – The youngest of five Blackthorne children, she is also the fraternal twin of Breydon Blackthorne. She is married to Dr. ST Wong.

Rafe Blackthorne {aka David Pearson} – He is the eldest of his identical triplet brothers, Rourke Blackthorne and Bastion RavenCroft. At fifty years old, he is a father of five (Dante, Dart, Drin, Breydon, and Meg). Recently retired from the FBI, he now runs his horse ranch full time.

Dante Blackthorne {aka Agent Frank Kastle} – Rafe's first born son, he is the identical twin to Dartanian Blackthorne. He works undercover with the CIA.

Dartanian (Dart) Blackthorne – The third son born of Rafe's set of triplets. He is an identical twin to Dante Blackthorne and a Sheriff's Deputy of Breckenridge County,

Drinian (Drin) Blackthorne – The second born in the set of triplets within the Blackthorne clan. He is a gentle soul, intelligent but slow (almost childlike), and a carpenter by trade.

CHARACTER LIST AND CULPRIT

Breydon Blackthorne – The fourth in the order of birth. He is the fraternal twin of Megorah Wong and a recent addition in the prosecuting attorney's office for Breckenridge County.

Jericho Henley (The Milkman) –Though he plays the part of a CIA agent, he's really an agent of a covert organization called Phenom; a black ops organization not formally recognized by the CIA.

Phenom – A corrupt organization that seeks to trap, enslave and control individuals with special abilities. In particular, they desire anyone connected to the Maxwell Blackthorne line; for it is extensive and of ancient origin.

Mitch (Mitchell) Gaylord – Pilot to Rafe Blackthorne.

Astraia (Smith) O'Kahner – Recently widowed, she is the mother of Aimee, Jake, and Adam.

Agent Ricardo Pegueros – He is a double operative. He works both within the Phenom organization as well as the Central Intelligence Agency (CIA) in undercover operations. He specializes in information retrieval and has a fierce desire to undermine and destroy Phenom.

Veta Rohann – Wife of Mitchell Gaylord and the mother of Casey and Aaron, her identical twin boys. She is strong in her faith.

Rourke Blackthorne – He is the second born of his identical brothers, Rafe Blackthorne and Bastion RavenCroft. Normally he lives in the Blackthorne Estates in Scotland, but recent events have him travelling.

CHARACTER LIST AND CULPRIT

Bastion RavenCroft aka Randulf Blackthorne – Long thought deceased, he is the third born of his identical brothers, Rafe and Rourke Blackthorne. He and his wife Inara had five kids as well: Kahner, Kalturek, Kalab(ernus), Drayke and Mackenzie. When he is not running his horse ranch he takes jobs as a mercenary.

Angel (Doe) Stryfe – She is a woman with no memory of her past and a child-like air as a result. She is married to Wilton Stryfe and has a one-year old son.

Ciara Marketti – In volume VI, Kayos Knows, she was known as Ciara Biardon. But something has changed, for events are playing out ten years sooner then expected and she has yet to have married.

Kahner RavenCroft – Eldest son of Bastion RavenCroft and one of a set of triplets, he is identical to his brother Kalturek in appearance. He works in undercover operations for the CIA.

Vortigern Black - Narrator of the RavenCroft and Blackthorne stories as well as a character within. But which one of the characters among this list lays claim to the pseudonym?

Eliza Dushku – The former wife of Kahner RavenCroft, and the mother of his children. Kids he long ago thought she hadn't carried to term.

Kalturek RavenCroft – Is the identical brother to Kahner Ravencroft, and one of a set of triplets including Kalab. He is also a Sheriff's Deputy of Loveland, Colorado.

CHARACTER LIST AND CULPRIT

Wilton Stryfe – The husband of Angel Stryfe and father of their son, Kal.

Chase Ryans, PI – Is a private investigator and bounty hunter who is married to Mackenzie (RavenCroft) Ryans.

Mackenzie (RavenCroft) Ryans – The youngest child of Inara and Bastion RavenCroft, she is married to Chase Ryans, PI.

Kalabernus (Kalab) RavenCroft – One of a set of triplets including Kahner and Kalturek. He is easy going and a painter by trade.

Drayke RavenCroft – Fourth born and the youngest son of the RavenCroft's, he is the fraternal twin of Mackenzie Ryans.

Inara RavenCroft – Bastion RavenCroft's deceased wife.

Maxwell Blackthorne – Illegitimate bastard son of an incestuous union between Major Thomas Weir and his own sister Jean Weir from the 1600's. (Both were notorious for being outed as a warlock and witch in 1670 and executed for it.) The product of this disturbing relationship, Maxwell, took up the name Blackthorne in his youth and became the founder of the family line. His birth connects the Blackthorne's and RavenCroft's to an extensive lineage through the Weir-deVere's.

AUTHOR
DELAINE CHRISTINE

Who is this lady,
who writes what she knows?
And what part of this warped story
is her, do you suppose?

For sure she's an author
much like Angel, one can see
With a spouse who did serve
in a North American country.

And though her eyes change color
dependent upon her mood,
she'll skip the hot toddies
for a dark coffee, hot and brewed

But add some amaretto
and she'll be doing just fine,
while writing one of her books
In the evening way past nine.